BOOKISH
BOYFRIENDS

AMULET BOOKS
NEW YORK

TIFFANY SCHMIDT

BOOKISH BOYFRIENDS

Cataloging-in-Publication Data has been applied for and may be obtained from the Library of Congress.
ISBN 978-1-4197-2860-0

Text copyright © 2018 Tiffany Schmidt
Jacket illustrations copyright © 2018 Danielle Kroll
Book design by Alyssa Nassner

Printed and bound in U.S.A.
10 9 8 7 6 5 4 3 2 1

Amulet Books are available at special discounts when purchased in quantity for premiums and promotions as well as fundraising or educational use. Special editions can also be created to specification. For details, contact specialsales@abramsbooks.com or the address below.

ABRAMS The Art of Books
195 Broadway, New York, NY 10007
abramsbooks.com

TO MY PARENTS,
WHO TRIED TO STOP ME FROM
READING UNDER THE COVERS . . .
BUT NEVER TRIED TOO HARD.

"SHE IS A GREAT READER,
AND HAS NO PLEASURE
IN ANYTHING ELSE."

—Jane Austen, *Pride and Prejudice*

1

Merrilee Rose Campbell, what are you doing?"

I barely heard Eliza's question over her pounding on my bedroom door. Not that she waited for me to answer it—the door or her question. My best friend flung it open and stood in my doorway wearing her brand-new uniform and an exasperated expression. Despite her frown, she looked perfect. Her skirt and shirt were as crisp as a new book's pages. Her blond hair gleamed in my room's twinkle lights.

My uniform—well, if Eliza's was a new hardcover, mine was a well-loved paperback. And my brown hair was only half dried because I'd gotten distracted—again—by the novel propped on my dresser. It was held open by my hair dryer and brush as I hopped on one foot and tugged a tall sock to my knee without taking my eyes off the page.

I offered her an apologetic shrug. "Reading."

She stormed into my room, eyebrows and voice high. "We're going to be late! On the first day!"

I nodded solemnly, then turned back to fiddle with the contents of my jewelry box while I gulped in the last paragraphs of chapter twenty-three.

"Merrilee!"

"I'm looking for earrings," I said. The hero, swoon-worthy Blake, *leaned in, closing his eyes—*

"You are not! I can see you in the mirror!"

"It's the end of a chapter!" I protested as she yanked the book away.

"Late! First day!"

"Kissing scene!"

"New school!"

If she was going to kidnap my book, I was going to retaliate. "There's no rush. We can always catch a ride with Toby and Rory. If he drives, we've got an extra thirty minutes." Nothing irritated Eliza more than my *other* best friend, Tobias May.

Her fair skin flushed prettily when she was mad—much like the heroine Blake was about to kiss. Of course, Blake's heroine was half angel, so *she* had a reason for being that gorgeous. Eliza was just the genetics equivalent of a Megabucks winner. Most of our former classmates at our all-girls charter school would've killed for her eyebrows alone.

She took a deep breath and shut her eyes before answering. "I already agreed to ride with Toby and your sister for the rest of the year . . . but this is *our* tradition. Doughnut Day! So, please, can't the kissing scene wait until later? I promise to listen to you talk all about your new book boyfriend on the walk."

I twisted my remaining sock into a pretzel. "He's pretty drool-inspiring. Hot, British, rich, brilliant, *and* an actor."

"You're not dressed or walking. I don't want to hear about him until you're doing *both*."

"Compromise." I picked up my hairbrush. "You read aloud while I get ready."

"Fine." She snapped the book open, and I fought the urge to clap. Eliza read better than any audiobook narrator—a fact I'd learned during last spring's reading-on-the-treadmill concussion mishap, when I was given strict instructions for "brain rest" while in the middle of an addictive series. She read with clarity and feeling—even when her own feelings about the books were those of complete disdain. Have I mentioned she's the *best* friend?

"Okay, here's what you need to know—"

Eliza held up her hand. "I don't need context. I'll read. You dress."

"No teasing."

"No stalling! You have five minutes or I'm heading to the Donut Hut without you."

"Relax," I said. "I'll be ready."

I brushed my hair into a ponytail and fussed with my shirt while Eliza skimmed the page. We could wear *any* white button-down shirt, but as I toyed with the navy-and-red crossover tie that was a mandatory part of my new uniform, I started to second-guess the Peter Pan collar on mine. And the red heart-shaped buttons. "Is fifteen too old for heart-shaped buttons?" I asked, then shook my head. "Whatever. I like them. I think of my style as toddler-chic. Lots of color and sparkles are a bonus." I turned to get Eliza's opinion.

She lifted her eyes from the pages and gave me a scan. "It works. It's a very you look," she said, then turned back to the book and scowled. "I'm not reading this." She flipped to the next page and her eyes went wide. "I can't believe *you* are reading this. I don't think this scenario is possible—*she doesn't notice she's not breathing?* And, biologically, that's not correct; the pupils of his eyes wouldn't *constrict*, they'd *dilate*." She pointed to a paragraph. "Also, the body dynamics here don't make sense. Is Blake an alien? Because he appears to have three hands: one on her neck, one around her waist, and the third—"

"Give it back before you ruin it for me. You're supposed to read it, not dissect it." I tossed the book onto my bed. It landed in the mound of throw pillows I used to disguise the lumpy, unmade state of my blankets. "Anyway, how do I look? I'm still not sold on uniforms."

"You're good." She paused. "But are those the socks you're wearing?"

I crossed one leg behind the other. Purple unicorns reached halfway up my left calf, while flying pigs soared around my right. I liked them both and had no idea where their pairs were hiding. "Yes?"

Of course *she* loved the uniforms—even in a boring, no-frills white shirt, school tie, and navy skirt, she looked stunning. Without a single fleck of makeup or hair product. She was flaxen haired, long legged, hourglass-y. Her eyes were large and expressive. And paired with her dark lashes and brows, their blue "fathomless depths" "blazed" and "flashed" in all the ways novelists described. She was a romance hero-ine, a fairy-tale princess, a Helen of Troy. Or, as stupid Brandy Erlich at our old school had dubbed her, "Brainiac Barbie."

It was obvious where she got her genius from, but I still

wasn't convinced her parents hadn't genetically engineered the biologically ideal appearance for their daughter. Except . . . beauty was the exact opposite of what they valued.

I couldn't do beautiful, or hot, or breathtaking. My nose was too perky, slightly upturned. I had freckles—not a coat of them, but a healthy sprinkling across the bridge of my nose. My brown hair was lost somewhere between light and dark, and it was a flyaway static magnet. My gray-blue eyes were too big and my mouth was too small.

I got "cute." I got "adorable." I got "feisty"—which doesn't even describe appearance. Or "pixie," which made no sense since I was average height, or at least I would be once I hit a growth spurt. Both my sisters were five-six, and there was no way I'd let them stay taller than me—it interfered with borrowing their clothing.

But if I couldn't be glamorous, or chic, or gorgeous, then I was certainly going to make the best of cute. If Eliza tried fighting me on my socks, she'd get to see feisty. I lifted my pointy pixie chin defiantly.

She sighed. "We don't have time to discuss your issues with matching—but, *boots*?" She went through the beaded curtain that served as my closet door and returned with a light brown leather pair.

"I'm glad the uniform doesn't stipulate footwear. At least my feet get to have personality." I straightened the waist of my navy pleated skirt and zipped my calves into the boots. "Can you believe we're going to be in classes with *boys*!? I bet the Hero High guys look amazing in uniforms. . . . Though do you think they're still the same unromantic mouth breathers we had in elementary school? If so, what a waste. *Someday,* I'll have my first kiss/boyfriend/love—hopefully before I'm ancient—but until then . . ." I shrugged and looked longingly at the book on my pillow. "Boys are so much better in books."

Eliza was hunting among the paperbacks and clutter on my desk, adding pens, notebooks, and the folder containing Reginald R. Hero Preparatory School sophomore schedule/ orientation papers to my satchel. I'd meant to do that last night, but . . . I glanced again at the book. Black cover, the title, *Fall with Me,* in fancy script. Oh, *Blake,* you plot-tastic distraction.

"Did you hear me?" I asked.

"Yes." She held out the strap and I ducked into it. "Boys are better in books. It's your latest maxim, I know."

"*So much better,*" I corrected as I grabbed a stack of bangles off my dresser and slid them onto my wrist. Eh, they clanged too much. I took them off. "Fingers crossed we find our own heroes at Hero High."

"Don't lump me in that *we*—I'm not interested. Adolescent girls involved in romantic relationships are more likely to experience depression and lowered levels of academic success." Facts her parents had drummed into her head the same way she drummed her fingers against my doorframe while I checked that my balcony door was closed and unplugged my twinkle lights.

"Ready." I tapped on the corner of the Fibonacci poster on the back of my door, shut it behind us, and started down the long hallway to the stairs. The walls were covered with photos of my two sisters and me at all ages of awkward and all seasons of apparel. Thank goodness Mom couldn't dress Lilly, Rory, and me in matching holiday outfits anymore. Nope, now Rory, Eliza, and I would just have matching uniforms, *every single day*. Gag.

"So if you don't want *real-life* romance, you should agree with me—about boys and books." I waggled my eyebrows, but she just shook her head. "Speaking of books, do you think we'll be reading a lot of them?"

"Probably. It's private school. Parents expect to see more homework. It makes them feel like they're getting their money's worth."

"I hope our . . ." I looked over my shoulder at her and shrugged. "Syllabuses?"

"Syllabi."

"Aren't full of stupid war stories. I mean, I love a good classic—you know how I feel about *The Great Gatsby*—but why do teachers always seem to assign war books by old dudes?"

"Classics become classics for a reason." Eliza paused to straighten a photo of Mom and Dad at their twentieth anniversary party. "And usually that reason has to do with our patriarchal society and the authors being privileged white men."

"Yawn. I want it noted: if we have to read *The Catcher in the Rye* again I'm staging a protest. I'm so over Holden and his privileged ennui." I jumped down the last two stairs, my skirt blooming out like the bell cap on a mushroom.

"Noted," said Eliza with a smile. "And agree. I loathe that—"

She was interrupted by my parents rushing into the foyer. They were already in work polos because our family-owned dog boutique opened early to catch the morning leashes and lattes power-walking crowd.

"There you are!" Mom's lipstick was the same peach color as in all the photos in the upstairs hallway. I'm sure it had been trendy at some point in the past twenty years, but I only cared that it was as familiar as her wide smile.

"Good luck to our sophomores." Dad tweaked my nose and grinned at Eliza, whose cheeks turned pink as she fought a smile. I loved him for making her a part of their "our," since her parents were off at the South Pole, more interested in being the first to discover new species than in being around for first days of school. I bumped a shoulder against Eliza's.

"You girls look so grown-up in your uniforms. Pictures? Pictures!" Mom fumbled in her pockets for her phone. When she didn't come up with it, Dad brought out his own and snapped a pic.

"Say cheese*boogers*," he said, undermining her statement about growing up. He grinned at the photo on his screen, which was probably a super-flattering shot of me gigglesnorting. "It's nice to know that even though you're a high school sophomore, you'll always be the little girl who laughs at her ol' dad's jokes."

"Emphasis on *little*," said my younger sister, Rory. She was slumped at the kitchen table eating some sort of sticks-and-dirt healthy cereal with her eyes half shut.

Mom turned and gave my sister a stern, full-name warning. "*Aurora*." Then Mom and Eliza said in unison, "Ignore her."

"I will," I said, but couldn't resist muttering, "I *do*, as often as possible."

Rory's eyes narrowed. "There's something wrong with you two. No doughnut is worth getting up earlier and walking."

I rolled my eyes. "Good thing you're not invited, then."

Rory turned back toward her cereal, unsuccessfully hiding her smug smile and pink cheeks. "When I'm sitting in Toby's car enjoying air-conditioning and someone who knows where we're going, I'll try not to feel jealous."

Now Eliza was the one rolling her eyes. It was her automatic reaction to Toby's name. Rory's was blushing.

"Now, girls . . ." said Mom. She sighed and clasped her hands together, pressing them against her chest. "You know, I met your father in high school. First day."

Rory mumbled, "We *know*." But I loved that story, so I nodded.

She kissed my cheek. "Maybe you girls will meet *your* special someones at Hero High."

I raised my eyebrows at Eliza as Dad added his kisses to both our cheeks. *See! I come by my sappiness genetically.* Eliza knew my family well enough to interpret the sentiment in a single glance.

"Good-bye, Mr. and Mrs. Campbell." She grabbed my arm and I let her drag me away, stopping only to give my dog, Gatsby, a kiss on his adorable muttsy nose. Outside on the sidewalk, I took a deep breath. Eliza groaned and gave a pointed look at her watch, but I stayed still, looking from my house to Toby's next door to the road that led in one direction toward our old school and in the other toward our new one. Counting two years of preschool and kindergarten, this was my thirteenth first day of school.

The number felt a little ominous.

"Ready for Hero High?" Eliza asked, her eyes already focused down the sidewalk like she was picturing the state-of-the-art bio labs that awaited us on the other side of doughnuts.

Ready? To be the new girl in an unfamiliar school where boys and the potential for humiliation waited around every picturesque corner? Not really.

I slid my satchel higher on my shoulder and lifted my chin. "Please," I said with a wink. "Hero High should be asking if it's ready for me."

2

Once we'd braved the lines at the Donut Hut and started walking toward our new school, Eliza looked at her watch and visibly relaxed.

"Told you we had time." I licked powdered sugar from the corner of my lips, savoring it and the rare experience of being the one who was right.

She took a delicate bite of her cinnamon doughnut. "I like being punctual."

Mine was a not-so-delicate bite, and I jumped backward as jelly filling shot out the other side. Luckily, it missed my uniform and landed only on my boot.

Eliza handed me a napkin and I knelt to wipe at the Ohio-shaped spot on my toe. Hopefully Mom or Google knew jelly-on-suede stain removal tricks, because now that I'd thought about it, the boots actually belonged to my older sister, Lillian.

I stared at the stain as every glossy photo from the school's website shuffled through my memory. Would I find a place among the smiling clusters on the benches or in the labs? I wanted one, oh, how I wanted one. But. Those students were as crisp as kale . . . and I wore jelly as a boot accessory.

Eliza pulled me up. "Stop rubbing it. That's making it worse."

I stretched the fingers of my non-doughnut hand wide, like I was reaching for something I couldn't grasp. This wasn't just about the boot. "You know that shimmy you get in your stomach and throat when you listen to Disney movie soundtracks? And you feel like you can do more—*be* more? That you should want to see how far you can go?"

Eliza paused and considered this. "Yearning?"

"Yeah, that's probably it." I fit the word in the Mad Libs of emotions in my brain. It clicked. "But I don't know what I'm yearning *for*." I opened and closed my hand, but it was still empty, whatever I needed elusive. "I want to spin on a mountaintop, or in a blizzard, or under the sea, or on a boat. I want a purpose. I want *so much more than this suburban life*."

Eliza smiled and ducked the arms I'd flung outward. "It's a little too early for improv show tunes."

I smiled back, but weakly. "You have science. Lilly has her wedding and law school applications. Rory has her art. I want . . . something that's mine. Something I'm good at. I *need* something. I hope I find it here."

I started down the sidewalk, because technically *here* was still two blocks away. "This is a fresh start. I no longer have to be known as the girl who still believed in Santa in the fifth grade. Or the one sent to the nurse because she couldn't stop crying over *Where the Red Fern Grows*. Or—who could forget the super-fun first week when I couldn't find my gym locker, and I had to wear my sweaty clothes to class? Can I just not be *that* person?"

I wasn't a fan of Lilly's future mother-in-law, but I was grateful for her insistence that Rory and I switch from the charter school we'd attended since sixth grade to this "much more prestigious" private school.

"I promise to remember where your locker is," said Eliza. "And I called to confirm that our schedules are identical."

"Thank you." Bless this girl for transferring schools with me and Eliza'ing her way into matching schedules. Of course her parents had *always* wanted her to go to Hero High and had only begrudgingly settled on Woodcreek Charter School for Girls because of studies about the benefits of an all-girls' educational environment on confidence and achievement. *But,* as they'd been happy to point out, those advantages weren't significant enough to make up for a lack of lab facilities, AP classes, or International Baccalaureate programmes—all of which Reginald R. Hero Preparatory School had in spades. This was a rare moment when my parents' lack of finances and Eliza's stubborn refusal to go without me were finally not obstacles in the Gordon-Ferguses' plans. So, if I was blessing things, I should include the financial aid and scholarship committees.

Eliza looked mournfully at her last bite of doughnut before popping it in her mouth and chewing slowly. She swallowed and asked, "May I make a suggestion?"

I gave her some serious side-eye, but her poker face was inscrutable. "Maybe."

She began, "You know you're my favorite human on the planet—"

I interrupted to add, "And Gatsby is your favorite canine."

She laughed. "Sure." Then she continued, "And I love your fearless optimism and imagination. But . . . maybe don't spend the whole day starry-eyed. I know you're excited about going coed and don't intentionally get so lost in your thoughts—but at least on the first day, try to focus on what people *actually* say—not the narratives you're inventing for them."

I dragged the toe of my boot along the pavement—then winced when it added a scuff to the stain. There was no way I could return these without facing capital punishment from Lilly. I'd have to bury them in the back of my closet with her pink blouse (blueberry pie) and Rory's white skirt (impromptu Slip 'N Slide—though to be fair, Toby had dared me).

Eliza cleared her throat and I blinked, realizing I owed her an answer. "Oh. I *do* try."

She laughed. "You know what? Be you. If they don't adore you, that's their problem. And we'll try every club until we figure out what you're yearning for. Now, what about me?"

Because that was the thing about Eliza—she gave lots of advice, but she also asked for my opinion and listened.

"Try not to be so sensitive if your parents come up." Since she was nodding and receptive, I added, "And be nicer to Toby."

Eliza scowled. "I can't believe we're going to have to see him every single day."

He lived next door. I already saw him every day, but I didn't remind her. I also didn't say, *You need to learn to share me*, because I'd said it—and they'd ignored it—a gazillion times.

"We're here." My stomach tightened as the long drive-way to Hero High loomed large across the street. I dropped the last piece of my doughnut back into the bag and stared at the stone arch and, beyond that, a campus that looked much too perfect and pristine for someone with scuffed and jelly-spotted boots, someone who frequently got grass stains by just looking at lawns and who hadn't yet managed to wear tights for an entire day without snagging them. Someone who occasionally still forgot to raise her hand and blurted out the answer in math class before the teacher finished explaining the problem.

I took a deep breath and a moment to absorb the beauty of the campus—*my* new campus. There was a double row of trees that arched over the drive leading to the stone mansions where classes were held. The grass was Technicolor green and so temptingly lush that I wanted to climb the gentle slope off to our left and roll down it.

Okay, so maybe there was a reason I was prone to grass stains.

"Ohhh, who's that under the maples?" I pointed across the drive to a guy pacing beneath the row of trees. It reminded me of a scene from a book—I just couldn't remember which one.

"Those are sycamores," said Eliza. "And the only male I know here is Toby, so your guess is as good as mine."

I studied the way the mystery student's head was bent. Sunlight and shadows played across the black curls that spilled around his ears. "Does he look upset? Do you think we should—" I stepped off the path in his direction, but Eliza grabbed my arm.

"No, I don't think you should bother the brooding boy

who's *choosing* to be by himself. He's a stranger, not a stray puppy."

But he was so *alone* beneath the trees. So alone and so picturesque with his dark pants and white shirt against the green backdrop and dappled shade. His tie wasn't fastened, just draped around his collar, and his sleeves were rolled up. A blazer was slung over a book bag at the base of a tree. The guy's face was hidden by the angle and those touch-me curls, so I couldn't see if his expression was as emotional as his posture and pacing, but I could practically hear his sighs as he clenched and unclenched a fist in time with his footsteps. It was something right off the pages of a half dozen romance novels. Only it was happening, real, live, right in front of me.

Color me emo-intrigued.

School with boys was awesome.

"Earth to Merri." Eliza shook my arm.

"He's so *mysterious*."

"You can't solve all the school's mysteries on your first day." Eliza spun me back in the right direction. "Today, let's focus on the mystery of locating our classes. He's probably just angsty about summer being over."

"I doubt it. Today's Friday. Who gets *that* moody about one day of classes? Though maybe his weekend plans are as exciting as mine." I wagged one finger in faux enthusiasm. "It's finally here—Lilly and Trent's engagement party is tonight."

I'd never understand what Lilly saw in Trent—what anyone did. Sure, he was handsome, in an entirely generic soap opera actor way. But before he'd put a ring on it—*it* being my sister's finger—he'd been on a list of the state's most eligible bachelors. Everything about Lilly's relationship and fiancé were yawn-inducing. The party would be a total snoozefest, too—full of his mom's politics and fussy food. Gah, neither the election nor the wedding could come fast enough.

I let Eliza drag me farther down the path but glanced over my shoulder. The boy was leaning against a tree. Not *back* against it. He was facing it, one palm pressed flat against the trunk as he bowed his head, the other hand fisted tightly by his side. He was *so* broody and *so* mysterious. The broodiest boys in books were also the ones who made my heart *c'thunk,* and this guy was a Brontë hero: Heathcliff and Rochester combined. The mysterious ones brought out my inner sleuth—and this guy made me want to dig up Sir Arthur Conan Doyle or Agatha Christie.

I wished he would look up so I could offer an encouraging smile or a friendly wave. Heck, if Eliza wouldn't have killed me for even thinking it, I would have given him a cheer-up hug. Since I couldn't, really, *shouldn't*—Stranger Hugger was *not* the reputation I wanted at Hero High—I just gave him one last look and vowed that as soon as possible, I'd solve his mystery.

3

The closer we got to the gray stone buildings of the campus, the faster Eliza walked. When we heard the voices of other students, her pace forced me to jog. She wasn't overanxious to get to homeroom; she was just anxious. Fast footsteps, clipped tone, jerky gestures—these were Eliza's tells. Distraction mode: activated.

"The *scenery* here is certainly better," I teased, raising my eyebrows and tilting my head to indicate yet another pretty guy made prettier and preppier by a perfectly cut blazer and pants. Since Eliza didn't answer, I poked her and added, "By 'scenery,' I mean 'guys.'"

The boy I'd indicated was standing in front of a trash can. And since I was still holding a sticky doughnut bag, this had all the ingredients of a perfectly book-worthy meet cute. As gorgeous as the tree boy had been, this one was an upgrade. Like, an are-you-kidding specimen of teenage perfection. If all the Hero High guys looked this good, I was in serious danger of flunking out. Or maybe I just needed some time to build up a tolerance? Like with caffeine. Either way, I gave this tall, dark double espresso my best attempt at a flirty, not-pixie smile and said, "Excuse me," as I leaned around him to toss my bag in the trash.

"Wait!" he called.

Oh, I waited. I *so* willingly waited for whatever would come out of his mouth next. And while I waited, I tried to picture how he'd be described in a Mick Flame novel. Everything about him was crisp and corners, from the collar and cuffs on his shirt—were those cuff links?—to the angles of his cheekbones and jaw line. Lips that any romance writer would write raptures over: just this side of sulky and, in a word, *bitable*. Eyes, rich brown, intense, alert like he was taking note of everything—and I didn't mind being noted. His posture would make an etiquette teacher drool; yet, like his clothing, it seemed a natural part of him. His hair was dark brown and neat—except for one piece that dared to droop onto his forehead. Oh, I liked that piece. I bet it annoyed *him*, but a girl could go swoony just thinking about fixing it. Even his voice was sharp—sharp enough to pierce my heart and make me—

"You can't do that!" I jerked backward from his scolding. His scowl made me want to apologize, even though I didn't know what for. "You're not going to leave it like that, are you?"

"If you could use a more specific noun than 'that' or 'it,' perhaps we'd have a clue what you're complaining about," snapped Eliza.

"That's *recycling*." He pointed to the can behind him, then aimed his intense dark eyes back at me. "Your trash was not recyclable."

"Oh." Breath whooshed out of my lungs in a relieved gust. "That's easy enough to fix. My mistake. Sorry."

"Don't you dare apologize for making a mistake," lectured Eliza, and I bit my tongue so I didn't say sorry to her as well. Usually I would, just to see her cheeks flush and hear her speech on female disempowerment through the narrative of apologies and self-blame, but leaning elbow-deep into the recycling can, I was willing to let this chance pass.

"You know, they should really mark these better," I chattered as I leaned deeper into the can, hoping my skirt still covered all the parts it should. *This* wasn't a scenario I'd tested for accidental exposure.

The guy's eyes widened like I'd just told a particularly cutting "yo' momma" joke or insulted his puppy. "Most of our students don't have difficulty reading."

I gasped—which was apparently the last boost I needed, because my fingertips finally brushed against my doughnut trash. I stood and crushed the bag in my hand before tossing it in the next can.

"Did—" I swallowed and took a deep breath, because I *must* have misunderstood. "Did you just accuse me of not knowing how to read?"

The accusation was so preposterous that I couldn't help but giggle. Everyone said I was practically born with my nose in a book. I stopped laughing when he didn't smile. His eyebrows arched like perfectly graceful, perfectly disdainful punctuation on his perfect and disdainful face. He tapped a polished loafer on the tiles that read "trash" and "recycling."

"Who puts signs on the ground? That's hardly practical." I looked to Eliza—who nodded in agreement—then back to the guy.

"Like I said before, most of our students don't struggle with this concept." And since he'd saved the planet from my waxed-paper bag, he gave me one last haughty sniff and started walking away.

I chased after him, determined to coax a grin and win him over, because this had to be fake. Some sort of new-kid hazing, or Toby had set this up as one of his pranks. "Hey," I called when I caught up. I held out my palm. "I didn't get a chance to introduce myself."

I knew I was vertically challenged, but no one had ever actually looked down their nose at me before. And, *gah*, the intensity in his gaze—if this was how he looked when he was *annoyed* with someone, imagine being on the receiving end when he gazed on someone he *adored*. Not that *I* wanted to be that someone. Not at all. Despite all the enemies-turned-love-interests books I'd read, I was okay with this guy keeping his pretty scorn to himself. Especially when he paired it with a slow, measured, *are you an idiot?* voice. "That hand was just in the garbage. Do you really expect me to shake it?"

"Actually, as you were so quick to point out, it was in the *recycling*."

He stared at my fingers like they were crawling with salmonella, which . . . maybe they were. The longer he stared at them, the more I was tempted to run for the closest sink or dig through Eliza's bag for her anti-bac.

In the half second before I convinced myself I could actually *see* the germs crawling across my nails—had that freckle always been there?—Eliza tugged on my arm.

But I didn't look at her. I looked up at him. He was looking at me too. Still arrogant. And maybe . . . as his dark eyes narrowed and searched mine—just a tiny bit surprised or confused or intrigued or . . . ? Whatever emotion had sparked between us, he blinked it away. Covered it with annoyance and amped up the wattage of his glower. I was tempted to rub my germy hand all over his perfectly pressed shirt. Except *my* parents trained me better than that.

"Forget it. He's rude," Eliza said.

His gaze slid from me, to her, to away. I did a subtle fist pump by my side. It might be bad *dog*-training advice to commence an eye-contact contest with a pup, but it sure felt good to win one against this jerk. "Did you hear that?" I demanded of Eliza. "He said I couldn't read."

Eliza looked gratifyingly pissed, and her angry looks were way more murderous than mine. A hazard of cute is that it is incompatible with scary. "You sleep with books under your pillow. You read more pages than anyone else in the Chester Elementary read-a-thon. You can recite Keats and Dickinson like the alphabet. You were the first in our class to complete all seven Harry Pot—"

I held up a hand to cut her off—and because I really wanted the anti-bac she kept in her bag. While I loved her defensive mode, I didn't need a recitation of *all* the evidence that he was wrong. Not that he seemed to care or even acknowledge that she'd spoken. Well, I wasn't going to directly acknowledge *him* either.

"Wow, the welcoming committee at Hero High is

top-notch," I said while slathering anti-bac all over my fingers. I'd said it louder than I should. Loud enough—I hoped—that it carried to his reddening ears as he walked away.

It certainly reached the ears of several other students, because I caught two girls giggling, and a guy stopped and asked, "Do you need help?"

"No." Eliza turned her back and tapped an impatient ballet flat on the path.

This new guy couldn't be more different from the Recycling Can Enforcement Squad. He was rumpled. One side of his shirt untucked. One cuff unbuttoned, revealing a wiry wrist and more of his rich brown skin. He had the hopeful eyes and eager smile of a well-loved puppy and looked like he was going through a puppylike growth spurt too. Oversize hands and long limbs he hadn't quite mastered yet. I glanced at his feet, because if shoes were the only nonstandard part of the uniform, I wanted to see what his said about him. Unlike the polished loafers of the jerk, this guy had on flip-flops. Their madras straps were shades of red, gray, and navy, which made me smile, because those were the school colors.

"Hey, I'm Curtis. What's your first class?" he asked *me*, which I appreciated since from my experiences around town at the mall and movies and parks, most guys forgot I existed once they'd seen Eliza. Maybe I just needed her to turn around whenever a boy approached.

"Um . . ." I never wasted headspace on things like schedules. Eliza picked our classes, then I followed her around and let her badger me into studying. She *loved* time management and any excuse to be bossy.

"Biology," she answered.

"Seriously? Bio first thing?" I stopped just short of stomping my foot. Instead I grabbed her shoulder and spun her around. "No wonder you were so excited to get here. Science before eight a.m. is cruel and unusual punishment!"

"I've got bio too. And I'll have to respectfully disagree—it's my favorite cla-ahh—" He got his first glimpse of Eliza and choked on his words or his tongue or his drool.

I winced. Yes, my best friend had a face and body that made guys stupid. But since stupidity and being objectified were her biggest turnoffs, this guy was not doing himself any favors.

"Um." Curtis cleared his throat and his voice came out octaves higher. "The bio teacher's—uh, really good. And you're . . . *wow.*"

Eliza glowered, and I cursed her parents for the way they'd drilled into her head that her beauty was a liability. They were away on research trips ten months out of the year and *still* managed to convince her that—since she fit a narrow beauty standard of privileged perfection with her Caucasian features and her blond-and-blue combination—no one would take her seriously.

I needed to change the topic before either of them made things worse. Clearly she was interpreting his bio-ramble as a reference to her parents, and clearly *he* was about to build an altar to sacrifice himself upon. I said the first thing I could think of: "Don't you agree the trash cans aren't well labeled?"

"Um." He blinked at me. "What?"

"Never mind." Gah, five minutes on campus and I was already ruining my chances of being seen as normal. I sighed and walked the last five steps to where the sidewalks intersected.

Hero High didn't believe in signposts. On the ground at the places where paths crossed, inlaid mosaics indicated direction. The design style paid homage to Reginald R. Hero, the school's founder, who'd made his fortune in artisan tiles. None of the ones in the ground were *his*, though. Those were in glass cases in museums or ornamenting the historic homes of the superwealthy. The ones students stepped on were reproductions. Tiles shaped like books with opened covers spilled pages toward the library. Balls bounced toward the athletic fields and gymnasium. The masks of comedy and tragedy nodded at the theater. They'd charmed me on my tour of the school. They charmed me again today. I did a clumsy spin on top of a globe-shaped tile. "I love these."

"They're a pain to clean, so don't get too many demerits, or you'll spend your Saturday scraping gum, moss, and weeds from the cracks." His grin was pure troublemaker—I bet he was a substitute's worst nightmare.

When Eliza tutted—like the idea of demerits made her itchy, which, let's be honest, it probably did—his smile turned sheepish and he ran a hand across his hair. It was dark, closer to black than the bronze of his skin, and short, but looked like it might curl if it grew longer.

A warm, tan hand landed on my shoulder and gave it a

quick squeeze. "Spoken by someone who's logged many hours in detention, so listen to Curtis, Rowboat."

Toby looked dapper—as always—in a uniform cut to show-case his long limbs and dark hair and eyes. But I'd never been so dismayed by his use of that nickname. Especially once I saw Curtis mouth it with a puzzled look. He turned to Eliza. "What is 'Rowboat' short for?"

Eliza ignored him and grasped my arm. "Let's go."

"Where are you headed? I can show you to your first class," said Toby.

"No need." Curtis took a micro-step closer to Eliza. "I've got this."

She pointed to a mosaic of test tubes and beakers. The smoke that poured out of the top pointed down the path on the right. "Thanks, but we don't need an escort."

"Maybe not," Toby said, "but I'm in bio, too, so you're stuck with me."

Toby and Eliza had long ago stopped treating each other with what most considered general manners or human decency. But they liked each other. Deep down they must. Possibly, *way* deep down.

"You're stuck with *us*," Curtis said, his grin turning imp-ish when he added, "Just wait till you check me out in my lab goggles. Sizzle."

"And suddenly I'm not looking forward to bio anymore," Eliza muttered.

"Ouch." Curtis said it lightly, but his smile flickered. "I'm hurt."

Eliza glanced at the paths and pointed left. "The health center is that way."

Toby laughed and reached for a high-five she would never, ever grant him, then chuckled again as he linked his arm through my other one, causing a brief moment of panic that they might *literally* play tug-of-war with me.

"Welcome to Hero High." Toby smiled at us. "I'm going to like having you here."

4

Eliza wore her post-biology high like a secret, tucked close to her heart so no one could tell how much she'd loved the class. It lasted through history, a trip to our lockers (so much shinier and bigger than our old lockers—though they still had that sweat-and-overripe-apple smell) and through Latin too.

All I could think on our walk to English was: Eliza's parents had better remember to call her tonight! I didn't care about the weather at the South Pole, the fickleness of their satellite phone, or how busy they were with their "important work"—I cared about Eliza. She deserved a phone call where she could rehash or gush—in her restrained, not-at-all-gushy way—about her first day at a new school.

The tiles pointing the way to English were a quill pen whose calligraphy spiraled off of a roll of parchment to form an arrow. While we walked the crowded paths, while Eliza was busy suppressing her still-lingering smile, I mentally composed an email about *priorities* and *What the double helix is wrong with you?* Because if they didn't call, I was overdue to give them a piece of my mind. It was one of my emails six years ago that had gotten them to grant Eliza the leniency to have a doughnut on the first day of school (as long as the rest of her nutrition followed their absurd regimen). I'd also been the one to convince them she was terrified of the python they gotten as a pet/experiment.

And as long as they hadn't changed their email addresses or blocked mine, I was more than willing to remind the famous Drs. Gordon and Fergus that their best achievement was being parents to the most awesome girl on the planet.

"Hey!" Toby called from a classroom doorway. "We're in here. I saved you seats."

My smile widened; Eliza's dimmed. "Just how many classes do you share with us?"

"Not as many as you have with each other, so calm down."

Ha! Point to Toby . . . except the seats he'd saved were in the *back corner*, and Eliza only liked sitting in what she called the "classroom T-zone"—first row across and single row up the center. There was some study or other that proved those seats were linked to higher performance.

"You'll be okay," I assured her, dismayed that all traces of her smile were gone. "At least they're together. Thanks, Toby."

"Ms. Gregoire is one of the most popular teachers on campus. I was only one building over, and it was almost full by the time I got here," he said with a shrug.

"Full" clearly had a different meaning in private school, because while almost all the desks were claimed, there were only twelve students in them. I leaned toward his. "What's she like?"

"You're going to like her." Toby nodded toward the door, which was opening to reveal a petite woman with red hair.

She balanced two leather bags, a stack of papers, and a coffee mug.

"Welcome, sophomores!" Ms. Gregoire punctuated the statement by dropping everything but the coffee on her desk. "If you're not a sophomore, scram. If you are, get out your laptop and turn it on. Open a file and add today's date. We've no time for laziness."

The class scrambled to do her bidding, and I was grateful I'd taken the time to download the software to make Eliza's and my laptops "school-ready"—*more* grateful Toby had installed some under-the-radar messaging program, which I opened along with my blank document.

"If you were in my class last year, you'll remember we surveyed American literature. This year's curriculum is going to focus on Brit lit."

There were so many things I wanted to tell Eliza. At Woodcreek Charter, I would've whispered, or scrawled a note, or texted in my lap. At Hero High, texting was "absolutely ver-boten." They broke out fancy vocab words and cellular signal blockers that were only turned off at lunch and dismissal.

I sent a quick: I'm so grateful for your hacker skills right now to MAYbeToby. He sent back a gif I'd have to ask him how to access.

Then I opened a messenger box to ElizaGF. My screen name riffed off Toby's nickname for me—one he'd given me back in preschool when he'd thought "Row, Row, Row Your Boat" went "Merrilee, Merrilee, Merrilee, Merrilee, life is but a dream."

RowboatReads: Do you think Rory has Ms. G. too?

What books do you think they studied last year?

Do you think next year is Australian? Canadian?

Or what about an Asian country?

Or African?

Or other parts of Europe?

French or German or Roman or Romanian . . .

Eliza still hadn't responded, though I could see the boxes filling up her screen, and the corner of her mouth twitched.

Narnia.

Neverland.

Hogwarts.

Endor.

I finally heard her fingers move on the keyboard. Score one for persistent badgering.

ElizaGF: I'm buying you a globe for your birthday.

Now PAY ATTENTION!

Then the spoilsport signed out.

For once, paying attention was easy. It wasn't her clothing—though Ms. Gregoire's jade-green dress with subtle gold pinstripes made me super jealous I was stuck in a uniform. And it wasn't her hair—awesome, deep red, worn in a crown of braids around her head. Or the tone of her voice—rich and breathy, like she was whispering magical secrets, though she wasn't actually whispering at all.

It was all of these. Plus the swoop and curl of her letters on the electronic whiteboard in handwriting that made me think of quills and inkwells. And her graceful hand flourishes that seemed to invite us all in to "take an educational journey with me."

No one laughed when she said this. Instead we leaned forward in our seats.

"This year you will fall in love—" She paused to take a sip of her coffee. I swear the mug had been regular brushed steel—but as she locked eyes with me over its rim, light reflected off it like it was covered in rhinestones. It made my mind spin, and for a moment time seemed to pause so her words could echo in my head: *This year you will fall in love. In love. In love.* She kept sipping as she stepped around her desk, closer and closer to my mine—I didn't dare break eye contact even though I still had messenger open on my screen.

When she was a step or two away, the mug blazed so bright that I had to close my eyes. By the time I'd opened them, she'd shifted her gaze to someone else. "—with books."

"This year you'll fall in love with books," she repeated. She put her mug down on her desk. I stared at it—plain dull silver with the school crest—then typed frantically in messenger.

RowboatReads: Did you see that?

MAYbeToby: See what?

RowboatReads: Her mug. It glowed! You didn't see it?

MAYbeToby: Um. No???

Well, he was useless. Luckily Eliza's nosiness must have gotten the best of her, because she'd logged back in.

RowboatReads: Did you see that thing with her mug? Tell me you did.

ElizaGF: ??? Did she spill coffee or something?

Ugh. I wanted to slam my laptop shut. They were both useless. How had they missed it? It had glowed, flashed. I hadn't imagined it. I hadn't!

Ms. Gregoire paused in the center of the room. "We'll be starting with a story you all *think* you know." She flung her arms wide and spun around—and if she'd sprinkled us with pixie dust and told us we could fly, I would've been the first one to the windowsill. "I'm going to break your expectations over and over and over again."

"What book?" asked a guy in the first row. All I could see was the back of his head, his neck, and his shoulders—but they were a *nice* head, neck, and shoulders: blond hair, muscles and lines and tanned skin that made the uniform do all sorts of attractive things. Maybe I *would* fall in love in this room after all.

Except he groaned when Ms. Gregoire answered, "Actually, Lance, it's a play. . . ." So, maybe not.

She hopped onto her desk and swung her feet—clad in gold-trimmed navy heels that inspired English bulldog levels of drool. She let the dramatic pause stretch until all eyes were on her, but not so long that we started to turn to one another and exchange *she's lost it* looks. "*The Most Excellent and Lamentable Tragedy of Romeo and Juliet.*"

She painted the title in the air with her fingers and then shushed the grumbles with a gentle plucking motion. "None of that—though each of your reactions, moan or smile, prove my point. You *think* you know this story. You don't." She paused to make eye contact with each of us. She was looking at me when she said, "But you will. You'll know it like you've *lived it* by the time we're done."

I turned to see if Eliza was equally spellbound, but she was typing.

ElizaGF: So much for academic rigor. We read that in eighth grade at Woodcreek Charter.

"I know some of you are probably already dismissing this as an easy class—after all, those of you who attended Mayfield Middle Academy already studied *Romeo and Juliet*, in, what, sixth grade?" Ms. Gregoire paused, and everyone in class except for Eliza and me nodded.

Eliza signed off again.

"Like I said before, you *think* you know this play. But you're wrong. And you're not preteens anymore. You're not going to be stumbling over 'thees' and 'eres' or have the bawdy humor slide over your heads. There is so much more to this story than Leonardo DiCaprio or that hideous remake with Chuck from *Gossip Girl*. Seriously, if you're going to try and cheat by watching a movie, skip that one."

We laughed.

"Okay, I had you turn on those laptops for a reason—and not so you can talk about me on whatever new chat program bypasses the school firewalls. I'd like you to write yourselves a letter about this play—quotes, feelings, themes, scenes, whatever comes to mind. *Romeo and Juliet* is a play that reveals a lot about the *reader*. It's a great way for me to get to know you and figure out who you are as learners and people and what you need. So I want you to take this letter seriously. Reviewing them will be illuminating for me—I'll draw from these as I shape your curriculum for the year. When you finish, send them to me via the class dropbox."

She paused and surveyed the room with a mischievous smile and, I swear, a twinkle in her eye. "I look forward to proving you all wrong."

5

"You know, these mosaics may be more picturesque than signposts, and I get the whole 'tiles as tribute to our school founder' thing, but they're really impractical." I wasn't talking to anyone in particular. We were smushed in a glob of bodies making its way from various points A to B (in my case, locker to lunch), and I assumed Eliza or Toby was listening. "For one thing: traffic jams like this. For another: leaves, snow, mud, puddles, or people standing on the tile you need to see."

"They aren't meant to be a long-term solution." The answer came from over my left shoulder. I recognized the voice by its condescension. Apparently recycling cans weren't the only things that got his starched undies in a bunch. Mr. Recycling Fanatic was leaning down to talk to me, his words brushing over the shell of my ear, making my stomach squirm and plummet and my breath catch in surprise. "Once the freshmen learn their way—or realize campus maps exist—they'll stop interfering with the rest of us getting to class. But since you have so many complaints, maybe you should return to your old school."

The way he'd said "complaints" reminded me of the way a

snotty earl had spat the word "peasants" on a BBC movie Lilly, Toby, and I had watched the previous weekend. I wanted to ask if all transfer students earned the same level of contempt, or if I was special, but Hero High's resident curmudgeon turned down the path's left fork without saying good-bye.

He was replaced by Lance—aka the owner of the neck and shoulders I'd momentarily admired in English class. They supported a head covered in disheveled blond hair and a face that was dominated by an open smile as he said, "C'mon, I'll teach you a trick." And while Lance's English class grumblings disqualified him from any crushes, I was always open to new friends. So when he lifted an arm, which sported some serious muscles and one of those surfer-y friendship bracelets, I followed his pointer finger to the edge of the path.

I bet this was how secret societies started—put teens in uniforms and have one crook a finger and offer a temptation. Really, I was only one step away from chants and rituals and handshakes and midnight hijinks in a hidden tomb. It was good Eliza had signed us up for Latin; mottos and solemn vows were always in Latin.

He bent his head toward mine. "We're not exactly supposed to walk on the grass, but it's lunch, I'm hungry, and it's *grass*. Are we really going to hurt it?" He took an exaggeratedly large step onto the lawn and waited, the heels of his fancy sneakers bobbing up and down. I laughed and took three normal-size steps to meet him.

Okay, so it wasn't the same as blood oaths or drinking from a sacred mug made from a skull, but . . .

From behind me, Eliza called, "Merrilee! Where are you—
What are you— That's not allowed!"

"Come on, Eliza," I said. "Or you can stay with Toby and
catch up later."

In a blink, disapproval became fury: pink cheeks, straight-
line mouth, *I'll kill you* eyes. She took a deep breath, looked
around, and tiptoed toward us. Pointing a finger at Lance, she
said, "Walk. Quickly. And I'm blaming you if we get caught."

"She doesn't mean it," I huffed, struggling to keep up as he
followed her orders and practically jogged across the lawn to
another path. "Except she kinda does." He sped up.

At the door to the dining hall, Lance paused. "You buying
or packing?"

"Packing." Though, since the air smelled delicious, maybe
I'd rethink that in the future. I sniffed again: basil, bread,
chocolate?

"Cool. I'm buying, but if you head to the far table on the
left side, that's where our group sits. Toby will find you there."

"Thanks," I said. Eliza was already stomping off, but I
caught up and gave her my winningest smile. "So, what do
you think so far?" She kept frowning. "Dude, it was *grass*. I'm
pretty sure it's been walked on for thousands of years without
harm. My opinions? Bio, blech. Meh on Latin and history.
Hooray for English! Can you believe we're studying *Romeo and
Juliet*? It's the most romantic story in the world. I would die to
have a boy love me that much."

"Seriously, Merrilee?" Eliza sighed, but her voice was less
anger and more exasperation—it was an amused echo of the

clinically cool voice her parents used whenever they combatted my imagination with their stupid facts. "Yeah, you would die—you'd be literally *dead*. You've read the play, you know how it ends. That is *not* romance. It's rash actions and lack of communication and incredible immaturity."

I shook my head, refusing to let her cynicism contaminate my imaginings. *I* had a balcony; why couldn't I find a boy to stand beneath it and say poetical things? "It all goes back to what I was telling you this morning: boys are so much better in books."

"Oooh! A book discussion? I want in!"

And, truly, was there any way my future lunch mates could've made a better first impression? There were two girls sitting at the table Lance had indicated. The pretty Asian girl with red-streaked bangs and matching glasses was the one who'd spoken. She was small and round—and seemed even shorter next to the tall, reed-thin girl who smiled shyly at us before looking down at her sandwich.

"Hannah Kim," said the first girl. "And this is Sera. I think you're in our English class and in my history too."

"And my bio." Sera's voice was a whisper. The two words made her soap-white skin blush, a thing I thought *only* happened to heroines in books. It made me adore her instantly.

"I love your bangs," I told Hannah, already debating which color I'd tint mine if I had bangs and my parents wouldn't kill me dead.

"Thanks! I did it while visiting my cousins in Korea this summer, but I think I might keep it. You're Toby's friend

Merrilee, right? He's so excited you're here. And if you like books, then *I'm* so excited you're here too. I love to read. I've got a book blog and everything. This one is so not a reader."

Hannah nudged Sera's shoulder. It made her blush again. "I read. Just not at your impossible book-a-day rate."

"Unless you value kissing scenes more than writing skill, do *not* ask Merrilee for book recommendations." My best friend smirked at me to show that she was—maybe-sorta—joking.

"This is Eliza, and she's just mad because I said *On the Origin of Species* was boring." I plopped down in the seat next to where she was unpacking her lunch. "For the record, it is."

"Agree," said Hannah. "I don't even need to read it to agree. So tell me more—what do you like to read? Or do you mostly stick to romance novels? If so, no judgment. We get enough of that from every other corner of the bookstore."

"Yeah, since it's a genre read mostly by women, it must be dumb, right?" We traded eye rolls. As I pulled my sandwich out of my bag, I added, "I'm actually reading an incredibly feminist romance series. It's about this guy, Blake, and this warrior half-angel heroine—"

"Esmeralda?" Hannah leaned in and nodded. "The Fall with Me series is awesome." She elbowed Sera. "See? I told you you should read it."

I elbowed Eliza. "See? I told you not to judge it from that one scene."

Sera took a deep breath and looked across the table. "Well, I . . . I'm with Eliza. I liked *Origins.* But I have no interest in reading about Blake."

"I'll wear you down eventually," Hannah said as she linked their hands on the top of the table. I was pretty sure I understood what that meant, but I've never let being "pretty sure" stop me from stating the obvious.

"Are you guys a couple?"

"Yes," said Sera. The intense blush was back, but her gaze was direct.

"Cool." It was good to know that even though Toby was perpetually single, this school wasn't a relationship wasteland. "And to answer your question from before, Hannah, I read anything. Anything *fiction*, that is. Classics, contemporary, fantasy, sci-fi, thriller. I don't really like war books, but I make an exception for, like, *Johnny Tremain* and *Henry V.*"

Hannah laughed. "Eclectic. I like it."

I shrugged. "And if there's a romance plot or subplot . . . I'm certainly not going to complain. Like I was telling Eliza this morning: boys are so much better in books."

"This *again*?" sighed Eliza.

Hannah snorted. "Well, I agree. Kinda."

I quirked an eyebrow. "Oh, right. *Girls* are so much better in books?"

She laughed and shook her head, making her red bangs dance. She tapped a pin on her blazer that read "Biracial/Bisexual." "I've got strong opinions on all sorts of fictional love interests. Sometimes the quote-unquote 'romantic heroes' are really disturbing—but there are also some truly hot characters that no real-life guy or girl could measure up to." She squeezed Sera's hand. "Not that I'd want them to. I'm happier with you than a paper person."

"See?" I told Eliza. "Hannah thinks some book heroes are better. And I happen to think that Romeo is right up there with Blake, and Rochester, and Gilbert Blythe, and Gatsby."

Eliza groaned. "Gatsby is a narcissistic mess. He is *not* romantic."

I fiddled with the zipper on my lunch bag and ignored her. "And Juliet's only *thirteen*. Yet she's already had way more romance than I've had in my whole life."

"Your *whole life* is fifteen years," said Eliza. "Plus, life expectancy back then was so different."

"True! It's like dog years. Juliet was probably comparatively thirty," said Sera.

"Stop killing the romance, both of you!" Hannah threw a blueberry at Sera and aimed another one at Eliza.

Toby caught it from mid air and popped it in his mouth. "Uh-oh, Hannah. You're getting Eliza's *don't encourage her* glare. What's this one up to now?" Toby put his tray on the table and dropped his hands onto my shoulders with a playful squeeze. "I heard 'romance.' Talking about me?"

I laughed and let my head settle back against him. "You feeling all right, Mayday? You're more delusional than usual." Toby and I talked dares, and movies, and fanfiction, and fandoms, and music, and—when we were feeling particularly dorky—math. We did *not* talk romance. Not if I could avoid it.

"Mayday?" asked Lance as he settled into the chair next to Sera. "Oh, Toby *May* . . . Ha! I get it."

"Sorry. That nickname's off-limits," I said. Eliza groaned.

"She made me sign in blood." Toby slid his hands off my shoulders and plopped down beside me. "I'm not allowed to respond to anyone else using it."

"Don't even pretend you didn't use ketchup," I said.

"*Interesting*," said Hannah. She was raising her eyebrows and looking back and forth between us.

"No, it's really not." Eliza rolled her eyes. I didn't actually look over and see her do it, but I could hear the eye roll in her tone. "Listening to Merrilee and Toby recount their childhood playdates and inside jokes is really not interesting at all."

"I want to know what has Eliza more scowly than usual," pressed Toby. He swatted my hand away from his brownie.

Rude! I was only going to take a bite. "I was explaining how boys are better in books."

"Specifically Romeo," said Hannah. "But I disagree. That book is called a tragedy for a reason."

"Their situation is tragic, but the characters are romantic," I countered. "So, Toby, since you were so interested, what do *you* think?"

I expected a banterish deflection, but Toby took a long sip of water, then frowned slightly. "I haven't *read* much romance, but you've made me watch more than enough of it. I always liked that Knightley dude from *Emma*. He's there as Emma's friend, and she just has to wake up and realize they should be *more*."

I wasn't clueless about how Toby thought he felt about me. I mean, Eliza referred to him as "the infatuation next door." Thankfully, not to his face. But last summer, he and I had had The Talk. He'd started to make declarations, and I'd cut him off and listed out all the reasons it would never work. I even used the words "We'd be a catastrophe of a couple." He'd nodded and agreed. And for most of the twelve months since then, he'd still been the pal who was responsible for all my scars and groundings and muddiest childhood adventures. But occasionally he poked at parameters I'd thought we'd made pretty firm. Occasionally he did things like press his leg to mine under the cafeteria table in a way that felt like it was angling for more-than-friends.

This was a conversation he and I needed to have—again— but not here. Not on the first day of school, not in front of an audience, with Sera and Hannah smirking, Eliza frowning. I didn't want him to ask his questions, because he wouldn't like my answers.

I smacked his leg and scooted my chair an inch away. A perfectly friendly, perfectly clear *knock it off* gesture that only made him lean toward me and open his mouth—

"Wait! Did I miss the part where we do names?" Curtis looked even more like an overgrown puppy as his flip-flops slid on the floor and he crashed down on the chair next to Hannah's, the momentum sliding her seat several inches. I felt Eliza stiffen next to me; apparently she still hadn't for- given him for walking us to bio. "Please, for the love of all things sacred and sugary, someone tell me their first names!"

"Huh, they really *do* use our last names in classes, don't they? 'Miss Campbell' sounds so formal," I said. Toby snorted and Curtis pressed his palms into a prayer posture. "Oh, right! I'm Merrilee. She's Eliza."

"Eliza," he repeated. "So, why was the whole science department lined up to shake your hand before first period?'"

She flushed like a cherub, just like she had when they made her walk a gauntlet of introductions before bio.

Sera snorted. "Clearly *someone* didn't read the school newsletter." She looked around the table for affirmation, but everyone shrugged. Hannah patted her arm. Sera's voice squeaked when she asked, "Wait, am I the *only* one who did?"

Eliza raised her hand and Sera exhaled loudly. I smiled around a bite of yogurt—it was such a heart-squish moment of watching two kindred spirits.

Except for Toby and me, everyone at the table was leaning in, openly studying Eliza like a bug. Sera shook her head. "Eliza's a Gordon-Fergus. As in, daughter of Violet Gordon and Warner Fergus. As in, the Gordon Principle? The Fergus Cycle? They're the most famous biologists on the planet. Well, living biologists. Darwin's still probably a bit more well-known."

"Ohhhh." Curtis's expression could only be described as "lit lightbulb." "Is that why Dr. Badawi couldn't speak coherently in bio this morning? She's normally, well, normal. At least she was when I was her lab aide last year."

Eliza shrugged. Her face was blank, but her knuckles were white.

"So, who are you?" Curtis asked me. "Are you someone special, too?"

I laughed. "Me? No."

"Hey!" protested Toby, at the same time Eliza said, "Excuse me?"

"Well, my older sister is marrying Senator Rhodes's son. Does that count?"

Eliza huffed. "Oh, stop being such a middle child! She's Merrilee and she's awesome. That's all you need to know."

"Welcome," said Lance. "No offense to the rest of you, but I'm ready for new people. *Any* new faces are exciting when you've been stuck with the same kids since sixth grade at Mayfield Middle Academy."

I was about to explain that the feeling was mutual and add that I'd been stuck with the same *female* faces since sixth grade—not that I was remotely romantically interested in anyone at this table—but Toby beat me to speaking.

"That's a good reminder," he said. Toby pointed to Eliza and me, then turned to his friends. "No. No. Don't even think about it. And *no.*"

I blushed. They laughed.

Eliza stood up. "Please tell me you weren't just playing some patriarchal role and pretending you have any say in my relationships. Because A) I'm not some commodity you get to trade or restrict, and B) Who gave *you* the authority to speak for either of us and our desires?"

Hannah and Sera clapped. Toby ground his jaw and looked away. I couldn't reach out and calm *either* of them without upsetting the other, so I ignored them both.

"Is now a good time to ask for your phone number?" Curtis faux-whispered to Eliza. "I mean, why not take this opportunity to prove Toby wrong by giving it to me?"

Lance laughed, but Eliza silenced them both with a glare. Before she could follow up with a verbal rejection, I jumped in. "How many classes left?"

"Math, media, and then Convocation," she said.

"And Convocation is announcements and speeches and stuff? It's where you said you nap, right, Toby?" I tipped my head back on my chair and whined. "So tired. Need more summer."

"Probably no napping on the first day," he said with a grin. "But sit next to me, I'll poke you if you start yawning."

6

After school, I opened the passenger door of Toby's car and leaned in. "Hey, Rory. Fun first day? Good. Now scoot!" I pointed from my little sister to the backseat. "I've got *permanent* shotgun. Right, Mayday?"

"Right-o," he agreed, reaching across Rory to give me a fist bump. "Rowboat's my hapless sidekick."

"Hapless? I'd like to think I'm rather hapful." I ignored my sister's glower as she pushed me out of her way and joined Eliza in the backseat. I was used to her glower. Rory was *born* ticked off at me. Mom swore it was her way of looking up to me, but Mom needed to update the prescription on her rose-colored glasses. "In fact, I'm so hapful, I've been adopted already. *Both* Eliza and I were hapful." I practically melted onto the tan leather seats of Toby's car. First days were exhausting.

"Stop saying 'hapful,'" said Eliza. "But I'm really pleased with our Knight Lights."

"What? I wanted to adopt you!" Toby dropped his keys but didn't pick them up. Instead he turned his puppy-dog eyes on me.

"Oh." My heart squished guiltily. I should've known. Why hadn't I thought of that?

"Too late! She's claimed." Eliza sounded elated. I shot her a look and she kicked the back of my seat.

"I've planned on being your Knight Light since you told me you were transferring. Who is it? Can't you tell them no?"

"Sorry! It's Hannah and Sera. I can't back out." I put my hand on his arm—the muscles were tight as he gripped the steering wheel. "Besides, I already know *you*."

"Um, can someone fill me in?" Rory asked. "Adopted? Knight Lights?"

Despite having asked those same questions when Hannah and Sera found me after Convocation, I rolled my eyes like she was clueless. It was an older sister's prerogative, plus she deserved it for stealing shotgun. I would've been there first, but I'd gotten lost in the exodus from the Convocation hall. I needed Eliza to point me in the direction of my locker, but I couldn't see her, or Toby, or Curtis, Lance, Hannah, Sera—*any* familiar faces. I would even have welcomed the cranky dude. He probably would've been delighted to give me directions . . . right into traffic.

It's possible getting separated had been my fault. I'd slow-poked, hoping to get a glimpse of my emo mystery boy. And it's really too bad I hadn't found him. We could've paced sadly together until Hannah located me, linked her arm through mine, and asked to adopt me.

"Well?" Now Rory just sounded pissed, and I realized no one had answered her. Eliza was too busy frowning at her phone and Toby was still staring at me like I'd cut his piano strings.

"There are cookies involved." That's how Hannah had presented it to me. And ditto Sera to Eliza, when the two of them had joined us. Not that Eliza ate cookies. More for me!

"It's a Hero High tradition," clarified Toby. "Sophomores 'adopt' a freshman or a new student. It's sort of like a mentor program, except less mentoring and more boxes of cookies in your locker and a person to ask if you have questions. We're called Knight Lights—because the school mascot is the Crimson Knight and we 'light your way'—cheesy, right? Though, I guess it could be worse—adoptees could be called serfs or vassals. You're sure you're taken, Merri?"

Eliza didn't mock Toby's awful joke or delight in telling him I was. She still hadn't looked up from her phone. I reclined my seat until I was practically in her lap. She wouldn't want me asking "You okay?" in front of an audience, so I just reached back and squeezed her hand. She didn't object, squeezed back. Uh-oh.

"Could you adopt me?" Rory's voice squeaked on the question, a nervous tick I hadn't heard since back in the days when she still wet the bed, still called him "Twoby," and still had the most adorable-obnoxious little kid crush on him. "I mean, Eliza and Merrilee have each other and you—but I don't know anyone. So if you can't have Merri . . ."

More squeaks. Each one made my stomach drop. My first day had been easy—but how had hers been? I hadn't seen her except one glimpse of the back of her head at Convocation. *Worse*, I hadn't even looked for her.

I uprighted my chair and poked his shoulder. "You with Aurora! That's perfect."

She rewarded me with a smile, and I congratulated myself on achieving the impossible—for as long as this lasted, I'd be her favorite sister.

Toby sighed. "You're sure you can't—"

"No," interrupted Eliza.

"Please, Toby! Hannah said some guys use Knight Light as a sketchy hookup thing. Please save my sweet baby sister from some skeezeball who just wants a piece of her."

"I'm *not* a baby! I'm only ten months younger than you!"

And no longer her favorite sister. It was a fun thirty seconds. Since she was already annoyed, I might as well . . . "I can't call you my *little* sister. It's not my fault you're a giantess."

"Can you kick her chair again?" Rory asked Eliza. "Five-six isn't tall. You're *short!*"

"The *S*-word?" I gasped. "How dare you. Toby, I take it back."

He laughed and turned around in his seat. "Rory, I'd be honored to adopt you, if you want me."

"I do!" Her flush turned to blush. "I mean, if you don't mind?"

"Of course not. Campbell ladies are my favorite."

Eliza muttered, "They're individuals—not a category."

Toby responded by fishing his keys from the floor and starting the car. "Eliza, am I dropping you at your house?"

"No! I need her!" I answered. "She's helping me get ready for Lillian's engagement party. I'm codependent when it comes to formal wear. Oh, hey, there's Curtis!" I spotted him as Toby backed out of the parking space, but he was too far away to call a greeting. "I like him. Not *like* like, but I like him as a human."

"He's a good guy," said Toby. Eliza grumbled, but he ignored her. "And his mom is the best baker. She's from Egypt and makes this almond cake, *basbousa*." He paused to drool over the memory, and I took the time to Google *bass-boo-sah* on my phone. But, yeah, I didn't spell it right. "I swear, even if I didn't like him, I'd still be friends just for his mom's cooking."

I glanced back at Curtis, glad to have another piece of info to add to my nosy-girl dossier. There was no question he was attractive: golden skin, dark eyes, mascara-commercial lashes, dignified nose. And baked goods, well, that was the clichéd icing on the almond cake. Still . . . not interested. He was too tall. And while he was fun and nice, there was no spark.

Plus, and this was really the *only* reason I needed: he was already smitten with Eliza. Didn't matter if she reciprocated, he'd never be *my* Hero High hero.

"Speaking of guys—" Rory chimed in. "The freshman class won't stop talking about the headmaster's son. Apparently he's gorgeous and brilliant and super aloof."

"Oh, really?" I turned around to look at Eliza. "Aloof? Gorgeous? Sounds like my mystery boy."

"Yours?" asked Toby, breaking jerkily at a stop sign. "How?"

"Not hers," Eliza clarified. "Not anywhere but in her head."

"Do you know him, Toby?" asked Rory.

"Fielding's one of my best friends."

"Really?" That meant he was one of the parade of guys I'd seen swinging by Toby's house before and after sports practices. Coming over for school projects and to shoot basketball in his driveway. That part of his life had always been so separate from our friendship. It was strange to think that now they overlapped. Stranger to think that I could've met mystery boy years sooner if I'd learned to dribble or gone to any of his games.

"Will you introduce me?" asked Rory. "The other freshmen will be so jealous!"

"Sure." Toby laughed.

"And me!" I added. "Side note: Fielding is an awesome name."

"I asked first," said Rory.

"So? I saw him first." I sighed and relived the memory of dappled shade and dapper boy. "Being all dreamy and self-reflective."

Toby's laugh faded. "I guess. He's a junior, so we may not cross paths or anything."

I snickered. "Don't be ridiculous. You just said he's one of your best friends. Our paths *will* cross." I leaned my head back. "Now, if you'll excuse me—since someone was poking me in Convocation—" Which had been just as boring as Toby promised. A mash-up of school assembly with announcements and Headmaster Williams's welcome speech, while seated on hard wooden benches and fighting an urge to make the sign of the cross or sing "Amazing Grace," because the Convocation hall looked remarkably like a church. There'd been Latin mottos and a school song—and, disappointingly, still no indications of a secret society. "Since I was up late with Blake, I need a power nap."

"Who?" asked Rory.

"Blake?" asked Toby. "Who's Blake?"

Eliza was probably behind me plotting ways to steal the novel and replace it with a science journal. I'm positive she rolled her eyes.

I shut mine and reclined my seat. "Wake me when we're home."

7

"Can you braid my hair like Ms. Gregoire's?" I asked once Eliza and I had answered my parents' avalanche of first-day-tell-me-*everything* questions and escaped behind my bedroom door.

Eliza's hair had the perfect amount of wave and texture for any hairstyle. It had so much glowy, angelic, look-at-me perfection when worn down. Naturally this meant she kept it in a ponytail.

My brown hair occasionally achieved shampoo-commercial shine after a brushing, but Rory and I had gotten our dad's hair genes, and the result was as stubborn as he was. Even NASA couldn't create a product that would make it hold a curl.

Rory had given up and cut hers into a chin-length bob that suited her heart-shaped face. Mine plus bob? I might as well buy pointy stick-on ears and start looking for a giant acorn to live in.

"No," said Eliza.

"No, don't cut my hair? I'm not. Wait, what were we talking about?"

"No, I can't style you like a teacher-clone. I'll try, but I doubt it'll stay."

"I wish you were coming." Or I wished I were staying home and curling up with a book.

"It's a family thing. I'm not family." Eliza's shrug was a lie. With her parents sciencing all over the globe, we were the closest thing she had to a family. She *should* be invited. Toby and his father were equally non-blood, and they were coming.

"Eh, I think in this case it's a politics thing," I corrected.

"I wish Trent had never asked me about my parents' opinion on his mom. And it's not like I *lied*. Her positions on the environment could be stronger. Yes, they're stronger than Stratford's, but *come on*, that's a pretty low bar."

"The thing is, Eliza," I began cautiously, "Trent *didn't* ask you. You volunteered."

"Oh." She blinked like she was fitting this new piece of information into her mental puzzle. "Well, it's not like I said they wouldn't vote for her. Of course they will—look at her opposition. Plus, she's the first female senator from our state—I'm all about shattered ceilings, and I support ninety percent of her platform. She's got an excellent track record of championing marginalized voices. But it doesn't mean she's above reproach."

My eyes started to glaze over. They did whenever people talked politics. Give me numbers, give me chemistry, give me history, give me computers . . . but politics, well, I associated that with Trent and his mom. I stifled a yawn with the back of my hand and waited for her to finish ranting so I could ask, "Eliza, did something happen after Convocation? You've seemed . . . upset since then."

Her hand tightened on the tube of Apocalypse Gel ("*You may not survive the apocalypse, but your hairstyle will!*"). The amount of product she smushed onto my head might prove their slogan right.

"It's nothing." Her fingers pulled and tugged as she braided and twisted.

"Are you sure? Because it seems like you're pretty angry. Like maybe you've forgotten there's a *head* attached to the hair you're ripping out—*my* head. Ow!"

"Do you want it to stay up or not?" She was holding my hair so tightly I couldn't even nod. "Then sit still."

Her fingers relaxed enough for me to hear her over the screaming pain of my scalp. "It's just . . . Dr. Badawi stopped me after Convocation. My parents contacted her to ask how I'd performed in my first day of class." She tried to sound bored, like she was commenting on a rom-com I'd forced her to watch, but I didn't miss her hand shaking in the mirror.

"Have they emailed or called you? To wish you luck on your first day?"

Eliza laughed. Her laugh was one of my favorite things about her—it wasn't beautiful or dainty; she snorted like a Canadian goose. But this bitter version didn't make me smile. "Don't be ridiculous. Luck's not a real thing . . . and they're busy."

"If they have time for your teachers, they have time for you." Note to self—write a scathing *look at your priorities* email to the Gordon-Ferguses tomorrow.

"There's still plenty of time for them to check in."

I winced at the hope in her voice. "I'll cross my fingers."

She patted my head. "And you're done. No wild dancing, and this might actually stay."

"I don't think the senator rolls with a wild-dancing crowd." I looked in the mirror, and my jaw dropped. "You're a miracle worker!" My crown of braids was perfect! Add in Eliza's precision makeup application, and I looked more elegant than cute.

She handed me the purse she'd packed, layered on one more coat of hairspray, and motioned for me to spin. I did, smoothing the demure halter top that tied in a flouncy bow and fluffing out the dress's swishy skirt to maximize its twirlability.

"You're perfect," she said.

Eliza wasn't big on hugs, but there were times I ignored this. Times I felt like she wanted me to ignore this. I threw my arms around her. She squeezed me back.

I walked her out—using the trip down the hallway and stairs as a trial run for my ability to balance in heels. Eh, close enough. Maybe I'd stand still.

Back upstairs, I passed Rory in the hall. I was about to say how much I liked her navy-and-teal strapless dress when she shrieked, "You can't wear that!"

I looked down. Nope, hadn't sprouted any stains or tears yet. "Why not?"

"Are you serious? Lillian!"

My older sister stuck her head out of her bathroom. It never seemed fair that she got her own while Aurora and I had to share. Not that I hadn't used hers while she was away at college, but now she was home till her wedding and working with Mom and Dad at the store until she started law school next fall. It was majorly inconvenient. "What?" she snapped.

"Tell Merrilee she can't wear *white* to your engagement party. You're the bride, not her."

I checked off rebuttals on my fingers: "Technically, it's ivory. It's only four days after Labor Day. *Style Magazine* says that rule is outdated. Plus, this is *not* the wedding."

"She can wear pajamas for all I care, as long as you're both in the car in—" Lilly glanced at the hall clock and paled. "Four minutes. We cannot be late. Punctuality is the senator's thing."

I didn't mean to shoot Rory an I-told-you-so look; it just slipped onto my face, possibly accompanied by a twirl so she could get the full effect of the swishy skirt. She huffed and stomped downstairs. I stayed put, counting in my head.

At eighteen seconds, Lilly yelled, "Merrilee!" and popped back into the hall. "You know I'm not serious about pajamas, right? You *cannot* wear pajamas."

"I know."

"But we really can't be late. I don't even know three-fourths of the guest list. FYI—your new headmaster's family will be there."

"Really?" I did a little shimmy, because that meant my mystery boy would be too. And this time Eliza wouldn't be there to stop me from decoding him.

"Really." Lilly smiled at my dance and added, "You look lovely, by the way."

I twirled while I said, "Thanks," then straightened the collar of her lilac silk dress and touched the blueberry-size pearls on the necklace Trent had given her as an engagement present. Lilly had curves like a slalom course, and this dress highlighted them all. "You look beautiful."

"I hope so." She started to pick at the fresh manicure on her nails, then folded them behind her back. "And let's be clear: you can wear white *today*, but not at the wedding."

"Won't you pick my dress color? I'm a bridesmaid, right? So you get to dress me as ridiculously as you want."

Lilly laughed. "I think I'm supposed to ask you, but *yes*. Be my maid of honor?"

We were still hugging when Rory called up the stairs with a thirty-second warning.

Who cared? It's not like they could start the party without the bride *and* maid of honor.

My excitement and power trip over my title lasted the fifteen-minute car ride to the Rhodes's country club. I also got the pleasure of seeing Rory pout when she heard my maid-of-honor news—dude, last week she'd hassled Lilly about every page she'd flagged in *Bride Magazine*, calling them "the embodiment of generic wedding." Did she really think she was MoH material?

But apparently I wasn't the senator's choice for the role. And when Mom made the mistake of using me as an explanation for our three-minute—three-minute!—tardiness, her reaction to the news was a bit cold. Like, the Gordon-Ferguses could leave the South Pole and come study *this* iciness.

"That's a lot of responsibility, and Merrilee is a child. I was thinking Trenton's cousin Gloria would be maid of honor," Senator Rhodes said stiffly. Everything about her was stiff, so this wasn't unusual. And since when did the mother of the groom have any say in the bridal party? I wasn't an expert on Senate stuff, but I knew how to recognize an ego-tripping control freak.

To Lilly's credit, she refused to budge, and Senator Rhodes declared, "This isn't the time for this discussion. You and Trenton need to mingle."

I wanted to mingle too! I wanted to link my elbow with Toby's and compliment his black suit and the olive-green tie that brought out the dark undertones in his skin and made his eyes pop. That boy was made for dressing up and wearing as arm candy. Preferably while gossiping, pranking, or acting as his wingwoman. While I had always preferred book boyfriends to real ones, Toby was fluent in flirt. He was a master class in dating dynamics, and one of these days, the lessons I learned from watching him and his adoring fangirls might stick. One of these days, I might even meet someone I wanted to give my first kiss to.

Instead the senator trapped me in a corner of the ballroom. It was me and a ficus—and I think the plant cared more about the senator's rules of decorum than I did. "A lady never points, or crosses her legs at the knees—ankles only. At any bridal functions, the maid of honor will not curse or wear anything that exposes her naval or cleavage. Always assume there are photographers. And that anyone asking questions is a reporter. If so, you do *not* answer them."

I nodded and tuned her out, daydreaming about *Fall with Me* and its hero, Blake—where do you live when your soul mate is a half angel caught in a battle between heaven and hell and you're a British actor who's always on set? Star-crossed love stories were the best kind. No wonder we were study-ing *Romeo and Juliet* hundreds of years later. I couldn't wait to spend some quality time curled up with Romeo. Too bad book boyfriends gave paper cuts when you tried to snuggle.

The senator droned on. "I'll need to vet your speeches for the shower and reception, so make sure you get copies to me at least a week prior."

Seriously? I was much more *let's wing it* than speechwriter.

"As a member of this wedding party, you represent my family and my reelection campaign—do not do anything that will reflect poorly on either."

I nodded like some dizzy bobblehead, but man, Lilly owed me BIG TIME. Like, *way* more than just the pair of boots I wasn't going to tell her I'd ruined.

The senator concluded with a disorientingly warm "Welcome to the team. Trenton and Lillian are lucky to have you as part of their special day."

I looked around. Had she been body snatched while I'd day-dreamed? Had I missed the part where she decided to like me? I mumbled, "Thanks" and tottered away—but really that stumble was on *her*, not me or the heels.

All I wanted was Toby, a crab cake, or anything wrapped in bacon or puff pastry—and to avoid Rory, since she was carrying a glass of something red and looking menacingly at my dress. Ideally I'd find Toby, overload a plate with appetizers, and we'd sneak away to a porch to eat them while plotting ways to thwart the senator. Plotting and subverting were Toby's specialties—and when I spotted his back in the bar alcove and saw he was double-fisting plates, I wondered if he'd psychically known to prep for these exact tasks.

I swept toward him, admiring the way my skirt swished and the magical qualities of this hair gel. I paused just before the bar alcove. Toby's back was toward me, and he was talking to someone. It would be entirely inappropriate to spring at him, cover his eyes, and make him *guess who*. Which made it all the more appealing.

Before I could pounce he said, "Oh, there's the senator. Hero High alumni at its finest." I froze. Yeah, I was done with the senator portion of the night. Toby continued, "That means Merri finally escaped. I'm going to find her. Come with me, I'll introduce you. She's the best."

Why, thank you, Mayday. I did a mental curtsy. I hadn't realized how badly I'd needed to hear that—how much the day's nonstop newness and the senator's criticism had rubbed me raw, made whatever I was yearning for rise to the surface.

Except whoever he was talking to responded, "No, thank you."

Toby laughed. "Do you even know who I'm talking about? Middle sister of the bride and new Hero High student. White dress. Brown hair. Normally it's down, but tonight she's got it up in loopy things."

Ivory! Why was everyone having such a hard time distinguishing ivory from white? And "loopy things"? I knew Toby and his dad lived in an all-male household, but were braids really that foreign a concept? Of course, he once made Rory cry by describing her hair as "nice and frizzy" after she'd spent the night sleeping in foam rollers. In his mind, "loopy" was probably a similar compliment.

"She's gorgeous. You've got to meet her," Toby finished in a voice that knocked the laughter from my throat and made me stumble on my heels. Eavesdropping time was more than over. I stepped around the corner.

"Yeah. I know the person you mean. I'm not tempted. But don't let me stop you."

My eyes flew to my insulter—a handsome guy in a suit. Like, paranormal hero handsome. Then I recognized him and cringed. This was technically the second time he'd refused to meet me. The first was when I'd extended a germy hand and a smile in his direction near the trash—nay, recycling—can. He was even more handsome than he'd been in his uniform. Normally I found basic black suits boring, but not on him. The glowing white of his shirt made his skin flawless in a way that shouldn't be allowed on any teenager. It made me want to ask what sort of detergent and face wash he used. And the Windsor knot of his gray pinstriped tie was too perfect to have been done on the first try. *He* looked too perfect for this ballroom, like he'd stepped out of a Bond movie or was about to step into one.

Except then he'd be charming, not insulting. I pivoted away before either of them saw me. I'd catch up with Toby once he'd found better company. And speaking of, why was that snob bait at Lilly's party?

Not tempted. Like I wanted to tempt him. Like he had even crossed my mind or would ever cross my mind. Who cared if he didn't want to meet me? I didn't want to meet him either. He could go back to marching around campus like he owned the place, like everyone should need his permission to breathe or attend class or whatever. I'd find much better people to fill my time.

I made my way over to the table mounded with shrimp and fruit and cheeses, but none of it seemed appealing. My skirt didn't feel as swishy, my heels felt unsteadier, and while I knew Eliza had painted on my makeup like an artist, I felt like a kid playing dress-up. Even my hair itched, and when I raised a hand to pat it, it felt crunchy and fake instead of elegant. *Loopy*. I slouched around the table to hover near an ice sculpture.

"There you are!" Dad strode over, holding a glass of red wine that he'd miraculously managed not to spill on his tie or shirt yet. What can I say, I came by my staining skills honestly. "What is with you girls hiding tonight? Where's your sister?"

"Last I saw, Rory was roving with a glass of punch." My voice sounded as squashed as my ego. I scanned the room and pointed. "She's been cornered by one of Trent's aunts."

"I mean your *other* sister." He said it lightly, but his lips were sticking to his teeth like his smile was too tight. "I've been looking for her for twenty minutes."

"Lilly? You've lost the bride?"

"She's got to be here somewhere, but . . ." He glanced around the room and took a long sip of his drink. "Your mom and I haven't been able to find her, and the senator's been asking."

"Oh!" No wonder that vein in his neck was pulsing. I raised my hand in salute—MoH reporting for duty. "I'm on it."

8

The party spilled out of the ballroom. People clustered like grapes around the small tables and benches in the lobby and out on the decks. But Lilly was in none of them.

I saw Trent standing in a bro-group, one more Ken doll in a herd of wax-statue attractiveness. Perhaps I *should* have gone over and asked if he knew where Lilly was, but . . . gah. He was such a paste eater. I swear his molecules were made up of manners and *this is my best side* poses. I didn't feel like getting stuck in a loop of "Allow me to come with you to look for her." / "No, thanks. I'm all set." / "Please, I insist." / "No, *really*, it's not necessary." / "Oh, but it is." / "Oh, but I'm going to smack you right in that toothpaste-commercial smile."

Yeah, definitely better that I dealt with my future brother-in-law in small doses.

Lillian wasn't in the bathroom either. And I felt like a creeper calling her name and checking under stall doors.

I wandered down an empty hall, past windows that over-looked tennis courts instead of golf greens. The only people in it were two guys in crisp shorts and polo shirts with racquet bags at their feet.

The first guy was deep in kiss-up mode. "You looked good out there. Get any better and I'll think you're gunning for my spot on the team. You're not, are you?"

But his friend with the dark curls wasn't paying attention. He lifted his eyes from the dusky flowers printed on the carpet. They were shockingly blue. They were shockingly clear. And then they were shockingly pinned to mine. Oh, I wanted to freeze the moment and stay caught in his stare. It made my toes curl against my shoes. The hallway suddenly felt way, way too warm.

I was five steps past before I recognized him as the guy from this morning. The emo-mystery. The headmaster's son! And if I met him now, I wouldn't need Toby to introduce us. . . . Except—Lillian! Maid of Honor! I wanted to turn around and have some magical meet-cute moment, but I was an MoH with a mission: find the bride.

I gritted my teeth and entered the locker room. It was empty.

He was gone when I came back out. Mystery *unsolved*. Opportunity missed. Sister *still missing*.

I found Lilly in the darkened pro shop. A pearl-wearing silhouette among chrome racks of polo shirts and spindly shadows of golf clubs.

"What are you doing? Everyone is looking for you. I don't think you're supposed to be in here. Wait. Are you crying? What's going on?" I shut the door behind me, praying it wouldn't lock.

Lilly wiped at her eyes. "I'm fine."

"You are so *not* fine." I pulled tissues from my purse and passed them to her.

"It's stupid . . ."

"You wouldn't be crying if it was stupid." I put a hand on her arm. "Tell me who I need to beat up."

She sniffle-snorted, a noise like a pug with a cold. "It's just . . . a lot of pressure. Senator Rhodes—she—she—"

I had to grit my teeth so I didn't jump into her pauses with my own complaints about the woman. How dare she be so bossy, so organized, have such well-behaved hair.

Lilly sniffed. "She really wants the best for Trent, and she means well, but it's hard hearing everything I'm doing wr-wrong."

I shifted my weight in my shoes—another complaint: the senator always wore heels and never teetered. "I hope someone fills her pillow with porcupines."

Lilly's raccoon eyes widened. "You wouldn't."

"If I knew where to get porcupines, I might." I handed her another tissue. "You shouldn't be crying at your engagement party because of her."

Lilly blew her nose. "It's not just that. It's being around Mom and Dad at the store all day, and they're so worried about finances, but they're fake-smiling and pretending everything's fine. And this wedding is so stupid expensive. And then Trent picked me up after work and we went in that boutique next door, and there was this stupid hipster pillow—a disgruntled cat with a mustache—like I said, stupid. But I picked it up and . . . Trent laughed and made it clear there won't be a place in our house for things like that. And one of his exes is here tonight and she made a comment about how 'Some brides really should be avoiding the cheese tray.' And I don't need a hipster pillow—mustaches are passé, I know this! And I don't care about Veronica's opinion of my thighs. I know my size. I love my size, my thighs, my belly, jiggle and all. Trent does too. It's just . . ." She raised a shaking hand to her mouth. "I wanted that pillow, you know?"

Nope. It sounded hideous. And I really wasn't following her ramble. "So . . . which are you upset about? The senator? The ex? Or the pillow?"

She snorted and blew her nose. "It's just . . . everything? Mostly everything. And maybe one too many cocktails on an empty stomach."

Maybe this was a good time for a MoH pep talk? Because I felt like a failure. Less than two hours after I'd been given the title, my bride was hiding and crying. "You know that you are the best big sister ever and that I adore you and Trent is the luckiest guy and you are the smartest and the prettiest and most amazing and neither of us would trade you for anyone in the world, right?" Okay, so I was no Shakespeare and that was no Saint Crispin's Day speech, but it was the best I could come up with off the top of my head in a dark golf shop. "Um, can I do anything?"

"No, but *I* can!" She said it firmly and raised teary eyes to mine, staring fiercely from between mascara gone clumpy. "You're right. I *am* pretty awesome. And I need to stop playing doormat. When we first started dating, I asked Trent's mom's opinion on *everything*. I just wanted her to like me so badly.

And now . . . Well, I let her get away with deciding for so long—what I wore, where we ate . . . I think the only words I said to her for months were 'What do you suggest?' She doesn't even know I have opinions . . . so why would she consult them?"

"It's not too late," I said, and she nodded so vigorously that I cautiously added more advice: "You don't have to get married."

"Yes. Yes, I do! And I want to. I love Trent. He's good and he's kind and he's patient and he loves me so much. He's the best person I know. I just need to—I need to tell the senator to back off and let us be *us*."

Lillian was taller than me, but she always somehow felt smaller. Not smaller weight-wise, except for that horrible period her freshman year of college when she came home all bones and angles and celery sticks and sadness. But despite therapy and the army of people who'd have swallowed fire for her, she'd never been able to shrug off even the slightest criticism. She wore her vulnerability like a fluorescent shirt. It always made me want to protect her and always made her a target for the cruel, the bullies—or in tonight's case, Trent's jilted ex.

As for Senator Rhodes, she could forget vetting my toast, and she was lucky I wasn't old enough to vote.

"I can do this!" Lilly said.

"Yes, you can!" I agreed.

"I'm not going to let anyone make me feel small or tell me what I think!"

"Absolutely!" I clapped. "Me neither!"

. . . Except I'd apologized for a garbage mistake that very

morning. I was still reeling from *not tempted*. Who cared if Mr. Recycling was tempted? Who asked that jerk to be tempted? But that feeling from this morning still clamped down on my stomach: the Disney songs, the itchy longing that practically sizzled on my skin. I *yearned*. Not for *him*, obviously. But for something.

Maybe Lilly had had the right idea after all, because hiding in here sounded great. "Let's just stay here until the party is over," I suggested.

"No. I'm fine." Lilly fixed a stray piece of hair and straightened her dress. "I'm better than fine. Just had a moment and too many toasts. I'll go back out there and stick to seltzer and eat some protein. And tell the senator that I absolutely don't want bagpipes at the church."

Bagpipes? I grimaced. "Yikes. Well, stop in the bathroom first to wipe your face. And here—Eliza packed my clutch. It's got makeup."

Lilly laughed. "She thinks of everything, doesn't she? Tell her thanks for me."

I nodded. "Want me to come with you?"

She shook her head. "I want a minute to pull myself together. I'll see you back out there, MoH." She leaned over and kissed my cheek before heading toward the exit. At the door she turned and whispered, "And Merri? I'd stuff a pillowcase with porcupines for you too."

9

The pro shop door opened and I turned to ask Lilly what she forgot, but Lilly wasn't a guy. A tall, shadowy silhouette of one. Standing between me and the door. Me and everyone I knew, everyone who could hear me scream "stranger danger!" And it was way too late to hide, since I was standing directly beneath a skylight in a dress that glowed as bright as the moonlight hitting it.

I took a step backward, snagged my heel on the strap of a golf bag, and then oh-so-gracefully, with full windmill arms and a slo-mo "Nooooo!" fell into a tower of golf ball boxes.

Which have really pointy corners! Corners that can pop open and crush beneath even five-foot people—causing small white balls to shoot out in every direction, like a popcorn popper whose projectiles were hard, loud, and bouncy.

"Are you okay?" The voice was closer, but I couldn't see anything but the rack of clubs that loomed precariously overhead. "I didn't mean to scare you."

Which I guess was a better thing to hear while lying on a pile of destroyed inventory than "Police! Hands up!" or "How attached are you to your skin?"

"I'm—" Well, I was bruised, embarrassed, still slightly

hyperventilating from the scare—and so, so grateful my dress hadn't fallen down or hiked up during that maneuver. I needed a stunt double. Or a bodyguard.

"Here, let me help you up." The guy stepped from shadows into moonlight and offered me a hand.

But I could only stare.

It was *the* guy. The one from the hall, the one from this morning. My mystery.

"Can you move?" He stepped closer and ran a hand through his curly hair, making it chaotic in ways that disarmed and charmed me.

"Oh, right." Maybe introductions were better done while I wasn't lying on my back in a ball pit made of golf balls. I brushed some off my dress, then accepted his hands. He pulled me up and steadied me as the world still wobbled. I thought it was because of how close we were and how hot he was, but really it was a golf ball beneath my shoe.

"There you are," he said, letting go of me—which made me want to whimper in protest. "Sorry again for scaring you. I . . . well, I saw you in the hallway earlier, and I wanted to meet you."

His eyes were ice blue, Siberian husky blue, the kind I thought only existed in books—and they stared back into mine.

The way he looked at me made my throat dry and my knees weak. Two clichés I hadn't really believed in before. My heart was racing, my cheeks were warm—four clichés! Was that what romance was? The moment you found out clichés were real? In that case, should I bite my lip and look up at him through lowered lashes?

No! Wait! Talk! It's not a conversation if I don't participate.

"I wanted to meet you too," I squeaked. My yearning felt like it had been dialed up to eleven. My nerves were at a thirteen.

He took a step closer and they shot up to sixteen.

This guy I'd noticed first thing in the morning, well before Rory told me about his freshman fan club and Toby gave his "one of my best friends" stamp of approval—this guy who was among the most beautiful humans I'd ever seen, had tracked me down. He'd seen me and then sought me out. And if Lilly could be brave about the senator and bagpipes, *I* could be brave about boys. Apparently the idiot in the other room was wrong. Not every guy thought I was icky. I kicked aside a golf ball as I swayed a step closer to him. "I'm really glad you were tempted."

Wait. What? Had I said that aloud? *I'm really glad you were tempted*? What did that even mean? This was why I'd die alone and unkissed. Because I had the social skills of a hyperactive puppy. I covered my face with my hand and mumbled between my fingers, "And I'm going to shut up now and die of embarrassment."

"Hey." His voice was so gentle I dared to peek between my fingers. He reached for my hand and tugged it from my face. Tingles! Those were genuine tingles at his touch. "Don't be. Tempted by you? Yeah, I'd say so." He stroked a thumb down the back of my fingers, and the blood beneath my skin ignited even before he added, "You're stunning."

I could check "heart skipped a beat" off my list of clichés. *This* was more romantic than anything I'd ever read in a novel. He was looking at me in a way I'd never been looked at before. Like the words "cute" or "amusing" weren't even in his vocabulary. I wanted to pause and thank the designers of this dress, the makers of this hair gel, and Eliza's nimble braiding fingers. And moonlight for making this shop glow.

And it wasn't just that he'd called me stunning. And tempting. Or that this night and setting felt crafted for romance. Or that I'd just vowed to be brave. Or Mom's reminders about her and Dad's high school romance. Or that I was tired of waiting for my first kiss. It was . . . everything. Like Lilly said, it was mostly everything. And mostly, mostly—I wanted to kiss this boy.

So even though my hands were shaking, I took the last half step between us. His head tilted down and mine tilted up. We had all the pieces needed for a novel's epic lip-lock scene: moonlight, mystery man, fancy dress. All I needed was to assemble them and add saliva. I raised an eyebrow, and . . . yes, I *did* bite my lower lip. I swear I didn't plan it. But then I opened my mouth and said, "I'm going to kiss you now—if that's okay."

"Yeah." When he answered, his eyes were black and hazy. Eliza was so right about pupils dilating. "That's *very* okay."

He cupped my face with long, strong fingers—so far, so good, that was definitely an A-plus hero move. Then he leaned in and brushed his mouth against mine. Also a classic maneuver. As he increased the pressure, our mouths began to figure out their own choreography, starting with the Hokey-Pokey and gradually progressing toward a waltz. And just when I'd managed to get out of my head and into the experience, ready to start looking for tingles, sparks, and all that fuss . . . Oxygen—I needed some. I turned my head away and took a step back, then a second, so I could lean on the wall and catch my breath. I tipped my head against it, feeling my braids brush something behind me, bobby pins poking my skull and prodding me back to reality.

"I should return to the party. People are going to be looking for me."

"But . . ." His face wrinkled in confusion. "Wait—"

"I really can't."

"But what's your name? When can I see you again?"

I was about to tell him, until I realized there was something wonderfully romantic about this moment. It was just like when Esmeralda had left Blake at the masquerade ball—right before masks were removed and identities revealed! This guy wanted to see me again! *I* knew we both went to the same school, I knew he was the headmaster's son and Toby's friend, but he had no clue about me.

"Oh, I'm not worried. I'm pretty sure you'll be able to track me down." The words felt so bookishly romantic in my mouth. I could practically see the plot points we'd skip across on the way to our happily ever after. I knew insta-love existed in books, but was it an actual phenomenon? Was this it? Maybe some part of me had *known* this morning—maybe that's why I'd been so drawn to him.

And the actual sparks and get-to-know-you stuff . . . well, that could come later.

"Can I at least have a hint?" he asked with a smile that made my insides go mushy.

"Hmm." I tapped a finger on my lip. "This should help . . . It's not only freshman in your fan club, Fielding." Man, I loved his name. "Transfer students think you're pretty great too."

I tossed my head and pushed off the wall—only to bounce back like a human yo-yo, because my hair was caught on something. But he didn't notice because he was too busy shaking his head.

"Fielding? Fielding Williams?" He practically spat the words. "I'm not *Fielding.*"

I'd been in the middle of trying to wrench myself free from whatever had caught my hair, but the vehemence of his words chilled me. My shoulders stiffened and I would've shrunk away from him if there was any room to do so. Instead, I reached back and grabbed the object ensnaring me and yanked on it—

With no further warning, the room blinked with the blue-white strobe of an alarm, and the scream of its siren filled the air.

I looked from his shocked face to over my shoulder, where my hand still rested on a fire alarm—a few strands of my hair stuck to the handle.

His curse was drowned out by the sirens. But I saw him mouth, "We need to go," and I ran for the closest door.

Which wasn't the right one.

Instead of leading into the club, it opened onto the golf course. I shrieked like a pug falling into a bathtub—because, sprinklers. *Cold* sprinklers. My heels sunk into the wet green as I scrambled backward, bouncing off the boy behind me and getting drenched. The sprinkler didn't sprinkle, it must have been high-efficiency or something, because it deluged. It dissolved all the hair gunk Eliza had used, and bobby pins began to slip free as my braids tumbled down in sticky clumps. I blinked, which resulted in mascara in my eyes.

Maybe he hadn't noticed? Or maybe I somehow still looked good—like the rain-soaked girls in music videos? Or maybe he was distracted because I'd slipped and practically tumbled into his arms. I guess it was sort of romantic, the way he caught me and all. I mean, from a third-party vantage point I'm sure it looked it—but mostly it was wet and clumsy. Not that I didn't appreciate him preventing me from high-fiving the ground with my face. But that wasn't how this moment was supposed to go—with him yelling at me for getting his name wrong—which meant he was *not* Toby's preapproved friend. Which meant I'd just kissed a total stranger. Who had, it bore repeating, *yelled at me*, before I'd gone and Merrilee'd a weird situation into something worse and wet.

"You okay?" he asked, herding me back into the strobe-lit pro shop.

"Yes," I yelled over the alarm, "but we have to go! Now."

"I'll find you," he vowed, then his voice went as icy as the water. "But I'm *not* Fielding."

And that was important right now, because . . . ? Mistaken identity was one of my favorite tropes, but he—whoever he was—was ruining it. "Noted," I said. "And . . . bye?"

He ran toward the locker rooms, while I ran down the hallway to the ballroom, which was empty of people. The last stragglers were pushing their way out the front door.

The drive was crowded with well-dressed and irritated

adults fretting about when they could retrieve their coats and purses, how long it would take the valet to sort keys and cars, and whether or not the fire trucks were blocking them in.

There was a subgroup within the crowd—those looking for *me*. My parents, Rory, Toby, and Lilly rushed to meet me on the steps.

"What—what *happened*?" Lilly asked.

I flipped a strand of sticky hair out of my face. "Um, hey, guys."

"Where were you?" asked Dad after he and Mom had each crushed me in a hug. "Why are you all wet?"

"I got confused and went out the wrong door." True. "And got caught in a sprinkler on the golf course." Also true. "I had to double back, and that's why I'm late." True again . . . just not the *whole* truth.

"And you went back *into* the building with fire alarms blaring?" Mom gave me a second hug. "Oh, Merrilee. Sometimes I think God gave you a double dose of intelligence but forgot to include any common sense. I'm so glad you're okay."

Toby frowned at this comment and pulled me into a hug of his own. "There are fences she would've had to climb if she'd gone around." He was way sensitive to anything he interpreted as an insult aimed at me. I wasn't. Yes, I did stupid, accidental, impulsive things, and yes, I scored ninety-ninth percentile on achievement tests—this combination of facts was sometimes frustrating, but it didn't mean my parents loved me any less.

Though how would Mom and Dad feel if they knew I'd just had my first kiss with a boy whose name I didn't know? My stomach dropped. *What the double-stuffed cookie was I thinking?* What happened now? I shivered in the cool September air.

"Fielding!" My head swiveled toward the voice. The same one that had broadcast through the microphone at Convocation. Headmaster Williams looked different in a gray suit than he had in a navy blazer and red tie—though the same round face that clashed with his in-shape-for-an-old-guy body and the same buzz-it-all-to-hide-a-bald-spot head perched above it. I hadn't exactly loved him during my enrollment interview. "Just a formality," Senator Rhodes had assured me, but my interview had sounded a lot tougher than Rory's or Eliza's. He'd seemed like he was sitting on a whole pile of resentment or hemorrhoids as he and the school board's enrollment committee worked through their list of questions.

He was wearing the same sour expression now when I followed his eyes toward his son. Black suit filled out to that perfect place between bulky and thin, where a girl could lean upon his shoulders but wouldn't worry that a hug would squash her. Not that I had to worry about hugs *or* friendly shoulders from this particular masculine masterpiece.

Because *of course* this was Fielding. And no wonder my mystery kisser had been offended when I'd mixed them up. Fielding Williams, guardian of the recycling can, mocker of the freshman crowds. Untemptable and contemptible—and perhaps psychic, because he turned and met my gaze across the crowded parking lot.

His eyebrows lifted so haughtily that I would gladly have traded the contents of my bookshelves to have the power to shave them off. This time I didn't buckle under his judgment or run away from it. I ignored the damp cling of my skirt and the water-gel combo that was dripping from my hair to slide stickily down my cheeks. There were dozens of people flapping and squawking and milling between us, but I met his gaze steadily and lifted my chin. *He* might not be tempted, but someone else was.

Headmaster Williams put a hand on Fielding's arm, breaking our staring contest. Which meant I totally won. They headed toward the parking lot, and I turned back to my family.

"Well, at least we all know *I* was right." Rory sounded so smug that I wanted to push her into the country club pool. "Wearing white was a *bad* idea. Hello, see-through dress. Hello, purple underwear."

I didn't even have a chance to look down before Toby shrugged off his coat and draped it around my shoulders.

I wondered if my mystery was lingering around here somewhere. If his face was being splashed with the red-and-white lights from the fire truck. Why had I decided to be a secret? It seemed so intoxicating: this idea that *I* could be mysterious too. That *I* could be the heroine instead of the quirky sidekick. The temptress. But what if he decided it wasn't worth the effort to find me? Or shrugged it off as impossible? I should've given him a clue. Even Cinderella left a slipper.

"Question for everyone but Rory: On a scale of one to a million, how ridiculous do I look?"

"I should go find Trent and Senator Rhodes," said Lilly. "I think they're talking to the firefighters."

"You look *safe*," said Mom, leaning around Toby to kiss my forehead.

"A little soggy, but that's my Merri—I'm not sure if you find trouble or it finds you." Dad tweaked a strand of my hair. It dripped.

Rory, who pretended to be too cool for all things pop culture, hummed a song that sounded suspiciously like Taylor Swift and rolled her eyes.

It was Toby who gave me the answer I wanted. I didn't care if it was a lie. "You look adorable. Only you, Merrilee. This could *only* happen to *you*."

They probably all nodded and chimed in with their *only Merrilee* stories of hijinks and mishaps. I didn't listen. I was too busy scanning the crowd for the one other person who'd be sprinkler-damp and kiss-drunk. My missing mystery.

10

*W*ake up! Calling in 15.

I pressed send and leaned my wet hair against the car window. It was tangled and goopy and left marks on the glass when I sat up and turned my phone over to check for a response.

Eliza knew that I knew what that request meant—her having to document a sleep disturbance in the daily log her parents made her keep and fill out pages of explanatory paperwork. She knew I wouldn't wake her unless it was A Big Deal.

Or, maybe this time I could convince her to fudge her log. Really, did they *need* to know exactly how many hours of sleep she got? Or every calorie she ate? Her weight? Her workout—duration/type/intensity? Never mind their random glucose/drug/cholesterol/who-knows-what screenings. If they wanted to know what their daughter did every day, they should be *here,* not in Australia, or the South Pole, or wherever they'd end up next. At least after the disaster in Brazil, they'd decided to stop dragging her along. The only *good* parenting decision they'd ever made was to leave her behind with a rotation of graduate student guardians when they went off to make their "important biological breakthroughs."

My phone beeped. **Are you okay?**

I limited myself to only three exclamation points on my response of **Yes!!!** Then I stared out the smeared window, pressing my fingers to my lips and replaying the kiss in my head.

Once home, Mom and Dad offered sleepy hugs and forehead kisses in the upstairs hall, accompanied by their familiar "Sleep sweet, little dreamer." Then they stumbled to their room muttering about "too old to wear heels like this" and "ties are just civilized nooses—so glad I don't have to wear one at the store."

It was hard for me to remember what tired felt like. Or believe I'd ever be tired again. I tossed Toby's coat on the back of my chair, hit the power button on my laptop, then dashed to the bathroom and pounded on the door. "Aurora, hurry up!"

I ran back to my room, pulled up iLive, and checked for new connections.

Oh, *please* let him find me. Please don't let this turn into me ducking behind trees and trash cans to avoid him on campus and some horribly awkward encounter when we finally do come face-to-face and he pretends we've never met. And then me becoming a fifteen-year-old spinster recluse who lives in some scary old house with lots of creepy porcelain dolls, doilies, and cats.

I'm a dog person!

I had a dozen new iLive connections. All from people with Hero High in their profile, but none of them were obviously him. The ones with selfie avatars definitely weren't.

The lacrosse stick was Lance, and the only other unknown was K_KNite, and his image was a graffiti-type scrawl of "Wuzzup?"—Oh, please, don't let my first kiss have been with someone who thought "Wuzzup?" was cool or clever.

There was a knock on my bedroom door and I opened it to catch Rory yawning. "Bathroom's all yours. 'Night."

I jumped and contorted to reach the back zipper on my dress and threw on my robe to go scrub my face and teeth while my phone rang against my ear.

"If you're waking me up, you'd better have a good reason," said Eliza.

I spat out a mouthful of toothpaste. "I do!" I answered. "Hang on, I'm getting in comfy clothes." I stepped into sleep shorts, pulled a long-sleeved shirt over my head, and tugged my damp hair out of the collar. "Hey." I paused, worried I'd be pressing on a bruise. "Did your parents call?"

"Yes." There was no missing the joy in her voice, and I sighed my relief. "So it was good I wasn't at the party—but what trouble did you get in without me?"

"Um, I may have kissed a boy."

"May have? It would've been your first kiss. Don't you know?"

"I do. I *did*." I opened the door to my balcony, ready to climb up on the railing and then crawl onto the roof. It wasn't an activity my parents exactly *approved* of, but I'd been monkeying my way up there and sitting braced between the roof's eaves since I was eight. The balcony addition for my twelfth birthday was supposed to be a bribe to stop—but instead it just made the climb easier. I no longer had to go out the window.

The railing worked as a perfect ladder. By now they'd given up lecturing and just pretended not to know.

"Explain!" ordered Eliza.

I leaned back against the railing and tipped my face up toward the stars. There's no way she'd wait for me to finish the climb, so my balcony would do. "Kissing is wonderful. It's like flying and electricity. You know that scene in *Willy Wonka* where they drink the Fizzy Lifting Drinks and start to float? It's like that—only without the threat of a chop-you-to-bits fan."

"Oh, Merri . . ." She sighed, but not in a secondhand swooning way. "I'm going to kill Toby."

"What does Toby have to do with any of this?" I paused with one foot on the bottom rail. "Wake up, Eliza! I'm trying to tell you about my kiss."

"Wait!"

I waited.

And waited.

"Exactly how long is it going to take you to finish your thought?" I asked.

"Whom did you kiss?"

"Um . . ." Apparently *not* Fielding. And not someone who was a fan of Fielding—which only earned him bonus points in my book. I loved Eliza more than cream soda, chocolate, and oftentimes Rory, but she was not going to be cool with an answer of "I don't know." I squinched my mouth to the side. "It's complicated?"

She sighed against the phone, and I knew she'd be rolling her eyes or throwing her hands up, or some other gesture of exasperation. "Take a deep breath. Start at the beginning."

I dutifully inhaled, counted to five, then exhaled with a whoosh. "Lillian! Lilly disappeared."

"Disappeared?" Eliza said incredulously.

"Oh, I found her. But wait, I need to back up. I forgot part. Really, it's all Fielding's fault."

"You kissed the headmaster's son?"

"No. Ew. Gross." I wrinkled my nose. "But I thought it was him." I scowled at the stars. "He said—"

"How's this for soon enough?"

I shrieked, because the deep voice wasn't from my phone. And it wasn't Toby either. His bedroom light was off, his balcony door shut.

"What's wrong?" Eliza demanded as I leaned over the railing and stared down: blue eyes, damp curly hair.

"You're . . . *here*?" I said.

"Hey, beautiful," he answered. "Next time give me a *real* challenge."

"Wow . . ." I gave my leg a subtle pinch, but he was still standing on the patch of lawn Dad was always complaining about having to reseed because Toby and I had worn a path between our houses. "I just expected you'd find me on iLive."

"Oh." He ducked his head. "You said 'find you.' I just assumed . . ."

I nibbled the inside of my cheek. Was this romantic or creepy? Stalkery or swoony? I couldn't tell if my stomach was sinking or doing flips. Hang up with Eliza and call 911, or hang up with Eliza and smash my mouth against his? Both felt hasty—which Mom often said should be my middle name. I decided the best option was not deciding until I'd given him a chance to explain. "I guess you figured out who I am . . . and where I live?"

"You won't be impressed when you hear how easy it was. I asked the first person I saw about the gorgeous girl in white"—*Ivory. Ivory, ivory, ivory!*—"and that person lives next door."

"Toby?" I whispered, like he could hear me through his door.

"His dad."

"Merrilee Rose Campbell! Whom are you talking to?" Eliza had probably been yelling the whole time, but I only just noticed.

"I've got to go," I told her. "Sorry. I'm doing research, getting answers."

Eliza said words. They sounded like agreement, so I added, "Uh-huh. Love you. Bye," and hung up without looking away from the boy gazing at me with poetry in his eyes.

"Should I leave?" He stepped onto the stone wall that ringed the patio below my room and grasped the bottom of my balcony. "I—I didn't mean to come on too strong . . . I wasn't planning on seeing you."

"Um, you were just going to stake out my house?"

"No!" He looked so horrified that I laughed and his expression relaxed. "I planned to leave a note with my phone number in your mailbox."

"Oh. That makes sense." Did it?

"May I come up?" he asked.

"I'm not in the habit of inviting anonymous guys onto my balcony at midnight." I wasn't in the habit of having midnight rendezvous with anyone other than Toby. I crouched down.

"Maybe we should start with introductions? Once we're not strangers, I'll reconsider."

He placed a hand flat on his chest. "Monroe Stratford. Junior at Reginald R. Hero Preparatory School."

I slipped a hand between the slats to shake his. "It's nice to meet you, Monroe." I liked the shape of those letters on my tongue, the way they sounded in my ear. Even better was "Merri *and* Monroe"—but I wasn't quite delusional enough to say that aloud.

"I think you can come up. Be careful climbing." I stood as he climbed and balanced on the other side of my balcony railing.

"Merrilee." It was the first time he'd said the name he learned from Toby's dad. Well, at least the first time he said it to me, and his voice was as intense as his gaze. Both made me totally aware of my snatched-up, mismatched pajamas and unbrushed sprinkler-hair—but then he smiled in a way that made me glow. "I think I'd always like to see you in moonlight. You look beautiful."

That statement would look so perfect written in a book; out loud it made me squirm. But one thing was perfectly clear—no guy who spoke like that could possibly have *wazzup* as his iLive avatar.

"Um . . . thank you?"

We played a round of ping-pong glances, our eyes bouncing toward and away from each other as we shuffled our feet. Gah. Was silence always so uncomfortable? I needed a question, *any* question.

"So . . . you play tennis?"

He shrugged. "My parents insisted I have lessons in all the 'social sports'—golf, tennis, squash. But I'm not on any teams; it interferes with play rehearsals."

"You act? Cool." Just like Blake in *Fall with Me*! And he was practically made of knee-weakening soliloquies and red carpet romance. I was so lights-camera-ready for that.

"I think so. My parents . . . not so much."

I couldn't stand another silence and didn't have another question. So I did the only logical thing—kissed him.

"Did you know," he said when we paused for stupid oxygen, our foreheads inches apart and his hands entwined with mine on the railing between us, "that your sister is marrying the son of my father's campaign rival?"

That was not the sweet nothing I'd expected. Political talk . . . not a turn-on. "Patrick Stratford"—I had to fight to keep my voice level, because I usually only said and heard that name with a sneer—"is your father?" I saw the resemblance now, not the curls or the inviting shape of his lips, but the jawline and the eyes. The impact of this washed over me slowly, sickeningly. I had to look away.

Patrick Stratford was enemy number one in Senator Rhodes's house and, as a result, our house too. I mean, besides the fact that he seemed incompetent and slimy, there was also the fact that every time he gained a point in the polls the senator, and everyone around her, was miserable. Monroe's dad had eviscerated Lilly's future mother-in-law in a pretty dubious attack ad last month. The fallout had been so bad that Trent had hidden at our house for a week of dinners. So really, everyone was punished.

"That's not a problem, is it?" Monroe asked.

"I hope not?" I didn't mean for it to come out as a question. I was still thinking of the hour-long dinner conversation about which veggies were actually fruits. Avocados, apparently. Trent was the embodiment of torture by boredom. How did Lilly stand it?

"Why would it be?" Monroe wrung his hands on the railing, his voice growing louder with each word. "I am *not* my father!"

"Shhhh!" But it was too late. Lights flicked on in the room across the yard from mine. "You need to go."

And I didn't mind that as much as I would've a minute earlier, because that was the second time he'd raised his voice at me. Though maybe they'd been valid? Both times I'd compared him to guys I considered vile.

"I'm sorry I yelled," he said, covering my hands with his and making no attempt at leaving. "My father . . . he just . . ." Monroe sighed and squeezed my fingers. "I know I need to go, but when can I see you?"

"Merrilee?" Toby's groggy voice drifted through his balcony door. "You up?"

"Um . . . yeah?"

"Let me find my glasses," he mumbled. "I'll be right back."

"Tomorrow?" I whispered to Monroe.

"My weekend is packed—campaign stuff and auditions for the school play." I'd never used the word "crestfallen" before, but it seemed the only way to describe his face.

"If you're busy, then Monday's fine." I tugged at his fingers, trying to loosen them from the railing.

He dropped down to the patio below. "I don't want to leave."

He may not have wanted to—but I *needed* him to. "I'll see you soon. Monday. Monday morning. Before school." Which would make this the first Monday morning I'd ever looked forward to. "But, go!"

My eyes flashed back and forth between Monroe's forlorn face and Toby's open balcony door. Toby reappeared, yawning and stretching as he stepped outside. "What are you doing up, Rowboat?" He was barefoot in Hawaiian-print pajama pants and a white T-shirt, sleep-staticky brown hair and crooked glasses.

I refused to look down, to let my glance or actions draw attention toward where Monroe was slipping away across my front lawn.

"Sorry I woke you."

"No big deal." Toby rolled his neck and rubbed his eyes beneath his glasses. "Everything okay?"

I wasn't a liar, and Toby and I didn't keep secrets. A car started somewhere down my street, and I glanced at my empty yard.

"Want to come over, Mayday? Have a roof talk?"

These words seemed to wake him up and make him stand taller. "Yeah, I think we should."

In the years since my twelfth-birthday balcony was built, Toby and I had tried a zillion methods of getting straight from his railing to mine. It's just dumb luck that none of them resulted in either of our deaths. It was much easier—and safer—for us to climb down from our own balcony and then climb up to the other person's. Toby clambered down and up, landing next to me. He was much more graceful than Monroe, but then again, he'd had years of practice.

"You okay?" He blinked at me through his glasses.

Could he tell I'd been kissed? Did I look different? *Good* different? Or *bad*?

"Fine," I squeaked.

"Climb up first, I'll spot you."

I scrambled onto the railing. His warm hands hovered, then landed lightly on my waist as I shimmied over to the edge of the roof and crawled up. The rough surface of shingles bit at my bare knees, reminding me: "Go grab the blanket from the foot of my bed."

He passed it up, then climbed beside me and helped spread it out.

"We're almost too big to share this space," I said once we were settled shoulder-to-shoulder in the nook where I did my best thinking. I rolled onto my stomach and pushed up on my elbows so I could see his expression. "I'm sorry about Knight Lights."

He shrugged and kept his eyes on the stars.

I turned his face toward me. "But why didn't you ask me weeks ago?"

"Because I'm an idiot." He shrugged again and pressed his cheek into my palm, reaching up with his own hand to hold mine there. "I thought I had more time—Headmaster Williams won't mention it until Monday. I guess I underestimated you, Rowboat. I knew you'd take Hero High by storm, but I didn't expect you to win everyone over in one day."

"Speaking of . . ." I pulled my hand away and covered my face, not sure if it was cruel to tell him—but it was crueler if he heard it from someone else. "I kinda kissed someone."

"What?" It was the same first question Eliza had asked, but hers had been a shout, and his was a whisper. I felt the liquid relaxation disappear from his body. He pushed himself up to sitting, propping his elbows on his knees. "Who?"

I rolled over and sat up too, but stayed farther back in the eaves. Something about his posture and tone warned that he didn't want me in his face right now. "Monroe Stratford."

"How could you possibly . . . ? When?"

"Tonight." It was an answer to his last question. I didn't have one for his first. Nothing more coherent than *yearning*. "It just sort of happened."

"Monroe? Really?" His voice sounded like he had more to say. He shook his head instead. "But you wanted to? You're okay?" He looked at me over his shoulder, all concern and comfort and Toby. I wanted to throw myself into a hug, but I'd probably knock us both off the roof, and it wasn't the right time. My actions tonight had solidified those friendship parameters he'd been tiptoeing around, and there had to be feelings involved. Feelings I didn't want to toy with.

"I wanted to," I confirmed, and the silence settled around us like a snowdrift, making me shiver and fidget till I blurted, "Everything's just moving so fast. It's been one day at Hero High and I already have a mortal enemy."

"Wait! A what?"

"Let's put it this way, you don't have to bother introducing me to He-who-must-not-be-tempted. Aka Fielding."

"You heard that?" His eyebrows drew together. "He's not usually like that. It's—"

"Please don't defend him. So he has one less groupie in his fan club. I doubt he'll even notice—and he wouldn't care if he did."

"It's not *you*, Merri. It's this thing with his father."

"I'm done talking about him, Mayday. And unless you feel like being pushed off the roof is a more efficient way of getting home, you are too."

"Fine. Topic change. So, Monroe. He's . . . he's not who I would've picked for you. Was it just a kiss, a one-time thing, or . . . ?"

I cringed, wondering if that was a warning, or him hinting that *he* would've liked the role. Neither sat well in my knotted stomach, but I kept my voice light. "I think it's an *or*."

"Oh." The shape of his shoulders against the sky made my heart ache.

"Should I . . ." Gah, I needed a guide map for navigating this weird transitional place in our friendship. "Do you not want me to tell you things about other guys? How do I make this easier on you? Do I give you space?"

"No." He reached back and grasped my hand like he was worried I'd disappear or leave him there. "Don't you dare. You've always told me everything. And we're friends. We're best friends. I'm not losing that. I'm fine."

My "Okay" was quiet, and his grip on my fingers loosened, then let go.

Toby and I had sat in silence on my roof before. Lots of times. When we were searching for shooting stars, or trying to stump each other by quoting lines from movies. Sometimes just the comfortable silence of lying sides pressed together with someone who knows the name of every pet you've ever owned—including your imaginary ones. I'd fallen asleep up here beside him. He'd dozed off next to me. We'd climbed up here and talked the day he'd discovered he was adopted—a fact that shouldn't have shocked us since his brown skin didn't match his pasty-pale parents' but still rocked our eight-year-old world. And here is where he'd shared that his parents were getting a divorce, and where he'd told me he'd chosen to stay with his dad. Where I'd whispered my fears about Lilly and an eating disorder and where we'd rehearsed ways for me to talk to her and my parents. Where we'd daydreamed all summer about going to the same school for the first time.

We'd done silence on my roof before, but it had never felt so heavy. I'd never felt so precarious. For the first time, I thought about what would happen if I fell.

"It's late. We should go to bed," I whispered.

"I'll go first and spot you."

If I fell, he'd catch me. These associations had been automatic for so long: Toby. Rooftop. Balcony. Toby.

Yet when my feet touched back down on my balcony that night, he wasn't the boy I was thinking about.

11

Gatsby and my parents' dog, Byron, weren't allowed upstairs. Most of the time Mom and Dad took pure Pomeranian Byron to the store, which was a specialty dog boutique in one of the upscale shopping strips in town, and left my hodgepodge of a mutt at home. This had nothing to do with pedigree papers and everything to do with Gatsby liking to leave his "mark" on Haute Dog every time he visited. He was also a Houdini when it came to breaking into the glass cases that held the fancy bakery-style dog treats—K-9 cannoli, doggy doughnuts, pupcakes—which he'd later puke up all over the doggy sweater display.

Fine, they could maintain their image (and inventory), and I'd maintain my belief that "no dogs upstairs" didn't apply to Gatsby on Saturday mornings when no one was home to tattle.

But if he was in my bedroom breathing stank doggy breath in my face, why wasn't I being drowned in slobber kisses? I opened an eye and batted away—not Gatsby's snout—a running shoe propped on my pillow. Gag. Did my feet *really* smell that bad?

"Morning, sunshine," said Eliza.

"What are you doing here?"

Her ponytail swung like a blond pendulum when she tilted her head. "Morning run?"

"No. Too early. Too mean." I squashed my pillow over my head.

"But you agreed last night." She bounced on the edge of my bed. "Get up!"

"I did?" Her face pinched in a frown and I remembered my hasty half-listening hangup. "I mean, I did!"

"How late were you up? You slept through my calls and texts, knocking on your door, and pinching your toes through the blanket. I was worried the stench of your shoes knocked you unconscious. I told you to stuff them with newspaper after running in the rain."

My response was half grumble, half groan.

She plucked the pillow from my head. "Our first meet is in *three days*. Get your lazy butt out of bed. Also, I believe you have some news to tell me?"

Kissing! It wasn't a dream. I had to tell her about how fate or luck or coincidence had thrown Monroe and me together in the pro shop. I loosened my death grip on my pillow and sat up. "So much to tell you, and I can't talk while running."

I thought that was a winning argument—that we'd be heading to the backyard, me with a big bowl of cereal, her with a veggie smoothie, plopping down by the pool while I told her all the details.

But I should never have underestimated Eliza. She smiled. "Then we'll run slower. Conversational pace."

If "conversational pace" was truly a thing, then I was bad at it. Perhaps I shouldn't have skipped so many of the workouts Eliza had encouraged over the summer. Or maybe it was that I didn't want to have a conversation; I wanted to *gush*. I wanted to dance and skip and generally float off the ground. I'd been dreaming about my first kiss for fifteen years, and I'd earned this moment.

"Tree!"

"Mailbox!"

Luckily, Eliza was excellent at preventing my death by collision with inanimate object.

"Honestly, Merrilee, could you *stop* shutting your eyes? Coach Lynn won't be impressed if you can't compete because you collided with a stop sign while reenacting a kiss."

While I was sticking out my tongue at her, I stepped in gum. "It was so romantic! Just like something in a book." I dragged my sticky shoe on the sidewalk to scrape it off, but that just made me stumble.

Eliza's mouth thinned. "Be careful, okay? It's one thing when you're infatuated with a book character, but Monroe's a *person*. He's not going to be perfect, you know? And I worry you're building him up to— *Bicycle! Merrilee! Bicycle!*"

That one was totally not my—okay, it was a little bit my fault. But no one was hurt.

"What's the rest of your day like?" I asked once we were back on my front steps. She was stretching and I was digging watermelon-scented stickiness from the treads on my sneakers with a twig. "I've got a shift at the store later, but want to sleep over?"

"Are you going to make me watch a rom-com and compare it to Monroe?" she asked.

"Yes," I admitted. "But I'll let you dissect it without shushing."

She tilted her head and considered this. Eliza hated romances but loved predicting their plots. And she was eerily accurate at spoiling them. "Okay, but we need to be on air mattresses with the basement lights off by ten thirty. I can't handle another set of sleep disturbance paperwork this week."

"We could just say we slept," I suggested.

"You don't— You can't be— That is *wrong!*" Eliza stared at me like I'd suggested a murder spree followed by some recreational car theft. "Falsifying experiment data is not funny." She pointed to the silver tech-band around her wrist. "Besides, you know they log in to my step and sleep counter."

I opened my mouth to say *It's not an experiment; it's your life!* But we'd had this argument many times. Eliza needed to believe that all these stupid calculations and records her parents demanded added up to science. That they justified their rules, justified leaving her behind with graduate student guardians "in a controlled, stable environment for her own homeostasis," justified rigid nutrition and sleep logs and tracking hair and fingernail growth and blood pH and every other task they threw at her in the name of some "-ology" or another.

"I'm just kidding," I forced myself to say. Because she was stuck with her parents' science baggage, and I'd inherited my mom and dad's romantic idealizations. And whether or not we approved, we supported each other. Always.

After Eliza went home on Sunday morning, I went upstairs to shower and get ready for church and another day at Haute Dog. The store used to be closed on Sundays, but Mom and Dad's latest attempt at keeping up with the big-box pet store in town was a half day on Sunday and staying open late on Tuesday and Wednesday. They *really* needed to hire more staff, or Lilly needed to have fewer wedding-planning obligations, because I wasn't going to be able to juggle school, cross-country, *and* all the extra hours of listening to pet owners debate which designer collar complimented their pet's fur or obsessing over shampoos and haircuts with Sonia, our zero-personality groomer.

I grabbed my robe and turned to beat Rory to the bathroom, but paused when I caught sight of something red on my balcony.

Roses. They were shaped into the outline of a heart and there was a crisp envelope placed in the center. I did a little *Eeeeee!* dance as I picked it up and then traced my name.

Hello, Monroe's handwriting! You are lovely and the shape of my name in your letters makes my heart go squish. I almost didn't want to open the envelope, because there was no way what was inside could possibly be better than what my imagination was drafting.

Hey Merrilee—

I hope you're missing me as much as I'm missing you. These roses are almost as pretty as your face. I can't stop thinking about kissing you. REALLY can't wait to do it again.

Monroe

So it was sweet, but . . . kinda generic? That was okay. He was seventeen, not Shakespeare. It was the thought that counted, and this was adorably thoughtful.

I stayed in that rose-scented fairy-ring of romance until Mom yelled up the stairs, "If you're eating brunch before we leave, come down *now*," and even then I was too busy smiling to do much biting and chewing. I didn't even stop grinning when a customer spent forty minutes trying sweaters and boots on his Chinese crested, then left without picking up his mess or making a purchase.

It wasn't until midnight that my smile faded into yawns. I was cold too—my cute pajamas weren't warm enough for September nights on my balcony—and the mosquitoes had found me. I'd finished my English homework—reading act one of *Romeo and Juliet*—hours ago and spent the minutes afterward imagining Monroe and me in those roles, imagining him *here*, now, reciting those lines, meaning them.

Come over, come over, come over, I begged Monroe via wishes on constellations I was inventing.

But he didn't. And it was a school night—a school *morning*. I climbed into bed and fell asleep with rose petals crushed in my palm and his letter crinkling beneath my pillow.

12

Who's ready for their first full week of school?" Toby asked as he poured himself a glass of juice. He poured a second one and slid it across the counter to where I had my head resting on folded arms.

"Ummsighgrumble." I hadn't yet reached the stage in my morning where I was using real words or full sentences. My bugbites itched. Why were Mondays so much meaner than other days?

Toby grinned and took a bite of toaster pastry, offering me the second from his foil wrapper. "So, are we stopping for a coffee-flavored sugar drink? You look like you could use it."

Since he'd shared his breakfast, I guessed I could try communicating with something other than grunts. "My hero. Yes, please."

"Yes, please, what? Why is Toby your hero?" Rory wasn't a morning person either, but you'd never guess that from the way she bounced into the kitchen like Tigger on Pixy Stix. She had a small scrap of silk stuck to her sleeve; I plucked it off as she passed. Had she really been working on one of her textile sculptures already? I'd barely managed to brush my hair. "Good morning, Toby!"

"Hey, Rory." He sat next to me, so close I could feel his body heat. I was tempted to snuggle against him—I still felt shivery cold from my hours on the balcony—but those instinctive friendship gestures no longer felt natural. "Rowboat, did you change your mind about Monroe? You can, you know."

I lifted my head, blinked, and backed away from the intensity in his eyes.

"What's going on?" demanded Rory.

The doorbell rang, providing a beautiful excuse for ignoring my sister and escaping the ferocity of Toby's questions and wishes. I darted into the front hall, scolding Byron, "No bark!" as I flung the door open with a grateful smile for whatever paperboy, neighbor, or Rhodes family member was on the other side.

Or . . . *Monroe.*

I wanted to line up every wannabe boy-band look-alike with too much hair product and an attempted swagger that made him look like he was fighting a wedgie. Line them all up, and show them: THIS.

This is the look all those guys were going for—the one they'd never achieve—because putting effort into looking effortless is always transparent.

Monroe hadn't tried. He was standing on my front step with hair that was shower damp and curling in ways that suggested his styling regimen consisted of shaking his head.

I wanted to stare, to study him up close, then retroactively add new details—the shape of his ears, the single freckle on his cheek, the cords of his neck muscles—to the shadowy face I'd inserted in my *Romeo and Juliet* fantasy.

"Impossible," he said, his mouth turning up in a smile that evicted all traces of chilliness from my body. "You're even more beautiful in the daylight."

"Hi?" I mentally ran through a bunch of versions of *What are you doing here?* But even sleep-deprived and shocked, they felt tactless. Plus, all I really wanted to do was kiss him. Was seven a.m. too early for an enthusiastic make-out session? I'd brushed my teeth.

Before I could sway any closer, Gatsby joined Byron in barking at Monroe and trying to herd us apart. Traitor dog.

"Stratford." Toby appeared at my elbow, doing that last-name-as-greeting, head-nod thing boys think makes them look macho.

"May."

Okay, so, it *did* look macho when Monroe did it. Especially since he'd simultaneously slid a hand around my waist and pulled me to his side, tangling my fingers with his and resting them on my hip. It was a gesture that felt romantic for half a second; but the aftertaste was possessive. I sidestepped to put a little distance between us.

"Hush, Byron! Gatsby! Merrilee, who's at the door?" Dad stopped short and dropped the newspaper he was carrying. Byron barked at the fluttering pages and ran to hide under the dining room table.

I gave a high-pitched laugh and went full ramble: "Good morning, clumsy. *This* is why you should never get an e-reader. Though who has time to read lately? I still haven't finished the book I started last Thursday. That's got to be a record for me." Maybe if I kept talking, he'd forget about the tall, handsome boy standing beside me?

Except the tall, handsome boy didn't know about this plan. And without letting go of me, he reached out his other hand. No, stop, T.H. Boy! And definitely don't pull me closer, or look at me like I'm an empty peanut butter jar and you're Gatsby about to steal me from the recycling bin.

"Good morning, sir. I'm Monroe Stratford."

"George Campbell." Dad's eyes widened as he took in our body language. "Jennifer, could you come down here, please?"

"Coming." Mom appeared on the stairs, putting in her left earring and frowning at Dad's newspaper mess before noticing I was stuck between Toby and Monroe like the red-cheeked filling in a tall-guy cookie.

"Hello," she said. "Merrilee, dear, who's your friend?"

"This is Monroe," I mumbled. "He goes to Hero High. He's my . . ."

Was there any ending to that sentence that wouldn't make me want to fling myself onto the nearest pointy object? Especially since everyone in the foyer seemed to be leaning in and holding their breath. Rory hopped off her stool and came to join us. She was still clutching her fork. It was pointy; it would do. . . .

"What did you say? I missed that," Rory prompted. "He's your *what*?"

Monroe squeezed me. "I'm the guy she's captivated. And who can blame me?"

Mom cooed like I was a toddler. "Merri! You have a boyfriend? Why didn't you tell me, sweet pea?"

"Um, I didn't say 'boyfriend.'" I looked up at Monroe with wide eyes. "I never said 'boyfriend.' You heard me, that word did not cross my lips." He just shrugged and smiled.

"Our little late bloomer," said Dad, and I wondered if it was possible to combust from humiliation. "We wondered when you were going to notice that boys existed outside of books."

"Seriously. It's about time," Rory said, perking up. Like she had any right to talk. Rory always had a line of artsy fanboy admirers trailing after her like paper dolls. But she never looked up from her easel long enough to notice them. Lilly and I were convinced that when someone with enough talent came along, Rory would put down the paintbrush and pucker up. She beamed at Monroe. "You should drive with him. Toby and I will get Eliza."

Why wasn't Monroe sprinting? There should be a cartoon cloud of dust behind him and steam coming off the bottoms of his loafers. That their overzealous, super-weirdo reactions didn't make him go dashing for the door won Monroe *all* the bonus points in the world. Not that he'd get to cash them in, because embarrassment this acute had to be fatal.

"How did you two meet?" Dad asked.

"At Lilly's party."

"Hmm." Mom's eyes narrowed as she wagged a finger between us. "Does this have anything to do with why you were MIA during the fire drill?"

"Fire drill?" asked Monroe. I elbowed him, and the confusion smoothed off his face as a lie slid confidently off his tongue. "Right. The fire drill. They should really plan those things for less inconvenient times."

"So true." Mom was moony-eyed. Rory was too. Part of me wished Lilly were here so she could meet Monroe and see an example of *real* romance—and maybe be inspired to dump her stodgy, insomnia-cure fiancé.

No offense to Trent.

"C'mon, Rory, let's go." Toby sounded as bitter as his disgusting coffee preference: *no* cream, *no* sugar.

"Later." Rory started to follow Toby's stiff march out the front door, then pivoted and paused in front of Monroe. "It's *so* nice to meet you." After shaking his hand, she hugged me before flouncing after Toby. Hugged me. Rory hadn't voluntarily done that since . . . ever?

"I—" It was still far too early, far too Monday for so much drama. "Mom, Dad, you can finish mortifying me later? We've got to get to school."

"Mortifying you is a parental requirement." Mom smiled and kissed me on the forehead. She hugged Monroe. "I hope we see you again soon."

Monroe's eyes rounded in surprise. "It was nice to meet you both."

"You too," said Dad. "Don't be a stranger—you're welcome any time."

"Thanks, sir." Monroe lifted my school bag from the foyer bench and slung it over his shoulder before opening the front door for me.

"You guys are too cute." Mom sighed audibly and cuddled into Dad's arms. "Think we'll have finished paying off Lilly's wedding before we start getting bills for Merrilee's?"

Oh. No. Please. No. That was an auditory hallucination, right?

I wanted to cover my ears with my hands and hum. Or go even more old-school, to the years of sandboxes and juice boxes, when it would've been acceptable to pull my skirt over my head and pretend I'd disappeared. Instead I cringed and kept walking, because if I didn't acknowledge their words, he'd assume he'd misheard, right?

Or did silence imply *agreement*? Gah.

Monroe's car was black and sporty. It had tinted windows and a gray interior. He let go of my hand just long enough to shut my door and start the ignition, then knotted our fingers and looked at me. I had no words for what had just happened. I mean, I knew my parents were romantics—I'd stumbled upon more than a few of the sappy love notes they still wrote each other, and they marked "date nights" on the kitchen calendar in pink glitter pen and engaged in gag-worthy PDA—but I hadn't known they'd gone pro in daughter humiliation.

And since I had no words and Monroe was clearly expecting some, I leaned in and kissed him. Apology quickly turned to something else altogether when his mouth opened against mine. My blush faded into a flush as fireworks crackled along our lips.

My head was filled with the sounds of applause. I thought it was my hormones cheering . . . until I saw my parents standing on the front step, clapping.

I pulled away and sank down in my seat. Monroe waved to them stiffly and backed out of the driveway, narrowly missing our poodle-shaped mailbox. His ears had turned red, which was actually kind of a relief. There's perfect, and then there's doesn't mind putting on a makeout show in front of parents. I was so glad he didn't fit in the second category.

"Thank you for the roses," I blurted, because silence was making my humiliation feel louder.

"Did you like them?"

"I loved them, but . . . I could've told you that at school?"

"I thought we agreed if we didn't see each other over the weekend . . . You said Monday *morning*. I thought that meant I should pick you up," said Monroe.

"It was a wonderful surprise. I'm just sorry you had to deal with my parents." I lowered my face into my hands and spoke around my fingers. "They were kidding about the wedding stuff." Um, at least I desperately hoped they were. "Anyway— that's my parents. What are yours like?"

His jaw hardened and he braked sharply at the corner. "My parents only listen to campaign advisors and media consultants. The flowchart of communication in my house only goes one way—and I'm at the bottom. But let's not talk about them."

"Okay. Um, do you have siblings?" Technically I knew this answer—courtesy of a quick Google search while getting ready for bed the night before. But I wanted to hear it from him. I wanted all sorts of get-to-know-you conversations.

"No."

I waited—because according to Wikipedia, Monroe had an older half sister from his dad's first marriage—but that was his full answer. "Oh." Maybe they weren't close? Maybe she was much older? Maybe I should break the lingering silence and tell him about mine? About Eliza?

Or ask him more questions—on a different topic, since family was clearly off-limits. But before I could, he said, "Cast lists are being posted this morning." He squeezed my hand and I watched his smile shrink. "Come with me to check it?"

"Of course." Ooh, my first relationship duty. I could do this. "What's the play? What role do you want?"

"I don't want to jinx it."

Him as an actor made so much sense—his expressive face, sometimes over-the-topness—he was very *theatrical*. "They'd be stupid not to give you the best role. I mean—look how good you were at ad-libbing about the fire drill."

This earned me a quick, fierce kiss as we waited in the line of vehicles filtering into the Hero High lot. And a not-so-quick but even fiercer one when he found his name on the page posted outside the theater.

With a whoop of delight, he twirled me off my feet. Normally I'd have told him to Put. Me. Down. Because being little did not mean I was a human kite. I had not signed off on going airborne. But he was too busy celebrating. "I can't believe it. Romeo! The whole time I was auditioning, I pictured saying the lines to *you*."

"Really?" Goose bumps rippled down my arms. "That's so weird, because we're reading it for English, and I pictured you when—"

"Hang on!" He turned to high-five a guy who'd just yelled, "Mercutio!"

"Woooo, Stratford!" There was a steady stream of people wanting to clap his back and congratulate him. Which I was sorta okay with, because this whole morning felt pinch-me surreal. I took a step back from the jubilant theater crowd. Someone was cheering. Someone singing. Someone dancing. Did none of them have respect for the silent sanctity of Monday mornings and the uncaffeinated?

Before I could completely escape, Monroe clasped my hand and drew me into the melee. "Juliet has nothing on you, love."

Love. Wow. He'd gone there. I loved my family and friends and books and cream soda and Gatsby and movie nights and bath fizzies. And none of those feelings felt like this. But they shouldn't, right? Like, sisters and suitors shouldn't inspire the same flutters.

Thankfully he hadn't used the word as a declaration. It was an endearment. One that rolled off his lips as naturally as my name and bounced in my stomach like a pinecone.

"I—I need to get to bio. Congrats on the role. I know you'll be great."

"How can I not be, with you as my muse?" I took a step away, but he grabbed my hand. "Hey, before you go. You know that whole 'boyfriend' thing from your foyer?"

"Oh." My face felt like an inferno. "I didn't . . . My parents, they . . ." I ducked my chin into my chest and prayed to disappear.

"Let's do it." He put a finger below my chin and tilted it up to meet his eyes. He didn't look embarrassed or angry—he still had the same glowy triumphant look as when he'd seen the cast list.

"Do what?" I asked, my eyes going owl-wide.

He laughed. "Us." He pointed a finger between our faces. "Make it official. You, girlfriend. Me, boyfriend."

"Oh. Gah. Um. I guess so?" It was so not the conversation I'd thought we'd be having, and I hadn't quite found my equilibrium. I mean, it was a *good* surprise, and I gave him a smile, but it felt Swiss cheesy—the holes punctured by his use of that four-letter *L*-word and this new "official" thing.

"Good." He pressed a kiss to my cheek. "Now that's taken care of, you can get to class."

"Yeah. Taken care of." I was just a mumbling parrot at this point, so it was definitely time to make an exit. He rejoined the others clustered around the cast list. They greeted him like a returning hero. I waggled some fingers and then took off down the path as fast as my polka-dotted flats would carry me.

Hannah and Sera were sitting side by side on the stone wall that ringed the gardens and greenhouse. Sera's leather sandal was wrapped casually around Hannah's red Converse. Their legs swung as they chatted with their heads bent toward each other, Sera gesturing with her long slender fingers and Hannah nodding and weaving together blades of grass.

She noticed me first. "Hey, adoptee! Happy first Monday! Here, have a bracelet. Unless you're a victim of allergy angst like Sera, in which case, *don't*." She held out a braided grass circle, which I happily slipped onto my wrist.

"Good morning."

"Any questions for your wise Knight Lights?" asked Sera.

"Actually, yes!" Thank goodness for this program and that my mentor was *not* Toby. "I want the scoop on the Hero *heroes*. And the villains as well, I guess." Though Fielding had done a fairly excellent job of outing himself.

"Whom do you want to know about?" Sera asked, and I bit back a smile. Correct use of "whom"? She and Eliza were such kindred spirits.

"Um, how about Lance?" How many decoy guys did I need before I mentioned Monroe?

"He's so pretty," said Hannah.

"And so kind. One of the nicest guys you will ever meet, but . . ."

"Well, he helps us maintain a bell curve," Hannah finished diplomatically.

"And the lacrosse team would be lost without him," said Sera.

Hannah hopped off the wall and held her hands up to Sera. "Who else?" she asked. "That can't be it."

While I was curious about Fielding and while I trusted Hannah and Sera, I *didn't* trust my luck. If things continued the way they'd gone so far, he'd show up just in time to hear the question and decide I was obsessed with him or something. Instead I asked, "How about Curtis?"

"There's *way* more to him than he wants people to see," said Sera. "Know the saying 'still waters run deep'? He's noisy *and* deep."

I nodded and crossed my fingers. "What do you think of Monroe Stratford?"

Hannah snorted and Sera smacked her arm. "Better question: What do *you* think of him?"

"You knew? Already?"

"Oh, Merrilee," said Sera. "We probably knew before you'd reapplied your lip gloss. Welcome to Hero High, where gossip moves faster than the internet."

"And the new girl snagging one of the hottest upperclassmen on the first day? That's tasty gossip." Hannah turned to Sera. "We picked awesome people for our Knight Lights."

"She doesn't mean that how it sounds." Sera rolled her eyes.

"I don't. Okay, not much." She wobbled a hand back and forth.

"But *how* did you hear about Monroe and me?" Eliza wouldn't have told. Neither would Toby. And they were the only two . . . unless *Monroe*? Had he bragged about snagging some fresh meat? My stomach turned and I raised a hand to my mouth, not sure whether I should wipe off his kisses or hold fast to my evaporating happiness.

"He was playing tennis with Khalil, whose three talents are: the violin, the ability to text shockingly fast, and gossiping." Hannah paused and arched an eyebrow. "And anyone who didn't know already did after you made out by the theater. So? Details?"

"Is he a good guy? Tell me he's a good guy."

"We know *of* him, of course—everyone does—he's pretty popular. But we don't really know him," confessed Sera.

"He's amazing in the plays," added Hannah. "Half our

class was crushing on him after seeing him in *Phantom* last year. Obviously he's handsome as sin. I want his eyelashes."

"I like your eyelashes." Sera poked her girlfriend before turning back to me. "Have you googled him? With who his dad is, he's probably got his own wiki or something."

"Of course!" Should I have admitted that? Probably not. I fumbled for a distraction. "We should get to class."

13

liza claimed she wasn't mad I'd ditched her to drive with Monroe—but it was possible this was just to shush me since I was "pretty please"-ing during Dr. Badawi's directions.

Regardless, she seemed truly over it by the time we made it to English and Ms. Gregoire announced, "I tolerated rows on the first day of class, but that's not going to happen again. Form the desks into a circle, please."

"No more T-zone angst," I said. She rolled her eyes but joined Hannah in directing the redistribution of the furniture.

Lance, Toby, and two boys I hadn't met did most of the heavy lifting, while Curtis made jokes and got in the way. Sera waited in the corner with a raven-haired girl who gave Eliza some serious competition for most gorgeous being in the universe. Only unlike Eliza, she *owned* it. I tried to copy her expert-level hair toss and ended up with it stuck to my lip balm.

In the other corner, a pretty black girl with doodles on both hands and a super-skinny, super-freckled white guy were engrossed in something on his laptop. I nudged desks this way and that, but mostly I was fascinated by watching Ms. Gregoire watch us.

Once we were circled up and seated, she tapped her pen on the electronic whiteboard to get our attention. "I forgot to take attendance last week. I know some of you from freshman year, but not all of you were in my class. So, let's get that out of the way, then I'll tell you *why* we're starting with Shakespeare."

Ohhh! I totally had insider info on that one. Messenger opened.

RowboatReads: It's because the fall play is Romeo & Juliet.

ElizaGF: Makes sense.

RowboatReads: Monroe is ROMEO.

ElizaGF: This means you're going to make me see it, doesn't it?

I wished I knew how to access those fancy emojis Toby had used last week, because I wanted a stuck-out tongue. Maybe there was even a Shakespearian emoji. I could e-bite my thumb at Eliza.

Or . . . I could pay attention, because Ms. Gregoire was pointing a gold-painted nail at my classmates. "Okay, if you're Michael, that makes *you*"—she pointed from the darkest-skinned of the desk movers to the freckled guy who was pasty pale—"Randolph. Now we're down to the last three. Hmmm." She looked between me, the successful hair flipper, and doodle-handed girl. "Merrilee, Ava, Nicole."

We nodded. I offered a smile to Nicole, who waved Sharpied fingers back at me, and Ava, who responded with a glower. All righty then. I was glad my chair was across the classroom from hers.

Ms. Gregoire perched on the edge of an empty desk and folded her hands on her lap. She was wearing another fabulous dress. This one was printed with antique postcards. "Over the weekend, I read your letters. Your opinions of *Romeo and Juliet* varied quite a bit. From 'the most romantic story ever written'"—I blushed, a few students laughed—"to 'the most boring play known to man.'

"Now let's talk about why we're studying this play." She stood and walked around the crater of the desks. I followed her movements with my eyes and felt each of her words as hot and close as if they'd been whispered in my ear. "This story lives and breathes. Hundreds of years after Shakespeare wrote it, we cry over characters so far removed from our own lives—because they're *not* removed from us at all. We relate to them. We *know* them. They're us. You're them."

"Like reincarnation?" I hadn't meant to ask, but she pounced on my question with bright eyes a-twinkle.

"Almost. Literature is powerful. Anything can happen when you open yourself up to it. Are you open?" It was a question for everyone, but she held my gaze. I nodded emphatically. "I can tell *you* are, Merrilee. And when you're ready . . . Well, you'll find your book."

With those cryptic statements, she turned around and picked up a stack of papers. I wanted to call out, *But I'm ready now! And I've found my book! It's this one!* Instead I chewed my lip. Sweat was collecting around my collar, but my hands were ice-cold.

Ms. Gregoire continued, "Some of you may think they're 'an impulsive, reckless boy and a girl without guidance or role models' or 'a story about lust, not love'—but, clearly no one in this classroom has ever done anything reckless or impulsive. You always listen to your parents, right? Especially their dating advice? And you're never, ever swayed by a person's physical attractiveness? Oh, wait, you have? You are? See, these characters aren't so different from you."

Ms. Gregoire flipped through her papers. "This one might be my favorite—" She smiled at Curtis. "'A cautionary tale about poor timing and why neither mail delivery nor drugs are reliable.' Yes, if you take nothing else away from *Romeo and Juliet*: send important mail with delivery confirmation, and don't do drugs."

She waited while we laughed, then began to move again. "I expect you all to find something to relate to in the books we read this year—but for some of you, the personal connections will feel . . . bigger. Life changing."

The circles she was pacing were making me dizzy. Her words were falling, hammering against my mind and heart. The classroom seemed so hot. So stuffy. The hair on my arms was standing on end. Why wasn't the clock moving? Why was my heart racing?

"By the time we're done studying this play"—she stopped in front of my desk and smiled down at me—"you'll know the story like it's your own. Like you've lived and breathed it."

Meanwhile, I was holding my breath. Like I'd forgotten how to exhale or didn't dare do it. And into this space of accidental self-asphyxiation, a message bubble popped onto my screen.

MonROMEO: I miss you already, my muse. My Juliet.

His timing was eerie. Did he somehow know that Ms. Gregoire was talking about us, was comparing our lives to those of this dramatic duo?

RowboatReads: You've got serious sleuthing skills. How'd you get my screen name?

MonROMEO: Moved heaven and earth. Impressed?

I typed VERY, ignoring Eliza's disapproving elbow to my ribs, and sent him my cell number when he asked, because, really, we should've exchanged those before now.

Ms. Gregoire clapped and I jumped. Ava paused with her lip gloss partway to her mouth, Nicole dropped her Sharpie, a new arm doodle half finished, and Michael froze mid-sneeze, trapping an "Ahhh!" behind his hand, waiting for a *choo* that didn't come.

"Bless you," Ms. Gregoire said anyway. "Now then, Twelve students, of varying levels of curiosity / In fair Hero High where we lay our scene . . ." She twirled to a stop in the center of our circle and clasped her hands over her heart. "So, act one. We all read it?"

Twelve heads nodded and leaned in. "Then, ladies and gentlemen, let's get discussing. What do you think the grudge was about? What could cause a rift so ancient and powerful that it's been elevated to something nearly sacred?"

Ms. Gregoire shook her head at Eliza's raised hand. "None of that. We're having a conversation: you don't need to ask permission to participate."

Oh, Eliza hadn't liked that rebuke, no matter how gently it had been given. Her voice was tight and her cheeks faintly pink. "The text doesn't account for a reason. It's simply an 'ancient grudge' that both families continue to propagate with their relatives and servants."

"That's a technically correct answer, but I want to know what you *think*. What reasons could these families have for choosing to hate so fiercely? We all know where this story is headed. What could fuel an animosity that will consume so many lives?"

"Politics?" I suggested with a frown, thinking of Lilly and Trent. "They ruin *everything*."

"But they already have a prince," argued Ava. "So neither family is going to be in charge of Verona."

I stole a glance down at my screen.

MonROMEO: Can I come over tonight?

My cheeks flushed as I remembered that kiss from the courtyard and his parting words.

"Love?" I suggested, the word soapy slick on my tongue.

"Like, way back one family rejected a member of the other?" Toby asked. When I nodded, he looked doubtful. "I don't know—would that create hatred? Or embarrassment and avoidance?"

MonROMEO: I've got rehearsal so I'm not free till late, but if you leave your balcony unlocked . . .

My mind was on what Ms. Gregoire implied about book-life parallels. Now balconies were back in play . . . I shivered and typed with hasty fingers.

RowboatReads: Maybe. We'll see.

MonROMEO: Please. We can practice—be my Juliet, I'll be your Romeo.

The words were too close to my thoughts. To Ms. Gregoire's

pronouncements. *We were them, they were us.* All the romance, all the family grudges, all the balconies. Hopefully a hundred percent less death.

The class kept talking and I turned toward each speaker, doing a great impression of paying attention, but my head was a mess of tangled thoughts and story elements.

"Money," said Randolph. Already I'd noticed he spoke in short sentences and absolutes. "Isn't it always about money?"

"Or religion," said Sera. "It seems like most wars are over one or the other."

"But both families have a relationship with Friar Laurence—this implies they're both Catholic," said Nicole. "And Romeo and Juliet's first conversation is full of him making allusions to a shared belief system: saints and pilgrims and prayers."

Ms. Gregoire smiled. "Great use of textual support. I'm loving all your ideas."

"Power," said Lance. "It's all about saving face."

"But *why* do they feel the need to 'save face'?" asked Eliza. "You're describing the reaction, not the motives. Which makes sense because the motives *aren't in the text.* This is pure conjecture."

Ms. Gregoire laughed. "Touché. I can see how playing revisionist with Shakespeare could feel objectionable. But I do want you thinking about the characters' motivations as you read tonight. *Why* do they commit so quickly and fully to each other? What drives them to make their pledges of devotion, despite the reasons—whatever the cause may be—they have to hate?" She trailed her fingers along the front edges of our desks, skipping from one corner to the next as she circled around the group.

Hannah suggested, "Maybe that's why he left it a mystery. So the theatergoers would be more intrigued and invested."

Eliza groaned.

"You thinking what I'm thinking, E?" Curtis shifted his desk closer to hers. "The only way to figure this out is a séance. Let's light some candles, get a Ouija board, hold hands, and ask Ol' Willy's ghost."

Eliza pushed away the hand he'd held out toward her. "No."

I looked down at my screen, at the cursor blinking on the messenger app. I still hadn't responded, but it showed that Monroe was typing again. I dragged my fingers over the keys. *Monroe or Romeo? Yes or no? To sleep perchance to miss a visit on my balcony? To be or not to be his Juliet?* But those weren't even the right play. I chewed my bottom lip and moved my pointer finger to the *Y* key. But my thumb was on the *N.*

"Merrilee," said Ms. Gregoire. "You're looking particularly conflicted. Would you like to share your insights?"

"Um." My fingers crashed down with a mess of letters that felt like they were knotted in a pointy ball in my throat. "Um, I was . . ." I looked helplessly at the computer screen in front of me. There was a new message from Monroe, a quote that I seized upon gratefully. "I really like this line: *'Ay me, sad hours seem long.'*" I clicked out of his message and looked up at the class. "It just speaks to Mon— er, Romeo's impatience. The way his emotions are the guiding force in his life." I swallowed. They were becoming guiding forces in mine too.

"And how . . . um, expressive he is too. All those . . . feelings," added Toby.

Eliza, for all her pointy elbows, was also ready to jump in and save me. "It's one of the first lines Romeo speaks, yet it's prophetic for his actions throughout the book. He's either bemoaning a wait or acting rashly. He has no in-between."

"Very good, you three." Ms. Gregoire nodded her approval, but her gaze lingered on me, and the hair on my scalp prickled. "That's exactly what I mean about connecting with the text and putting yourself in the characters' shoes. There's so much more of this to come!"

14

Ms. Gregoire had barely finished her "Tonight, read act two. I'll see you all tomorrow" before I was grabbing Eliza's arm and dragging her out of the building.

"The dining hall's that way," she said. Then, "Grass! Grass! We're on the gra— Are you going to throw up? Pass out? Breathe, Merrilee. Put your head down. Breathe slowly."

I didn't think I was going pass out. Maybe? It would certainly explain why I felt so dizzy.

"Monroe is Romeo," I whispered.

"I know. School play. You told me. Congrats to him. But why are you so pale? Did you skip breakfast?"

"No. You don't understand. He *is* Romeo. Not just in the play."

"I officially have no clue what you're talking about." Eliza tugged at the fingers I'd wrapped around her arm.

"In real life. He *is* him. You heard Ms. Gregoire. 'This book lives and breathes.'"

"She didn't mean the characters *literally* live and breathe."

"And Friday she looked right at me and said I'd fall in love—and her mug went all strobe-y—*just like the fire alarm at*

the country club when I met Monroe! And what about the whole
'We *know* them. They're us. We're them.' Or 'you'll find your
book.' And our families: the Rhodeses and the Stratfords—
they're political opponents. We kissed without knowing each
other's names. Balconies!" Air sputtered out of my lungs. I
whispered, "How did she do it?"

"Our English teacher didn't *do* anything." Eliza rubbed at
her temples. "Repeat after me: Ms. Gregoire is not magical,
and Romeo is a fictional character."

"I'm not saying she's magical."

"Oh. Good," said Eliza. "If you're done, can we go eat?"

I trailed after her down the path to the cafeteria. And
whether or not she heard me, she didn't respond when I
added, "It's not magic if it's *real.*"

I could lie and say I didn't spend lunch craning my neck
to try to get a glimpse of Monroe, but I won't. Luckily Toby
figured out what I was doing before I pulled any muscles.
"Stratford wouldn't have this lunch. Juniors eat later than us."

I nodded, pouting, and stole a bite of his red velvet cupcake. But part of me was also kind of relieved. It's not every
day that you learn your new boyfriend and you are epic, star-
crossed lovers. I needed a little bit of time to process and
figure out how to casually tell him, "Just say no to poisons."

Speaking of poison . . . I was still curious about the death
glare I'd gotten during English class intros. I turned to Hannah.
"What's Ava's deal? She looked like she wanted to kill me and
wear my skin as a cape."

Hannah choked on her water and sputtered out a laugh.
"Um, gross. Ava's pretty self-important. Her dad's the head

of the school board. She's been queen bee since kindergarten and has never been a fan of new people. She'll either warm up to you . . . or not."

I rolled my eyes. "Those sound like good odds."

Curtis leaned around her to add, "And she is, or at least *was*, a fan of Monroe's, if you catch my drift." He paused to take a huge bite of his sandwich, then said, "Like, she liked him. *Like* liked him."

I held up a hand. "I get it. So there's probably no chance she and I will ever be besties?"

"Literally zero," said Curtis cheerfully. "Good thing you've got us."

It was sweet of him to say, especially since I was already sick of trying to calculate how long until my outsider status was upgraded to friends forever. Dad always said, "Patience and Merrilee will never be bedfellows. Or roommates. Or even casual acquaintances." So, the sooner I got to know them all, the sooner we'd be friends, and the sooner I'd get to hear secrets and understand the whys behind things like Sera blushing and excusing herself to get milk when everyone began to talk about their sports teams and practice schedules.

I flashed Hannah question eyes and she leaned in. "Sera's exempt from the sports requirement, and it makes her uncomfortable. She's an unbelievably good ballerina. Once she gets to know you better, I'm sure she'll tell you about it."

"Oh. Okay." And it *was* okay, I got it . . . but I didn't want to accept it. I wanted Sera to trust and tell me *now*. I wanted them *all* to. Especially because if things *did* go full *Romeo and Juliet*, who knew how much time I— No! I wasn't going there.

By the end of lunch, I'd facilitated a table-wide phone number swap and had four new connections on iLive. Curtis's page was bugs and baked goods. Lance's lacrosse and anime. Sera's dance and NASA. Hannah's books, books, and books. I wanted to pause and study them—the crib notes get-to-know-you guide. When I said it aloud, everyone laughed.

"Short stack with the friendship shortcuts," said Curtis, holding out a hand for me to fist-bump, while totally sleuthing on Eliza's page. "I like it."

I glanced at Toby, who was pulling a Sherlock on my iLive page—which made no sense because he'd been the first friend I added when I set it up two years ago. "What are you looking for?" I asked.

"Um, nothing." He jammed his phone's off screen, but not before I glimpsed where on my iLive site he'd been: checking my relationship status. We sighed in sync, both of us wishing we could change the other's feelings, but in very different ways.

"Can I say something gushy?" I asked the table, then didn't wait for a response before stumbling forward, my words rolling over one another like a litter of puppies. "I'm really glad I'm here. And I'm really glad I found all of you."

Sera responded first. "I'm really glad you're here too. Both of you."

And the rest of the group joined in, Curtis with a joking "Does this mean we get to keep you?" Lance with an aw-shucks "Ditto," Hannah with shrugging and laughing and "Girls, you're stuck with us." Eliza with her formal "You've all been so welcoming. I appreciate that." And Toby with a nudge of his shoulder against mine and a "Friends forever, Rowboat."

And since we were totally on our way to being insiders, I felt justified in linking my arm through Sera's on the way out of the dining hall and saying, "So, I hear you're a ballerina! Tell me all about it!"

By the time we'd made it to math, I knew how long she'd been dancing: "Since I was three."

By media, I knew her fave ballet: "*Giselle*! I'd love to play the title role. Or *Coppélia*."

And by Convocation, why she loved it: "The way it's both art and order. The choreography is fixed, the positions and movements don't change, but every dancer is unique—even while trying to look uniform." As we made our way down the Convocation hall aisle, I'd received an invitation to her next performance. "If you want. You don't have to. No pressure, like, at all."

The invitation was priceless because she'd volunteered it. Like she wasn't just tolerating me at her lunch table for Toby. Like we were already friends. Like she wanted to continue to be.

And this was *exactly* what I wanted too. I could easily see Hannah and Sera becoming—well, not besties, because Toby and Eliza had that position on lockdown, but close thirds. People whose families considered me one of their own for dinners and sleepovers and lazy weekend goof-offs. By the time her recital rolled around, I'd totally have that role cemented.

Except, maybe I didn't know Sera quite as well as I thought, because as we settled onto a bench in the Convocation hall, Hannah reached over and plucked at Sera's fingers, wrinkling her nose as she said, "Your dad looked like he was on the warpath today."

"Her dad?" Come to think of it, I knew Sera was short for Seraphina, but I didn't know her last name. I meant to follow up on this, but I was distracted—we were *all* distracted by a commotion behind us. It started with some clomping, some "excuse mes" and protests.

Then grew to, "Merrilee! Merrilee? Where are you, Merrilee?"

I turned to see Monroe scanning the crowd as he climbed over the rows like a conquering warrior.

"Does he mean you?" asked Lance from behind me.

"I don't think there's another Merrilee at Hero," said Curtis. "And definitely not another one dating the BMOC."

"The what?" I asked.

"Big man on campus," Curtis said. "Power player. You know . . . Stratford."

Actually, I *didn't* know. There was a whole heck of a lot I didn't know about him, apparently.

"Huh, wouldn't have pegged you for a party girl." Lance tilted his head and considered me.

I opened my mouth to ask *party girl?* and for some more BMOC details but was cut off by Curtis whistling. He'd climbed on his bench. "Yo, Stratford, she's over here." He fingergunned down at me and added, "I figured I'd help him out. It's not easy to find a short stack in a haystack."

"Um, thanks?"

Hello, Hero High! This was not how I planned to make my center-stage debut—red cheeked and soaked in a sudden

sheen of stress sweat, with my best friend pug-eyed with horror beside me and my boyfriend—that word still snagged in my
thoughts—calling, "There you are!" from across five benches.

There were audible female sighs and giggles. Hannah
leaned across Sera. "Whoa. Someone turn on the A/C—it's
hot in here."

But at least one other girl in the crowd wasn't swooning:
the one seated next to me. She yanked on my arm. "That's
him? What is he doing?"

I nodded for Eliza without taking my eyes off Monroe. He'd
been handsome in the pro shop's darkness; gorgeous in the
midnight air; a beautiful surprise on my doorstep this morning. But standing on the bench with his face illuminated by a
smile and all of him glowing in the soft light coming through
the nonreligious stained-glass windows, he was something
godly, something beyond breathtaking. The window lit his
white shirt with rainbow splashes of color, made his dark
curls look blue-black, and caught all the angles and planes of
his face and neck. The light loved him, and I—I didn't. But it'd
only been two days. Maybe I'd figure out how to not choke on
the word "boyfriend" before I worried about that.

He stepped over the last bench between Lance and Curtis,
then climbed down in my row.

"Hello, love."

Oh, was that going to be a thing now? "Love"? At least
it was better than "short stack." *We get it, Curtis. I'm small.
Clever. Keep it up, and I won't root for you to win over Eliza.*

"Love" should've sounded classy, like a British endearment. The type of thing I'd insisted our heroes call their

heroines in Toby's and my old fanfic days. Instead it felt a bit too try-hard. A bit too loud. The sun must've slid behind a cloud, because the stained-glass glow around him faded into shadows. The only things glowing were my cheeks. "Um, hi?"

He kissed the top of my head, which was a *look how short you are!* thing. I hated it. Not that he knew this bugged me. But Eliza did. She looked him up and down. Slowly. "Monroe."

I saw his smile wane. "You must be Eliza." His voice sounded friendly enough, but his grip on me had tightened like he was trying to squeeze the last globs of toothpaste out of a tube. "Since you and I share remarkably good taste in our favorite person, I hope we'll get along."

Eliza arched an eyebrow. "Oh, you prefer Rosalind Franklin to Watson and Crick too?"

I would have laughed and explained the who-*really*-discovered-DNA's-structure joke to Monroe. I might have complained about him making a scene. I mean, I'm all for the *idea* of romantic gestures, but maybe not such big ones on my second day at a new school?

There were lots of things I could've done next, *if* the headmaster hadn't interrupted. "Stratford! These sort of antics are unacceptable. Climbing on furniture, yelling in the Convocation hall. What were you thinking?" He stood at the end of our row and called across the heads of four students.

"Sir, I was declaring my affection for this beautiful girl. I apologize for the disruption."

"Yes, well…" Headmaster Williams clearly hadn't expected Monroe to respond with frank talk about *feelings*. He looked momentarily baffled. "Go to my office and think about more appropriate ways to express it. When Convocation is over, I'll discuss this with you."

"Yes, sir." But he lingered for one last squeeze and brush of his lips across my cheek. Instead of romantic, it felt a little defiant and a lot possessive.

"Go *now*, Mr. Stratford," Headmaster Williams said sternly. "Your nonsense has already delayed Convocation enough."

Monroe lifted his hand to his mouth, then tilted it toward me before he trudged down the aisle and out the large arched double doors at the rear of the room. I'd always thought of blowing kisses as something toddlers did. Or girls. The type of girls who could wear body glitter unselfconsciously and had mastered the art of winking without looking like they had something in their eyes. But Monroe was a whole new category: *hot*. The guy who talked emotions. The gesture drew my eyes to his mouth and filled my head with memories of how nice those lips had felt against mine.

I just wished those memories were louder than the whispers. Sharper than the not-so-furtive glances. (Ava's took "if looks could kill" to murder-spree levels.) Clearer than Sera looking at the headmaster, who still stood in the aisle, and squeaking, "Hi, Dad."

He nodded at her before heading to the podium. I dragged my eyes from the back of his blazer to meet hers. "Wait!" My voice was slightly on the wrong side of whisper—people who had stopped staring turned to look again. I ducked down in my pew and said, "Wait. If *the headmaster* is your father, that means you're related to *Fielding*."

I tried to infuse my voice with at least half the scorn he'd demonstrated toward me, and I must've succeeded, because Sera paled and bit her lip. "Oh no. What did my brother do?"

"He—he—" Eliza tried to elbow me from the left, but I dodged her bone dagger—seriously, the girl could market her elbows as weapons. "No, never mind. Nothing. I'm over it . . ." I faced forward and attempted to listen to the headmaster for a full thirty seconds, but he had Fielding's chin, and they both curled their lips the same way. I turned back to Sera. "Except he's . . . he's . . . awful! I mean, I adore you, Sera, but your brother's a jerk."

Having said my piece, I turned back to the front just in time for the singing of the school song. I still didn't know the words, but I faked it like a pro.

By the time the headmaster strutted back down the aisle, I thought my run-ins with the Williams family men were done for the day—but before we'd cleared our row, I caught a glimpse of the other owner of the Williams's square jawline and chin. He was standing at the aisle looking down on us as he, well . . . looked down on us.

"You!" It was more of a growl than a greeting, because I'd swallowed a breath mint down the wrong pipe and my throat was all scratchy and raw. His fault.

"What?" Hannah broke off her rambling story about soccer camp. "Oh. Hey, Williams."

"Hi, Hannah," he replied. I was still glaring at him, trying not to cough up bits of my esophagus or show any other sign of weakness, but he hadn't even glanced at me. "Sera, you left a pointe shoe in my car. Thought your class tonight might be tricky with just one."

She laughed. "Ha! A bit. Thanks! It must've fallen out of my bag." She accepted the shoe. "And I guess you know Hannah's and my adoptees? Eliza and Mer—"

"We've met." My iciness crackled and his jaw tightened, and he finally *did* look at me. But with the way his eyes flashed and nostrils flared, I wished he hadn't. And just knowing that he'd been *here* when Monroe did his whole . . . whatever. That Fielding had seen that, had probably *laughed* at it, made flames lick across my cheeks.

"Indeed," he said stiffly. "How are you finding Hero High so far?"

He was back to not looking at me. Looking everywhere *but* at me. Probably because the last time he'd seen me, I'd been giving the whole country club parking lot a sneak peek at my underwear through my water-soaked dress. Or maybe because the last time we'd spoken, he'd accused me of being illiterate.

I narrowed my eyes. "It's fine. Easy. Really easy. Not even the slightest bit challenging."

"Well, that's good." The corners of his mouth twitched. "Seeing as it's been two whole days of strenuous syllabus review and rigorous get-to-know-you games."

While my thoughts and feelings were as snarled as the fur of a Maltese that'd missed an appointment at the groomer's, my voice was coolly calm as I said, "You must hate those games. You know, since you think getting to know people before you judge them is a waste of your time."

He pressed his lips into a thin line.

Point. For. Me.

Sera looked between us and sighed, her fingers knotting in the ribbons of the ballet shoe. "I'm sincerely sorry for whatever is going on here."

I reached out and squeezed her hand. "*You* don't need to apologize. *You* have been nothing but sweet and lovely. It's not like you get to choose who you're related to. If you could—"

"It's 'whom,'" Fielding interrupted, his words as tight as his jaw. "And the same lack-of-choice sentiment applies to classmates." His hands looked like they were just resting on the edge of the pew, but his fingertips were white with pressure. He squeezed them into a fist and walked away without even attempting an explanation, apology, or good-bye.

I wanted to call him rude, but actually that had been me. "Sorry," I muttered. "He's just so . . ." Disappointing. Handsome. Pretentious. Pretty. Obnoxious. Gorgeous. *"Exasperating!"*

I watched his back retreating. What a waste of good bones and muscles and tailoring. The girls, however, watched me: Hannah with curiosity, Sera with confusion, and Eliza—"I'm proud you stuck up for yourself, Merrilee." Which, really, that was the participation ribbon of praise. She added, "And Sera, it isn't *your* fault."

"He was really that awful?" Sera asked.

"I wouldn't suggest he join any welcoming committees," I said. "And I feel bad for whoever *his* Knight Light adoptee was."

"Well, that was me, and he was great, but . . ."

"Family discount," said Hannah. "He adores you. It's *other people* your brother has issues with." When Sera frowned, she kissed her cheek and added, "I'm not saying he's a bad guy . . .

but you have to admit no one's ever going to confuse him with a teddy bear." She turned to me and arched an envy-inspiring eyebrow into her envy-inspiring red bangs. "Though I've never heard anyone dislike him quite so *passionately* before."

I pulled my book bag higher up my shoulder. "I don't know what you're talking about."

Eliza had her head tilted, studying me like a specimen in one of her experiments. "You *are* being unusually vocal about how much you dislike him. Is this about the recycling debacle? What don't I know?"

Oh, so many things. She didn't know about Fielding's mosaic path commentary, or what he'd said at the party. The way he'd been the haughtiest of haughties in the parking lot after. She didn't know how everything with Monroe felt like it was moving at warp speed. And since she refused to believe me about Ms. Gregoire's book-life connection powers, she didn't know all the ways my thoughts were spinning like a wobbly top—

"Merrilee?"

Capulet.

"Merri?"

Montague.

"Rowboat?"

MonRomeo.

A piercing whistle split the air. I jumped, stepping on Hannah's foot and whacking Eliza with my satchel.

Curtis pulled two fingers from his mouth. "You okay there, short stack?"

I glanced around at all the eyebrows-up faces. I mentally rewound a minute and realized they'd all been calling me while I was lost in my own headspace. "Totally fine." I forced up the corners of my mouth. "C'mon, Eliza. We've got cross-country."

15

eaves crunched under my sneakers. Fall was just getting
started, so these were the quitters—the leaves that had
let go early and changed directly from green to brown
without pausing on the gorgeous colors in between. They
had less of a *crunch* and more of a slip, since they weren't even
nice and crisp, like good autumn leaves should be. But the
sky was blue, the air was warm, the trail around campus was
picturesque, and the cropped leggings and T-shirt I'd filched
from Rory's drawer were cute. If it weren't for the fact that I
was breathless and sweaty and my running partner was pissed
and practically sprinting, it might have been enjoyable.

"You know that today isn't actually a race, right?" I asked
Eliza, pausing to catch my breath before adding, "I mean, why
don't we try that 'conversational pace' thing?"

"Conversational? Sure, let's talk. Let's talk about what
went down in Convocation."

"I was thinking we should talk about . . ." Gah, I should've
planned this better. I glanced around for a topic. "Leaves. Do
you know what any of these trees are?"

"Are you *truly* pretending we're not going to have this
conversation about Monroe?"

"I think that's a sassafras?" I nodded toward a tree. "How fun is that word? *Sassafras.*"

"It's a tulip poplar. So, about Monroe—"

"Can't we talk about something else? How about bio? Read any good studies lately?"

"Nope," she said.

"I hate you," I panted, struggling to keep up with her anger-fueled pace.

"I've got ten years of friendship bracelets that argue differently."

"Fine, then I'm stopping." I made a show of flopping into a mulch bed. Then bending forward to stretch my calves so I couldn't see her face. "What'd you think?"

"What'd I think of the guy who was hauled out of Convocation for creating a spectacle?"

"Those wouldn't have been my words, but . . . yeah?" I peeked up at her, then went back to studying my shoelaces. "Keep in mind I want you to like him . . . Um, not that I want you to *like* like him, but you know."

"I'm sure he's a perfectly nice guy—but you need to *slow down.*"

"Why?" I stood up and staggered a bit from blood-rush dizziness. "Because it's not the pace *you* want me to go? If you had your way, neither of us would date until we'd finished our doctorates. I *like* him. He likes me. Maybe he *more* than likes me."

Eliza's anger was always calm—it burned like frostbite; it slapped with facts. But standing on the trail, with no one around but trees and whatever woodland animals we hadn't scared, she kicked ferociously at the ground, spraying small pieces of dirt, rocks, and sticks. "Do you want me to have a panic attack? Because if you keep saying things like that, I—"

"You'll do what? Tell my parents? They've already met him. They loved him with their usual over-the-top flair, and he didn't freak out. Did you notice he didn't flip over *you*, either? He was absolutely intimidated by you—but not by your appearance, it was your position as my best friend that made him nervous."

"Oh." I watched this fact sink in. For once a guy hadn't been overawed by her. For once my *cute* hadn't played second fiddle to her *beautiful*.

"Look, Eliza, I'm sorry if you think it's too much, too soon, but that's not the way the story goes." I began to run again, faster this time. Frustration was apparently a pace booster.

"The story?" She groaned. "Are you still fixated on that? Okay, let's just pretend for a second you're right—you're not, but let's pretend. Comparing your relationship to *Romeo and Juliet* and claiming it's romantic—that's the equivalent of saying that *Macbeth* is a play about finding your motivation. Or that *The Tempest* is about hurricane preparedness. Or *King Lear* makes a great gift for Father's Day. I can keep going; *Julius Caesar*, that's—"

"Please don't."

Eliza was the one who stopped running first this time. She fixed me with earnest eyes. "Just be careful. I know I'm no good at this romance stuff—but you have the best heart of anyone I've ever met. I don't want him to hurt it."

I gave her a hug, and she let me, sweat and all.

Then she added, "And drop the whole 'we're *Romeo and Juliet*' thing. Monroe is not Romeo. This is not magic. Next you'll be telling me Toby is Knightley because he lives next door. Or is he Laurie? Curtis is a clown . . . does that mean he's Puck? Bottom? The dark-haired boy and the redhead from Latin class are dating—clearly that makes them Gilbert and Anne from Green Gables. Is Lance short for Lancelot? Who's his Guinevere? Who are Sera and Hannah? Which fictional character will you reduce me to? If you're going to commit to this, cast everyone. Or are you just special and the *only* one affected?"

I narrowed my eyes. "Just because you're a super genius doesn't mean you're always right." I ground a stupid tulip poplar leaf beneath my shoe. "You read your fancy science journals and think you're so above all things romantic. You scoff at the books and movies I like and are critical of all my crushes. Well, this isn't *your* area of expertise. It's mine."

We didn't talk the rest of our run or during the drive home—which was especially awkward since Nancy, the latest in a revolving door of doctoral students the Gordon-Ferguses hired as Eliza's temporary guardians, didn't do small talk *or* listen to the radio. Literally, the only words spoken were my "Hello, Nancy" and my "Thanks, Nancy. Let's talk later, Eliza."

At least that last one got a soft sigh and a nod. And three minutes later, my phone buzzed with her apology. I was already stripped down and standing next to the running shower, so I quickly responded and conceded that maybe/ definitely she'd made some valid points before I said we'd talk later. There was only so much hot water, and I wanted all of it to combat sore muscles and the trail mud striping my legs.

Thirty—okay, forty-five—minutes later I was mud-free, moisturized, and relaxed.

And Eliza and I were *fine*. I knew this because she'd texted, **We're fine, right?** to which I'd put down my lotion to reply **YES** . . . and a bunch of random emojis. Which was really just to mess with her. Eliza may have been fluent in Spanish and the periodic table, but she didn't speak emoji. I smiled when three minutes later she texted, **I give up. Love + Bug + Coffee + Cake + Confetti + Volcano + Indonesian Flag + Train + Whale = what?**

It = I adore you!

And I did. I adored the whole world right then. Well, with the exception of animal abusers and Fielding. How could I not? The sun was setting in Cheeto-flamingo colors out the bathroom window. The hair dryer was warm and the polish I'd just slapped on my toes was bright pink. I had the best best friends, a new school I liked, my family kicked butt . . .

Plus Monroe. Now that I was over the initial mortification from Convocation, maybe it hadn't been that bad. It was sort of sweet, right?

"Sweetheart?" Mom knocked on the door.

I pulled it open. "Almost done, I swear."

She gave me a tight smile, followed by the four worst words in the history of conversations: "We need to talk."

16

Mom followed up with "When your father gets home." Which, really, Mom? All the panic, none of the answers.

"Is everyone okay?" I asked.

"No one's hurt. But why don't you go start homework until he's back from the store."

"Oh—*kay*?" I stretched the word as thin as my patience and crept down the hall as slowly as possible, but she didn't crack. Which was probably just as well, since Mom did discipline and Dad did "one more chance" and "Oh, don't give me the sad puppy-dog eyes." There was a reason that Byron and Gatsby sat under his chair at dinner—he had "pushover" written all over his pullover sweaters.

But whatever it was we needed to talk about, it was churning into a panicked stomach as I pulled on a pair of purple-and-green-striped leggings and an oversized sweatshirt.

What had I done this time? I was no stranger to my parents in lecture mode, but I usually knew *why*. Did they hear about Convocation? And if so, would they care or would they *Awwww*? I still wasn't sure which side I fell on or what trouble Monroe had gotten into.

I grabbed Brontësaurus Rex, the stuffed dinosaur I'd had since I was eight, and mashed her beneath my chin as I paced my room. I wanted answers. I'd wanted Monroe to be an answer. The solution to that awful vacant feeling I'd described to Eliza. But it was still there, and gnawing beside it were Ms. Gregoire's words from class, Monroe's from Convocation, Eliza's from our run, and Mom's from two minutes ago.

I used the next ten minutes to take the laziest stab at math homework. I wrote the problems on the page, did *some* calculations, and even solved a couple. But, yeah—focus and I weren't friends. And when my phone rang, I didn't just answer it, I pounced on it like Gatsby on a chew stick. "Hello?"

Technically, last year Mom and Dad had implemented a No Cell Phones During Homework policy—which was really more of a Rory policy than a me one. Because Eliza wouldn't dream of texting or talking on the phone while she was studying, and Toby . . . well, he just climbed over, no phone necessary.

The policy was on the honor system, but the consequences of being dishonorable were severe—losing our phones for a whole week. Rory had been in cellular jail at least once a month last year. I'd only been caught one time—but I had a feeling Monroe was going to make being obedient tricky.

"Hey, love. I've missed you."

"Oh. Thanks?" It had only been three hours . . . which was more than the total time we'd spent together. I flopped on my bed and bit my lip before asking, "How much trouble did you get in for Convocation?"

He laughed. "Williams is useless. Don't worry about it."

"Um, okay?" He hadn't *seemed* useless when I was interviewing. He'd seemed intimidating and intense. And exactly like the type of uptight, pretentious authoritarian who'd have a child like Fielding. Clearly Sera was a changeling who'd been left with the wrong family. Or the jerk genes carried through the male branches of the Williams family tree.

Monroe groaned. "Rehearsal was endless. The director wants us all off-book, like, yesterday. I'm not complaining, but I do have the most lines in the play. Six hundred and fifteen. Even Juliet has only five hundred something."

That was another parallel between the play and us—more proof Ms. Gregoire was right and Eliza was wrong—because he definitely did more of the talking.

"So," Monroe continued, "when can you sneak out? Because I can't wait till morning to kiss you again."

"Um—" But I was saved from answering by a knock on my door. "I'vegottogobye."

"Merrilee? Can we come in?"

It's a good thing I had ninja-like reflexes, because apparently Mom's question was rhetorical. As I shoved my phone in my sweatshirt pocket, she opened the door and entered with Dad. "Hi, pumpkin."

Mom sat on my desk chair and then heel-walked it over to where my books were spread out on my bed. Dad moved my math book and sat down.

I flicked my phone over to silent. "What's up?"

"Mom made you chocolate milk." Dad held out a Snoopy glass with a bendy straw.

Pouring milk and adding chocolate syrup was about the

limit of Mom's culinary skills. She also made a mean bowl of cereal and could rock a plate of cheese and crackers. And mac 'n' cheese, if you liked it on the gummy/rubbery side of edible. But her gesture didn't feel comforting or like it heralded a *quick* conversation.

I took the glass and sat on my rag rug. "What's going on?" I tugged the sleeves of my sweatshirt over my hands. It had been Toby's back before a growth spurt, but I'd notched the collar and swapped his chewed drawstrings for ribbons, so it was irrevocably mine now.

Mom frowned at my math homework. She drew asterisks beside the problems I hadn't finished, just like she had when I was little and wrote threes backward. She looked up and said, "You didn't tell us Monroe was a Stratford."

"Um, he introduced himself to you as Monroe *Stratford.* So what?"

"The senator's not happy about it. Monroe's the son of her rival."

"Wait. You went into parental DEFCON mode because the senator doesn't like my boyfriend's father?" I laughed and waited for them to join in. They didn't.

My pocket began to vibrate. My phone screen lit up through the fabric. "Eliza," I said with a fake smile so big my teeth felt dry. "I'll call her back after my homework's done."

"Is she okay?" Dad's brows furrowed. "It's not right—her alone in that big house with just a grad student while her parents—"

"I like this latest grad student." Someone mark this date on the calendar, because it was the first and last time I'd ever defend Eliza's mom and dad. But it was also true. "Nancy's way better than the last couple."

Dad frowned. "Eliza knows that if she needs something, she can come to us, right? I worry about her." Normally I loved how he considered her his fourth daughter, but not right now, when he was holding out his hand for my cell, which was buzzing again. "You know what, answer the phone. I should tell her myself."

I powered it off. "She's fine. Just impatient to compare math answers. So let's get this over with so I can do them. You were saying something about the senate campaigns?"

Mom pressed her lips together. "They haven't exactly been friendly. All the objectification of the senator. The attack ads are toxic."

"And?" I shrugged. Wasn't politics always toxic? "Am I going to have to start avoiding everyone who isn't a Rhodes voter? Are we going to ban anyone wearing a Stratford pin from the store? Toby's father supports Mr. Stratford. Are the Mays uninvited to the wedding?"

"Of course not; Toby's practically family." Dad had arranged my eclectic collection of throw pillows in neat rows. They were all shapes and sizes, made from handkerchiefs and cloth place-mats I'd bought at yard sales during my sewing phase.

I snatched up Brontësaurus and fiddled with her spikes. "So, you won't tell me who I can be friends with—just who I can date?"

"We're not doing that either." Mom wheeled over to my desk and was capping pens and putting them in a mug from the local bookshop.

"What *are* you doing? Because when I left this morning you were practically designing Team Monroe T-shirts, and now you're . . . *this!*"

Dad's mouth quirked till Mom shot him a look. Normally I thought it was adorably, obnoxiously, cheesily romantic that they had such perfect ESP. For an old-people couple, my parents were pretty cute—I wanted that someday. The love notes on my bathroom mirror and steering wheel. The butt pinches in the kitchen when he thought no one was looking. The hand holding in the grocery store while discussing prices and coupons. Someday many years from now, I wanted to be sitting in my future daughter's bedroom, giving my future husband a pointed look that said, "your turn to be bad cop."

But first I wanted wild romance and passionate kisses, big gestures and racing-heart excitement. Roses on my balcony, declarations in Convocation, sneaking in and out, phone calls under covers, and a love story worthy of the best-seller list. I wanted the butterfly feelings and moonlight rendezvous. Monroe was a willing partner in crime, so the only obstacle was the pair of scowls lecture-cleaning my room . . . and the fact that these gestures were way more appealing in my imagination than they were in reality.

Dad cleared his throat. "We're not trying to give you mixed messages, but . . . the senator raised some valid concerns." He moved from organizing my pillows to the contents of my book bag that I'd dumped on the bed, but he paused and turned toward me, *don't disappoint me* eyes lit up like high beams. "Is there anything you'd like to tell us?"

"Like?" I squeaked. My head was spinning with all sorts

of off-limits ways of answering my own question: *Like, the senator's a complete control freak. Like, she's going all Capulet-Montague, and we know how that turns out. Like, your little girl is currently contemplating her boyfriend's request to sneak out and make out.*

Oh, definitely not that last one.

Dad's eyes dimmed, and I felt it like a gut punch. I'd failed this test enough times to know I'd missed the chance he was giving me to fess up and come clean. And I would've—I usually did—but this time I truly didn't know *about what*.

Mom frowned. "Your sister's party? You lied to us. You stood there and lied to us about the fire alarm."

"Ohhh." It was less word, more gasp. The sound you make when bitten by a mosquito or when stepping in dog poop.

"That," said Dad, "is what has us so conflicted right now. You like this boy, and that's important. But . . . the first thing you did after kissing him was lie to us."

"Technically, I never said I *didn't* do it." I gave my best attempt at a *don't ground me* smile, but it probably looked more like a post-Novocain grimace.

"Merrilee!" warned Mom. "Know how we found out? Senator Rhodes has the security footage from the club. She called to let me know you'd pulled the alarm while making out."

I cringed so hard-core that I think even my molecules shuddered. "First, please don't ever say the words 'making out' again. Gross. Also, the senator saw it?" My stomach was twisted in more loops than my bendy straw. "Did she tell you it was an accident? Because it was."

"You lied to us," said Mom, in that disappointed voice that always made Byron pee and Gatsby tuck his tail between his legs and slink away. If I could've followed his example and fled, I would've.

Instead, I squeaked, "I'm really sorry. And you should know, it's not Monroe's fault. It was *mine*." I had no doubt they'd believe this. Mom always said my middle name should be "Instigator."

"Not your best move, kiddo. But . . ." Dad squeezed a throw pillow shaped like a Sriracha bottle. "We were young once too—"

Normally I loved these stories. Proof that way back in the day, he and Mom had had their own epic hijinks, but right now, I just wanted them to leave so I could call Monroe. I needed someone to cringe with me.

Dad kept talking, but I wasn't listening. His voice faded into a chuckle that sounded slightly sniffly. "I can't believe our little dreamer is dating. I was starting to think no real boy would ever be able to compete with your book crushes."

My eyebrows shot up, because I was dating Romeo, so clearly books and boyfriends didn't have to be separate.

"This is your *one* pass, Merri," said Mom. "And you're lucky Mr. Rhodes is on the country club board, and they voted not to add any fines on top of the fire department's."

My mind had wandered back to English class, to imagining my parents' reactions if I repeated Ms. Gregoire's words and told them, *This story lives and breathes. We know them. They're us. You're them.*

"Huh?" I snapped back to the here and now. "Fines?"

"It costs money to respond to false alarms. All the fire trucks and man-hours. Who do you think pays for that?" Mom kneaded the back of her neck and sighed. "And with the wedding and school expenses . . . Really, this was the last thing we needed."

I swallowed around a guilt-shaped lump. "How much?"

Dad shook his head. "We don't have the bill yet."

I fiddled with Brontësaurus's floppy, stuffingless neck. "You can take it out of my paychecks."

"No doubt you'll help, but until we see a dollar figure . . . It could be significant," said Dad.

"In the meantime, Merri, just . . . *think*." Mom patted my hand. "I know you're our impulsive little imp, but better judgment and decision making, please."

"And since you can't do either of those things on an empty belly, what do you want for dinner? Your sisters scrounged leftovers, but I can whip up something," offered Dad. "Stir fry?"

"Not hungry. Thanks." I stood and opened my door. "If we're done, I need to do homework." Or have a panic attack, or pretend that none of this was happening, or call my boyfriend. If that was multiple choice, I was all about option D.

17

Even though I'd just promised to behave and make better choices, and I doubted that my parents had even reached the stairs yet, I pulled out and powered up my phone, bypassing the new texts (seventeen) and voice mails (eight) to dial the boy who'd left them all.

"There's my girl." His words were like stepping into a hot tub. I needed to feel warm and wanted after that lecture. "Finally. So, what time can you leave without getting caught? I can be on your street in eight minutes."

Inexplicably, I thought of Fielding. Of his expression when he'd judged me from across the parking lot—like somehow by standing there dripping wet and looking idiotic, I'd confirmed some deep-seated conclusion he'd already drawn about me.

I thought about my parents. My mom's "I know you're our impulsive little imp, but—"

Dad's "I'm not sure if you find trouble or trouble finds you."

Eliza's "You don't intentionally get so lost in your thoughts, but—"

I didn't like their expectations being stacked against me. The fact that people—my parents, my best friend—treated me like a fiasco was inevitable. Even Toby—who was fiercely defensive of me—felt like I needed defending.

I desperately wanted to tell Monroe yes. Tell him, "Make it seven minutes," and then monkey down from my balcony and across the lawn and into his heated leather seats and embrace. Have him distract me from my parents' disappointment.

But I wanted romantic adventures, not disasters. Hijinks, not mishaps. I wanted my parents to look at me with pride for my accomplishments, not resigned tolerance for my mistakes. Sneaking out felt like the wrong side of this equation. I sighed and slashed my arm through Dad's careful pillow arrangement. Being responsible was no fun. "I can't."

"What? No. You can. Even if you have to wait till later. I'll stay up all night."

"I really can't. I shouldn't even be on the phone. I just got a huge lecture—my parents found out about the fire alarm."

"Oh." He sucked in a breath. "And I'm guessing they're pissed?"

"Yeah. They're most upset about my lies. But it's expensive too. The fines—"

"I'll take care of it. I'll have someone call the club tomorrow." I could practically hear the shrug and hand wave in his quick answer. "Dad will make a donation to the firefighters' retirement fund, and this will all disappear. Seriously, don't worry about it."

That's what money was to him, a wave of the hand, a "don't worry about it." I was used to the rich. The May rich of international banking and Gordon-Fergus rich of prizes and sponsorships. Rhodes old-money rich.

We weren't. We'd inherited the house from Mom's parents, but that had been her whole inheritance and it had been before I was born. We were stretched thin by Lillian's college tuition bills, thinner by her wedding, thinner still by the expenses of Hero High that weren't covered by scholarships. We weren't poor. I'd seen the YouTube videos about global wealth distribution and #FirstWorldProblems and knew we were much better off than most people. And as long as humanity didn't decide to stop spoiling their pets, we'd probably scrape by. But I'd never be waving my hand to dismiss an unknown sum, as though no matter how many zeros were involved, it was no concern.

"Now that that's taken care of—what time can I pick you up?"

"No!" There was impulsive and there was stupid. This was trespassing in stupid territory and had set up a base camp in Not Listening. "I can't! Monroe, seriously—I mean, aren't *your* parents mad?"

"They don't know."

"Well, if-slash-when they find out—won't you be in trouble?" How could he not understand that me sneaking out right now was going from frying pan to firebomb?

"They won't find out. Dad's assistant will write the check. Besides, he'll get political clout from the donation. Come on. No one's home at my house. I'll pick you up and we can—"

The knock on my door had me jamming the hang-up button *and* burying my phone beneath a pillow, because that was not a conversation I was ready to have or have overheard.

"Merri?" Lilly knocked again.

I squeaked, "Come in."

"Am I interrupting?" Lilly looked around the room. She had a mug of tea cupped in her hands. I wasn't sure if it was for me—and I wasn't thirsty after chocolate milk—but I snatched it and took a big sip to disguise my flush.

"Not really. A little bit. This much." I held my fingers up an inch apart. "What's up?"

"I wanted to apologize for dumping all that on you the other night."

"Oh." I shrugged. "It's fine. I'm the MoH; that's literally my job."

"Yeah, well. I was being ridiculous. All that over a cat pillow. Anyway, Trent and I worked it out."

"Good. Can I see it?"

"The pillow? We didn't get it. We talked, and—"

"Talked?" My sister deserved a boy who'd buy her a dozen cat-mustache pillows. Who'd have the picture turned into wall art. *This* was why I didn't understand Trent or the ring on her finger. Where was his big apology gesture? "What store was the pillow from?"

Lilly laughed. "I know what you're thinking. Don't get me the pillow; I don't want it. I never really did, because it was never about the pillow. I was swept up in the idea of buying something for our future place. But it's *ours*, mine and Trent's—not just mine. So after we talked it out, we went shopping and picked out some lamps we both like."

I wrinkled my nose. "Lamps?" Wasn't Lilly actually supposed to be *old* before she became old and boring? I blamed Trent. He was a horrible influence. That would never be me.

Monroe would never be a Trent. He'd have filled my room with the pillows and the wall art *and* gotten it tattooed on his arm. We'd name the kitten something cute and couple-y—Verona! And every night before I went to sleep, I'd kiss the tattoo and he'd curl that arm around me.

Poor Lilly. I'd have to make notes to pester Trent before Valentine's Day and anniversaries—left to his own devices, he'd probably buy her blenders or vacuum cleaners—end tables to put the freaking lamps on. Was it bad form for the MoH to talk the bride into picking a different groom?

"Anyway . . ." Lilly drew out the word in a way that meant she knew she'd lost my attention. "I also wanted to check on you about Monroe. This whole thing seems really sudden. I didn't even know you knew each other . . . and now you're dating? Is he anything like his dad, because I've heard—"

"It's totally fine. Good. All good. Great!" Um, where was a thesaurus when you needed one? Because as Lilly had just clearly demonstrated, *she* was not the person I'd be going to for romance advice. "Marvelous, even."

"You sure?" Lilly was twisting a strand of her hair around her finger. She'd been doing it the whole conversation, but it was only then that I noticed the tip was turning white. Only then did I notice the teeth marks in her lipstick, and the way her voice was straining.

I stopped trying to shoo her out the door. "I promise. The situation with the fire alarm and the senator sucks, but at least I'll never have to call her 'Mom.'"

Lilly shuddered. "Something for me to look forward to, right?" She sighed and leaned against my dresser, absently putting lids back on powders and lining up my lip glosses and mascara. By the end of the night, my room would be uncomfortably organized. "Do you know she signed us both up for Bridal Body Boot Camp?"

"Are you kidding me? What did you do?" I glance apologetically at the pillows on my bed. My phone was probably buzzing away underneath them. But Lilly needed me, and would any MoH worth her weight in taffeta and tulle act differently?

"I told her that she could go if she wanted, but since I was a bride and this was my body, I already had a quote-unquote 'bridal body'—no boot camp necessary."

I gaped at her. "Did you really?"

She bit her lip, then beamed. "Yup. I need to start setting boundaries *now*. And I tore up her list of suggested wedding hairstyles. I'm capable of choosing my own, thanks very much."

"Go, *you*!" I gave her a hug.

Unlike Eliza, Lilly was a hugger. The type that held on tight and didn't let go right away. *She* was the one I used to run to with scraped knees. Not because I didn't love my parents, but because they rushed to the bandage part too quickly, and sometimes all I wanted was someone to acknowledge my pain, not fix it.

"Lills, I'm proud of you."

"Thanks." She took a sip of my/her tea, then handed it back. "But I should probably let you get to your homework . . . Isn't your fancy new school supposed to be hard? To hear Rory talk, it's med school combined with law school combined with rocket science."

I rolled my eyes. "It's been two days. We've barely even started—" Except why was I prolonging this conversation? "But you're right. I shouldn't get behind. Good night."

I was turning toward my bed to pick up my phone when Dad opened my door. "Hi, sweetie."

I sighed. "Seriously, is my room Grand Central Station tonight?"

"I'm not staying. I just wanted to drop off this." Dad pulled a plate from behind his back. It was heaped with a giant's portion of spaghetti, smothered in olive oil, peas, and fresh Parmesan. "I know you said you're not hungry, but you've got a big day tomorrow, and I wanted to make sure you carbo-loaded."

"Big day?" I tilted my head.

"Your first meet!" Dad crossed my room and peered out onto the balcony. "It's supposed to rain later—going to make for a muddy course tomorrow." He'd been waiting his whole life to have offspring he could cheer for in *any* sort of athletic competition. No wonder he was more excited about my first meet than I was. Honestly, I'd almost forgotten. While he checked the weather on his phone, I grabbed a pen and wrote *pack uniform* on my hand. "They wouldn't delay the race for a little mud, would they?" he asked, forehead knotted.

"Promise there'll be a meet tomorrow, puddles and all." I grabbed the pasta from his hands, taking a bite so large I almost choked when I spoke around it. "This is really good, Dad. Thanks." I paused to chew and swallow. "But I need to do my homework."

"Right. Of course." He stamped a kiss on my forehead. "I'll let you focus so you can get to bed and rest up for the big race. Sleep sweet, little dreamer."

I managed to swallow the noodles, but my mouth tasted of guilt and garlic. "Thanks. Good night."

This time I looked up and down the hallway before shutting the door. Having endured *three* visitors, I was good for the rest of the night, right? Wasn't that the rule Dickens established way back in *A Christmas Carol*? Three and done?

I stared down at my pasta and tried to convince myself I had an appetite. Tomorrow was a three-mile race—but today had felt like a marathon. I picked up my phone and dialed.

"Hey, before you even ask, I'm not coming out tonight. So please don't put me in a situation where I have to say no to you again."

"Fine." Monroe managed to cram an impressive amount of sulkiness into four letters.

"But . . . we could talk?" Maybe I needed to try this maturity stuff. Especially if it would give me answers about what it meant to be a modern incarnation of Romeo and Juliet. I didn't want to go through life fearing poisons and daggers—avoiding everything from sewing needles to piercings to splinters. "Tell me about your family. You said they're busy—what's that like?"

Because while having my bedroom feel like Grand Central Station wasn't ideal, I couldn't imagine having parents who weren't involved and wouldn't sit there and listen to me recount every detail from my day like it was fascinating. I

mean, they still hung my doodles on the fridge. And I was no
Rory. Maybe if I got him talking about his parents, he'd even
tell me about his half sister. It bothered me that he'd edited
her out of his family.

"No offense," said Monroe. "But the last thing I want to do
with you is talk—especially about my parents."

I wasn't sure if I should be seriously offended or just
moderately miffed. But I *had* hung up on him several times
tonight, so maybe he was entitled to a little frustration. "Okay,
then. I have another idea. A compromise. I've got English
homework and you've got lines to learn. . . . Do you maybe
want to read the play to me? Act two?"

"Huh." I could practically hear his annoyance melt away
as he absorbed this idea. "Clever *and* gorgeous. And mine.
Love, that's brilliant. Get comfy while I find my script."

I wished he was here. That when I lounged on my bed, the
elephant pillow beneath my cheek could've been his chest.
My hand resting on his arm where I'd imagined the kitten
tattoo.

He'd started reading while I was still fumbling through my
book, trying to find the right page. I caught up as he finished
the chorus and reached the first of Romeo's lines.

*"Can I go forward when my heart is here? / Turn back, dull
earth, and find thy centre out."* He changed his voice and read
Benvolio's line, then again for Mercutio.

I rested my chin on my hand and closed my book, closed
my eyes, and immersed myself in the richness of his emotions and voice. Never had Shakespeare felt more alive. The
politics were in place, Monroe was full-on Romeo . . . and

all the other characters too. But the more he read, the less I felt connected with the play. I wasn't digging Juliet—how *her* guy didn't want to talk either, not beyond compliments and demands. And how she let herself be so easily swayed by his plans. When Monroe read her most famous soliloquy, my thoughts were a distorted echo of her lines. *I would no longer like to be a Capulet.*

Eliza was dead wrong. Magic was real. But not all magic was good. I'd wanted this. I wanted what I saw in every romance book, and this was right off those pages. But while this moment felt full of every ingredient for enchantment—it wasn't quite sticking. Everything was moving too fast, and instead of letting myself get swept up in the momentum, I was clinging to my misgivings. I wanted to swoon . . . but I couldn't quite fall.

18

Toby, you don't need to bother introducing me to Fielding; Clara already claimed him." Rory's declaration broke the silence on the drive to school the next morning. I was busy yawning and texting. And texting. And texting. There was a delicate balance between wooing and try-hard, and Monroe had tipped the scales the wrong way. The texts had started seconds after we'd hung up.

What are you doing?

Math homework.

What are you doing now?

Still math. problem #3

They hadn't stopped. Not even when I'd answered **Sleeping**.

Today brought a dozen texts during breakfast to convince him that I was fine riding with Toby. In fact, I *wanted* to drive with Toby. In fact-fact, I was *currently* driving with Toby and, no, I wasn't going to ask him to pull over so Monroe could pick me up.

I put down my phone and wrinkled my nose. I'd forgotten that Rory wanted an intro and to join his freshman fan club. "Ugh. Believe me, you're not missing much with Fielding." I didn't know who this Clara girl was, but I would not be sad or surprised if she flunked out of school. I mean, she had to have been an idiot if she wanted a guy who looked at you like you were dog vomit. Except . . . maybe he *didn't* look at other girls that way. Maybe it was just *me*. I swallowed. Dad must've bought the juice with pulp again. That was totally what was stuck in my throat.

"Um, really?" said Rory. "Because from what I've heard, he's hot, smart, and president of just about every club on campus. He's like Hero High royalty."

"Royal pain in the . . ." I shook my head. Who cared if that was true? "Regardless, you can't *claim* people."

"Says the girl who claimed Prince Eric, the Beast—in both human and nonhuman forms—all Prince Charmings, and the entire house of Gryffindor?" Rory was wearing fingerless gray knit gloves. I'm not sure if she thought they looked cool or if they were part of her artist costume or what, but when she ran a hand through her chin-length hair, it stood out straight with static. I didn't tell her.

My phone had beeped twice during this exchange, but I ignored it and turned around to look in the backseat. "You're totally Slytherin, so why do you even care? Not you, Eliza; you're Ravenclaw."

"I'd like to point out that those are *characters* and fiction," said Eliza. I hated her parents' sleep log and rules, but gah, for a second I was jealous of it. And of the fact that she looked bright-eyed and well rested while it was taking all my energy not to drool when I yawned. "Not that I disagree with Rory that it's ridiculous to claim them—but I'm going to also agree with Merri here. What do you mean Clara *claimed* him?"

"And who is Clara?" asked Toby. "Does she even know Fielding?"

"Not if she's lucky," I mumbled.

"He would hate everything about this conversation," Toby said. "Poor guy. He's actually really shy."

Rory said, "Awww." I rolled my eyes.

My phone was beeping again. I scrolled through text after text. The latest said, **Waiting to surprise you at your locker.**

Except now it wasn't a surprise. "Do we have time for drive-through coffee?" I asked, tugging on Toby's arm. "Please, please, please. You'll be my hero."

"Late night?" Eliza asked.

Rory kicked my seat and said, "Merri and Toby were up as late as I was. My math homework is going to murder me."

My eyes widened. Note to self: turn down speakerphone. At least Rory had given me the perfect Monroe–cell phone cover story.

"I wasn't—" Toby began, and I pinched his arm. He frowned at me, but finished, "aware we'd been so loud."

Rory's voice sweetened as she responded to him, "I was going to bang on the wall, but Mom said Merri had a rough night and to leave her alone."

"Rough night?" Toby and Eliza chorused.

Why were ejector seats in cars not a real thing? Especially since interloping younger sisters were. "Hence my need for coffee," I answered, and Toby put on his turn signal to head to Cool Beans' drive-through.

Once we'd parked at school and finally gotten rid of Rory, I filled them in as best I could in the two minutes' walk toward our lockers. "So, in summary, I'm now a felon, I've pissed off a senator, I'm exhausted, Monroe apparently thinks I'll forget him if he goes five minutes without texting. And I'm not liking this play nearly as much as I thought."

Toby gave me a side hug. Eliza offered comfort in the form of facts. "It isn't a felony—"

"I wish I could be that coffee cup." Monroe's words hit my ear as he slid an arm around my waist, twisting my bag off my shoulder and slinging it onto his. I jumped and almost sloshed my mocha on him, so I guess he managed his surprise after all.

"Oh, hi." I held up my cup. "Do you want some?"

"No, I'm just jealous it gets to be the first thing your lips touched this morning."

"Oh." I was way too aware that Eliza and Toby were listening. That she'd snorted into her herbal tea and he'd pitched his half-finished coffee in the trash. "It's really not. That was lip balm. Then toothbrush, then breakfast, then toothbrush again, and I'm sure there was more lip balm. And my parents' cheeks . . ." I paused to count on my fingers. "There are probably a dozen things I've touched with my mouth before this cup."

"Then I'm jealous of them all." We were at the edge of the sophomore hall. The intersection where the bright red of the juniors' lockers transitioned to the silver of my class's. Thickets of students bumbled around us—those who were at my level of morning coordination almost stumbled into our little roadblock. They greeted Toby and Monroe, threw general hellos in Eliza's and my direction.

There was one student, however, who walked by without

a greeting. Face averted, footsteps fast. I doubt he would've acknowledged us at all if Toby hadn't reached out and given him a bro-smack on the shoulder. "Hey, Fielding!"

"Oh. Hi, Toby." Fielding did a grim scan of the rest our group before giving a stiff nod. The whole exchange took less than five seconds, and his eyes didn't so much as flicker my way. If they had, I would definitely have noticed, since my eyes were suctioned on him. And then he walked away.

"See," Toby said to me. "He's shy."

I snorted. "That's one word for it."

I turned to look at him over my shoulder, to see if I could spot any hint of Toby being right, but the movement was cut short by Monroe grasping my face with both hands. It was a gesture that had felt sooo tingly on Friday, but now I just wanted my face back. Especially when he used his very best theater-projection voice to broadcast, "I can't wait another minute to kiss you good morning."

"That's our cue to leave," said Toby. "C'mon, Eliza, let's get to class."

"Don't be late," she warned; but I wanted her to grab my hand and drag me away. Why didn't she? That would be the ultimate Eliza move—prioritizing punctuality over a kiss.

Except—my cross-country lecture. This was her form of respecting me, showing she'd listened. Gah, we needed to work out some sort of Bat Signal, a gesture I could make that meant *You were right, I was wrong. Save me!*

I used to dream about endless boyfriend texts and being kissed and complimented. But now I wanted . . . space. Or at least texts that communicated instead of pestered. Kisses that I reciprocated instead of tolerated. And compliments that felt like they were about *me*, not saying fancy words for an audience of onlookers.

The hallway was emptying around us. I pulled out of his grasp and slid my satchel back off his shoulder. "Have a good morning. I'll look for you between classes."

Monroe clamped a hand over mine. "Don't go yet! The warning bell hasn't even rung."

"But bio is all the way across campus. I really need to."

"But I need *you*. Let's skip and go get waffles."

During summer storms, Gatsby glued himself to my side like a barnacle. I seriously couldn't even pee without him wedged between my leg and the toilet paper roll. And sleep? Not possible with a quivering, sixty-pound, drooling fur ball trying to burrow beneath my pillow. During thunder and lightning, Gatsby needed me. On a random Tuesday morning, Monroe did not. "Skipping's really not my thing."

"Come on, Dr. Badawi won't care if you're late. Say you got lost."

Oh, the devil on my shoulder wanted to tell *him* to get lost. But the better part of me just reapplied lip gloss and blew him a kiss— Yeah, I couldn't pull that gesture off. I wouldn't be doing it again. He was all basset hound eyes and pouty lips, and maybe if I weren't so tired, and it weren't so off-limits, and I weren't already in a litter-full of trouble about the country club, I would've relented. But I waved and backed away. "I've got to go. I'll see you later."

I didn't even make it to the first tile on the path before my phone chirped with an I miss you already text. Actually, it wasn't "I miss you already," it was **Parting is such sweet sorrow,** but personally, I thought the moment the cell phone signal blocker kicked in and cut off his texts was pretty sweet.

That didn't stop him from messaging me on my laptop. Constantly. By the time I got to English, I was stressed out and fed up.

RowboatReads: I think we're going to get in trouble. Please stop.

MonROMEO: O, teach me how I should forget to think

RowboatReads: I'm serious. Stop. Now.

MonROMEO: Let me be ta'en, let me be put to death; I am content, so thou wilt have it so

Either we hadn't gotten to that part of the play or I'd forgotten it. Either way, *I wiln't have it.* And I was about to tell him—

"Merrilee, would you care to weigh in with your thoughts?" Ms. Gregoire asked.

Again! Getting caught off guard twice in one week meant I wasn't nearly as stealthy at messaging as I thought. I needed to turn in my ninja card. We'd been doing a reading of the first three scenes of act three.

I hadn't been cast as Juliet, which seemed super strange. In fact, Ms. Gregoire hadn't given me a role at all. And not that I'd been sulking, but it had made me slightly less reluctant to engage with Monroe via messenger.

I glanced at my screen. There was a new quote there. It had worked before. . . . I crossed my fingers and read, "'*So tedious is this day / As is the night before some festival.*'" I wisely left off the rest of Monroe's message, the part where he suggested skipping Convocation.

"That's a lovely line, but I'm not sure how it's relevant."

Ms. Gregoire stood slowly, in a way that disarmed me, so I was unprepared when she crossed the circle in two strides and flipped my computer around. "I see." I wilted under her look of disappointment. "Class, I need to step out of the room for a moment, but I'd like you to continue the discussion. The topic, for those of you who may not have been paying attention, was Romeo's agency. Was he as cornered as he believed? Did he *have* to murder Tybalt?"

The pause while Ms. Gregoire exited with my laptop was full of humiliation. Luckily it was brief, discussion resuming before the door shut.

"Romeo has so much more agency than he admits. His level of privilege is absurd. He's protected from the consequences of his actions by his gender and his parents' wealth. He should have been *killed*, not exiled, and yet his reaction is to throw a crying tantrum like a toddler."

It wasn't Eliza. It was Ava. And while her words may have distracted from my shame, her glare was as sharp as a dart.

"Juliet's not much better," Nicole argued. Her hands had a new Sharpie tattoo today, one that danced as she gestured while speaking. "She says she'd rather her parents be *dead* than Romeo be banished. I'd say that's equally pathetic—it's why they're so well matched."

"Except—" It was Eliza this time, one finger held up in the air, her other hand searching through her book. "Juliet has practically no agency at all. The only power she can wield is whether or not to kill herself. She has the last line in the act: *'If all else fail, myself have the power to die.'* I know we haven't gotten that far, but it's not like I'm offering spoilers here.

Maybe her statement about Tybalt's death, and the hypothetical sacrifice of her parents too, is more a statement about wanting control—and the fact that her best chance of *any* agency was through a marriage to Romeo and using *him* to escape from her family."

"Go, Legally Blonde!"

Curtis was giving a slow clap, but froze and lowered his hands when she whirled toward him with a paint-curling glare. "Don't ever call me that again."

I shot him a look of sympathy. Eliza had zero tolerance for anything remotely like a blonde joke. He returned my sympathetic look as Ms. Gregoire walked back in.

"Nevertheless, he's right, that was quite a good point, Eliza." She placed my laptop on her desk. "Let's hear from one of the men in here. Do you feel the same way?"

"It's Romeo's loyalty that's being tested—not just his temper. This wasn't the same as Tybalt insulting Mercutio on iLive or something. He *killed* him. Romeo is honor-bound to avenge the death of his friend," said Randolph.

"Maybe I'd accept that argument if he hadn't blamed Juliet's beauty for making him 'effeminate.' That sounds more like toxic masculinity than loyalty," said Curtis.

Eliza lifted an eyebrow in approval, but when she caught me watching, it slammed down.

"It's too much." I was saying the words before I'd even finished the thought in my head. "Too fast. I just wish they could slow down. Take a time-out. Think about what they really want. The more choices he makes, the more cornered she feels."

"Indeed," said Ms. Gregoire. "That's a fine place to end. Tonight I'd like you to finish acts three and four."

In the shuffling of pens and books and laptops being packed, Ms. Gregoire approached my desk. "I'd like you to stay after for a few moments." She gave a small, disappointed headshake. "Headmaster Williams will be joining us."

Did classrooms always take this long to empty? I couldn't decide if I wanted everyone to linger, or to hurry up and leave. I ignored the sympathetic looks they were offering on their way out the door. Well, everyone but anti-new girl, pro-Monroe Ava.

Eliza paused in the hallway, making a show of dumping an imaginary pebble out of her shoe and fiddling with the contents of her bag.

"Ms. Gordon-Fergus, go to lunch. Merrilee will be along shortly."

"Yes, Ms. Gregoire," Eliza said, but she didn't walk away particularly fast.

Ms. Gregoire didn't fill our wait with small talk. She worked at her desk and let me focus on my guilt and keeping my breakfast from reappearing.

By the time I heard the clacking of footsteps in the hallway, I'd worked myself into a massive panic. My nostrils flared and my eyes were glassy before Headmaster Williams entered the classroom, looking so official and intimidating I wanted to confess to every lie I'd ever told.

He nodded a greeting. "Merrilee, you're aware of why Ms. Gregoire asked me here?"

I nodded and sniffled.

"I reviewed your messages to Monroe Stratford and sent the file over to Headmaster Williams as well," said Ms. Gregoire.

Forget crying, I wanted to *die*. They'd read my e-love notes with Monroe? I would not vomit. I would *not* vomit. I would not think about any of the things he'd written or the things I'd written back. Oh, I was going to vomit.

Ms. Gregoire cleared her throat and I looked up from the floor tiles. "It doesn't seem like there was any cheating."

"Cheating?" I shook my head so fast my hair lashed my face, sticking in my lip balm. I spat it out and added, "I know Monroe sent some quotes from the play, but he had no idea what we were discussing in class."

"Our concern wasn't that *you* were cheating, but that *he* was," clarified Ms. Gregoire.

"I don't understand."

"Were you aware that Monroe was messaging you while taking an exam in his calculus class?" asked Headmaster Williams.

"A test?" I winced. Why, Monroe? *Why?*

"An online exam. During which having *any* other program open constitutes cheating. This was a policy his teacher explained before distributing the link to the exam."

"I didn't know. And I *was* telling him to stop messaging." Was that throwing him under the bus? Whatever, it was *true*! If he'd stopped the first time I asked, or the sixth, or the twelfth, I wouldn't be the filling of this disapproval sandwich. "And I wasn't planning on skipping. I was literally typing no when I got caught. It's probably still in the window."

"We saw that—" Ms. Gregoire paused, and I didn't dare exhale in case she added a "but."

Headmaster Williams cleared his throat. "*But*, you both signed the Hero High Honor Code. Do you remember the consequence for cheating, Ms. Campbell?"

Nope. I had no clue, but judging from the pulsing vein on the side of his forehead, now was not the time to admit to signing without reading. "I didn't know he was taking a test. I swear. And I'm in precalc. I wouldn't know how to help him if I wanted to—which I didn't! Or *wouldn't* have, because I really didn't know he was taking a test."

There was a long silence as the headmaster's head continued to look like it might explode and I fought against the flood of blather that was gathering on my tongue. Eliza always said that when confronted, answer *only* the question asked and don't give any additional incriminating details. Whoops.

"Facts are facts and behaviors have consequences, Ms. Campbell." Judging from his expression, it was too bad the Convocation hall was *not* a church, because it would've been a good time to slip in there and start praying.

Ms. Gregoire stood up. "Maybe, just this once, because Merrilee is a new student and perhaps the policies weren't completely clear to her, we can exercise leniency with her punishment. If I might—since it was my class she disrupted —I'd like to be the one to assign the consequence."

The headmaster nodded. "I'll grant that."

I turned to Ms. Gregoire. Was that a glint in her eye? I shivered. She was supposed to be twinkle-eyed, not glinty.

"What will the punishment be?" My voice wavered as I

made a mental list of evil teachers in books—*Matilda* with
Trunchbull and her chokey, Harry Potter's Umbridge and
her blood quill, *Little Women*'s Mr. Davis, who struck Amy
March's hand and made her throw her limes out the window.
I clenched my fingers tight and tucked them behind my back.

"I'm going to have to think on it. You're an interesting
case, Merrilee. More complicated than I originally thought.
But . . ." She studied me a moment. "You might be ready."

I didn't know what that meant, if it was a compliment
or something I should apologize for. I bobbed my head and
body—part chicken, part acknowledgment, and part clumsy
curtsy.

Headmaster Williams handed back my laptop. I took
it with shaky hands. "I'll also be calling your parents, Ms.
Campbell. This is your one and only chance. Next time—"

"There won't be a next time!" Probably not the best idea
to interrupt him, but I was fizzy with anxiety, and that made
me blurt.

"Come see me tomorrow morning before homeroom, and
I'll have your punishment sorted," Ms. Gregoire said. "In the
meantime, run along to lunch before Miss Gordon-Fergus
comes searching to make sure we haven't tortured you."

"*And*, if you're capable of it, do manage to stay out of trouble," added the headmaster.

"Thank you!" I was so relieved I threw my arms around
Ms. Gregoire. Yup, I hugged a teacher. Probably something
that's frowned upon, post-kindergarten. I would've hugged
Headmaster Williams too—but I didn't want to get greasy condescension on my uniform.

"All right now." She laughed and gently pried my hands off. "See you in the morning."

"Thank you," I said again as I shoved my laptop into its sleeve, then paused with it halfway zipped. "But . . . what about Monroe?"

"Unfortunately, Mr. Stratford was quite aware he was taking an exam. And he's had three years to learn the school policies. He seems to have a penchant for getting into trouble with regards to you, Ms. Campbell."

The last part may have been true, but that didn't mean it was my fault. No meant no. In all domains. And I'd said "no" and "stop" more than once. Whatever happened was on him.

19

When I arrived at lunch, the table fell quiet. Curtis spoke first. "Everything okay?"

"Yeah. Sorta." I studied my bag so I could pretend they weren't all staring. "I don't really want to talk about it." Not with Sera there—because I liked her and didn't think I could be polite about her father just then.

Hannah offered me the cupcake from Toby's tray. "Well, I'm fully prepared to go into Knight Light crisis mode."

"Thanks, but that's not necessary." Though I'd absolutely take a frosting-only bite of Toby's cupcake before returning it—and the fact that he didn't object meant he was worried too.

Eliza nudged my foot under the table; I nudged hers back. Best-friend speak for *We'll talk later*. She offered me a grape, which was her way of saying, *Oh, you better believe we will*.

I zombied through the rest of my classes, but once we hit the cross-country locker rooms, all bets were off. Eliza and I changed at record pace, like the actual race was to see who could get in her singlet and shorts fastest. And then, while our teammates were still stripping down, she suggested, "Let's do a warm-up lap," and dragged me out the door.

Silly me for not realizing she actually meant the running part of it. I puffed after her. "Just when I'm starting to like running, they have to make us go and do something stupid like race." I glanced over my shoulder at the school gates and almost stumbled over a root.

"You're going to give me high blood pressure, I swear it," said Eliza.

"Well, I don't like the part where I fall constantly. But I like that it's time with you, even though I'm slow and you can run so much faster."

"You're getting faster." She ran quietly for a few steps before adding, "I like that it's time with you too. But I won't be slowing my pace during the meet, just FYI."

"Oh, I *know*." I grinned. "You've got a competitive streak three-point-two miles long, so I'm guessing you plan to win?"

"I might not *win*," she said dismissively. "But I have been doing supplementary workouts too. The anaerobic strength training my parents require. Some yoga for flexibility. And occasionally sprints on the treadmill if we spent more time chatting than running."

"Eliza!" I studied her face. "That sounds like too much."

She ducked her head. "Yeah, my parents thought so too when they saw my exercise log."

"They did?" I tugged the waistband of our uniform shorts—they were *short* and rode up.

"They're not monsters, Merrilee. They leave me here because they think it's best *for me*. And maybe monitoring my nutrition and sleep and exercise and the rest of it seems extreme to you, but science and data are the languages they communicate in. They're never going to be the types of parents who want to cuddle and kiss and say 'I love you' all the time. I know they're not *your* parents, but that doesn't mean they're not showing they care by wanting to know I'm healthy and thriving and in optimal condition."

Like a car. But I didn't say it out loud. "And they think you're overexercising?"

"We had a long talk yesterday—yes, they actually called—and they sent me a couple of journal articles on compulsive exercise and its link to disordered eating and body image. I hadn't increased my caloric intake enough and my BMI had dropped slightly. It's still completely within the normal range, but they were concerned." She lifted her chin. "See, they *do* care."

"They have the best daughter in the world; they'd be idiots not to," I said. "And they've got shelves and shelves of awards that prove they're not idiots."

"Thank you." They were quiet words, but I saw the shift in her posture, her shoulders rolling back and her neck straightening.

"So you're going to back off with the exercise?"

"And add more protein and calories to my diet."

"Good."

"Thank you," she said again. "For wanting to talk about this, not Monroe."

"Hey!" I wasn't sure if I should be hurt or insulted. Both? "I'm your best friend. I *always* want to talk about what's going on with you. Boys will *never* be more important. Ever. You're stuck with me like dog hair on black pants. Like—" I searched my head for an Eliza-worthy comparison. "Like parts of an atom."

"You're saying it would take nuclear fission to split us?" I loved her laugh—it was loud enough to scare the squirrels in the trees. "Did you just compare us to an atomic bomb?"

"Yes. I'd destroy the world before I gave up your friendship."

"Good to know." She laughed again as we circled back to the field house. The rest of the team was spread out on the grass—apparently this particular patch wasn't off-limits?—stretching and hydrating. Eliza stopped short of them. "Are you okay? With English class and everything? If you still don't want to talk about it, we can discuss whatever book boy you're crushing on."

There was so much I wanted to say, but I didn't know where to begin. Instead I scoffed. "You think I have time to read with all this?" I gestured at the campus. Though maybe I *would have* if I wasn't up all night with Monroe. Hannah was still updating her blog and recommending new books, after all.

"Merri?" It was just my name, but it pushed me past some tipping point I hadn't realized I was approaching. The country club consequences, the lack of sleep, the lecture from the headmaster, getting caught by *Ms. Gregoire*, the teacher I liked most. I blinked wetly and swallowed. "It's all a mess. Like, a Gatsby-got-in-the-trash-size one."

"Come on." Eliza glanced at the team, then pushed me into the locker room. "Talk."

I sat on the bench and summarized as best I could between blowing my nose and sniffling. Eliza paced and passed me tissues.

"I always said I wanted romance—something like *Romeo and Juliet*. And I know you think I'm delusional, but Monroe *is* that. He's all about the big gestures and exaggerated compliments. . . ." I pulled my legs up on the bench. "But I want fewer declarations—more actual talking . . . I wanted to get to know him—and he just wants to put on a show. It feels like he's never *not* playing a part. Like his life is method-acting Romeo." I scrubbed at my eyes. "He's everything I always said I wanted in a boyfriend, but it's not enough. It's not . . . right."

"Merri, you're allowed to change your mind about what you want. It's part of growing up." She sat down next to me and I leaned my head on her shoulder. Eliza had threaded her fingers together and was tapping her thumbs—her thinking gesture. "Remember that time you tried to make cookies with *all* your favorite foods?"

"Pineapple-chocolate chip-ginger-gummy bear." I scraped my tongue against my teeth to wipe off even the memory of that taste.

"What happened when you ate them?" prompted Eliza.

"I got sick . . . but I still think maybe we underbaked them."

"That's not my point. You *love* allegories. I'm trying to give you one. Pay attention!" She shook her head. Her ponytail smacked against my cheek. "You *thought* you'd like all those foods in the same cookie—but you didn't. Maybe the same is true with boyfriends? I'm not telling you what to do, but I'm here. And I'm sorry he didn't listen to you and respect your boundaries."

She didn't need to tell me what to do. This decision was

obvious. Sure, Romeo and Juliet had overcome harder obstacles, but they'd ended up dead; so *really*, what kind of role models were they? Plus, I was starting to hate that play. I tightened my shoelaces, repeating her words to myself.

I'd be borrowing that whole part about boundaries when I called to break up with him.

20

Sprinting across the lawn toward the starting line *definitely* counted as a warm-up. And the timing couldn't have been better. We joined the runners as the starting gun fired—so while I caught Coach Lynn's angry glares, she didn't have time to back up her murderous expressions with words.

But Coach Lynn's looks had nothing on Mom's and Dad's. They were standing at the top of the course's big hill. My first thought was: *Yay, they both came*; then, *Are they going to yell for me, or at me?* And you know what makes running up a steep hill even harder? Double parent disapproval waiting at the top.

And you know what's *not* super motivating on the second half of a race? The knowledge that the faster you run, the sooner you'll be face-to-face with those parents and their lectures.

Mom began, "We're furious with you," before I'd found water or stopped panting like an overheated pug. Attacking when I didn't have the breath to argue back—not fair.

"A call from the headmaster? On your first week of school? Merrilee Rose Campbell!" Mom middle-named like a boss, and it always made me cringe. "Is this supposed to convince us that you're trustworthy and this boy *isn't* a bad influence? If so, you've failed."

Eliza tossed me a water bottle and lowered her gaze as she walked by, heading toward the team. They were stretching and sharing a container of homemade cookies. They got *cookies*, and I got public parental humiliation.

"Take a breath, both of you," suggested Dad.

"I'm. Trying," I panted. "Some of us just ran a race."

Dad's mouth wiggled in that way it did when he was trying to look firm but was actually amused. Like when I'd stuck *real* worms in the kindergarten bully's pudding dirt. "You looked great out there."

"Thanks. I'm sorry I got caught messaging."

"Sorry you got caught? Or sorry you did it?" he asked.

"Honestly?" Eliza says whenever I start a sentence with "honestly," I should stop talking. One of these days I'm going to remember to take her advice. "Sorry I got caught. Everyone uses messenger. It's like not chewing gum with braces, one of those rules no one follows."

"So you're okay with cheating? That's what you're telling us? Everyone at your school cheats and you're okay with that?"

"I wasn't cheating, Mom."

"Monroe was taking a test!"

I'd hoped Headmaster Williams would leave that part out. "I didn't know that."

"*He* knew. And I know you know this was wrong," said Dad. His hair—the same hair I had, which didn't do anything but flop and look brown—was sticking up. Like he'd been pulling on it. Hopefully it had been while he was cheering, rather than in frustration.

"He was quoting Shakespeare, not suggesting we elope." What was it about parents that made you want to disagree with them—even when you agreed with them? There was no other explanation for why I was defending the same guy I'd decided to break up with three miles ago.

"He hasn't done that, right?" Mom was rumpled too; even on her best day, her eye makeup tended to be a bit smeared or crooked, but now it was smudged like she'd been rubbing her eyes or pinching the bridge of her nose.

"Of course not!" I glanced at the team huddle and pep talk I was missing. The cookies were going to be long gone by the time my parents finished convincing the contrary part of my brain to *not* break up with Monroe.

"Another deep breath might be a good idea," Dad suggested. "Merrilee, we're glad you found a boy who makes you happy, *but* we don't like the behaviors he seems to be encouraging."

I looked down at my muddy sneakers, which were suddenly fascinating. . . . Dad in his usual Dad-ness had gotten to the heart of the issue without even realizing it. Monroe didn't make me happy, and he'd encouraged far worse behaviors.

"And you need a consequence," he finished.

"Like what?" I looked up at him with my most innocent expression as I stood on one foot to stretch my quad.

Dad wrapped an arm around my shoulder to steady me and looked at Mom with an expression that clearly said, *How can you possibly expect me to punish anyone this adorable?* Sometimes being a Daddy's girl paid off.

"You're grounded," said Mom. "Through the weekend."

And sometimes it didn't. "Grounded? No. Please?"

"How about this?" Dad countered. "If you want to see any of your *other* friends between now and Monday, that's okay. We don't want to stop you from forming friendships with your new classmates. But you're grounded from Monroe. Good?"

Mom tilted her head as she considered this. "I'm okay with that."

I was one hundred percent okay with being grounded from him. But it wouldn't do to be excited about a punishment, so I looked down and scraped my shoe along the sidewalk for effect. "Fine."

"Good," said Mom. "Now grab your stuff. You're working at the store tonight."

Mom and Dad were waiting in the car. I'd promised to just run in, throw on my Haute Dog uniform, and come back out. They'd assume I'd grab a snack or a bathroom break, but still—I had ten minutes. Tops. It probably wasn't enough for a serious conversation, but I was sick with impatience—literally. My stomach was twisted into knots, and if I had to throw up, I'd rather do it in the privacy of my own bathroom than at the store. I pressed one sweaty hand to my stomach and dialed with the other.

"Hello." He answered on the first ring, and I paused for one last check for butterflies or sparks or any sort of wistful feeling. Nope. Just stress-nausea.

"Hey, Monroe." I sat on the corner of my bed and tucked Brontësaurus Rex under my chin. "I've only got a minute, but we need to talk."

"Hi." He sounded sullen. Maybe he knew what was coming? "I'm not Romeo anymore."

"Good, because I don't want to be Juliet." Not his, not anyone's. I mean, *really*, who voluntarily models their love life after a tragedy? "So, we can just be—"

"No, you don't understand, love."

My "—friends" was buried beneath his interruption, and clearly we were *not* on the same page, or even in the same book. Not that his "love" had sounded all that loving.

He sounded even more frustrated when he added, "What I'm telling you is: '*And for that offence / Immediately we do exile him hence.*'"

"Um, what?" I stood and toed off my socks. Shimmied out of my shorts and into khakis.

"Catch up, Merri. Act three, scene one, the Prince."

"Nope. No clue what you mean." And I wasn't super keen on the tone he was using. I clicked him onto speakerphone while I rummaged in my drawer for a store polo and a bra.

"I got kicked out of the play. The idiot headmaster kicked me out of the play."

"That was your punishment for messaging?" I sucked in a breath and froze with my singlet tangled around my neck and one arm. I remembered how ecstatic he'd been to get that role—you know, a whole thirty-six hours ago, back when I was still excited about us.

"And I'm suspended for a week—but can you believe the play?"

Personally, I thought the suspension was the bigger deal, especially on the year before he'd be applying to colleges—but to each his own.

"And you know what my parents said when the headmaster called them? This is via their assistant, obviously, because neither of them had time to call me. They said 'good.' They thanked him. They said this was the last play they were going to let me do anyway, and they're glad I'm done with that nonsense."

The part of my stomach that wasn't a ball of stress clenched with sympathy. This was his dream they'd ridiculed. And since he was clearly devastated by this, it meant I'd have to live in breakup limbo a little while longer, because I couldn't pile on more problems.

Also, Dad had double-beeped the horn. Next step was Mom coming in to fetch me. I doubted she'd be happy to find me on the phone with the person I was grounded from. I'd call him tomorrow, after he'd had time to process everything. We could break up then. I sighed into the collar of my shirt but offered a sincere "I'm sorry."

"You should be. I mean, how hard is it to hide your computer screen?"

"I'm sorry?" I said it again, but with *very* different inflection. "I must have misunderstood, because you can't possibly be blaming *me* for the messages you sent, despite me asking you to stop, and despite the fact that you were taking a test."

"You're the one who got caught."

Any reservations I had about this breakup vanished into a red haze of rage. If I were to rewrite the play at that moment, I'd have had Juliet stab Romeo, not herself. Or maybe she'd just push him off her balcony the first time he tried to climb it.

"I'm also the one ending this phone call. Don't call me back. Don't text. Don't come over. I'm sorry you lost your part in the play, I know you must be really disappointed, but I'm not taking the blame for your mistakes."

Before he could give any sort of big Shakespearean response, I hung up.

21

It might not have been especially professional to work while smelling like a sweat sock, but I didn't care. Mom and Dad dropped me off out front and I stomped toward the store, ready to unleash a hurricane of complaints to Lilly. But the door was locked. I let myself in, flipping the "Bark in woofteen minutes" sign.

I wanted to call Eliza or Toby or anyone who would let me rant then tell me how special and wronged I was. Instead I picked up a cloth and vigorously cleaned the pup-pastry case until the bell over the door rang and in bounded a chocolate Lab that clearly needed to be lavished with ear scratches and belly rubs while his owner picked out kibble.

Lilly breezed in ten minutes later. "I'm late, but I've got dinner, do you forgive me?"

"Depends. What's in the bag?"

"For you, cream soda and chicken potpie." Okay, she was forgiven because those were my comfort foods.

"And for you?"

"Oh, I ate with Trent."

I hated that even years after she'd been through treatment, my first reaction was to worry she was lying. And that there was no way to ask her without making it a big issue. I knew that sometimes those questions, making it sound like I *expected* her to be skipping meals, could be a trigger. I hated that her connection with food might never be simple or straightforward. I hated that it haunted our relationship.

She put the bag on the counter and ducked to make eye contact. "I really did. Caesar salad with shrimp. Want me to breathe on you so you can smell my garlic breadstick breath?"

I hated that she knew what I was thinking. That I now felt guilty for caring. "Yuck. Don't you dare. And thank you for dinner."

"Of course. So, am I forgiven?"

"No big deal. We only had one customer. Mrs. Diaz needed dog food. She brought Bear."

"Not for being late. For the country club." Lilly's shoulders were up, and her head was bowed down like she expected me to rant and yell. "I heard about the fines."

"You're not the one who pulled the fire alarm. And Monroe took care of the fines. He said it was 'no big deal.'"

"Must be nice," said Lilly.

"Seriously." I uncapped my soda. "Though you'll know soon enough. How many days until you're a Rhodes?"

Lilly picked up my fork and poked a hole in the top of my piecrust. A puff of steam came out and she yelped when she took a bite. "Let that cool. Eight months, but we're not taking their money. I mean, I'm obviously not, but Trent won't either. His parents said they'd only pay for law school if he chose one of their alma maters."

"And Trent's got something against the Ivy League?"

She grinned and leaned in. "He does when it comes with a side of expectations that he'll join his dad's law firm. Don't tell them, but we're going rogue. We'll be taking out loans and likely living on noodles, but it'll be worth it."

"You mavericks!" I told her around bites of chicken. I totally didn't know that Trent had a backbone or enough personality to dream up something so scandalous. But if he was going to go rogue, I was glad it was *for* her, *with* her. It might not have been roses, but it was sort of romantic.

Store traffic always picked up after five p.m., so Lillian and I were busy. I stole bites and sips between wrestling a Chihuahua into rain boots, choosing the right collar to compliment Fizzy the chow chow's fur, and helping a nervous middle-aged man pick out a heart-shaped chew toy for his new boyfriend's goldendoodle.

The door chime jingled, and I put on my best customer smile. The one that charmed people into telling me their pup's life story and hopefully picking up extra treats while they chattered. But my lips slid back over my teeth. "Oh. It's you. Why are you here? You weren't on the schedule." And if she was going to stay, maybe I could leave early?

"Hello to you too." Rory's voice was set at snark level ten. "I'm doing a new window display, if that's all right with you."

"Oh. Right. And hi." I gave a limp wave. "Are you hungry? I've still got some . . ." I gestured down at the crumbs of my chicken potpie, not that she ate chicken. Whoops. "I think I have a fig bar in my bag?"

"Thanks, but I'm fine." She went into the back room and came out wearing a spattered smock and carrying her bucket of brushes and paints.

"Hey, Rory. When did you get here?" Lilly had been carrying a load of cardboard to the Dumpster behind the store. "Perfect timing, because I was just going to tease Merri about the boy in her room last night—and no one teases Merri as well as you."

I'd been frantically making every *shut up* gesture known to man, but by the time Rory set down her paint and turned around, I'd resorted to covering half my face. "Really, Lilly? Have you met our sister? Rory's catchphrase is 'I'm telling.' If she were a super villain, her name would be the Tattler."

"Geez, wonder why," Rory muttered. "Maybe if you two ever actually included me instead of treating me like I'm six—"

"Maybe if you didn't act like you were six, we'd actually include you."

"Maybe you should both hit the pause button." Lilly jutted out her jaw and propped her hands on her hips. "Neither of you is too old for me to send to time-out."

I turned to Rory. "Remember how she used to do that whenever she babysat?"

Rory smiled. "We spent more time *in* time-out than out of it."

"Remember going through Lill's dresser?" It was one of the few times when Rory and I got along and had a united goal. That goal was figuring out how to slingshot cereal from Lilly's bras.

Rory doubled over with giggles. "That was the best."

Lilly took her hands off her hips and smiled. "Are you done fighting, then? Because I've got good gossips on Merri."

Rory had put down all her brushes, but she was wringing a paint rag between her hands as she walked over to join us by the counter. "Fine, I won't say anything to Mom and Dad." Her mouth was twisted like she'd tasted something sour. "What were you and Toby doing last night?"

"Toby?" Lilly laughed. "Why would she need to hide Toby?"

"You're both wrong." I waved a hand. "No one was in my room *last* night. Just speakerphone." I raised my eyebrows and attempted a nonchalant voice. "But other nights . . ."

"No way." Rory gasped. "Monroe?"

We had to take a conversational pause because Mrs. Makris came in with my all-time favorite customer, eleven-year-old Christina, and my all-time favorite dog patron, Marcie. Christina was blond-haired, gray-eyed mischief, still in her soccer uniform with a dripping vanilla ice-cream cone in her hand. Marcie was a German shepherd—whip smart and the world's biggest marshmallow.

"Merri! You have got to read this book!" Christina was tall for a fifth grader and a voracious reader. More than once, customers had thought we were the same age when we stood around chatting about books. Today she was waving a copy of Raina Telgemeier's latest graphic novel, which I'd loved. Marcie licked my knee impatiently while Christina and I flipped pages—and let's be honest, the pup wasn't the only impatient one. Rory's sighs echoed off the glass and her paintbrush tapped out her annoyance as I maybe/possibly/

definitely dragged out my conversation with Christina to avoid the one I knew would be happening after the Makrises left. Ten minutes, a twenty-pound bag of dog food, and two indestructible toys later, the chimes rang on the closing door, and Rory and Lilly pounced.

"Fine. Monroe came over after the engagement party. You can't tell Mom and Dad."

"Obviously," sniffed Rory.

"Also, I want to clarify—it's not like I invited him; he just showed up."

"Really?" Lilly frowned. "How do you feel about that?"

I bent over and began fixing a basket of neckerchiefs that Marcie had upset with her tail, because I had bucketfuls of feelings but not the fun, gossipy kind.

"Merri!" Lilly took the basket from my hands. "Spill!"

Rory was kneeling on the floor opening jars and spreading out a drop cloth. "I need to paint and talk, otherwise Mom and Dad aren't going to pay me. But I've been asking around about Monroe. I heard he throws great parties. Invite only. Very exclusive."

"Really?" No one had mentioned that to me, not that he and my new friends seemed to travel in the same circles. And I guess Lance had made that "party girl" comment in Convocation the day before. But wait, how did Rory know? "Where'd you hear that?"

"My friend Clara has an older brother who's a junior, and he told her and she told me. Plus, this guy Byron in my advanced painting class."

"Byron? Like Mom and Dad's dog? Wait—you're in advanced painting? I thought that was for upperclassmen." Though it took one glance at the lines Rory had sketched onto the store's front window to understand why they'd made an exception. Even at the most basic level of curves and lines and angles, it was clear she had a plan for the space—and that it would be gorgeous. Worthy of canvas and keeping instead of window paint and washing.

"It is upperclassmen. Well, mostly. There's one other freshman."

"Congratulations!" Lilly swooped in for a hug. "That's so great!"

"It is," I agreed. "But why didn't you tell us?"

"Um, no one asked?" Whoops. And there was that gut punch. No one did left-out guilt as well as Rory. She spun back toward her window, where pink and purple lines were shaping into the curls of a poodle. If I wasn't wrong, that blue-and-green outline would be Marcie. "But anyway, Monroe's parties! You *have* to bring me."

This whole scene was a demonstration of how different we were. I couldn't draw a straight line; she only had *least* favorite dogs. I would rather curl up in my bed with a book—she wanted in to the upperclassman party scene. "No."

Rory scowled, and Lilly threw up her hands. "You guys were getting along for ten whole minutes. I give up."

"It has nothing to do with you, Rory." But her scowl didn't fade. "It's because A) I'm grounded and B) I'm about to break up with Monroe, so I doubt I'll be invited."

"Wait, what? Why?" I couldn't tell if the spatter of yellow

across the window was intentional or not, but Rory's eyes were wide.

"I'm ready for my balcony to be a little *less* trafficky. Well, except for Toby. If you know what I mean." And for all Monroe's messages and texts to disappear. Despite all the time he spent talking, he didn't actually *say* anything. I mean, he still hadn't told me about the half sister that Google had definitely confirmed existed.

"No, I don't know what you mean!" The smudge of green she'd wiped by her temple—*that* couldn't be on purpose. And I tried not to be offended by the high-pitched urgency of her declaration. I mean, parties are cool and all—I guess? For people who aren't me—but shouldn't she be a little less hysterical about *my* breakup and her loss of party connections? She rubbed her hands on her apron and demanded, "Are you saying there's someone else?"

I laughed. "Between Monroe's visits and texts—I've had zero time to meet anyone new."

Her eyes narrowed. "That's not a no."

Lilly clapped her hands, making us jump and look at her. She'd be an excellent kindergarten teacher if the lawyer thing didn't pan out. "Rory, what we say when someone's going through a breakup is: 'Are you okay? Do you want to talk about it?'"

Rory lifted her chin—and for a second I thought of Fielding and his pretty, pretty haughtiness. She gritted out, "Are you okay? Do you want to talk about it?"

"No, thank you," I said to Rory's annoyance and Lilly's "Are you sure?" dismay. But I'd talked enough and thought about it exhaustively. All I needed now was to tell him "We're done."

I waited for Rory to retaliate, but instead she added a third dog to the window display. One that looked uncannily like my Gatsby. It was the Roryest of supportive gestures—an artistic show of camaraderie. And while neither of us would ever acknowledge it verbally, we did trade smiles before we got back to work.

22

After closing, I was going to do some homework (maybe), take a shower (definitely), then read a book. Though not Blake's story, because I was taking a break from romance in both real life and in novels. I told this plan to Lilly and Rory on the drive home. "Seriously, the shower is mine, don't fight me on it."

"Um, have you smelled yourself?" Rory asked. "Don't worry, we won't."

Before I grabbed my bathrobe and PJs, I picked out a book from the stack Hannah had loaned me. One with spaceships on the cover and no mention of lovey-doveyness on the back. I propped it on my pillow before treating myself to the longest, hottest shower our water heater would allow, using all Lilly's fancy scrubs and lotions.

I put on my ice-cream sundae pajama pants with my "I don't care who dies in the book as long as the dog lives" T-shirt. Next, I wrapped a towel around my hair and tied the sash on the robe Rory called "too ugly to exist." In my opinion, it was the most comfortable piece of tie-dyed orange-and-navy chenille that had ever been stitched into a sack-like shape.

I daubed on my pee-yellow zit cream that smelled worse

than stinkbugs. . . . The only thing that made it tolerable was how well it worked. Actually, I'd read that toothpaste worked too, so I used Crest on the last few troublesome spots on my forehead. Eliza would be so impressed by my experiment—or, more likely, she'd laugh. Since I already looked polka-dot ridiculous, I added some diaper cream to the faint mark Monroe had left on my neck. I wanted all traces of him gone, and Mom swore diaper cream worked on anything.

"Mom, Dad, I'm going to bed," I called from the top of the stairs so I'd have their attention. Then I struck a dramatic, hands-up, hip-cocked, *ta-da!* pose at the bottom.

"Such a beauty, folks," Dad said to an imaginary audience. "The line starts to the left."

"I'm not sure where I'm supposed to put your good-night kiss with all these spots." Mom chuckled, then planted one above my left eyebrow.

Dad chose my left cheek. "I've got barbecue sauce in the fridge that would cover up that stink and add some nice red to the collection you've got going on. Want me to go get it?"

"Ha. Ha."

"Or let me grab my pen." He yanked one out of his crossword puzzle book. "Let's play connect the dots."

"When you're old and drooling, I'm not going to wipe your chin," I threatened.

"That's why I've got three of you. So I can tease one, annoy another, and still have a spare for my drool-wiping needs."

"It's good to know you've got a plan," I said. "Good night. I'll see you in the morning."

"Sleep sweet, little dreamer," they chorused.

"And good job in the race today," Dad added, while Mom said, "I'm glad to see you're taking the grounding so well."

"Yeah, well, you know, I'm getting more mature and stuff." I hummed and headed upstairs, thinking about the book on my bed. I hoped there was space fashion. I had a weird obsession with books that described futuristic clothing and space suits.

I opened my door to a room that glowed like a forest fire. There was a guy at the center of the blaze, his smug smile illuminated in the flickering light.

"What are you doing here?" I hissed. I shut my door and looked around, taking in the dozens and dozens of candles on every horizontal surface. "What *is* this?"

"This"—Monroe swooped across the room and flung his arms around me—"is romance. *'She doth teach the torches to burn bright.'*"

He attempted to dip me, which caused my towel to drop from my head, landing dangerously close to a candle. "No. *This*," I hissed, "is a fire hazard."

I pulled out of his grip and bent to blow out the one that was leaking wax onto my rag rug. Then the one dripping onto my bio homework, the one on the cover of my Latin book, and the one perched precariously on a pile of magazines. "You shouldn't be here."

He brushed off my comment, tracing his hands down the sleeves of my bathrobe. "Your dad said I was welcome any time."

I jerked away from him. "He did not mean late night in my bedroom. Plus, I told you—"

"Shhh." He put a finger to my lips, and, my hand to God, I almost bit it. He leaned down for a kiss. I turned away. He didn't seem to notice. Instead, he sniffed. "What's that smell?"

"Something's burning!"

"No." He shook his head. "It's peppermint and . . . vinegar?"

But across the room, a candle on my dresser was blackening the edge of a photo stuck in my mirror. The paper was curling, the image darkening, starting to glow in a thin line of red.

I ran to grab it. Dropped it on the floor and stomped it out.

He hadn't even noticed. "It smells like sulfur. Did you change your shampoo?"

"Monroe!" I pointed to the ashy remains of the photo on my floor. It was Toby and me on Catalina two summers ago. We had been laughing, all open mouths and sun-kissed skin on the deck of his mom's sailboat. Now all that was left was a scrap of white sail and soot. I began blowing out all the candles. When the room dimmed, I reached over and flipped the lights on.

He gasped. "Your face!"

I'm sure I turned a lovely shade of red beneath my yellow, blue, and white dots and shower-snarled hair. I crossed my arms . . . in my robe. My too-ugly-to-exist robe. But he wasn't supposed to be here, he'd practically lit my room on fire, he wasn't listening to me, *and* he had the audacity to critique my appearance?

"It's cute—the pajamas too—it just surprised me," he said with a winning smile. "'*Beauty too rich for use—*'"

I waved a hand to cut him off. "Cute." Ugh. That word.

I scowled over the top of two more wicks. Seriously, had he bought stock in a candle factory? And how could he *possibly* smell my face cream over the smorgasbord of candle scents? "It's time for you to go."

"No. You cost me the role of Romeo. You owe me."

"I owe you what? My participation in a relationship I want nothing to do with? That sounds super fun." I wasn't sure if his words were intentionally threatening, but I wasn't backing down. "I asked you not to come. I was really clear about not wanting to see you."

Monroe grinned. "You *said* that, but I know you. Really you want—"

Oh, I'd seen this logic in romance novels—the hero going against the heroine's wishes because *he* knew what she *really* wanted. It was supposed to be swoony. Nope. Just infuriating. I pointed to the balcony doors.

"Leave. Is that clear enough?"

"But I'm your Romeo." He shook his head. "I'm supposed to show up on your balcony."

"You're not supposed to do anything after I say no. . . ." I paused. "And I said no. And I said leave. And, in case you've missed the subtext: now I'm saying we're breaking up."

Monroe stomped out onto my balcony, and even though it was big enough for at least four people, he absorbed all the space. All the air. "I'm not leaving until you tell me what I can do to fix this. I'm getting my role in the play back, and I'm getting *you* back."

"Good luck with the play, but we're over."

Monroe absorbed my words slowly. He shook his head.

Said, "Merri, no." Punched the side of my house. Kicked a trio of candles on the floor. Really? Out here too?

But I was done. I wasn't going to provide an audience for his temper tantrum. "You need to leave, or I'll call my parents. Or better yet, *yours*."

His head shot up, and his eyes were round with shock and betrayal. "But why?"

I told him the truth in the simplest words I could find: "I don't want this."

Backlit by the night sky, his hair looked inky, a striking contrast to his eyes, which glowed bright with hurt. "You don't want me?"

"I don't *know* you!" I tugged my hair, making the shower snarls stand out straight. "I liked the idea of you. And I tried, but you never let me in, and now I'm not interested."

"Don't say that!" Monroe went full emo when he added, "'*Be merciful, say "death".*'"

I'd felt a lot of things about the play, but right then, when Monroe Wouldn't. Stop. Quoting. It . . . I wanted to go *Fahrenheit 451* on every copy ever printed. I picked up my phone. "If I dial your dad's office, will someone be able to patch me through? Because I've said everything I have to say to you—maybe it's time I call him."

The color drained from Monroe's skin and he scrambled over the railing. I hated that I'd had to resort to *I'm tattling*, but I hated even more that he had entered my bedroom without my permission, then refused to hear me. It was such an invasion, such a violation, such a lack of respect for me and my boundaries. Oh, wait. Eliza had said that earlier and I'd meant to parrot it to him. Whoops.

But since he was finally leaving, I wasn't going to stop him and restart the conversation. Instead, I followed him over the balcony and across the lawn, stopping at the edge of the flower bed so I could make sure he truly left. A car was pulling into Toby's driveway as Monroe opened his door, but I kept my focus in front of me, on the boy raising a hand to wave sadly out his window before he pulled into the street. I watched his headlights shrink, then disappear.

My cheeks were wet. My chin. The corner of my mouth was salty when I licked my lips. It may have ended quickly and awfully, but he'd still been my first kiss, my first boyfriend.

He'd still broken my heart. Not in the sense of love lost; but I had lost something—my naive first-kiss-equals-happily-ever-after daydreams. Those merited a tear or twelve—even if it smeared everything on my face and made me more of a mess.

A car's doors closed. I heard footsteps. "Rowboat? You okay?"

I shook my head and blindly threw myself in the direction of Toby's voice, knowing his arms would open and settle around me.

As expected, I knocked into a chest and arms came up to catch me—but they weren't the right arms. Toby's arms had never felt like a jolt of electricity up my spine. And these arms didn't snuggle me in, they didn't settle in familiar positions around my shoulders. I slid my hands up a chest that was unyielding, rippled with ridges of muscles. Ridges that held rigid as my palms continued to check that, yup, this was the wrong guy. Definitely the wrong guy . . . but definitely fit in all the right places. And if my fingers wandered and lingered a bit . . . well, I'd blame that on my emotional state. It had nothing to do with the muscles beneath my fingertips and sensations sizzling across my skin. Nothing at all. The hands on my arms braced me but gently pushed me away as their owner took a step back.

When I looked up, my stomach dropped. I wanted to drop with it. To go down on hands and knees and crawl away, because of course it was Fielding Williams I'd just flung myself at. Even worse—I'd gotten zit cream on his shirt. His perfectly fitted lacrosse uniform—seriously, did he have his jersey tailored? Because, wow. And also, surprise! Why did he *always* see me at my worst?

He dropped the arms that were steadying me and we both took a step backward. Neither of us met the other's eyes as I mumbled, "Sorry, wrong guy."

"Over here, Rowboat." Toby was a few steps behind Fielding, and when I barreled into his waiting arms, he wobbled and winced.

"What's wrong?" Toby and I asked simultaneously. I followed up with a sniffle and a half-hearted, "Jinx—but are you hurt?"

There was definitely something off about the way he was standing. While he had his arm comfortingly around me, I felt like I was supporting him. When he didn't answer immediately, I asked Fielding, "Is he hurt?"

"It's my knee. But Merri, what's—"

I was not ready to answer any questions, so I asked another. "How did you hurt your knee?" Again with the delay, so again with my redirection. "How did he hurt his knee?"

"We had a lacrosse game at St. Joe's Prep. I fell."

"Is there a reason you're asking me questions he's perfectly capable of answering?" Fielding's voice sounded deeper than I remembered. His eyes looked darker.

"Because Merri puts the 'imp' in impatient," said Toby. Apparently Fielding wasn't satisfied with that answer, because he continued to stare at me, his expression inscrutable. And since I had absolutely no poker face, I resented his.

"Because you're here, he's got a broken knee, and I figured you might have some purpose beyond decoration." Had I just admitted I found him pretty? Of course I had, because that was the sort of night I was having. Maybe he hadn't noticed?

Regardless, I wasn't going to be the one to look away first. Not even when his brown eyes were boring into mine. He belonged carved in marble in some museum, which would be an improvement, because then I could safely admire him. Also, cold stone seemed about right for his heart.

Not his eyes, though. They weren't cold at all. They blazed, crackled on the night air between us with an intensity that scorched my skin. I felt trapped in his gaze . . . but wasn't quite sure I didn't enjoy it.

"It's not broken. We stayed after the game to get it checked by the trainer," said Toby.

Fielding blinked. I gulped in a breath and pressed a cool

hand against my hot cheek; it came away sticky with tears and melted toothpaste and zit cream.

Fielding turned toward Toby. "You shouldn't be standing on it. You need ice."

"I'll do that." I needed a purpose. And privacy, so I could tell Toby what had gone down in my Yankee Candle Bedroom. "Thanks for driving him home. I've got it from here."

"Um, Rowboat." Toby squeezed my shoulders, then stepped back. "My bedroom's on the second floor. You're half my size." He held up his palms in a *don't shoot* gesture. "Not making a height joke, just stating a fact. I need Fielding's help with the stairs."

"Oh, right." Well, if Fielding got a job, I wanted one too. "I'll get ice."

"Thanks."

I stopped in my bathroom and wiped off smeared tears and polka dots. Yanked a comb through my hair. I grabbed a clean towel, then ran to the kitchen. Dad was washing dishes and had a podcast about small businesses cranked extra loud, which explained why he hadn't intervened despite all the yelling—and why he jumped and spilled dish soap when he noticed me. He turned it down and flicked a handful of suds my way. "I thought you went to bed?"

"I got thirsty." I looked away as I answered, filling the biggest glass I could find with ice.

"Ah, there's a book, isn't there? Don't stay up too late reading."

"I won't."

From there, I ditched the cup on my desk and climbed down my balcony and up Toby's with the ice-filled towel. Fielding was putting a glass of water and a bottle of aspirin on Toby's bedside table, which annoyed me because *I* should've remembered those. Toby was sitting on the edge of his bed grimacing at the shoes beside his socked feet.

"I could've helped with your sneakers." I shot a *what good are you?* look at Fielding. "I've got it from here," I told him. "You don't have to stay."

"She's right. I'm not moving until the doctor's tomorrow, so I'm all set. Thanks for getting me home and everything."

"Sure." If it were Curtis or Lance, this is where they'd do a bro-dude handshake. But Fielding just gave a stiff nod. "I'll bring your work by tomorrow."

"I'll do that." I wasn't sure why I was being so possessive. I'd never had the whole pee-on-my-friends urge before, but Fielding brought out the worst in me. Every single emotion that wasn't kind or patient or sweet. I felt like one of Rory's abstract paintings—the ones she'd done in all reds and grays and blacks.

"But you're not in his French or music classes," said Fielding.

"You're not in his English, bio, and math. Three is more than two. And I live next door."

"Plot twist," interjected Toby. "How about you both bring my stuff? That way Fielding can drive you home after practice, Merri."

"Oh, he really doesn't need to do that." If my face looked

as horrified as Fielding's did, then it still only showed half the horror I felt.

Fielding took a deep breath like he was fortifying himself. "That's fine."

"Be right back, Toby. I'll walk him out." Which was about as weird as it got, because it put me alone with Fielding and required me to walk *through* Toby's house. I couldn't remember the last time I'd used his stairs. They were covered in the same white carpet I'd dropped a grape juice box down when I was eight. The stains had been professionally removed, but I could still picture the purple splash marks.

Fielding gestured for me to precede him. Of course he did. Then he could glare at my back. And it robbed me of the chance to glare at his. I whirled around at the bottom of the stairs, fully prepared to catch him. But while he was staring, he looked pensive, not angry.

I hated him a little more for it. How dare he be an enigma while I was practically a master class in how *not* to have a poker face?

He held the front door for me. How dare he have manners. How dare he have grace. How dare he breathe. "You don't have to drive me home."

"It's fine."

"No, really."

"Toby normally drives; you don't have your license. It's fine."

"But—"

Fielding gave me one more appraisal. One more look that

212 | TIFFANY SCHMIDT

told me I didn't measure up. "Are you aware your socks don't match?"

"What?" Looking down was a reflex reaction: there were mermaids on my left foot and teapots on my right. Of all the ridiculous aspects of my outfit, *that* was what he chose to point out? "They're not supposed to."

"They're sold in matching pairs."

Seriously, what the double negative was wrong with him? My kindergarten teacher always said, "You'll never know unless you ask," so I did. "Ugh. What is *wrong with you*?"

He blinked at me. Like *I* was the one being rude. Fine, I guess I was. So when he responded with a stiff "I'll see you tomorrow," I stopped him with a hand on his arm.

"Wait." I could feel the muscles tense beneath my fingers, but his skin was so warm and he felt so steady that it was hard to convince my knuckles to unbend and let go. "Thanks for bringing Toby home."

He paused, confusion on his face as he searched my words for double meaning. "Of course." His tone was missing its usual haughtiness. For a second, when his expression was soft and open, I wished we'd met differently. I wished he didn't feel like a mortal enemy, because I wondered what it would be like to be his friend. The sort of person he'd drive home injured and help up to bed.

My cheeks blushed and I looked away, barely managing a nod when he asked, "His dad won't be home until midnight—you'll be around if he needs anything?"

Maybe we'd learn to tolerate each other in the smallest of doses after all.

"And—" He hesitated, and I tapped my foot impatiently while he cleared his throat and memorized the cracks in our sidewalk. His eyes were blazing when he looked up. "I don't know what happened with you and Monroe tonight, but I hope you're okay."

"Oh." The earnest sincerity in his voice crowded out all my thoughts and words. He was halfway into his car before I remembered to call out, "Thanks."

23

ow are you?" Toby asked once I had both feet over his railing, the tail of my bathrobe trailing behind me.

"I'm . . ." *Relieved, exhausted, confused.* I laughed and shrugged. I'd gotten home from the store at nine—so much had happened in the two hours since then. "How are you?"

"Pissed at the St. Joe's midfielder who tripped me with his stick." He rearranged the ice on his knee—wincing from either cold or pain. "You were crying, Rowboat."

"Yeah." I sighed and sank down next to him on the bed. "Monroe and I broke up."

Toby's jaw went hard. His nostrils flared in a way I recognized from our stubborn spats. I watched him inhale and exhale slowly before he said, "I'm trying not to go all machismo here and say 'I'm gonna have a talk with him.' But *you were crying.* He made you cry."

"Don't." I leaned my head on his shoulder and wished we were on the roof. Every conversation felt better up there. "I'm really fine. I initiated it. I'm happy about it."

There was a surge of hope in his eyes that made my

stomach drop. I scooted down a few inches, and when that didn't feel sufficient, stood up. And if his transparent feelings weren't enough, my mind was falling back into familiar patterns. If Monroe and I had been all star-crossed and Verona, and Toby was threatening to confront Monroe . . . then that made him Tybalt. And Fielding was, I don't know, Benvolio. Maybe Mercutio? No, definitely Benvolio; he was useless. But Tybalt, he . . . I leaned over so I was eye to eye with Toby. "Don't wind up dead, okay?"

"Usually I can follow your Merri-logic, but I have no idea what you're talking about."

"Tybalt. Juliet's cousin."

"I know who Tybalt is—we *are* in the same English class— but why are we talking about him?" He struggled to sit up.

"Just . . ." No, I wasn't going to tell him my theory. Because it *wasn't* my theory anymore. I was so done living my life like that play. "Never mind. Monroe and I are over. Everything is good."

"You're sure?"

"A thousand percent sure. Now what can I get you before I head home?" I glanced around his room, wanting to do *something* helpful. "You've got water and pain meds and ice."

He looked up at me with those puppy-dog brown eyes, the ones that had talked me into a lifetime of trouble and turned liquid every time we got caught. He reached for my hand and laced his fingers with mine. "Stay?"

For a few long seconds, I blinked at him. "Toby, we're not— I don't . . ." Gah, apparently being single for ten minutes meant he was back to pushing at boundaries. "I'm not—"

"Kidding." He grimaced and shifted. Or shifted and grimaced. I wasn't sure which came first, but there was no humor in his word, and he'd dropped my hand like it was contagious.

"I'm—I'm going to go." Because I was annoyed and frustrated and sad. There was no room for these new emotions on top of the Jenga pile of feelings today had already built, and I didn't want the whole thing crashing down on his head. "I've got a whole Yankee Candle massacre to clean up in my room."

Toby scrunched his face. "A what?"

I shook my head. "Feel better. And call me if you need anything. Okay?"

He nodded, but right before I slid my second foot over his balcony railing, I thought I heard him say, "I'm sorry."

My heart cracked a little, because we were trapped in a space where I couldn't change his feelings, and he couldn't change mine. Maybe he heard me, or maybe he didn't, but I whispered back, "Me too."

"Did you sleep on it? Maybe change your mind about Monroe?" Rory's questions and eyebrows were pitched way too high for this early in the morning. Way too hopeful after a night I'd spent not sleeping. She was a champion eavesdropper, and for the first time in my life, I was wishing she had gone all Harriet the Sibling Spy on me so that she'd already know the answer. Instead she'd probably been all noise-canceling headphones and, if the ink stains on her fingers were any indication, nose deep in a sketchbook.

"It's done. It's over." There. Four words and that topic should be finished.

Except this was Rory, not Lilly or Eliza. They'd notice that I was practically vampiric between my pale complexion and under-eye circles that makeup wouldn't cover. I'd also given up attempting to button my shirt straight after three tries, and I hadn't yet mustered the effort to tie the laces spilling from my shoes.

"Noooo!"

Gatsby added his "Aroooo" to Rory's whine, and the chorus was just about all my throbbing head could take.

My phone beeped. "It's Toby."

"What?" Rory's eyes rounded in shock. "Toby? But you said you and he—"

"The text." I held up my phone and read the group message. "He says he's not going to school, but our ride should be here in a minute."

Eliza, ever efficient—had already responded that she'd walk. I was halfway through typing that I'd join her—because I badly wanted the chance to talk to her about last night. But if I walked, Rory would too. I groaned and backspaced through my message. I'd tapped out the **Who's** in "Who's driving?" when a knock sounded on our front door.

If it was possible to have PTSD flashbacks to two days prior, then I was having one. I didn't care about Byron's barking or Gatsby's howl, or Rory's pouting as she slammed her books into her bag and grumbled. All that mattered as I tiptoed to the door with fingers crossed and breath held was that the person on the other side of it *wasn't* Monroe. That this wasn't another game of him showing up uninvited and ignoring everything that came out of my mouth. *Anyone* would be better than Monroe.

I exhaled, chomped down on my lip, and flung the door open.

"Good morning."

Well, maybe not *anyone*.

Fielding was crisp and shiny. A portrait of prep-school perfection. Whereas I was a rumpled, misbuttoned mess—still wearing the socks he'd objected to last night. I hadn't even managed to wash my face. There was probably drool crusted by my mouth. Drool I'd be adding to right now if he were anyone other than him, because, man, the morning light loved his angles. Dust motes practically did the shimmy just to be sharing the same air. Not that they'd dare to land on his immaculate blazer.

Fielding cleared his throat and repeated, "Good morning?"

I needed him to be less than superhuman, because I was definitely some subspecies right now. I pressed the corners of my mouth into something like a smile and mumbled, "Excuse me for a sec," before shutting the door. Luckily he hadn't attempted to cross the threshold—maybe he was part vampire and needed to be invited? Regardless, whether startled vampire or startled human, he'd been eyebrows up and eyes wide when the latch clicked in his face.

I unlocked my phone and power-typed: T, what did you do?

Toby's three dots were quickly replaced with an answer: Consider it my apology for overstepping last night.

"This is an apology?" I'd aimed the question at Gatsby,

who was trying to get me to move so he could continue howling at the door handle or lick to death the new person on the other side. I'd said no to sharing a drive home with Fielding, so Toby thought that was a yes to a ride in the morning? And maybe Toby had perfected cyber-hearing, because my phone lit up with another message.

I knew you'd forget to get another ride.

Which, fine, okay I had. But I could walk. I could definitely walk and—

& after the messenger debacle yesterday, I didn't want you late for your meeting with Ms G

Oh! I'd forgotten about that. And the clock on my phone told me I didn't have time for a proper meltdown. Not unless I wanted to add tardy to unkempt, half awake, and disobedient. My stomach wrenched itself into a knot, and there went any chance of choking down breakfast or imbibing the sweet heavenly nectar called coffee. Not unless I wanted it to reappear all over whatever gorgeous shoes Ms. Gregoire was wearing that day.

I turned to Rory, who was standing in the kitchen with her book bag in one hand, a pear in the other, and a smug look on her face.

"You coming?" I asked. "Or does Clara forbid you from interacting with him?"

"Oh, Clara's moved on to Keene." Her lips twitched. "Besides, I wouldn't miss this train wreck for the world."

"All right then." I yanked open the door. "Sorry about that. We're ready now."

I brushed past him out the door and headed down our

steps to his car. I wasn't a car person, but I'd been expecting something non-fancy, boring, reliable, favored by middle-age accountants. Instead, it was sleek. Silver. Not flashy, but elegant. I wanted to run my hands over the paint—which was doubly tempting since fingerprints would probably give Fielding hives. When I reached for the handle to the back door, Rory had already grasped it. "I know how much you like shotgun," I hissed.

"No." She hip-checked me and yanked the door open. "It's all yours. I insist."

"Fine." I slid inside a car that was as immaculate as Fielding's clothing. The red stitching on the black leather interior was a surprise. I traced it with my thumbnail before folding my hands in my lap. The car had a *don't muss me* vibe, and I was feeling very muss-ish.

My phone was buzzing in my pocket. I glanced down. Toby. **You okay? How's life post-Monroe?**

Which was sweet and thoughtful and oh-so-very Toby . . . except another thing that was oh-so-very Toby was forgetting to exit out of a group message and send me an individual one. And of the four people in this message group, there was only one who hadn't heard this news.

Eliza's individual message popped up instantly: **What happened? Are you okay?** And when I didn't reply fast enough: **I'll wait outside Ms. Gregoire's room.**

I thumbed from the *O* to the *K* and hit send, adding Toby-Eliza rivalry and jealousies to the jumble in my stomach. I directed my irritation at my surroundings. At the driver who waited exactly two seconds at stop signs. At his rearview mirror and dashboard, which looked like they were polished daily. At the public radio that was barely eking out of his speakers—the hosts sounded like they were whispering secret news.

"So . . ." I'd never before heard Fielding hesitate while speaking. It was enough to make me quit my murderous staring contest with the windshield and turn toward him. He was white-knuckled, like having a conversation with me was physically painful. "Last night, with Monroe . . ."

Seriously? He couldn't possibly be asking me to share feelings and talk about my breakup, right? We'd barely exchanged a few dozen words, and they'd all been antagonistic. I gave him my sunniest smile. "Everything's totally fine."

"I see." Two words and a clenched jaw. It was a surprisingly satisfying reaction.

"Clueless." Rory leaned forward and quietly singsonged the word, making my cheeks flush because I'd forgotten she was there. And while the word had been under her breath and in my ear, I wasn't sure if it was *for* me or *about* me. Or just her being Rory and trying to rattle me. Regardless, I made a mental note to be equally supportive the next time she was riding in an enemy's car, fresh off a breakup, and headed to a disciplinary meeting. And since I was the bigger—well, less tall, but definitely better—person than either of them, I spent the rest of the ride humming to myself and *not* saying all the things I would totally regret.

24

knocked on Ms. Gregoire's door. "It's Merri. I'm here to be punished."

"Now, that doesn't sound like a very fun way to start your Wednesday." Ms. Gregoire was smiling as she swung the door open, coffee mug in hand. I stared at it, waiting for it to go from brushed metal to magical rhinestone hypnosis, but it didn't. Because magic wasn't real and apparently neither was romance.

She stepped out of the way and gestured me inside, but I wasn't sure where to go, and hesitating made every voice in my brain spiral into a louder panic. I sort of dashed over to my desk—sitting down and putting my bag beneath it like this was class.

Ms. Gregoire took Toby's usual seat beside me. "If I reassure you we don't use torture at Hero High, will you relax? Your shoulders look like they're trying to invade your ears."

I thought I was supposed to laugh, so I did, but the sound was thin and sickly. And my shoulders wouldn't budge when I tried to pull them down.

"I've chosen the book for your punishment."

"A book?" My shoulders dropped immediately. A book

wasn't punishment. Well, unless it was *The Catcher in the Rye.* Ugh. I hated Holden with a fiery rage.

"Well, yes." Ms. Gregoire folded her hands on top of the desk. "What sort of punishment were you expecting?"

I didn't have an answer for her because I hadn't let myself expect. But sometimes the space around expectations was worse. Because sometimes that space was filled with so many possibilities and "what ifs" that it was impossible to focus. And sometimes when you've already started the day with the non-punishment punishment of driving with the headmaster's son, it feels like any *actual* punishments might actually kill you.

"As I was saying, I've chosen your book. If I've interpreted your responses in class correctly, you're feeling a bit disillusioned by *Romeo and Juliet.*"

"I am *sooo* over them. Like, can't they hurry up and die already?" I'd call that a stress overshare and pretend it didn't happen. Hopefully Ms. Gregoire would do the same. "I mean, it's a beautiful play and I'm really enjoying our—"

Ms. Gregoire cut me off with a wry smile and a wave of her hand. "It's not as romantic as you thought, is it?"

"No! It's not romantic at all." I grimaced as I thought back over the events of the night before. "I should've listened to Eliza. She's almost always right."

Ms. Gregoire took a sip of her coffee and shrugged my statement away. "You needed the experience of learning for yourself. But you were overidentifying with the play. That was not your story."

I said, "Agreed," but I was already replaying what she'd

said and trying to remember which word she'd emphasized. *That* was not your story? Or That was not *your* story? Was her implication that I wasn't Juliet—noted and thanking my stars—or that *Romeo and Juliet* wasn't my story, but something else was?

Ms. Gregoire bent to rummage in her bag. "The book I've chosen for you is a romance. One of the greatest romances of all time."

I groaned. "Can't I have a stupid war book instead? I'm really not feeling the romance right now."

She smiled wryly and shook her head. "You'll thank me for this one day, I guarantee it. This is the perfect story for you, and reading it . . . well, it will be eye-opening. I have the feeling you'll relate to it at a personal level, and it might even make you reconsider what you believe to be true."

"You said the same thing about *Romeo and Juliet* . . . and that did not turn out well."

"No." She wagged a finger at me. "I didn't. I told the whole class they would relate to the book. I told all of you that I'd learn about you from your reactions to it. But I didn't say it was a book *for you* specifically."

"You did!" I stood up, almost knocking over my chair. I was well aware I was being ridiculous, but it didn't stop me from pointing at her mug. "You and your coffee and that stupid play have ruined everything."

She shrugged and took another sip, totally unaffected by my tantrum. "I told you that you thought you knew the story. I told you I'd prove you wrong."

"Why? Why make me go through all that."

"One—it's part of the sophomore English curriculum; not everything is about you, Merrilee. Two—you weren't ready. While I don't believe like Mr. Bennet—you'll meet him soon—that 'a girl likes to be crossed a little in love now and then,' I do know that the girl who wrote me a love letter to *Romeo and Juliet* on the first day of school "—she paused and raised her eyebrows at me—"was not ready for a nuanced and actual romance."

I scowled just thinking about that letter and how simperingly silly I'd been. How shortsighted and idiotic and ignorant. Juliet should've burned her balcony and never looked back. I sat and dropped my head in my hands. "I don't want a romance. I'm done with it."

"No, you're finally *ready* for it. As I told you before: when you're ready, you'll find your book."

I wondered if Ms. Gregoire had ever heard the term "oversell," because that was a lot of pressure to put on a book. Plus, this whole conversation felt like confirmation of what I'd told Eliza—magic *was* real—but I was too tired to feel shocked or smug. "So I just read the book for punishment and whatever happens, happens?"

"You need to read it *and* write me reflection journals."

"Fine." Yeah, except no part of me felt *fine.* Every molecule between my hair and toenails felt like it was vibrating with expectation and anticipation and fear. "What is it?"

"One of my personal favorites." Ms. Gregoire pulled out a fuschia hardcover. "*Pride and Prejudice* by Jane Austen. Have you read it before?"

"No." I'd attempted to make Toby watch the miniseries

with me once. We'd had popcorn popped and our butts on the couch when he caught sight of the six-hour run time and issued a hard veto.

She twinkle-eye smiled as she passed over the book. When my fingers made contact with the pages, I jolted like I'd been given the world's strongest static shock. Except paper doesn't conduct static electricity—does it? I'd have to ask Eliza. It made the hair on my arms stand up, and the world spun in front of my eyes. I put the book down on my desk, and it stopped. I picked it up, and it hummed between my fingers, vibrating on some very high frequency. I put it down. Nothing. Creeping my fingers along my desk, I place two on its cover—tingles.

Realizing I must look bananas conducting these experiments—realizing I *might be*, since books were not supposed to be a form of electroshock therapy—I looked up at Ms. Gregoire.

. "Don't be intimidated," she said. "This is going to be good for you. You'll find it edifying and eye-opening."

"Intimidated?" I repeated, continuing to touch the book. It was like when you had a cut in your mouth and you couldn't keep your tongue away: Still hurt? Yes. Still hurt? Yes. Only this wasn't painful, it was sort of thrilling. I pressed a hand flat to the center of the cover.

"I'm really looking forward to reading your journals and seeing what you have to say and all the ways you're connecting to the story. You're ready for this, Merrilee. Give it a chance." She winked at me. "And if the headmaster asks, I've given you a grueling, time-intensive assignment that's made you feel completely repentant."

"Oh, I do. I am." I scooped the book off my desk and hugged it to my chest, a warm glow flooding my system. "Thank you."

She smiled. "Good. I'll see you in class."

I waved a few fingers and echoed her good-bye.

When Eliza had said she'd wait outside Ms. Gregoire's room, she meant *right* outside it. I almost caromed into her when I opened the door.

"Hey, you," I said cautiously, not quite sure where she was on the Toby-jealousy spectrum. "Hey, best friend."

"Are you okay? I'm sorry."

This didn't feel like an expression of sympathy. This wasn't an *I'm sorry this happened to you*. It made me quirk my mouth, because Eliza didn't apologize easily or often. "Why?"

"Because so much happens late at night and I'm never available. You can't just call or text me." She looked down at her shoes and then up at my face. "I feel like your first breakup is a milestone I should've been there for. What if you needed advice?"

"You gave me some before the race." I started walking. Not necessarily toward something, like our lockers or bio class, but away from the noise of campus filling up with classmates and chatter. "And I had plenty more. Lilly, Rory, and the random customers Rory polled at the store. Then there was the audience of Toby and Fielding. It was quite the spectacle."

She scrunched her nose. Elegantly. Picturesquely. And nose-scrunching should be neither of those things. Gah, if I didn't love her, I'd be toxically envious. "That sounds horrible."

"It was. Did I mention I was in my bathrobe?"

"The hideous one I keep trying to smuggle into the trash?"

"That'd be the one." I paused beside the Reginald R. Hero statue, leaning against his bronze arm to prop myself up. Yeah, I was penciling in a Convocation nap.

"Are you okay?"

I considered this. I wanted ice cream, cookie dough, movies, pajamas, and to stay in bed—but these clichés weren't breakup dependent—I *always* wanted them. It helped that Monroe was suspended and I wouldn't have to see him for a week. "I'm okay. And the fact that I'm fine proves what you said all along—Monroe was way too serious, too fast. I was smitten with being smitten—not with him. But I appreciate you not saying 'I told you so.'"

"Oh." She smiled. "I'm thinking it."

I laughed and gave her a sideways hug. "I know you are." I shut my eyes and stretched my arms out, trying to mentally insert myself into movie montages of heroines on the verge of life-changing accomplishments. But the images fell flat, and I dropped my arms and looked at Eliza. "I wanted him to be my thing."

"Your 'thing'?"

"Like we talked about on the first day of school—how everyone else has a thing. Remember? I was having the Disney Princess pre-adventure moment? Well, still having it."

"Why can't books be your thing?"

"Because I don't *do* anything with them. I just read them. Even Hannah has a blog. I don't . . . *do* anything. I want more."

"Oh, Merri—" Concern dented her forehead.

"I know. I don't actually need you to give me a lecture—I'm pretty sure I can give it myself. People can't be things. If I want a thing—I should be going to the club fair and signing up and trying stuff out." I hugged the book from Ms. Gregoire a little tighter. It no longer felt like it was vibrating or humming, but it was a book, and they brought me comfort. "How'd I do?"

"You did perfect," she said. "And I'll come with you to the club fair."

"Thank you." But that was aimed at the first part of her statement; I wasn't so sure about the second. Not that I *didn't* want Eliza with me. But she already had things. I was going to find mine. I wasn't sure I wanted to share. Or to go with someone who knew my whole history of flubs. Who'd be standing in front of the photo club remembering the time I exposed a whole class's negatives by getting tangled in the dark room's blackout curtain. Or at baking club gagging at the thought of my everything cookies.

"Can I do anything else?" she asked.

"Help me with my bio homework? Mine was a victim of candle-wax drowning." Eliza raised an eyebrow, but I shook my head when she opened her mouth. "You don't want to know."

"I do so," she insisted. "And you'll tell me later, but I'll let you finish the homework first." As she sorted through her bag for her notebook, I flipped open the cover of *Pride and Prejudice*, tracing my fingers over the first words: *"It is a truth universally acknowledged . . ."*

What were *my* universal truths?

My family rocked.

Eliza and Toby had my back.

Dogs were better than cats.

Socks didn't have to match.

Cream soda trumped cola.

And maybe—despite what had happened with Monroe and Romeo—I'd always be a romantic.

25

eady to leave?"

I'd been in the middle of dissecting a series for Hannah while playing with the thumbholes of my running shirt. Telling her how book one of Apocalypse Chasers had been so strong, but two felt like total setup for the series. And book three? It mashed up every cliché and trope and served them like pre-chewed salad. A boring, pre-chewed salad, just iceberg lettuce and shriveled, tasteless tomatoes. Hannah was doubled over, hands on her shin guards. She stood and wiped her eyes. But she didn't repeat her plea for me to type up my rant for her blog. Instead she looked over my shoulder. "Is Fielding talking to you?"

"What?" I glanced at where he was leaning against the side of the bleachers a few feet from us, a long black bag at his feet. "No."

He caught my eye and lifted his chin in a gesture that almost felt like acknowledgment but probably was just him showing off his jawline. "Merrilee? Ready?" he called.

"Oh. Maybe so? But I don't know why. . . . Hang on." I drifted from the doorway of the girls' locker room over to where he waited. "I don't need a ride. I'll go home with Eliza."

"I'm headed to Toby's house anyway."

"You don't need to. I can bring his schoolwork." I reached for the familiar backpack sitting on the bottom bleacher. Toby had used this faded red style for years. When one wore out, he replaced it with a clone. I'm sure he had at least two backups in his closet.

Fielding snatched it up before my fingers could close around the top strap. He slung it onto his own shoulder and frowned. "I'm headed that way already."

"But—"

His frown deepened. He added a jaw clench when Eliza and Hannah wandered over. Eliza's eyes were bright, her cheeks red in a way that I didn't think had anything to do with our run. "We've got to go, Merri," Eliza said. "Nancy's here, and she said my parents told her they'd be calling."

"That's so good!" I squashed my urge to hug her by bouncing on my toes and grabbing her arm. "Later, Hannah. And . . ." I looked at Fielding. "Bye?"

"I'm literally going to be driving next door." He held up one palm, placing one, then two fingers on top of it—a pantomime to show me what "next door" meant. "You don't want a ride?"

I could play charades too. I'd act out *heck no*—arms in a giant X, head shaking, maybe a palm out like a stop sign. Oh, the options.

"You're going to the Mays'? Tell Toby we miss him." Hannah's eyes glittered as she looked from Fielding to me. "And, for reals, Merri, just go with him."

I narrowed my eyes at her, not sure if it was some sort of misplaced gesture on Sera's behalf, or just her love for drama and gossip. Whatever the reason, she could kiss that guest blog post good-bye. Regardless of my obsession with the series, I wasn't an apocalypse chaser in real life. And me getting in a car with only Fielding McSnobpants was asking for disaster.

"Merri—" Eliza grimaced like her next words were distasteful, but she said them anyway. "Could you ride with him? It'd get me home faster. I don't want to miss this call."

Fielding didn't even wait for me to concede with a bitter "Fine" before he was smugly picking up his enormous bag and adding, "I'm parked this way."

"Call me later," I told Eliza. I shrugged when Hannah mouthed, "Sorry."

Fielding was already clearing his throat impatiently from the door to the gym and pointing to my cross-country bag. "Do you need me to carry that for you?"

"What? No." I shouldered my satchel and picked up the duffel, muttering, "Wish me luck," as I waved good-bye to my friends and marched over to the world's haughtiest chauffeur.

He waited at his trunk for me to slide my bags beside his. Then waited for the click of my seat belt before starting the engine. He adjusted the mirrors—twice—looked over his shoulder, and slowly backed out of his space. Then he . . . drove. That's it. No radio. Not even humming or drumming a finger on his leg. Hands at twelve and two, or six and nine, or whatever the heck time they're supposed to be at according to the driver's ed manual I hadn't opened yet. But if that instructor were here, he'd be impressed. I was bored. I never thought I'd say "I miss Rory," but I missed Rory. It's not like she had fixed the awkwardness that morning, but at least then I hadn't had to endure it alone.

Fielding didn't look affected. Not that he'd have noticed I was. He didn't look my way—not even at stop signs. The silence hung so loud that when I squirmed, I wanted to shush the rasp of my clothing on the seat. Was this some new form of psychological torture? Well, I wasn't giving in. I wouldn't be the one to talk first. And fine. He'd gotten his way. For whatever reason, he wanted my sweaty butt in his passenger seat. *Congratulations.* I was seat belted and sealed inside his pristine car. I hoped he enjoyed the sweet scent of victory when it was mixed with five miles of perspiration and came with muddy shoes on his immaculate car mats.

He didn't look muddy or sweaty. Not soggy and drippy like Toby after practice. His gray Dri-Fit shirt didn't have telltale armpit circles or grass stains. The only clues it shared were about his seriously fit body underneath. In fact, I wanted to sue the manufacturer, because holy hound dog, that should be illegal. Or maybe it was the maker of his blazers I'd be seeing in court, because how dare they obscure this? I'd been seriously missing out at my old all-girls' school.

No. No. Erase that thought. He should put the blazer on now, so he'd stop distracting me. He was probably doing it on purpose. I hated him.

Had he even practiced? Or was he simply decoration, a lacrosse lawn ornament? A *GQ* mascot. I frowned at his profile—his hair was the slightest bit damp around his right ear. It curled just a little along his neck—a tiny rebellion I hoped majorly annoyed him. I shifted closer to the console to check out his shoes. Either he had mud on his sneakers, or he hadn't worked out. Except his stupid long legs and knees were in the way. I couldn't see his feet. And he smelled like paper. Like a library or a bookstore. But not the old crumbly section of a used store with incontinent cats. Like crisp pages and unbroken bindings. It was a delicious scent—one that was wasted on him. One that I leaned a little farther over the center console to take another whiff of.

"Are you trying to smell me?" he asked.

"No. Are you trying to smell *me*?" Which not only didn't make sense, because he was keeping his nose on his half of the car, but it was a horrifying thing to have asked. Because what if he could? What if his answer was to grimace and say, "Unfortunately, I can smell you without trying"?

While I surreptitiously tried to sniff myself—which was neither surreptitious nor pleasant—Fielding shook his head and shifted his grip on the wheel. He muttered something that sounded suspiciously like "weirdo."

And, okay, I was totally being a weirdo, but I'd also won. I'd made him speak first. Which meant it was fine to ask, "What was in that toddler-size bag you put in the trunk? Well, not sized *for* a toddler, but the size *of* one. I'd ask if it was the dismembered body of the last person you drove somewhere, but it clanked when you put it down."

"Maybe the last person I drove was a cyborg."

"Um, maybe?" I couldn't tell if that was his attempt at a joke, but if so, judging by his furrowed brow and wince, even he hadn't found it funny.

"It's my fencing gear. I'm headed to my club after Toby's."

"Fencing?" I didn't know if I was delighted or disgusted by this new piece of strangeness. I liked the idea of him in a suit—complete with face mask so I wouldn't have to see him looking at me like he was shocked I knew how to use words. "Like, with real swords?"

"Points and all."

"How . . . posh." It was kinder than "strange," yet equally true. "Do you play polo too?"

"Horses or water?"

"Oh, um . . ." I trailed off and played with the window, but two ups and downs later, he was still waiting for an answer, and I wasn't sure I knew the difference. The only "polo" I'd ever played was Marco. "Either? Both?"

He shifted his grip on the wheel, probably imagining tightening those long, elegant fingers around my neck. "No."

I swallowed a grunt of annoyance and turned to face the windshield. Clearly he'd wanted me in this seat so he could mock me. Well, if I didn't say a word for the last three minutes, then he wouldn't have anything to mock.

He waited until the street before mine. Until the silence around us felt as rough and hard as rawhide dog treats. Then he cleared his throat. I watched his neck muscles move as he swallowed before asking, "So, how do you like Hero High so far?"

Oh, I had thoughts for him. But since this question felt like it came from Headmaster Williams and would be reported back to him, I went for the subtle subtext of: "Some parts are way more welcoming than others."

"I see," he answered, but I didn't think he did at all. Not

that it mattered. He could stay as oblivious as he wanted up on his high horse, so long as he didn't trample me or make me ride with him again. After another long pause, he added, "Perhaps that's because your enrollment was so dependent on your connection with Senator Rhodes."

I scrunched my eyebrows. Was his hatred just political? If so, he'd be thrilled to know how little the senator and I got along. Though Monroe had said his dad would hate me too. . . . Maybe I was just politicians' anathema? Wait. I needed a response. "I take it your family is voting Stratford?"

Fielding recoiled like I'd slapped him or fed him slugs. "Of course not."

"But if your big issue is with Senator Rhodes—"

"My big issue is with nepotism."

I scoffed. "I'm not related to the senator. Not even tangentially—not yet."

"Fine. Not nepotism." I watched the bones of his jaw shift sideways. "But her influence. You're here to make the trustees and alumni happy."

Something in my chest felt pinched, but I gritted my teeth and responded, "Funny, I thought I was here to get an education." I squirmed in my seat. "Well, not *here*. I'm *here* because you wouldn't let Eliza drive me home." And, dear dachshunds and all things furry, why was he taking a left at this fork? In what universe did it make sense to take the long way home?

He was still grinding his teeth, and between them came the faintest near-growl sound. It was kind of cute, actually. Like when a bull terrier puppy is trying to be ferocious but fails. I grinned. "But you're not voting Stratford?"

"I'm not voting—period. I'm seventeen. But even if I was eleven months older—*of course* I wouldn't vote Stratford."

"Because . . . ?"

I thought his jaw was going to dislocate from the way he clenched it as his face turned redder and his nostrils flared and he finally opened his mouth and exploded. "Because I'm not morally bankrupt!"

"Oh." I shrank back toward the window. "That's a good reason." Maybe I should've looked beyond the cute family photos and bio section of Patrick Stratford's website. I knew Eliza wasn't a fan. Despite his dad's support, Toby wasn't either. My parents had voted Rhodes in the last election—which was before Trent was in Lilly's life. What exactly did Monroe's father stand for? And what did Senator Rhodes? Maybe that was a good question for Trent at this Sunday's brunch. Lilly would be thrilled if I made an effort to talk to him. Come to think of it, Trent would be too, since anything that made Lilly smile made him *beam*. And, fine, that was sort of adorable.

Fielding glanced at me at every stop sign. Sometimes a full head turn, sometimes just a shift of his eyes. Each pause felt like it held potential, and each time my pulse surged. But then he'd switch his attention back to the road and press the gas pedal.

Finally, after the most circuitous route and five lifetimes' worth of awkward silences, Fielding pulled up in front of Toby's house.

"Thanks for the ride." I was out of the car as soon as he moved the gearshift into park. I grabbed my bags from the trunk. And now I was the one pausing, looking at him as he emerged from the car, sunlight glinting off the sunglasses he'd put on after turning onto my street. In the car I'd only seen them from the side; from the front—gah, they suited him.

"Why are you looking at me like that?" he asked.

My gaze fell to the ground like it wanted to stop, drop, and roll. "Like what?" I asked innocently, searching my brain for any answer that didn't involve objectifying him or drool.

He shook his head. "Forget it. Are you coming?" He pointed at the Mays' house, but I took a step backward, off their driveway and onto the grass.

"No." Another step, and another, till I'd crossed the threshold between the brighter green of the Mays' lawn service landscaping and my own patchy grass. "Tell Toby I'll be over later, but I've got to get to work."

It was an excuse, not a lie. I snuck one last look at Fielding, still standing by his car door. Still watching me. Then I turned and darted up my front steps faster than I'd run at practice.

While I might not have been a liar, I was most definitely a coward.

26

There was an unspoken agreement that Rory and I didn't fight when we were the only two working at the store. Actually, that rule seemed to hold up pretty well when we were the only two anywhere. It was like any other person was a catalyst—or was it an accelerant?—who made the two of us react. Eliza would know the right chemistry word, but if she showed up, she'd also assume that role. Maybe I should've used a mathematical analogy. On our own, Rory and I were rational numbers; we could do all sorts of calculations together and come up with solutions. But any third party was like pi—add them into our equation and the answer became irrational.

Rory had brought us dinner tonight—cheese quesadillas—but like anything she made, they were art. The sprinkle of chili powder, the arrangement of salsa and guacamole and sour cream along the side of the plates in strategic dollops.

"It almost looks too pretty to eat," I said. "Except I'm hungry." This was the same logic we used for eating at the counter, instead of the back room like we were supposed to.

She smiled and bit into her own—which I'm sure had vegan cheese and yogurt instead of sour cream, because Rory was on a health kick. Except maybe it couldn't be called a kick if it'd lasted more than a year? Regardless, I appreciated that she didn't try and foist it on the rest of us. I liked my cheese in cheese form, and don't get me started on the time I accidentally chomped into a meatless hot dog.

"Do you think the front window needs more pumpkins?" she asked, tilting her head to consider it.

"Not unless you feel like painting them."

She shrugged. "Not really, but I hate rainy nights when no one comes in." She wandered into the back room and fetched our school bags.

I had all sorts of biology I could catch up on and a precalc problem set that Toby had texted me was "killer." But it was the book from Ms. Gregoire I pulled out. Not *Romeo and Juliet*, even though I was supposed to be finishing the play tonight—no need: everyone dies and blah, blah, blah, good riddance. This was the fuschia-covered copy of *Pride and Prejudice*. I ran my fingers over the embossed title, feeling the blood rush beneath my skin as I flipped it open.

"It is a truth universally acknowledged . . ."

I was ten minutes into my introduction to the Bennet family and their meddling mother when Rory shoved her math book away. I peeked over the cover. "Want some help?"

But she'd already picked up a felt-tip pen and was doodling on a store bag, so I felt no guilt about turning the next page when she said, "No. It's fine."

The most exciting moment of the night was Mr. Stuhltrager's reaction to the sketch Rory had done of his bichon frise, Charlie, while the two of them prowled around the store. And while I wanted them to hurry up and walk their six legs out the door so I could get back to Lizzy Bennet and her four (four!) sisters, I had to admit the sketch was good enough to warrant Mr. Stuhltrager's "I can't believe you did that—just now! On a brown paper bag. I would frame this. I wonder if I still can trim it down and do that. You should offer this as a service. People would pay big bucks. I would pay big bucks! Here, take this as a tip."

I couldn't see the number on the bill he pressed into Rory's hand, but I don't think that mattered to her as much as the words, which had made her cheeks bright red and her mouth squirmy as she fought the urge to beam.

"You *should* offer that," I told her afterward. "Call it Pup Portraits or something."

"Maybe." She shrugged and entered her code into the cash register, swapping the twenty in her hand for two tens and offering me one.

I waved her off. "That's all yours. I can't draw a stick figure. But seriously, talk to Mom and Dad. They'll be here to get us in like ten minutes. I think it's a good idea."

If they chatted about it on the way home, I didn't hear. I was too busy reading in the backseat about the eldest Bennet daughter, Jane, falling in love with the charming and rich Mr. Bingley. I liked Jane, and I was totally cheering for her and Bingley—but I didn't relate to her. They were both too sweet. Too well-behaved. Too quiet and hesitant and gentle. I was all about the main character, Lizzy, and her sass and books and Lizzyness. When that awful Mr. Darcy snubbed her, I gasped.

"You okay back there, Merri?" Dad asked from behind the

steering wheel. I realized belatedly that we were home and parked and Rory was already out of the car, whereas I hadn't even unbuckled.

"Oh, right." I flicked off the overhead light I'd been using to see the pages and blinked at the night as I got out of the car. Toby's bedroom was still glowing, and I could hear the faint strains of his keyboard through the crack in his balcony door. "I'm going to go check on the patient."

Mom nodded. "Poor guy. Want us to take your backpack?"

"I've got it. There was talk of doing math homework." When I turned thirteen, my parents had sat me down and asked me how I felt about Toby. They checked in again every year or so. Since I'd never wavered from "platonic" or given them a reason to doubt me, they didn't restrict our visits. It was a gift of trust I appreciated, especially since they were exactly the type to indulge in boy-next-door fantasies about me and him.

"Don't stay too late," added Dad. "But in case you do, sleep sweet, little dreamer."

Mom stamped a kiss on my cheek. "We'll see you in the morning."

Toby was sitting at his keyboard with his bad knee propped on a laundry basket. He had the volume turned down, but the fact that he didn't have headphones plugged in indicated his dad wasn't home. Mr. May was a big supporter of the arts—as long as they were performed by people other than his son.

"Look at you, up and about." I set my bag on the floor and took a seat in his twirly desk chair. "Feeling better?"

"I'm pretty sure it's the pain meds, but maybe? They don't

think anything's torn, just sprained." Toby switched the keyboard off and carefully edged his knee brace around the legs of its stand. He stood on one foot and hopped across the room to his bed.

"If you're not going to use your crutches, you should at least let me help."

"Help me by checking my math," he countered. "Or by entertaining me. I'm so bored."

"Movie?" I suggested, reaching for the trunk of cosplay pieces that sat in the corner of his room. I understand that most people don't put on costumes to watch a movie, but most people aren't as fun as Toby and me. Donning a top hat or bandolier or fake mustache or cape before pressing play was part of our routine. And after the awkward way we'd left things the night before, I really wanted routine.

But Toby shook his head. "I watched disgusting amounts of TV today. Tell me about school. Anything good happen?"

"Not really? It was pretty much school—a little less quarrelsome because the you half of the Eliza-and-Toby bickering squad was absent, but—"

"Hey, you survived the rides with Fielding. See, he's nice."

I rolled my eyes. "You think everyone—except Eliza—is nice. I bet you even like Ava."

He shrugged. "She's fine."

"Point made." He was totally like Lizzy's older sister, Jane. Pretty, kind, and way too trusting. Of course that also described my actual older sister. And she had the bland boyfriend too. Trent was definitely a Bingley. Speaking of Austen . . . "Want me to read to you?" That would be two birds with one stone. Toby nodded, but before I could reach in my backpack for the novel, he picked up a comic book from his bedside table.

"Dig out some masks from the trunk, will you?" he asked.

Toby only made it four pages of *Pow! Bam! Crack!* before the eyes behind his superhero mask began to yo-yo up and down. By page six, they stayed shut, and I swapped his book for my own. I tried to read with the same punchy cadence, but it was hard to add *Zip! Slam!* to scenes about Jane catching a cold while visiting Bingley at Netherfield and Lizzy having to go act as nursemaid.

Once I was sure he was definitely asleep, this nursemaid was ready to find her own bed. I carefully removed his mask and tugged a blanket over him, then paused to check the math homework on his desk—pulling a my mom and asterisking the ones he needed to redo. I could've done my own problem set at the same time, but lingering in his room while he was sleeping felt creepier. I'd do mine in the morning while eating breakfast. At least, that's what I told myself while I put on PJs and brushed my teeth.

But instead of opening Hannah's book and seeing what the space crew was up to, or rescuing Blake from the dust bunnies beneath my bed and finishing *Fall with Me*, I opened my laptop and began to type up my first *Pride and Prejudice* reaction journal:

It is a truth universally acknowledged that being a middle child comes with its own set of challenges. Well, maybe not "universally," but it's known to me and Lizzy Bennet and all the other middlers of the world. Like Lizzy, I'm bracketed by sisters: an older one who feels controlled by others' expectations and a younger one who seems to get away with anything. Stuck in the middle—well, my job is . . .

I typed until my eyes started to go blurry. When my phone buzzed on the desk beside me, I picked it up, grateful for a distraction that saved me from myself, because my navel-gazing had started to feel like a belly-button-lint excavation. There was a difference between writing all the ways I identified with the main character and using the journal as a therapy session where I identified *as* the main character.

Maybe after reading the journal entry, Ms. Gregoire would rethink the punishment. Or refer me to health services. One or the other.

I rubbed at my eyes, shut the lid of my laptop, and read the text. How's the patient?

My eyes flicked to Toby's darkened windows before I responded. Who is this?

Fielding Williams.

Funny how having *his* name on the screen changed the tone in which I read his first question. From curious to gruff. Begrudging. Like he was frustrated by having to ask. I wondered why he had—except: *dark* windows. Toby had medded and bedded. So Fielding Williams was stuck with me. I typed: Ambulatory. Mostly. I think he's planning on school tomorrow.

Excellent. Thanks.

I didn't want him to have the last word, but I wanted something wittier than *you're welcome.* I wanted something that would make him spend the rest of the night feeling inferior to my cleverness. I typed and backspaced. Typed again. Until the pressure of minutes ticking past on the clock felt more pressing than wit. Gah. And I knew he'd have the three dots on his screen. A dead giveaway that I was being an angsty try-hard. I gave up and sent: Have a good night.

I watched my phone for the dots that would indicate he was typing back—because, really, common courtesy dictated a "you too." And then I could walk away and pat myself on the back about being civil. Maybe even reward myself with some midnight ice cream. But there were no dots on the screen. And after four minutes of watching and waiting for them to appear, my posture was hunched, my grip on the phone was knuckle cracking, and my lip was chewed like a German shepherd puppy's squeaky toy.

I tossed the phone onto my bed. Fine. He could just be like that. I didn't care. But since I was now wide awake, I might as well do my math homework. And really, there's nothing like sheer irritation to fuel calculations. By the time I'd completed the last factorial, I was beyond ready for sleep. But when I went to plug my phone in, I saw I'd missed a text.

Even though I'd just put on lip balm, I pressed my face into my pillow to hide the rogue grin that I couldn't stop from stretching my cheeks. I rolled over and peeked at the screen again. Yup, it really did read: You too. Sweet dreams.

27

There was no one around when my alarm went off Thursday morning. Well, no one but Rory. It was like the scene in *Home Alone* where Kevin realizes he's been left behind while everyone else went off to Paris. Except substitute Kevin for *me* and Paris for Haute Dog. Which is kinda, sorta, not exactly French.

Clearly Mom and Dad and Lilly had forgotten that I don't have a license or a car—and that Toby was currently hobbling on crutches. So even if Rory and I could make the trek to school—he couldn't. Either that or they'd assumed Eliza's current grad student, Nancy, was driving us. Maybe/definitely because I'd told them she was? And then forgotten to follow up and tell them she couldn't when I found out Eliza had a dentist appointment.

"No big," Toby said—after I'd climbed down my balcony, up his, and then traipsed through his super-white house to find him in his super-white kitchen drinking cranberry juice that looked like it was begging to be spilled on the alabaster countertops so it could drip down the cabinets and pool like melted rubies on the tile floor. "You and Rory can ride with me and Fielding."

Oh, he was wrong. It was a big. A *very* big. I'd already endured my yearly quota of Fielding, and I wasn't going to voluntarily get in his car again. Plus, his "sweet dreams" text was burning a hole through my iPhone.

"I think I'll walk," I said. "It's nice out."

"Oh, really?" Toby tilted his head toward the kitchen's picture window and the raindrops starting to polka dot the flagstone patio outside.

"Hello?" Rory ducked her head in the front door. "Merri? Toby? Anyone?"

"In here," he called.

She toed off her shoes and stepped inside. "Oh, phew. I was starting to worry that *everyone* had forgotten me."

Whoops. It's possible that I'd climbed out my balcony while she was still in the shower.

"No worries! We've got you. Juice?" Toby held up his glass and pointed with a crutch to the cabinet where she could find one of her own. Not that Rory drank juice. But from the radiant smile she aimed his way, you'd have thought he'd offered her a kidney. Hmm. Perhaps there was some present tense to her kiddo-crush on him after all.

"Um, I would, but—I think Fielding's here?" She nodded out the door toward the car idling in his driveway.

"Great." Toby leaned back against the counter as he tried to figure out how to handle his cup and his crutches. I jumped up to intervene before the kitchen turned into a splash spectacle. "Can you tell him we'll be right out?"

"I'm—" My cheeks grew hot. *Sweet dreams*. Two words and

Fielding had me itchy and bashful. Probably on purpose. "I'm still going to walk."

"No you're not," he answered. "Because you're going to carry my backpack, and I don't want it wet."

"Fine, but—but I get to pick our next movie night movie."

Toby laughed as he crutched out the door. "So, something new and different? Did I miss the part where I ever get to pick?"

I followed with both our bags and some serious misgivings.

Toby grimaced as he booty-scooted into the backseat, trying to hold his knee as still as possible. I stood uselessly, holding his crutches with one hand, while I held the other extended in some awkward pose of *I'd help if I knew how.* Rory walked around the car and took the seat beside him. That left me and shotgun. And the complete mystery of which version of Fielding I'd be facing this morning. The one who snarked about recycling and politics and felt I wasn't worthy of his school? Or the one who wished me sweet dreams?

I mean, what if that text had been sarcastic? And eleven letters didn't make up for a week of rude. It probably *was* sarcastic, seeing as how I wasn't tempting to him and all that.

The passenger door cracked; Fielding was leaning across the seat to push it open from the inside. "Get in. Unless you're planning to get in the backseat so you can smell him too?"

"Smell me?" Toby tugged the crutches from my hand and tossed them on the floor, then shut the door.

I sighed and settled into shotgun. So, based on the fact

that he'd decided to go with making fun of me before "hello"—it was probably a safe assumption that the text had been mocking as well.

I clipped my seat belt and spat out, "I already know what Toby smells like." I swear if there were a book of bad comebacks, I'd be the author. It'd be multiple volumes, but people would die of secondhand embarrassment before they finished the first chapter.

"I feel like there's a story here." Toby laughed. "So what do I smell like?"

"Licorice."

Rory said "Mint" at the same time, and he laughed louder.

"The toothpaste will last about ten minutes. Then Rowboat's got to be right."

"Of course I am." The implication that I might not be was insulting. "Too bad it *tastes* disgusting, because I kinda like the way you smell. Or maybe I'm just used to it." It was the smell of Saturdays in PJs, pillow forts, movie nights, bike rides, campouts, and rooftop talks.

I glanced at Fielding. He was scowling at the steering wheel, the windshield, the road beyond. I glanced in the backseat: Rory was scowling at me too—so status quo—and Toby was fiddling with his knee brace, a smile on his face. I wondered if he abstained from licoricing while dating. If not, had his past girlfriends found the taste of secondhand licorice tolerable? I grimaced at the thought, turning forward again. Fielding was in my peripheral vision, but I refused to look at him. What did *he* taste like?

Gah! Had I really just thought that? My brain was such a traitor. I turned my red cheeks toward the window.

Rory broke the silence by clearing her throat. "Thanks for driving us. My parents are already at their store. I think they're trying to figure out some sort of Hail Mary play to be able to afford next year's tuition . . . and, you know, food."

Rory was such a Lydia. Maybe that's what I'd write my next *Pride and Prejudice* response journal about. How Lizzy Bennet and I both knew the frustration of having little sisters and all the ways they humiliate you. For example, please, Rory, by all means, discuss our family's money problems in front of the Snob King. He'd probably love reporting that to his dad: *Good news, we might be rid of the Campbells after all!* And even though he probably knew we were scholarship kids, him hearing that we were scrambling to pull together tuition money made my cheeks burn.

I shot her a look. "It's not that bad."

"Clearly you didn't hear about the latest wedding plans. Some fancy orchestra. And a live dove release. To symbolize peace or whatever."

"You can't be serious," I said. That was so cheesy and dramatic—so *not* Lilly.

"Why stop at doves?" suggested Toby. "When there are so many other cool animals you could unleash on your wedding guests. Turtles for patience. Skunks—tolerance. Spiders for courage, because they're freaking terrifying."

"Your family runs a *pet shop*," said Fielding as he turned

off our street. "Are people truly worried about their feelings on peace?"

I straightened my shoulders at the disdain in his voice. "It's not a 'pet shop,'" I snapped. I was proud of Haute Dog and what my parents had built. But that didn't mean I hadn't endured plenty of elementary school playground teasing throughout the years. *They should've called it "Ugly Dog"—then they could sell you.* I sat up a little taller; I wasn't seven years old anymore. If Fielding wanted to dish it out, I could serve it up too. "It's a specialty dog boutique."

"You're missing my point," Fielding said. "Why would any-one care about their feelings on peace? What could they pos-sibly do? Let snakes out? Force cats and dogs to cohabitate?"

"Ooh," Toby called from the backseat. "Snakes for flexibil-ity—Lilly would love that."

I ground my teeth. "We don't have snakes or goldfish or cats. *Dog* boutique."

"Maybe you *should* sell those things." He was madden-ingly calm as he continued his lecture. "If you diversified, you'd expand your customer base. Make it Haute Dog and Cat-sup. Double the clients."

The hair on the back of my neck prickled. I wanted to yank up his emergency brake and shake him. (And while I was shaking him, lean in to see if he smelled as stupidly good when not post-workout). "How do you know the name of my parents' store?"

"Is it supposed to be a secret?" The edges of his mouth pressed in and he lifted an eyebrow. "That could be your problem right there. Hard to get business in a secret store. Perhaps some advertising is in order."

I gave a slow clap. "Please continue to mansplain everything wrong with my family's business. Clearly we should've hired you as a business consultant. Because it's all sooo easy to fix. It has nothing to do with the big-box pet store that opened. Or rising rents. Good thing you're so smart and didn't even have to visit the store to tell us how to run it."

Fielding was quiet for the length of two blocks. Finally he said, "I meant to be funny. Clearly I misjudged. I apologize."

"Oh." I glanced in the backseat, where Rory and Toby were both watching us with wide eyes and shoulder nudges. It was possible I was a wee bit sensitive about all things financial, because the second half of my *Pride and Prejudice* response journal had been comparing the Bennet sisters' financial situation—with all their father's money set to be inherited by an odious male cousin, Mr. Collins—to my own feelings of guilt about how the Hero High bills were keeping my parents up at night.

Just like Lizzy and Jane feel pressured to marry well—i.e. rich—so that they won't be a burden on their parents, I feel like I need to justify the money my parents are spending on tuition. Like, I should get the very most I can out of the Hero High experience and everything it has to offer. But I'm not sure what that looks like yet. . . .

I chewed my lip and looked over at Fielding. "Maybe I overreacted. I'm sorry too."

This led to another two blocks of front-seat silence, but at least Toby and Rory had started to chatter. I surreptitiously watched Fielding; he gave his complete attention to the road, but at stop signs he switched it—completely—to me for a half second. And even in that brief an interval, it was breath-stealingly intense.

At the last stop sign before school, he swallowed and said, "I have a dog."

"What? Seriously?" I conjured up images of Hungarian vizslas, Rhodesian ridgebacks, English pointers. Something aristocratic, finely boned. Something you'd see in an antique painting of men in top hats. "What kind?"

"He's a basset hound."

My mouth dropped open. Basset hounds were the Winnie the Pooh of the dog world. Everyone liked a basset hound. They were charming and patient and goofy-looking. *This* was his dog? I leaned on the center console. "You have never been as interesting to me as you are in this moment."

He gave a curt laugh. "Thanks?"

Toby cut off his conversation with Rory to interject, "Man, is his dog fat and lazy, though. He could give Gatsby a run for least obedient."

"He's high-spirited!" Our identical protests overlapped as we defended our respective pets in eerie synchronicity.

So eerie that we looked at each other, then immediately looked away and decided not to speak for the rest of the ride. Sure, we might have found common ground in our mischievous pups. Sure, we could've traded stories about the time

Gatsby got his head stuck in the empty oatmeal cylinder and kept running into walls. Or how every time Dad washed the kitchen floor, Gats slid across it and slammed into the fridge. Or how he was scared of crumpled tissues. Plus whatever it was that Fielding's dog did. But what was the point of common ground when neither of us wanted to stand there?

I turned more firmly toward the window. I bet his dog wasn't even that naughty.

28

Despite being a Monday after a completely forgettable Friday and a boring run-work-homework weekend, it had been *so* close to a good day. It had started with Rory and me having a civilized breakfast, during which she let me help her with her math homework. We made it through five problems without fighting or her storming off. A new record. This was followed by a ride from Eliza's grad student, Nancy, instead of Fielding, during which Eliza announced that *Her! Parents! Might! Be! Coming! Home!* The exclamation points faded as she clarified it was just for a visit. I squeezed her hand and forced the punctuation on my *But! Still!* until she was smiling again.

Hannah had brought me the second Spectacular Starfleet book. Ms. Gregoire had praised the *Pride and Prejudice* response journal I'd handed in last Thursday and was excited to read the one I'd handed in today—which focused on Mr. Collins and Monroe (though I was discreet enough not to name him by name):

Lizzy had the intelligence to reject Mr. Collins's super-awkward marriage proposal, despite the financial security he

would've provided for her family. I wish I were more like Lizzy, because I <u>shouldn't</u> have dated the first Hero High boy I met. . . . I bet the next time Lizzy faces a proposal, she'll say yes. Maybe it'll be that charming soldier, Wickham, the one who hates snobby Mr. Darcy. I bet it'll be swoonily romantic. Hopefully the same is true for me too!

I made it through five periods with no drama, no exes popping up on my messenger window, no pop quizzes, no embarrassing wardrobe malfunctions. And Eliza and Toby had kept their quarreling to a tolerable level. Heck, after five days of Monroe's nonstop texts requesting/begging/demanding I talk to him, even he had responded **FINE** to my latest unwavering **No**.

But as media class ended and we packed up to head to Convocation, an office aide knocked on the door. She had a whispered conversation with Mr. Welch, which ended with him pointing to me. The thin-lipped redhead headed to my table, giving me a smugly superior smile as she handed me a folded piece of paper. One she'd clearly taken the liberty of unfolding and reading.

"Have a good day," she trilled.

Grumbling under my breath and ignoring the nosy glances of my classmates, I unfolded the slip of paper: *Headmaster Williams would like to see you immediately after Convocation.*

Either the headmaster wrote in the third person and very swirly script, or he'd taken the time to dictate this message for someone else to transcribe. Which couldn't possibly be more efficient, but I guess that was his way of proving just how important and powerful he was? I mashed the note into a ball before passing it to Eliza.

She smoothed it. "Why?" she asked.

"Don't know."

"Well, you can't be in trouble." She said this emphatically and wiped her hands on her skirt like that idea was discarded. "You haven't *done* anything new. I've been watching."

I shrugged and shoved my things into my bag.

"Wait!" She studied my face. "Did I miss something?"

"No." I slung my bag over my shoulder. "At least I don't think so?"

"Then don't worry," said Eliza. "If you didn't do anything, you can't be in trouble. It's probably just . . ." But she couldn't finish that sentence, and I couldn't *not* worry.

Instead of listening to announcements, whisper-gossiping with Hannah, counting Curtis's furtive admiring glances at Eliza, or napping, I spent all Convocation trying to unlock the mysteries of Headmaster Williams's imperious expressions. The topic of his lecture today was spider safety. Or maybe campus safety? Driver safety?

Whatever, it was something about safety. But I was too distracted to pay attention. Gah! Which meant I wouldn't be prepared to answer any questions if he brought it up in our meeting. That was probably his plan all along—distract me with the cursive note, then nail me for not paying obsessive attention to his lecture on cooking safety or . . . ?

I grabbed a pen from my bag and scrawled *Ask Eliza* on my hand, then faced forward, determined to be totally in the zone for the rest of Convocation.

"—and I think you'll agree with me that this is a topic of utmost importance. One that hopefully you have a much better grasp on after this past hour." The headmaster paused to absorb the polite applause of my classmates, then cleared his throat and added, "Please rise and join me for the singing of the school song."

"Come in. Sit down." The words were orders, but the headmaster's tone was all genteel hospitality. He rose from his chair and ushered me to a seat, taking my satchel and placing it on a small side table. "Can I get you anything? Some water?"

"I'm fine. Thanks." I shifted on the slippery leather of the seat, trying to find a sophisticated way to stay perched when my feet didn't quite hit the floor. I wanted to fold my hands in my lap, but instead I clutched the arms of the chair to steady myself.

"Hmm," said Headmaster Williams. It was a noncommittal sound that probably meant something super important, but I had no idea how to interpret it. I followed his gaze to my hand. *Ask Eliza*—the crooked letters I'd scrawled practically screamed "ragamuffin." People who sat in this chair in this office were not supposed to use their skin as a notepad.

They must teach them in headmaster school about how to make stressful situations worse, I thought to myself, *until innocent girls forget what they were been planning to ask their best friends, and are sitting in an office that smells of furniture polish and decorum, and are tempted to lick the ink off their hands out of sheer embarrassment.*

I refrained.

"Um, good talk today," I said. "In Convocation."

He puffed up. "Well, yes. Cyber safety is an important and relevant topic to today's youths."

Cyber safety! That made so much more sense than cooking or spider.

"If you change your mind and get thirsty, don't hesitate to ask." Headmaster Williams took his own seat on the opposite side of his barge-like mahogany desk. He rolled in closer so his elbows could rest on the leather blotter. It was surrounded by fancy inscribed paperweights of crystal and brass. Awards—just like the framed certificates on the wall behind him—that proclaimed what a great school Hero High was and what a great leader helmed it. "So, I bet you're wondering why I've called you in here today."

"A bit, sir." "Sir" still felt like an act. Like I was a character from a Dickens novel. But everyone else used it—even Sera. And if his own daughter felt the need to "sir" him, it wasn't optional for me.

"Well, you aren't in trouble; so if you've been worried, get that thought right out of your head." He laughed and gave me what I'm sure was meant to be a genial smile, except . . . I *had* been worried, and clearly he knew I would worry. So if I didn't *need* to worry, why hadn't he added something to that effect in his note?

"May I ask why I *am* here, sir?" I could've stopped there, but since all my self-control was tied up in keeping my hands from reaching out and leaving smudgy fingerprints on his gleaming awards, I went ahead and added, "Because I'm supposed to be at cross-country practice, and I don't want to miss warm-ups if you don't need me."

"I won't keep you long. I just wanted to follow up and see how *you* feel you're fitting in here at Hero High. Offer a little advice, if I may."

No, you may not didn't feel like an acceptable response, so I didn't bother to give one.

"I hear from Ms. Gregoire that she's assigned you an extra reading project as consequence for the messaging incident."

"Yes, sir. *Pride and Prejudice.*"

"Ah, a classic. And I understand that your work on it has been exemplary so far."

"Thank you, sir."

"Had you studied it before?" The tilt of his head made it clear he was expecting a certain answer. "Maybe in your old school? Or seen the movie?"

"No. I haven't read it or watched it."

The way he sat back in his chair made it clear this was *not* the response he'd anticipated. With another person, I might have explained my rule about not seeing a movie before reading a book. With another person, I might've elaborated on my reaction to the story so far—how I didn't understand how *Pride and Prejudice* was billed as this great romance, because while I adored Lizzy and Jane, all the guys so far seemed like slime. Except possibly the charming Wickham. But I'd barely met him.

"I've heard from your other teachers that you've had a surprisingly successful first week academically."

I felt my eyebrows shoot up at "*surprisingly* successful"

—had he not looked at my transcripts from my old school? I kept my voice level as I said, "My classes have been interesting." Which was a total overstatement, but what was I supposed to say: *Thanks for thinking I'm an idiot; I'll enjoy proving you wrong?* Actually, that was tempting. . . .

"So all that truly remains is to integrate you into Hero High's student population. And luckily, you've got quite the team here to support you." He leaned forward like he was about to impart some ancient wisdom, maintaining eye contact and silence for five seconds beyond uncomfortable. "Merrilee, we're all here to help."

"Noted. Thanks," I answered, which might not have been exactly the apex of the manners or whatever else he was hoping I'd absorb while sharing his oxygen and wisdom.

"Well, yes." He straightened up, displaying posture that rivaled his son's for rigidity. "I understand that my daughter, Seraphina, has graciously offered you entry into her peer group. It's made up of reliable and respectable Hero High students. The type who everyone enrolled should aspire to be like."

My mind immediately rewound to media class, where Sera and Hannah had been writing Darwin-meets-Dracula fanfiction instead of completing the assignment on famous alumni. Or lunch, where Toby, Lance, and Curtis dared one another to eat increasingly revolting combinations—today Curtis had won with mustard, yogurt, and Nutella, but he hadn't turned green until Eliza announced that their behavior was "disgusting." Just thinking about it made me want to gag—or laugh—but Headmaster Williams was watching me, waiting me out. Clearly this was the portion of the lecture where my participation was required. "Yes, sir. They're all quite . . . impressive."

"I know you're not accustomed to an environment like this: the academic rigor, the trust and freedoms we gift our students, and the value we place on our honor code and school reputation. But with some concerted effort and dedication, I believe that you'll eventually adapt and be able to assimilate into the student body."

In other words: I lacked the smarts, morals, and social graces, but maybe if I tried real hard, I could be trained. Just like the clueless puppies at the store's obedience classes—supercute, but at any given moment, they might just pee on the floor or nip someone. "How generous of you." I bit my words into sharpened syllables, not that he noticed.

Headmaster Williams nodded magnanimously—a word I'm certain he assumed I didn't know, but one that perfectly described his supercilious manner. "I encourage you to make the most of this privilege. Observe and emulate Sera and her friends. Ask yourself, 'What would they do?' before acting. And if you're unsure of the answer—consult with your Knight Light. Hannah is a great girl. You should be honored that she selected you to mentor. Seek to truly benefit from the opportunity to learn from her."

It was a good thing I already liked Sera and Hannah—and that I'd met them before his sales pitch. Every contrary part of my soul wanted me to reject them just on principle. I wanted to take every particle of Headmaster Williams's advice and do the exact opposite.

Since I wasn't quite that self-destructive, I simply kicked my foot and said, "Sir, you've made your point. I'd rather not tie up any more of your valuable time; may I be excused to head to cross-country practice?"

He leaned farther forward in his seat. His eyebrows and voice lowered as he asked, "Do you know my favorite part from *Pride and Prejudice*?"

"I—" I looked around his office for the crystal ball he must have thought I'd consulted. "I can't begin to guess, sir."

"There's a scene in which one character—a young lady—greatly oversteps the boundaries of propriety. And another character justifiably calls her an 'obstinate, headstrong girl.' I find it to be one of the most satisfying lines in the whole of the literary canon."

I knew this was a thinly veiled insult. Emphasis on "thinly." But I just nodded politely. "I'm only on chapter twenty-two, sir. I don't think I've gotten to that part yet, but I'll keep my eyes peeled."

"You do that." We exchanged the fakest and weakest of smiles and sat for a silent count of six with our expressions getting tighter and tighter. "I'll let you get to practice now. Cross-country is a sport of endurance and mental discipline. Stick with that, and you'll go far—both literally and metaphorically."

He was still laughing at his joke when I snatched up my bag and shut his office door behind me.

I stormed across campus, muttering under my breath. But there wasn't really anyone around to care if I combined "headmaster" with "moron" and "pompous windbag" and "overinflated ego that I'd love to pop with a very sharp pin." I was glad I'd worn my patent-leather flats today. They made satisfying clacking sounds as I stomped to my destination. Except, when I arrived, there was a new, obnoxious obstacle in the way.

"That's my locker," I said.

"I'm aware. I've been waiting for you."

How was it possible that Fielding's posture and voice made it seem like *I* was the one who was imposing on him—as in, how dare I not appear immediately when he wanted me? Next time he'd have to coordinate a bit better with his father.

"Seriously? Are you guys going to do some sort of Hero High *Christmas Carol*? The ghosts of private school past, present, and future?" I swallowed as a bitter thought threatened to gag me. "Is Sera next? Please tell me she's not involved and does actually like me."

"I don't have any idea what you're talking about." He dropped his chin, but not his voice. "As usual."

I gritted my teeth, because he was such a waste of good looks. Such a waste of good tailoring, good posture, good diction, good dental hygiene. "Well, if you're done guarding my locker, can I get in it?"

He stepped back and I pounced on my lock, spinning the dial with hasty, indiscriminate fingers. But he didn't go away. Instead he inhaled deeply and said, "You baffle me."

The words were rich with emotion, a rarity from someone so starched and measured. I glanced at him, at his brown eyes that seemed wide and searching, like I was the word that stood between him and crossword puzzle mastery.

For a moment I hesitated, considered saying something soft and kind—but then I remembered his father's lecture. All the ways I'd just been insulted with politeness and circumspection. This *had* to be the setup for another account of all my failings. "I baffle you? And that's *my* problem because . . . ?"

"No." Fielding shook his head—that stubborn piece of hair falling down and bisecting his eyebrow. Making him look less polished, making the frustration in his expression seem more human. "It's not. That's not what I meant. It's just . . . I want to figure you out. I'm trying to. You're worth the effort. You're worth . . . everything."

I was screening these words, trying to find the hidden agenda. Then, since nothing I came up with made sense, I felt the urge to escape.

"I've got to go," I told him, my mouth dry. "I'm late."

"Please." He put a hand on my arm, and we both jerked away from the spark of static that jumped between our skin. "I've thought of nothing else all weekend. You have to hear me. Give me a chance to tell you how I feel about you."

"How you *feel* about me?" I squinted, as though it would make things go back to normal, because Fielding didn't sound like himself. All that swallowing hard and pausing, the desperation making his words rushed and blurred. He didn't look like himself either. He was pale. His fingers were fidgeting in infinite knots. And was he—was that actual sweat along his hairline?

"I've been trying—doing everything I can to *not* feel anything about you. But you've captivated me. I mean, you and your sister's admission to the school exploited the worst form of nepotism. Neither of you is the caliber of student who'd get selected from general admissions. And since you've been here, you've done nothing but cause trouble."

He was practically muttering to himself, totally unaware of the temper brewing beneath my skin—totally unaware of *me* in general. I mean, why bother looking at the person you're insulting?

He gulped in a deep breath and finally turned from the tile floor, pinning me with those deep brown eyes. "But that doesn't matter. I wish it did, but it doesn't. I can't stop thinking about you. And not just the ways you're going to be the sort of alumna the school will want to disavow. Or how you picked the absolute worst possible Hero High student as your boyfriend. Or how your socks never match, you refuse to use a door and stairs to exit your room, you can't differentiate recycling from trash cans, and I never understand half of what you're saying. Despite this, I can't stop thinking about dating you—kissing you. Figuring you out. And since no matter how I try and force you from my head, everything is failing—"

He paused to inhale again, and I watched his chest rise and fall beneath the stark white of his shirt. I realized then that my jaw was wide open—giving me, I'm sure, all the attractive qualities of a gaping fish.

"Merrilee, I don't see any other choice but to bring you as my date to the Fall Ball."

His chest was heaving, like he had completed a run. But other than that, his expression seemed calmer. As though his monologue had drained him of anxiety, and now the rest of the conversation could be a formality. This smug attitude only made my cheeks burn hotter. I turned my back on him and forced my stiff fingers to open my locker, select random books, and slide them into my bag. In my head I was counting. It was another of Eliza's recommendations: counting before responding. Since doing so in English didn't touch the temper-tempest that was brewing in my mind, I tried Latin.

Fielding cleared his throat. "Merrilee?"

"You *like me*? Is there something wrong with you?" I shook my head—that hadn't come out the way I'd meant. "How is that even possible? I'm barely civil to you. We can barely tolerate being around each other. What could you possibly like about me?"

He opened his mouth, but I held up a hand and shook my head. "No, don't answer that, because it doesn't matter. This"—I pointed a finger between us—"is never going to happen. My answer is no."

"No?"

"Not that you actually *asked* me a question—but the answer is still no. I won't go to the dance with you. Not 'no thank you.' Not 'I'm sorry but I can't' or 'I wish I could.' I'm not giving you any of the usual polite excuses."

Fielding's jaw hardened. And I mentally added jawline and throat to the list of attractive pieces that had been wasted on him. "May I ask why you can't even bother to be polite?"

"Why should *I* be polite when you weren't? You just went out of your way to insult me, my family, and my ex-boyfriend. I'm an embarrassment to the school? My family doesn't belong here? We're not the right caliber of people? My taste in boyfriends is awful? . . . Well then, find some comfort in the fact that *you* are the last guy I'd ever want to date."

His posture went from straight to stiff. "I see."

"No, I don't think you do. For someone so obsessed with the Hero High student population and whether or not they measure up to your exacting standards, *you* are the biggest jerk of all." My words were embers and sparks; I couldn't spit them out fast enough, but they still burned. I took a step forward into his space, expecting him to back up, but he held his ground, and it only made my heart beat faster. "How dare you judge me? How dare you tell me I'm not good enough to be here? You know nothing about my intelligence or Rory's giftedness. Who are you to slander Monroe? And nepotism? That's quite the accusation coming from the *son of the head-master*—would *you* be enrolled here if he wasn't your dad? If there's anyone at this school who's a lower-caliber human— it's you."

Fielding brushed some invisible dust off the sleeve of his shirt. Seriously—how did it stay so crisp, even at the end of a long day? Mine was a wrinkled mess. I watched his Adam's apple bob, watched his chin lift to even higher heights. "Thank you for clarifying exactly how you feel. I understand perfectly, and I won't bother you again."

I wanted to throw a book at his retreating back. At his shoulders, which were still so straight and proud. But once he was out of sight, I gave in to my other urge—the one that suggested I slump down on the floor in front of my locker. I looked up and down the empty hallway, and since there was no one around, I pulled my knees to my chin, exposing my underwear to the dust bunnies. A move I was sure no *proper* Hero High girl would make. But I needed to just lower my head for a second. I needed to regroup and process what had happened.

I'd been planning on a rage-cardio power run, one where I spewed all the headmaster's words on Eliza and let her indignation fix my hurt feelings. But now I just felt too raw, too exhausted. Instead of doubling my anger, that horror show of a conversation with Fielding had drained it. I wanted to curl up in my bed and escape into a book. And once I'd latched on to that thought, nothing else would do. I wanted hours and pages with the indomitable Lizzy Bennet. I wanted to watch her turn down suitors and scoff at invitations to dances. Take that, Collins! Take that, Darcy! Take that, everyone who told her or me that we weren't good enough!

And since I was already messing up everything else, why not skip practice? I texted Eliza that I wouldn't be showing up, then called Lilly and begged for a ride home.

29

skipped downstairs the next morning after a night spent between pages—and not the ones in my textbooks. Sometimes you just need to blow off equations in favor of Austen. Latin wasn't going anywhere. And, fine, maybe *Pride and Prejudice* wasn't going anywhere either, but after a few hours with Lizzy Bennet, I felt much more equipped to face school. If she could head to Hunsford to stay with the creepy Mr. Collins after rejecting his proposal and put up with all the backward compliments and unwelcome advice of Darcy's pretentious aunt, Lady Catherine, then I could handle a few judgmental Williams males. I'd channel my inner Lizzy and keep my chin high and sass strong. I couldn't say that I'd ever derived any similar inspiration from conjugating Latin verbs.

Rory was already at the table when I bounded into the kitchen. I smiled at her. "Good—" She practically growled over her mug of tea. "Or not," I amended. "Late night?"

"Stupid school with all its stupid homework. How does anyone have time to do anything but study?" She narrowed her eyes. "Don't answer that. We're not all supernaturally smart."

Clearly we were not in for a repeat of yesterday's civil tutoring session. And it was probably best I didn't share my homework strategies: two parts procrastination, one part flying through my math set while blow-drying my hair. Instead I poured myself a cup of juice and selected one of Dad's poppyseed muffins. I left an empty chair between us because I'd learned from years of experience that Rory's toes and heel bones were particularly pointy. "Well, we're not all artistic geniuses either."

Apparently "artistic genius" was an insult this morning or something? Because her eyes only narrowed further, her lips pulling back into something that resembled the way Gatsby snarled when he got spooked by his own reflection, or an empty trash can, or the vacuum.

Not that I had any plans to tell her this comparison. Instead I picked up Mom's tablet and logged in to my Hero High email. I hadn't checked it in a few days, and there was quite the collection of school bulletins, club flyers, funny forwards from Lance, goofy links from Curtis, and book recommendations from Hannah. And at the top, a shiny new email from a Williams.

But not Sera. Not the one whose first name might as well be Headmaster. Nope.

So much for Fielding promising to leave me alone.

I squished my OJ from one cheek to the other and kicked at the table legs. Just seeing that email made me want to behave in as uncouth a manner as possible. Not that he was there to judge me, or for me to prove that I wasn't affected by his judgment—but at least the behavior had the added benefit of annoying Rory, who rolled her eyes and stood. "I'm going to wait outside."

I was left with silence, a glass of orange juice that now tasted sour, a muffin that no longer looked appealing, and an email that I absolutely didn't want to read.

But I didn't want to spend the morning guessing what it might say, so I took a deep breath and clicked.

Dear Merrilee,

Before you begin to worry, I do intend to honor my promise not to bother you anymore with talk about feelings for you. It was a mistake—

Oh, swell, it was written in pretentious mode. Also, just what every girl wants to hear, that she's a mistake.

But there were a few things that you mentioned yesterday that have bothered me all night. I wanted to clear up any misconceptions that lingered between us.

As to your enrollment: you must know that Senator Rhodes used her considerable influence as an alumnus and as a politician to get you and your sister admitted to the school. There's a strict enrollment cap on each grade level—which, until this year, has never been violated. You and Aurora are the "plus ones" of your respective grades. Typically these application proceedings are kept confidential, but everything about your applications caused such a division within the school board that details leaked out to a small circle of students. Your and Rory's applications arrived months past the admissions deadline and didn't include the pre-requisite essays or recommendation letters. Your interviews were conducted as formalities—after the board had already assured Senator Rhodes of your both being granted positions in the school.

Essays? I'd never even heard *mention* of any essays. Senator Rhodes and Mom had taken care of filling out the applications. All Rory and I had done was sign them. I didn't know that we'd been given some shortcut version. I didn't like that I didn't know this.

I don't mean to imply that you're not intelligent or capable or that your time at RRH Prep won't be beneficial to you and the other students—but looking at this objectively, were you and your sister the most qualified candidates in the application pool? Is it fair that you got to skip the rigors of the process and were gifted openings that were created just for you? I don't like the implica-tion that the school board can be purchased with influence and sway.

Though, since it seems likely that this is all information you weren't privy to, the fact that I've held you accountable for it has probably rankled.

"Rankled"? "Privy"? I wanted to know if he naturally wrote like that, or if this was a thesaurus-assisted email. I wanted to hear how he talked with Toby and Curtis when they were alone. When I wasn't there to *rankle* him with my unearned presence.

I apologize and will keep in mind that, despite being the beneficiary of the senator's actions, you weren't the one behind the manipulations. I know your welcome to RRH Prep hasn't been the warmest. I apologize for that as well, and while I'll keep my word and keep my distance, please know that if our paths do cross, I'll be kinder. As for why I like you—since you challenged that notion as well—you are passionate and funny. I spent much of the time we've been together trying not to laugh—with you, not at you. Except half your jokes are at my expense, and I don't think you want me to find them humorous.

Also, your loyalty is so admirable. I've seen the way you stand up for your friends. Finally, your determination. Despite the lack of welcome you've received, you've won everyone over. I didn't know that you were the very thing our school was missing until you arrived. I'm glad you're here. I say all this not to sway your feelings—you were quite clear—but to answer your question. I hope I've done so to your satisfaction.

I knew those were compliments and I knew they were kind, but they sat in my stomach like a ball of thorns. I was so much more comfortable with our animosity. Changing the rules—being sweet and stomach-fluttery when I wanted to be all fisticuffs and anger—was such a stupid, Fielding thing to do.

As for my father: you referred to a meeting with him. While I can only conjecture as to what it was about, I'm fairly certain I can make an accurate guess. Father takes his duties as headmaster a bit too seriously at times. His focus on the "ideal" student can be singular, and I'm hoping his words didn't make you feel as though you don't measure up. I know it's not my place to apologize for him or make excuses for his actions, but I did want to assure you that his opinions are not my own. They are certainly not Sera's. My sister has only the highest degree of fondness and admiration for you.

One last thing, and I'll cease to bother you. You accused me of spreading slander about Monroe Stratford, and I can see why it would seem like my words were motivated by jealousy or pettiness. They were not. As you know, all students are required to sign an honor code at the time of their enrollment. For most of our classmates this is a formality, but Monroe saw it as a challenge. From the beginning of his freshman year, he's made it his goal to break every standard listed there. It is my greatest embarrassment to have firsthand knowledge of this fact because for our freshman year, he and I were friends. To my shame, I didn't report him to my father for purchasing papers online, copying off others' tests, skipping class to meet with girls, or hosting parties where he had a checklist of illegal and off-limits substances.

While I knew these actions were wrong, I admired his charisma and ability to be well-liked—these traits don't come easily to me. The final straw was on Admitted Students Day our freshman year, when the incoming class toured the campus. Listening to him charm and flirt with the eighth graders in attendance—then turn around and make lewd comments about them—was revolting. Especially when one of the girls he was discussing was my sister. He'd set up Corrupting the Headmaster's Daughter as the ultimate challenge.

I confronted him and said that if he ever approached Sera or her friends, I'd go directly to my father with what I knew about his activities. And, until he met you, he'd kept his word and stayed far away from her circle. He and I no longer associate, but as far as I'm aware, the parties and reckless behavior have continued.

I hope you'll understand that I'm telling you this in confidence, because I think you deserve to know—but it's not just my story, and I'd rather Sera not hear about how she was disrespected and discussed.

I nodded at the computer screen. Of course I wouldn't tell her. I wouldn't tell anyone. Of course he could trust me. I didn't know why he would, after the things we'd screeched at each other, but I would keep his secrets. The final paragraph contained more of the same apologies, followed by Fielding Williams, which was strangely unsatisfying, like I wanted to see his signature in his handwriting instead of the tablet's default font.

The whole letter was perfectly polite. It made me want to beat something with an etiquette guide.

And if it was true? It had to be, right? Because those sorts of lies would be so easy to check. But Sera—sweet, eighth-grader Sera—the thought of her being the object of a bet made my stomach churn. Especially when the lips that had placed that bet had been pressed to mine last week. In our short time dating, he'd more than proven how little he respected or followed rules. How little he'd respected me.

Wait! Was *I* a similar challenge? Claim the new girl? The new girl who didn't really deserve to be at the school?

"Rowboat?" I looked up from the tablet to see Toby standing in my kitchen, car keys in his hand and creases across his forehead. "Didn't you hear me beeping? Or Rory ringing the doorbell? Or Gatsby going ballistic?"

"No," I answered honestly. "Sorry."

"You okay?" His eyes scanned the kitchen, coming to rest on the tablet, and then his expression relaxed into a grin. "Oh, you were reading. What's today's book about? Vampires? Were-elk? Pixies—of the manic dream girl or wooded variety?"

I closed the mail window and stuck my tongue out at him. "If you're looking for a recommendation, I'm happy to make one." It was an easy tease, and he laughed as he grabbed my bag and tossed me my coat from the hook by the door.

"You didn't even notice." He did a stiff jig in his knee brace. "Look, no crutches."

"Wow." I was still blinking out of a mental fog, like when a book or movie holds onto your thoughts with sticky fingers, making it so much harder for reality to feel real. Only Fielding's email *was* part of my reality. Just not a welcome or comfortable part.

"Come on, bookworm. We're going to be late."

I stood, but my legs felt shaky. Like the words in that email had shifted the tiles beneath my feet. We were going to be late to a school where I'd cheated my way into admission. And my ex-boyfriend . . . "Toby—" I took a deep breath before asking him a question I already knew the answer to. Rory had provided it. "Does Monroe have big parties?"

"Yeah. They're supposed to be *wild.* I've never been invited to one. Why? Are you and he back—" His shoulders slumped, my bag trailing inches closer to the ground.

"No!" The thought made my stomach clench like Toby's fist. "Not at all."

"Oh. Good. I mean—" He shrugged and played with his hair. "Let's go before Rory hijacks my car."

"Good plan." But now we were both being falsely cheerful, and I just wanted to crawl back upstairs and hide beneath my covers.

"Wait. Breakfast. Do you want to bring it?" Toby pointed to the muffin I'd plated before getting sucked into Fielding's confessional.

I shook my head. Food and I were not friends right now. The three sips of OJ I'd managed were planning a tsunami in my stomach. I'd been so wrong. About myself. About Monroe. And maybe/probably/likely . . . about Fielding, too.

30

My stomach had been rumbling for a full five minutes by the time the bell rang for lunch, but it did a quick one-eighty into churning when Ms. Gregoire stopped by my desk. "Merrilee, can I keep you after class a moment?" She turned to Eliza and smiled. "She's not in trouble, I promise."

Eliza dropped her watchdog posture and raised her eyebrows at me. I knew exactly what she was thinking: that this was the type of reassurance Headmaster Williams should've included with his meeting request yesterday. "I'll grab your lunch and books from your locker so you can head straight to the cafeteria."

"Thanks." I pulled my English notebook out of my satchel, then handed her the bag. "Will you drop this off?" Just because I'd skipped cross-country the day before didn't mean I needed the extra workout of hauling around that massive thing.

"Sure." She eyed Ms. Gregoire, who had drifted over to the window, where she was watering the row of potted ivy that grew gracefully along the ledge. Eliza's scrutiny was repaid with an open smile and a wave.

"I promise to send her along soon."

Eliza nodded, turning to the only other student still lingering: Curtis. He was waiting to hold the door for her. Had probably been waiting this whole conversation, and had earned a scowl for his trouble. I bet they'd bicker the whole walk to the lockers. I bet I'd get to hear all about how infuriating he was during cross-country. I bet she'd smack me if I shared my theory about her protesting just *a bit too much* about how obnoxious she found him. Well, not literally smack me, but the verbal-takedown equivalent.

But that didn't mean I wasn't right.

Ms. Gregoire cleared her throat, and I turned away from the door. The dress she was wearing today was peach with teal parasols. I'm not sure why I was so sure they were parasols, not umbrellas, but I was a hundred percent convinced. She crossed one dark purple ankle boot over the other and smiled at me. She smiled a lot, but when it was *at* you, it just felt different. Authentic. Sincere. It was more than a facial expression, it was a gift, telling you she had all the time in the world for you and you had all her attention. I exhaled any lingering tension and sank back into my seat.

"Merrilee, I've been loving your journals. Have you considered joining the school literary magazine?"

"Not really?" But Hannah had suggested it too, after she'd squealed over the guest post I'd written for her blog. The club fair was coming up next Friday—maybe I'd stop at the booth? "But I've had fun writing these journals. I finished another one last night . . . but I didn't know if it was too early to give it to you."

"Please do." Ms. Gregoire waited while I fished it out of my notebook, then she hugged it to her chest. "Your writing has verve and voice, and your perspective on *Pride and Prejudice* is fresh and unique."

"Thanks," I said. Then, because I felt the need to add this disclaimer almost anytime I talked about the book: "Though I still don't get why it's considered this 'great romance.'"

"None of them are your . . . cup of tea?" Ms. Gregoire reached for her travel mug and winked at me over its lid.

"No. I guess for a millisecond I thought Wickham wasn't too bad, but . . ." But I'd had my fill of charming guys who came on too strong in real life with Monroe. As for Darcy . . . he just upset and confused me. Thinking about him made my head ache, so I avoided it as much as possible. I hadn't even included his name in my last journal, and I definitely wasn't going to talk about him as a romantic interest right now.

"Wickham? Blech." Ms. Gregoire wrinkled her nose. "Where are you in the plot now?"

I hesitated a moment while deciding what answer to give. "Um, Lizzy is still visiting Mr. Collins and her friend Charlotte. I still can't believe poor Charlotte married that weirdo!" Though I understood that she hadn't had the luxury of choosing love over stability. "Darcy and his cousin Colonel Fitzwilliam are visiting his aunt next door. And the colonel just accidentally revealed to Lizzy that it was Darcy who ruined Bingley and Jane's relationship. What a jerk."

"Oh. Only there?" Ms. Gregoire set down her cup and

picked up a copy of the book. She paged through it until she reached that section, then *hmmm*ed as she looked at me over the cover.

I turned away from her piercing gaze, feeling my palms go sweaty. "Is that not far enough?" It's not like it was chapter two or something; it was halfway through a four-hundred-page book.

"Life here is just—it moves faster." Ms. Gregoire was fanning the pages, looking at them and shaking her head just a little. "I don't want you caught unprepared."

"Unprepared? How?" The parasols on her dress seemed to shimmer as she tapped the book against her knee. The fabric hadn't looked metallic before. Maybe the sun was hitting it differently now? Because it almost looked like they were twirling. The movement was hypnotic. I blinked and rubbed my eyes. "Is there some sort of *Pride and Prejudice* trivia contest coming up that I should know about?"

"No, I'm not talking academics—" She hesitated and frowned. I could practically see her choosing her words with care—weighing the taste of them on her tongue before speaking. "I'm talking *life*. Your life. But I don't want to overstep. I know you've already had a faculty member giving you lots of unsolicited advice this week."

I was torn between telling her "Overstep, please!" because hers was advice I'd actually welcome and listen to, and the shame of realizing that not only had the headmaster delivered that embarrassing lecture to me, but he'd talked to my teachers about it too. Shame won. I looked down as my cheeks heated. "I didn't know he'd said any-thing to you. . . ."

She reached over and squeezed my hand before sitting back and taking another sip from her mug. "Let's just say I won't be surprised if your next response journal is about Lady Catherine de Bourgh."

My chin shot up and my lips parted, because the pages I'd just handed over *were* about Darcy's aunt. I hadn't made that real-life connection. Sure, I'd been angry at Headmaster Williams when I wrote it, but . . . had I subconsciously chan-neled that into my writing? I thought about the words that filled my pages:

Lady Catherine gives out unwelcome advice like a Pez dis-penser: with every regal nod of her head. Telling Lizzy how to be better at piano, that she should have had a governess, that her younger sisters shouldn't be out in society attending balls before she and Jane are married. Telling Collins to marry and the sort of wife to find. Even her nephews aren't immune to her "guidance."

But she harps on Lizzy especially, always trying to make her feel small under the guise of "help." And how dare she? What gives her permission to make Lizzy a target? There's such a power imbalance between the two of them, and I hate a bully. Lizzy's pretty good at holding her own, using wit and confidence to prevent Lady Catherine's words from affecting her. I wonder if I'd be that strong.

I didn't need to wonder. I'd lived this. It *had* upset me. I continued to stare openmouthed at Ms. Gregoire as dots connected in my head.

"I—I—" I knew words. Lots of them. But none would come out of my mouth. I identified so strongly with Lizzy . . . and if Headmaster Williams was like Lady Catherine de Bourgh . . . Tingles spread up and down my back—the same way they had when Ms. Gregoire spoke about *Romeo and Juliet* being more than just a book. About us seeing ourselves in its pages. I threw my gaze on her coffee mug—waiting to see if it would shimmer and sparkle like it had that day. It didn't, but her dress had. And the book's cover had shocked me. My head felt dizzy, the room too stuffy. Ideas too oppressive. If I was Lizzy, if Headmaster Williams was Catherine de Bourgh, then who else . . .

No. I wasn't going there again. Absolutely not.

Ms. Gregoire set the novel on the desk beside her and stroked its cover with one gray-painted nail. "I choose this novel for *you* for particular reasons. . . . I don't want you to miss out on them."

"No." This time I said it out loud. Because books were books. They weren't real. They were words and pages and things that couldn't change, couldn't climb from between the covers. The whole *Romeo and Juliet* thing had just been first-day jitters plus my overactive imagination.

The reason I had goose bumps up and down my arms, the reason my head spun and the cover image of a man and woman in silhouette suddenly seemed to pop like 3-D, the reason Ms. Gregoire was looking at me so intently and nodding her head . . . low blood sugar. I was hungry. I'd stayed up too late and needed to eat.

"I'll read faster," I told Ms. Gregoire, because the sooner I was done with this book, the sooner I could stop searching for parallels to my life. "But I really need to get to lunch." I really needed to get to Eliza, to her reassurances that this was just me being fanciful, because, after all, what did I have to go on? Practically nothing. And as long as I didn't go looking for more connections, or acknowledge the ones I'd already experienced, then I could totally dismiss this as a by-product of my growling stomach.

"Merrilee." The urgency in Ms. Gregoire's voice made me freeze partway out of my chair. "Your story—don't let it scare you. You're here at Hero High for a reason. You're in this class for a reason. You have so much to contribute to this school, to your peers—don't let *anyone* tell you that's not true, or discourage you, or make you feel like you don't belong."

So clearly Headmaster Williams had shared quite a bit about his lecture with her. I appreciated her pep talk. I needed to hear it. "Thank you."

She tipped her head and smiled knowingly. "Your ending here isn't written yet—but I know it's going to be a glorious one."

I mirrored her smile. "And hopefully not for another three years, at graduation."

"But"—she added as I approached the door—"don't get bogged down in your own prejudices either. First impressions often don't tell the whole story. Keep an open mind—an open heart. And finish the book. You're about to get to one of my favorite parts."

I knew which part she meant. Now my smile was warped. My stomach was queasy. My farewell wave was a limp wiggling of fingers as I ran to the dining hall chased by those words and ideas.

I shrugged off Toby's "You okay?" and Curtis's "In trouble again, short stack?"

I ignored the scalpel-like glances Eliza aimed my way, probing and dissecting every word, gesture, and expression I contributed to our lunch table conversation. I'm not sure what conclusions she drew, because as I stood up, I couldn't recall a single topic that had been discussed.

"Oh, for Pete's sake, *what* are you thinking about?" she finally demanded, having followed me from the table to the salad bar. I needed a breadstick, or soft pretzel, or really any carbs in stick form. "You're clearly having some daydreamer crisis. Can you please tell me what it is?"

With an invitation like that, she couldn't possibly blame me for asking, "Do you think it's possible that I'm some sort of Lizzy Bennet reincarnation?"

She stopped still, her eyes and mouth screwing up into beautiful bafflement. "Wh-what?"

"You know how with Monroe things were like *Romeo and Juliet*—or at least they were for a little while. Do you think I'm now Lizzy?"

"No." Eliza's face went blank for a second as she processed

what I'd said and hopefully did a mental review of the book. I'd been summarizing it for her daily—she knew all about Lizzy's crew of sisters, the failed romance between Jane and Bingley—and haughty Darcy's part in that failure—the trip to Hunsford to visit Mr. Collins and Charlotte, and all of Catherine de Bourgh's lectures. But then she shook her head and the confusion returned. "No, I don't. Where is this coming from?"

I looked away from her, because I'd lied to Ms. Gregoire about how far I'd read. And there were two chapters I hadn't yet recounted for Eliza. The one in which Darcy makes a shocking, out-of-the-blue, insult-infested declaration of love for Lizzy. And the one where he follows up her understandable rejection with a letter that gives backstory—explaining his feelings for her and Wickham's malicious past. I hadn't been ready to explore *that* in response journals yet. And I certainly wasn't ready to get into it with Eliza, because I also hadn't told her about Fielding's declaration or email. It just felt too . . . personal. It didn't feel fair to expose him like that. Especially not with what he'd revealed about *me* and Hero High. And if he was keeping my secrets, I'd keep his.

Besides, that wasn't even what I was thinking about when I'd asked about book-life parallels. I was purposely *not* thinking about that part of the plot. There was no point in thinking about that part of the plot . . . seeing as how he'd called me a mistake in his email. I shook my head and gnawed a hunk off my pretzel. "I'm not talking about the romance—I just mean, like, Lizzy and her family and Headmaster Williams."

"Merri—you realize this sounds insane. I'm not using that word as ignorant slang; you truly sound delusional."

"I just think—"

"Fine, let's try this out. Who am I in your fantasy? Where do I fit? And based on the way you've been describing them, if you say Mary or Lydia, you know I won't forgive you."

That was easy—clearly Eliza was Lizzy's oldest sister and best friend, Jane, the prettiest girl around. Except . . . Jane was known for always being good-natured. She saw the best in everything and was almost unendurably optimistic. And Eliza . . . notsomuch. Maybe Lilly was really more of a Jane. Eliza could be . . . hmm.

Right now she was tapping her foot—a little smugly, I might add. When I shrugged, she pressed further. "And Toby? How would you cast *him*? Is he your Mr. Collins?"

Mr. Collins, Lizzy's awkward, intrusive, sycophantic cousin. The one she'd rejected. I turned the pretzel over in my hands, flinging salt everywhere. "That's not fair. Just because *you* don't get along with Toby, there's no reason to be cruel." And maybe Toby was my Jane—the whole injury thing had required me to take care of him like when Jane caught ill at Netherfield.

"So, zero for two." She propped a hand on her hip and raised an eyebrow. "Still liking this theory?"

"Maybe you're not in this recast. Maybe it's just me." . . . And Headmaster Williams. Except that wasn't much to build a theory on. And the longer we talked about it, the more ridiculous I felt. "Fine. I'm not Lizzy. It was just a stupid daydream. Happy now?"

Eliza studied me some more. The wrinkle at the top of her nose meant she didn't believe me. I braced myself for battle, setting my feet slightly wider and crossing my arms. But she only reached over and straightened my school tie. "I think you need more sleep."

That was it? She was going to let this go that easily? But she never let things go. I gave her a dubious smile as I said, "Probably."

"Can I just ask—"

Ah-ha! I knew it was too good to be true. Eliza was like a bloodhound, and there was no way she'd drop a trail before she made it to her mark.

I waved a hand. "Go ahead."

"Where is this coming from?"

"The headmaster, mostly." Almost entirely. If he could just say one thing that was supportive and without agenda, I'd drop the whole idea forever.

Eliza pressed her lips together, flattening her eyebrows into a streak of disapproval. "He needs to back off you. If he doesn't, and if you don't say something to your parents, I will."

Except Eliza didn't know my admission was a scam. At her parents' insistence, her application to Hero High had been on file since last year. She'd been accepted as a freshman and deferred admission to stay at Woodcreek Charter with me. I'm sure she'd written the essay and gotten recommendation letters and all of that. She didn't know that I'd unknowingly cheated and hadn't earned the right to matriculate.

"I'm fine." I linked my arm through hers so we were side by side and she couldn't read my face. Because while I wasn't lying, this next line didn't feel quite honest. "I didn't want the book thing to be true anyway. Happy?"

"Well, yes," she admitted as I paid and we made our way back to the table.

"You okay?" Toby mouthed as I sat back down.

I nodded and pasted on a grin, turning to see what new revolting concoction Lance and Curtis had created. "Yogurt, hot dog, and cheese doodles?" I asked, wrinkling my nose. "Please, for the sake of everyone else at this table, do *not* eat that. I do not want to see that coming back up."

"I'll second that motion," said Sera.

"First, you didn't include the relish or the Pop Rocks. Second, you think a little concoction like this is going to best me? Please, I've got a stomach of steel." Curtis grinned over the spoon he was raising to his mouth.

"Is that supposed to be an accomplishment?" asked Eliza. "Overriding the evolutionary response to rid the body of food it judges to be harmful?"

The spoon in Curtis's hand wavered before his grin disappeared and he set it back down. "Well, when you put it that way . . ."

But I missed whether he decided to flirt with food poisoning or listen to Eliza. Because something else had snagged my attention: Ava.

She had one of those look-at-me laughs, so even though she was seated across the cafeteria, I did. It would've been just a glancing glance—except she was standing with Fielding. I hadn't responded to his email from this morning. Was I supposed to? I sucked in a breath and gripped the edge of the table. My first instinct was to duck beneath it, but he wasn't paying any attention to me—he was entirely focused on her.

She was laughing *with* Fielding. Not *at* him. I did a double take. He was standing perpendicular to me. Almost as if he knew that four tables away, I'd be trying to see his face, so he'd made it impossible. The crisp line of his blazer held shoulders that were relaxed, not shoved stiffly backward—aka how he always stood when talking to me. And *more* interestingly, the corner of his mouth looked like . . . Could he be? Was it possible? I leaned to get a better view. Leaned a bit more, because it looked like—

"Careful there, Rowboat, you're going to end up in my . . . well, lap." Toby laughed and steadied me.

"Oh, your knee! Sorry."

"S'okay. I'm fine. Just don't want you landing on your head. . . . What are you looking at anyway?" He followed my gaze across the room and stopped laughing. "Are you and Fielding fighting again? I have to say, of all my friends, I never expected *he*'d be the one you didn't get along with. Ava, sure. Especially since she's been infatuated with Monroe for years. But Fielding? And you? I don't get it."

"It's fine. He hasn't done anything." I said it quickly, breathlessly. He'd done nothing new except *smile*. At someone who wasn't me. Which made me realize that he'd never smiled at me, or even *around* me. Like it was some big secret what his lips looked like when curved upward. Maybe his teeth were pointed like a vampire's or a werewolf's. That would actually explain a lot. But I wanted to see it. I wanted to see what happened to all his edges and angles when he wasn't actively scowling. Stupid Fielding and his stupid secret smile.

If he'd only *smiled* at me instead of going into his recycling can lecture—maybe we would've had a different story. Maybe I'd be reading a different book for punishment. Or maybe I wouldn't have been in a situation where I'd been punished at all.

"What's the deal with those two anyway?" I pointed with a piece of pretzel. Yesterday afternoon, he'd liked me; last night, I was mistake. Today . . . had he moved on to Ava? I dropped the rest of my pretzel on the table.

"Deal? There isn't one, as far as I know. He's probably just dropping off a note from his dad or something." Toby studied my face in a way that made me want to bury it in my yogurt cup. Instead I enacted a polite retreat: hiding behind my water bottle. But his eyes still narrowed in that *I know you too well* way. "Why? Want me to find out?"

Hannah bumped into my other side. I hadn't realized she'd scooted her chair so close, but she was practically nose-to-yogurt cup. "Oooh! Who are we talking about? I can find out too!"

"I got you covered," said Curtis, leaning across the table and creating a drumroll with his fingers. "Her dad's prez of the school board. His is the headmaster. Ergo, they end up waiting around for a lot of the same meetings and events."

He settled back in his seat and shrugged. "If she's finally over Monroe, I could see them happening."

"Oh." I may have sputtered a little bit of water onto the table. And inhaled some as well. I glued my eyes on our lunch debris as I choked and coughed, because I didn't want to see if Hannah and Toby approved of an Ava-Fielding ship.

Reaching below the table, I snaked a hand into my bag and stroked the cover of *Pride and Prejudice*. One thing was certain: I had to finish it as fast as possible—I needed to know how it ended.

31

onroe's suspension ended Wednesday, and so did the brief respite from his texts: I need to see you. We need to talk, love. Fine, I'll find you. By lunch, I was either ready to join the spymaster ranks of Inspector Gadget and James Bond, or I was ready to have a double-O meltdown. I'd spent the past four hours attempting to peek around corners or creep in and out of classrooms.

"What are you doing?" Eliza asked. "You've been weird all day."

"Skulking," I answered, trying to keep my voice light even though my hands were shaking. "And skulduggery."

"Well, stop it. You've already gotten in more than your share of trouble."

I rolled my eyes at Eliza and they landed on *him*. Not Monroe him. *Him* him. The other person I wasn't prepared to see. The person whose email had spent the past thirty-six hours cycling through my head like one of those scrolling billboards that bends around corners in Times Square.

Fielding wasn't even walking toward me. I mean, he was headed my direction, but not on the same path. So unless he went on a rule-breaking jog across the lawn, we weren't going to have to interact.

Didn't matter. I went full sweaty and dry mouth. My pulse soared. Like the butterflies from my stomach had launched an invasion on my veins, stampeding and leaving me breathless and reckless. And while my brain screamed adrenaline-laced messages to *run!* and *hide!* my defiant feet dragged to nearly a stop. My rebel eyes stayed glued to him. And my heart . . . it squished. Or maybe it squashed? Regardless, it beat in ways that made my chest feel too tight.

True to pattern, since I was a five-ish feet of pure panic, Fielding noticed me. His humiliation-seeking radar locked on me and didn't let go. His brown gaze meshed with my gray-blue, and even from across the lawn, I was caught like burrs tangling up in a golden retriever's coat. His eyebrows drew in, and his shoulders shifted from their perfect posture—creeping up toward his ears.

Maybe I wasn't the only one who didn't know how to handle it now that too much honesty and vulnerability clogged the air between us. Though it was lopsided vulnerability: all the confessions—all the declarations—had come in one direction, from him to me. And maybe he needed reassurance, needed to hear me say I wouldn't use that arsenal of emotions and secrets against him.

I offered him a thumbs-up—and immediately regretted it. Completely uncool. There was a good reason that the last time I'd done a non-emoji version of the thumbs-up was when I was eight and posing next to a birthday cake. But this realization came a few seconds too late—because his eyes had dipped from mine to my hand before pulling back up.

Then again, maybe me in goober form was what he needed? Because the left corner of his mouth lifted in response. Not a smile. Not really. But it was in the smile family—a second cousin twice removed or something. And the drum inside my chest didn't care about the difference. It squished. This was definitely a squish. One so powerful it made me stumble over my feet, or a sidewalk tile, or the idea that I'd been a shortsighted idiot when it came to him.

Curtis caught my arm. "Whoa, short stack. Steady there."

I didn't feel steady at all. My worldview was going through seismic shifts—it felt only right that the ground beneath my feet should be tilting as well. I felt like Lizzy must have when she took a walk after reading Darcy's letter and realized how wrong she'd been about so much. How wrong she'd been about Darcy and his feelings. It took me an extra second or two to find my balance and the courage to look back over to where Fielding had been standing. By the time I did, the moment had passed. He had continued on his way.

I'd just come from English class, where Ms. Gregoire had handed out copies of the letters we'd written about *Romeo and Juliet* on the first day of class. "Now that we've finished reading the play," she'd said, "I'd like you all to reread and write a response to your reflections from our first day together."

Instead of handing me a letter, she'd paused at my desk. "Since you and I have already discussed the evolution of your feelings about the play, Merri, I know this assignment will be more personally meaningful if you focus on *Pride and Prejudice* instead. Even if you're not quite finished yet."

Since the very thought of anything Romeo-related made me want to run for the closest paper shredder, I was game. I'd wanted to write about Lizzy's initial bias against Darcy, or about the chapters I'd read last night, where Lizzy returns home and fills Jane in on everything that had gone down with her and Darcy while she was at Hunsford. How I still hadn't found the words or time to tell *my* sisters or Eliza about Fielding's Darcy-style declaration and email. Lilly, because she'd been spending the night at Trent's lately. Rory, because our relationship wasn't really the secret-sharing type. And Eliza . . . *honestly*, because I thought she'd take *my* side. And I didn't think I deserved it. I wanted a Jane-like reaction. Jane had worried about Darcy's hurt feelings and disappointment. The good news, I'd reassured myself as I wrote page-filling nonsense about the trip to Derbyshire that Lizzy had been invited to take with her aunt and uncle, was that Fielding barely knew me. It's not like he could really care that much about my rejection. As he'd written, I was "a mistake." He'd probably already moved on to Ava.

I may have even shot her a glare across the classroom as I thought this; if so, she'd definitely smirked in return.

The whole time I'd been pretending to do the assignment, I'd had a sinking feeling in my stomach. It was the type of plunge that occurred when I was standing on the end of our diving board and Rory or Toby snuck up behind me and bounced. Like gravity was no longer something

I understood—like it was too late to slow down, go back, or change the crash-splash outcome. It felt a lot like the moment I'd just experienced on the path with Fielding—one I was still experiencing, as I scanned the yard for any glimpse of his back.

32

I hoped Lilly's future mother-in-law would never run for president, because I would not wish Secret Service coverage on my worst enemy. My friends meant well—but from the moment Toby overhead Eliza asking me, "Wait . . . *why* are you skulking and skulduggering?" he knew.

"She doesn't want to see Monroe. He's back in school now, isn't he?" Toby put a hand on my elbow and pulled me to the side of the path. "That's why you're so skittish today. You practically jumped out of your skin when Curtis knocked over that book in English. And you went white when I surprised you at your locker this morning. What's going on?"

"I—I . . ." My voice came out as a squeak and I held out my phone, cued to Monroe's text messages. "I've just said everything I want to say . . . and I don't think he's heard any of it."

"Block his number," said Toby.

"And we've got your back," added Lance. "Okay?"

I agreed. And then it—all privacy and breathing room—was over.

Twenty-four hours later, I was still marveling at the speed at which they'd organized themselves into teams to walk me to and from every class. When I got up to get some salad dressing at lunch on Thursday, Hannah came with me. Lance shadowed me to the water cooler when I needed to refill my bottle. Toby decided it would just be easier to keep his books in my locker, since he was accompanying me on all trips to spin its dial.

But when I reached for the girls' bathroom pass in math and Curtis grabbed the guys', I'd had enough. "Seriously? I've been potty-trained for thirteen years—I've got this," I told him. "Honest."

Which of course meant that Monroe was waiting in the hall when I shouldered the door open, still drying my hands on my shirt in avoidance of the world's slowest hand dryer.

"Merrilee, love, we need to talk." He was still dark curls and Siberian husky eyes—but today he looked more like an under-groomed Pekingese than an artfully styled emo-stud. Clearly there had been some frustrated hair tugging going on. And clearly I was over him, since I felt less than zero empathy and didn't hesitate before answering.

"No. Nope. Not even a little." Damp or not, I used one of my hands to push him out of my way. He didn't move.

"Please," Monroe begged. "I've been out of my mind this last week. I need you—"

"You really don't. And I really don't need or want you." He was tall; I wasn't. This wasn't news to me. But I hadn't realized he was the type of guy who would use that size difference to his advantage. That he'd think it was acceptable or even remotely okay to cage me in the corner behind the bathroom door with his wide shoulders, kicking one of his feet between mine and looming over me with angry eyes and a furrowed brow. This stance and expression were every bit as dramatic as all his declarations of feelings and his theatrics during our breakup.

I couldn't believe I'd really found the pretty words and big, flashy, rash deeds romantic. In that moment, I found it threatening. And I was more than a little sad that I'd given my first kiss to a guy who didn't know me well enough to know I'd *hate* my size being used against me.

Or if he did know—he didn't care.

"I wasn't done," he said, leaning down so his fetid breath hit my forehead. "I need you to talk to the director. Take the blame. Tell him you made me do it. Say whatever you need to to get my part back. I *have* to be Romeo. I was born for that role."

Maybe he was—because this was all tragically pathetic. And what was *Romeo and Juliet* about, if not reckless actions and failure to take responsibility? Qualities I'd also ascribed to Wickham in my last reaction journal—clearly the literary world was lousy with this stupid species of men. The real world too, since Monroe was an A-plus expert in both.

"No." I kicked at his foot. "And move!"

"Yes," he continued. "It'll be like when Juliet goes to—"

"Oh, wrong answer." Because anything Juliet did, I would do the opposite. I'd outlined my paper on the play last night— my topic was the lack of strong, supportive female influences in Juliet's life. Maybe if she'd had a mother who paid attention—like mine, who'd brought me cocoa the night before and then held my copy of *Pride and Prejudice* hostage until breakfast because "You haven't been sleeping well lately, and

I know you, you'll stay up all night reading"—or an example of a healthy relationship like Lilly and Trent, or a friend like an Eliza, a Hannah, a Sera, heck, even a Rory—or a Jane Bennet. Maybe if Juliet had had anyone in her life who listened or told her she could be more and deserved more than a boy who climbed in through her window and gave her lots of poetry and empty promises . . . maybe then she would've found or fought her way to a happily ever after.

I scowled up at Monroe—wondering if he realized that sometimes the littlest dogs had the sharpest bites. "I'm not playing this game anymore. Let me go."

He stepped closer. His knee brushed the inside of my leg and I shivered—but not a good, anticipatory shiver, like when stomach butterflies flapped in giddy spirals. This was the shiver of them all dropping dead.

Monroe placed a hand on the wall on either side of my head. "I don't think you're listening. You *will* do this."

"Merrilee."

Only one person in the world said my name like that. Would I always be so aware of him? Would the sound of his voice always make my pulse fast-forward?

Monroe and I both turned to see Fielding standing in the hall, looking like an advertisement for prep school perfection. One that would make so many students promise every penny in their bank accounts plus their souls for a chance to be his classmate. At least, until he raised his eyebrows expectantly like he was doing now—as though he were waiting for me to salute or curtsy.

"Yes?" I wondered how this looked from his vantage

point—like a threat . . . or like we were about to make out. This mattered in a way that made the corners of my eyes smart.

"You're wanted in the office," he said.

"I am?" I ducked under Monroe's arm. He was too busy scowling at Fielding to try to stop me. Once I was safely on the other side of his armpit, I exhaled in relief, then inhaled in anticipatory anxiety. "Gah, what does Headmaster Williams want to lecture me on now?"

Fielding shrugged. "I'm just the messenger. Here's the note." He handed me a folded piece of white paper.

I frowned down at it. Hopefully it gave some sort of explanation for whatever wrong Headmaster Williams had decided I'd committed this time—but I wasn't going to read it in front of an audience—especially not an audience of an ex-boyfriend with reality and boundary problems and . . . well, Fielding.

I crumpled the note as I closed it in my fist. Fielding winced, and I fought the urge to roll my eyes. I bet he'd have a panic attack if he saw how I curled and folded and fidgeted with the church program each Sunday, so that by the end of service, it looked like remedial origami.

"Forget you, Merri," said Monroe. "I don't need you—there are other Capulets."

I whirled back toward him. "What does that even mean?" I asked. "Never mind, I don't want to know."

He grinned. "Wait and see—I *will* be Romeo."

"Good-bye, Monroe," I said, spinning on my heel and heading down the hallway toward the headmaster's office. I shuddered, trying to ignore the ominous tone in his parting words.

Fielding followed, but he didn't crowd me. He was far enough behind that when I unfolded the paper, I had to turn around and wait for him to catch up before I could wave it at him and ask, "What *is* this?"

"My calculus homework, actually. So if I could have it back before you rumple it any further, that would be much appreciated."

I tucked the pages by my side, out of the reach of his grasping fingers. Both because I wanted to avoid the frissons that always seemed to be exchanged when we touched, and because I was still in pre-punishment panic mode. "I don't understand. Why am I taking your homework to the office?"

"You're not. You don't actually have to go—" He exhaled loudly. "You looked like you wanted to get away from him. It was the best excuse I could think of. My homework was the only thing I had on me to use as an office note." He held out a hand again, but I was too busy catching up to respond. And my body was still in post-Monroe defensive mode. When Fielding stepped forward, I stepped back.

As I watched his mouth fold down with hurt, comprehension clicked into place, leaving me embarrassingly breathless when I said, "Wait. So, you—you *saved* me."

He looked at the floor. "That's a slight overstatement."

"Fine—but you were nice. Don't try to deny it!" I pointed at him with the rolled-up paper in my hand.

He snorted; it was a delightfully undignified noise. "Turns out I'm only a—What was it you called me, 'lower-caliber human'?—on Mondays. It's Thursday, so you're safe."

I giggled, then paused. "That was a joke, right?"

"Yes." The corners of his mouth flickered. Gah, so, so close to a smile. "But not a good one if you have to check."

"Keep practicing." I uncurled his homework—whoops—and smoothed it out against my stomach before handing it back. Just like I'd expected, *frissons* when our hands brushed. Ones that made us flinch away even as our eyes remained fixed on each other. Finally a door opened down the hall, breaking the spell.

"I should get back to class," I told him. "But thank you."

"Any time," he answered. There was nothing casual or throwaway about the word. Its sincerity practically echoed off the tile floor. "Any time, Merrilee."

33

You *live* on campus? For serious?"

"Well, not in the media lab." Sera blushed and giggled. Both were adorable. It made me want to study her, analyze how she could have so many of the same facial features as her brother, but how they could be so much softer and more welcoming on her. There was that same nose that so often pointed skyward on him. And those same rich brown eyes that I'd want to sink into . . . if his weren't always filled with icy judgment. "My house is on the far side of campus," she continued. "Behind the theater, near the health center."

"So there's literally no escaping school for you." I grimaced and drummed my fingers against the tablet we were supposed to be using to program something or other. It beeped in protest, and the screen turned red. Not good.

"Except for dance."

"True." And maybe that was why she spent so much time dancing—to get away from home. Except . . . Fielding had never been anything but kind to her. I mean, I'm sure he was still as obnoxious as siblings *should* be, but when he'd brought her shoe to Convocation that day and the way he talked about her in his email—he got bonus points for those.

Not that I was keeping score. He didn't need points. Bonus or not. I wasn't thinking about him. I definitely wasn't thinking about him after our run-in in the hall yesterday or my conversations three days ago with Ms. Gregoire and Eliza.

If *I* was a mistake, then any continuation of that line of thought would definitely be one.

"At least it's a short commute," I added. Though that meant those days Fielding drove me, he'd left campus to bring me back to it. Why would he . . . oh, right. That was back before he'd realized feelings for me were a mistake. I wanted to literally head-desk; instead I forced myself to pay attention to Sera.

"It's actually a pain when it's raining or snowing. It's a much longer walk from the house than the student lot. But I get to sleep later and never have to worry about a parking spot, so there's that."

I'd spent my first two periods yawning discreetly and pinching my legs to keep myself awake. Sleeping in sounded marvelous. "Those are pretty sweet perks."

"Do you want to come over after school? I mean, after practice? Cross-country and my Friday dance class get out around the same time. We could hang out?"

"Um, I—" I hadn't seen Fielding yet that day. Not even a glimpse of him between classes. And I knew just how impressive that feat was, because avoiding Monroe on campus still felt like a full-time job. One I was pretty darn good at, thank you very much. The only glimpses I'd seen of Monroe that day were near the art building and at the freshmen lockers as he chatted with a group of girls. Fielding? I hadn't even seen his shadow. Not that I was searching for him or anything.

"You don't have to." Sera looked down. The tips of her ears were as red as the screen of our still beeping tablet, and her shoulders were curled in like a poked pill bug. "I didn't mean to put you on the spot like that."

"No—it's not that. I want to. It's just . . . it's not *you*?" It was an excuse that was probably a bit too clearly aimed at the other members of her family, but I'd rather be honest and insult *them* than offend her.

"Oh!" Her chin popped up. "Fielding won't be home. My father too—he won't be there. No one else will be home."

I pulled on a grin. "Sounds good then."

"Perfect!" she replied with a smile that could've lit the moon. One that made me wish I'd ever seen a similar expression on her brother's face, made me wonder if he ever *had* had a similar expression. And if not, what it would take to get him to stop being so uptight all the time. Just the thought of it was exhausting.

"I don't know how you talked me into this." I laughed as I ended up splayed over the arm of the couch for the third time. The couch I should've been nowhere near, because we'd pushed it and all the other furniture clear across the room to make space for Sera to teach me a dance routine.

"I don't know either, but it was the best idea ever." She'd collapsed into a pile of giggles on the floor. A graceful pile of giggles in an adorably stylish dance outfit complete with gray ombre tights. My cross-country garb was laundry-day unchic. A pair of striped green leggings with a Haute Dog shirt I'd had to retire from store-wear because it had gotten holey. More holey than I'd realized, because I hadn't planned on sneak peeks of my fuchsia sports bra shining through.

I twitched it back into semirespectability and said, "I warned you that I wasn't coordinated."

"My stomach hurts from laughing." Sera paused to catch her breath and dab at her teary eyes. "I thought you were exaggerating."

"Not even a little." I peeled myself off the sofa and stretched to make sure that all my parts were still functional. It didn't look complicated when *she* did it. And that was the best part of this—getting to see how mind-blowingly *good* Sera was at dance. And watching her laugh. Her giggle—which was really the only way to describe her mouselike noises—curled into a cackle once she really got going, doubled over and hiccuping.

"We should stop before you get hurt. Or break something." She sniffed and pressed her lips together, still hiccuping. "I'm going to get us some water."

"Good idea. Maybe I'm not really that bad. Maybe I'm just dehydrated." I kept my face deadpan and watched Sera's eyes grow wide, but I could only hold the expression for a moment before cracking into a grin.

Her echoing hee-hee-*hic!* floated back down the hall as she trailed off toward the kitchen.

I set about trying to reassemble the topsy-turvy family room, pausing now and then to attempt at least *part* of the routine. I could do the individual pieces. Could step left, right, back and forward. My arms floated up and down—not as gracefully as Sera's, but they were capable of the movement. I could pivot and swing my hips.

I heard footsteps behind me. "Where does this lamp go?" I asked, still trying to combine a hip thrust left with an arm swing right.

"By the end table."

I froze. Arm still extended, hip still pushed out. I didn't want to turn around. Maybe if I stayed facing the back wall, Fielding would just go away?

"You weren't supposed to be here," I told him. "I checked."

I sounded like a petulant child. I braced myself for his retort. A very justified "I *live* here" or "You're in *my* house."

Instead he said, "I didn't mean to interrupt."

His words weren't accusatory—they were almost apologetic. It was his tone that made me stop posing like some sort of awkward flamingo and turn around. Now the only part of me that looked like a shrimp-loving bird were my super-pink cheeks. And the swatches of equally pink sports bra making an appearance through my shirt's extra ventilation. "Sera was, um—trying to teach me to dance." I fluttered my arms in some sort of doofus gesture that apparently was supposed to indicate dancing but really probably looked like a chicken trying to fly. In case it wasn't pathetically obvious, I added, "I'm not very good."

I ducked my chin and waited for the ridicule I knew him to be so talented at administering. I'd served myself up on a platter—all that was left was for him to feast on my humiliation.

"I hope she's more patient teaching *you* than she was when she tried to teach me."

"What?" The word bubbled out on a surprised laugh. "Sera tried to teach *you* to dance? You let her?"

"It was *one* time." The corner of his mouth twitched. "And let's just say I hope you've got more rhythm than I do, because she was *not* impressed, and I was doing my best. Honest."

I pressed a hand to my mouth, because if he wasn't going to laugh at me, it wasn't fair to laugh at him—but oh, I wanted to. "Can I get a demonstration?"

"Absolutely not."

"That's okay," I told him, peering up through my eyelashes. "I've got a pretty good imagination."

Now he was full-on laughing, and I was grinning. "Are you picturing me dancing? Stop! I forbid it." But instead of looking threatening, he did a mock leap as he returned a throw pillow to the couch. And looked super pleased when my grin dissolved into helpless chuckles.

But, gah, wait a minute. Was this flirting? Was I flirting with him? The peering, the banter, the prancing. When I stopped laughing and took him in as a whole, he was wearing the type of smile I'd wanted to see on him for so long. One that was open and warm and made it feel like the sunrise was tracing its way up my skin, leaving a path of heat behind.

"So that's what your smile looks like," I said. Because my brain had lost its filter. Or I'd just gone and lost my whole dang mind. As soon as I called attention to it, his smile fled, like that stupid groundhog on February second. Six more weeks of arctic chill. Which was a crime against humanity, because his smile was *that* beautiful. I wanted to commission Rory to capture it in a painting. One I'd hang on the back of my bedroom door and study all night.

Wait. *No.* I forced myself to think *just kidding*, in case he could read my thoughts. Because I was *a mistake*. This wasn't going to happen.

"Merrilee." His face and voice had gone serious. He was always so serious. I wanted to be a reason for him *not* to be so serious all the time. It felt like a challenge I could accomplish. One that would be worth the effort. Make him guffaw, make him joke, make him fill his mouth with marshmallows and do the Hokey-Pokey and run through lawn sprinklers and ride the park swings after sunset . . .

"Merrilee," he repeated, interrupting a perfectly good mental montage to ask, "Would you like to meet Fitz?" I stared at him blankly. "My dog?"

I blinked slowly. "Your dog's full name is Fitz Williams?"

The corners of his lips twitched. "I guess? I can't say we call him by his 'full name' that often."

"Fitz Williams?" I squeaked. Because hadn't he read *Pride and Prejudice*? Didn't he know . . . I shook my head.

"No, you don't want to meet him? He's somewhere around the house." Fielding turned away and cupped his hands around his mouth, "*Fitz!* Not that he ever comes when he's called."

His house.

I choked on a gasp or my tongue or the idea. Because the pieces clicked. And they kept falling, like a row of dominoes that were going to lie flat and reveal a message that read: *Hey, idiot, did you catch on yet?* All the ideas I'd been repressing. It wasn't just his dad being Lady Catherine de Bourgh, or Rory as maddening as Lydia. It wasn't just my kinship with Lizzy. It wasn't just his dog being named Fitz-dangit-Williams. Like *Fitzwilliam* Darcy. The parallels hadn't stopped with his declaration and emailed letter. They'd continued into the section I was reading—when Lizzy and Darcy are accidentally reunited while she's on vacation with her aunt and uncle. When she agrees to tour his ancestral mansion, Pemberley, after being reassured he isn't home.

Spoiler alert: he is.

"Are you okay?" Fielding asked, stepping closer and crinkling his brow. But not with criticism—with concern. The two looks were so different, and the current one disarmed me. I didn't want to be disarmed. Or charmed. I wanted him to prove me wrong. "Has Monroe bothered you any more?"

"No." It came out as a whisper. Monroe had completely ignored me. But I'd seen him a third time that day. Sitting by Rory in Convocation.

"No? To which question."

"Both." Though they were related. Monroe's sudden disappearance from my life . . . What if that wasn't a good thing? Not that I wanted him back—gag—but Pemberley, Fitzwilliam . . . a missing scoundrel. One who'd said he'd find "another Capulet"—could that be code for *another Bennet sister . . . aka another Campbell*? Because, if so, there was a whole separate *Pride and Prejudice* plot thread I could only pray was not being replicated right then.

"Merrilee?" Fielding held out a hand, but I backed away.

"Don't do this."

He stepped backward. "What am I doing?"

"Don't be nice to me now," I begged. "Don't go Darcy." The crinkles on Fielding's expression had transformed again. Now they were confusion. I wanted to create a map of all his expressions. Figure out the alchemy of earning the smiles and soft gazes. Except. Gah. No. I hadn't even finished the book!

"Merrilee, I—"

"I need to go. I think I need to go?"

"Are you sure you're okay? Can I do anything?"

I groaned and remembered one of the last Darcy-Lizzy details I'd read. "Promise you won't invite me fishing!"

"That I can promise," Fielding said. "But I really don't understand what's happening right now." He was all concern, his hands fisted on his shirt like he was trying not to reach for me—totally oblivious to the fact that he was crushing wrinkles into those starched sleeves.

"I've got to go."

"So, I figured you might be hungry, and since Eliza's not here to tell us sugar content—*oh!*" The dishes on Sera's tray clattered as she stopped short. Her eyes darting from her brother to me and back again. Taking in the fact that we were *both* frazzled. And while I may frazzle easily, I'd never seen him rumple.

"I'm sorry, I have to go," I told her, bending down to scoop my sweatshirt off the floor and trying to orient myself so I could remember which doorway lead to the front hall where I'd left my satchel.

"What did you do, Fielding?" She set the tray on a table and stomped toward him, hands on her hips and eyes furious.

"I honestly haven't got a clue." He turned from her to me. "But I sincerely apologize."

"You didn't—" I pivoted between them both. "He didn't. Nothing. It's me. I just—I figured something out."

"You don't need to defend him," Sera protested. "I know he's been perfectly awful to you since you started here. You're such a jerk, Fielding. Why do you have to ruin everything?"

"He really didn't!" I protested. "He's been nothing but kind today. Truly." I crossed fingers over my heart and gave her my most earnest basset-hound look. "Sorry."

I curtsied and exited. Because why not? Why not be awkward and make a strange situation even stranger? As my feet pounded across the quad toward the library, my brain raced even faster.

I didn't know how the story ended, but I knew what happened right after Lizzy's visit to Darcy's house. If Fielding was in fact Darcy and my life was a parallel to *Pride and Prejudice*, there was a more immediate danger than whatever was making my heart thump crazily at the thought of Fielding.

Because it was suddenly painfully obvious: Monroe wasn't Romeo. He never had been. He was Wickham. And what happened next in the book was that Wickham, Lizzy's ex-suitor, turned out to be a scoundrel—a truth that Darcy had revealed in his letter. A secret that Lizzy had kept secret. And because of that secrecy, Wickham was able to run away with her youngest sister. How many times had I compared mine to Lydia?

"Rory!" I burst through the heavy double doors of the library and bellowed her name across the oak shelves, marble floors, and stained-glass windows. My shout hung in the silence like dust motes and old-book smell, and I should have cringed under the ensuing scrutiny, but instead I was busy searching for my baby sister.

I exhaled when I spotted her at a side table. She was trying to duck behind a book. Her hands cupped across her forehead as she covered her eyes in a pose Lilly and I called "the ostrich."

"Oh, thank goodness." I modulated my voice to a much more reasonable volume as I approached her table. "I'm so glad you're here."

"What?" she demanded, sinking still lower in her seat. "What do you want?"

"Um." My skin began to prickle with the eyes of so many eavesdroppers. "To see you?"

She rolled her eyes and slammed her books and note-books into an angry, lopsided stack. "Is Dad here?"

I glanced at the clock. "Not for another five minutes."

"I was studying," she seethed. "And you just—you *humiliated me.* Why do you have to make everything into such a spectacle?" As she crammed her books into her bag, a yellow paper fell out. I only had time to read "Academic Warning" before she scooped it up and shoved it back in her front zipper pocket. She leapt up and stormed past me out the door.

I caught up with her on the front steps—which was really ideal. It gave us a bit of privacy to have the whole *Stay away from Wickham—I mean Monroe* conversation. But her body language didn't exactly scream, "I'm feeling chatty!" Before I figured out my opening—I mean, how do you tell your sister she plays the role of the fool in your life story?—Dad pulled up.

"Shotgun," I said weakly, but she ignored me, stomping down the steps and yanking open the front door. Even the way she clicked her seat belt sounded angry.

Except as soon as Dad asked her a question about her art project, she practically bloomed into a fountain of art lingo. Mediums and textures and lighting and shadow and all sorts of things that made sense and were important to her but weren't any language I spoke.

My head was full of *Pride and Prejudice.* I'd left off with Darcy and Lizzy at the Lambton inn. Lizzy had received a letter from home and been inconsolable, confessing to Darcy that Wickham had run off with her youngest sister—ruining her reputation and that of the family. Darcy felt "wretched" as he watched Lizzy's pain.

A day ago, I would never have dreamed it, but seeing the crinkle-cut concern Fielding had worn so nobly today . . . I could see him looking wretched. I could see him wretched with worry over *me*—and the image was warm, like sitting in a sunbeam with a lap full of dozing puppies. But that didn't mean it was worth Rory's ruin. *Why* had she been sitting with Monroe at Convocation? Why hadn't I pulled a Monroe and climbed over benches to stop it?

I had to prevent her from making a major mistake.

Which meant we needed to talk. It meant that Rory needed to shut up about perspective and proportion and Dad needed to hurry up and get us home.

It also meant I should probably prioritize finishing the book. Because as quickly as my heart spun and composed and imagined endings, my mind rejected and refused them.

My thoughts and feelings were such a tangle of contradictions and conflicts and *gah, why did Fielding have to be so kind today?* Why was that last glimpse of him—standing there in his wrinkled sleeves, watching helplessly while Sera berated him and I spouted nonsense and acted in ways that confirmed every one of his first judgments—why was that so endearing?

Why hadn't I listened better to Ms. Gregoire, and why had Eliza been *wrong*? Eliza wasn't ever supposed to be wrong. She had science on her side. And according to her, that always trumped imagination.

Apparently not.

"Merri, you getting out of the car tonight? Or just going to camp out until it's time to head back to school Monday morning?"

"Huh?" I looked up to see Dad grinning from his open car door. He was standing on the driveway. We were home, and I needed to do a Wickham intervention. "Oh, thanks for the ride."

I bolted from the backseat and ran into the house, calling a greeting to Mom as I toed off my sneakers and dashed up the stairs. I caught up with Rory in the hallway, snagging her arm and dragging her backward into my room as she squawked and protested. "What are you doing? What is *wrong* with you? Merrilee!"

I slammed my door shut behind us and leaned against it, ignoring the heads of the pushpins that were digging into my back as I trapped her in place. "We need to talk."

"Have you lost it?" Rory shook her short hair out of her face and glared down at me. Her hands were ridiculously strong from the clay work she did, and it was taking all my strength not to let her pry me out of her way. "If this is about that academic warning, I'm not talking about it with you, and don't you dare say anything to Mom and Dad."

"Oh, we *will* talk about that. But not right now." I set my feet wider and pushed my back even more firmly against the door. Since I was probably already going to have pin-shaped bruises, I'd at least make sure she heard me. "I need you to stay away from Monroe. I know he's handsome, but he's not—he's not a good guy for you." He wasn't a good guy for *anyone*, but I couldn't go into all that right now. Nothing about her death looks and pinching fingers communicated that she'd be open to hearing me get vulnerable and confess how badly he'd treated me. "He's really a jerk. You have to believe me."

Her eyes and lips thinned to sharp lines. "What are you talking about?"

"I know things." I nodded like a bobblehead. Bookish things, but about a book she hadn't read, so there was no real need to complicate that by trying to explain. "And Ms. Gregoire agrees with me."

"You *know* things? And one of these things you *know* is that I need to stay away from Monroe? And you discussed this with *our English teacher*? Well, guess what, Merrilee? Regardless of what you think you know, I don't spend all my time pining after guys who are in love with you."

"Guys? I'm talking about *one* guy. I'm only talking about Monroe. I only have one ex." Except there was also a dark-haired, dark-eyed, *not* dark-hearted boy who'd recently confessed to some feelings. . . . "Have you been reading my email?" No. I'd logged out. I knew I'd logged out.

"Oh, get a clue." Rory's voice had dropped to whisper-angry. Which was the apex in the hierarchy of her rage. Typically when she reached this point, I wanted to be as far away as possible. She glanced behind me at the balcony—like maybe she was considering making a break for it via that exit. Or maybe studying the house next door? It made me wonder, not for the first time, if her childhood crush on "Twoby" was really past tense.

"Toby would agree with me," I said.

Her face went ashy as she whipped around to glare at me. "I don't need your leftovers. I don't need you discussing me with our teachers. I don't need your life, or your friends."

"I didn't say you did." Though maybe I had implied it a little.

"I've made my own." She lifted her chin. "In fact, I'm sleeping over Clara's house tonight."

"Clara's? You promise? And promise that you won't go near Monroe."

"I'm sleeping over Clara's house," she repeated. "Which means you're going to have to cover my shift at the store tomorrow."

Normally I'd protest. Or I'd like to think that normally I'd protest. But not when faced with whisper-anger. Not when I'd just really insulted her. "Fine. But you owe me next time I need you to cover."

"Whatever." Rory yanked on my arm again, and this time I let her budge me. "Some of us actually *do* have plans."

I exhaled. Her plans were for gossipy girl time. Not to run away with Monroe/Wickham and throw the family into an uproar. Leaving Lizzy crying and Darcy wretched. And then . . . I didn't know. I had to read the rest first.

"I've got plans too!" I called after her. "Important ones." Ones that involved cream soda, snacks, comfy PJs, a certain book, and finding out just what happened next.

34

ory didn't say good-bye before leaving. Not that I would've looked up from my book to acknowledge her. I only took a break for dinner and when Gatsby went full howl-protest because he wanted a walk. Even then, I told him, "Make this quick," as I knotted my bathrobe over PJs, jammed my socked feet into flip-flops, and clipped his leash.

Gatsby, however, would not be hurried. He was doing a close inspection of every shrub on our block and being tinkle-indecisive. "Come on, boy!" I urged. "I just need to know if they ever find Wickham and Lydia." Somewhere between Mrs. Bennet's panic and Mr. Bennet's trip to search for his youngest daughter, I'd realized Rory *hadn't* promised me about Clara's house or staying away from Monroe. Which, of course, had me whipping out my phone to demand a vow, but she didn't answer my first two calls. It went straight to voice mail on the third.

"Merrilee?"

I jumped and whirled around with my finger on the trigger of the pepper spray attached to the leash. Gatsby whirled too—yanking me in the direction of the voice so that I was a pepper-spray wielding projectile before I realized that, as usual, it was me: mess; Fielding: witness.

"Oh. Hi. Sorry I almost Maced you."

He shrugged stiffly. "No harm done. It's good that you're prepared."

I tilted my head and wanted to push him beneath a streetlamp, because I didn't detect any sarcasm in his voice, but we lived in the sleepiest town in the world, so he must've been mocking. I only carried the spray because Eliza had made me promise. But once upon a stupid idea, Toby and I had tested it on ourselves, and yeah, Fielding would *not* be teasing if I'd pulled the trigger.

"What are you doing here?" I asked. "I promise you, I don't need a ride anywhere."

"Right, because my sole reason for being in your neighborhood is to function as your taxi service?" But even this was lighter—like it might be accompanied by a nudge and a wink if he were the type to do those things. "I was dropping off Toby's lacrosse equipment. It was still all in his locker, and Lance thought it was starting to stink."

I laughed. "You had a game tonight, right? Did you win?"

"Nope. It's hard when your top scorer is out for the season."

"Poor Toby." I glanced over at his window. His lights were on, but the door was shut. Likely he was headphones-deep in keyboard composing.

Fielding nodded, and then we were quiet except for Gatsby's snuffles. Gats sniffed in circles as he searched for just the right spot, wrapping his leash around us both.

"So, did you need something?" I stepped over the leash again and pushed Gatsby away.

"Oh." Fielding faltered, and the hand he'd been using to scratch Gatsby's ears dropped. "No. Not really. I just saw you and thought I should say hi. Especially after you ran off earlier."

Thought he *should*. Not wanted to. Gatsby was nudging Fielding's palm with his snout, trying to get those feel-good scratches back. I knew how he felt, because part of me wanted to poke at him and see if I could ever possibly revive some of his interest. I didn't want to be a *should*. Or a mistake.

We were both ignoring Gatsby at this point. I was too busy looking at the stars and blinking in attempts to keep my eyes dry. We'd had such a good moment that afternoon. Then I went and ruined it with weirdness. In the book, when Lizzy had said good-bye to Darcy in the Lambton inn, she "felt how improbable it was that they should ever see each other again on such terms of cordiality." I felt the same way; Fielding and I had missed our chance at friendship or more. The day had just been a sad preview of what I couldn't have.

Except instead of leaving, he stepped closer. "Merrilee—"

"Wait," I interrupted, because I still had eighty pages left in the book. I hadn't found out if Lydia got rescued or Lizzy got kissed—but the intense look on Fielding's face wasn't one he'd give to someone who was a casual acquaintance, or even "just" a friend. "I know you said I was a mistake. But . . . put me out of my misery. Am I reading this wrong?"

"What?" His eyebrows pulled together. "What are you talking about?"

"In your email. You said *this*"—I gestured between us—"was a mistake."

"No." Fielding shook his head emphatically. "Not *you*. Never you. How I went about telling you how I feel was a mistake. You are . . ."

My phone chimed and buzzed in my pocket, shattering the moment and Fielding's statement.

I am . . . ? I am what? I wanted to shake him until he spit out a word. Hopefully a complimentary one. But *feel* was present tense, not past. The emotion in my chest was a lot like hope. My phone vibrated and beeped again. And again. And again. *Rory!*

"Hold that thought," I said. As I reached for my phone, Gatsby's leash hit the back of my knees. Before I could nudge it down low enough to step over, he'd lapped me again—this time at thigh height. "Stop it, Gatsby!" My next two words were "sit" and "heel," but he must've heard "squirrel" or "lunge like there's free steaks"—because he yanked forward, pulling me with him. I only traveled the space of eighteen inches before I was halted by a collision with a hard object. Fielding's chest.

His hands shot up to steady me, then he reached back and grabbed Gatsby's collar. "Stay!"

I was planning on it. With my cheek against his chest and my hands fully Velcroed to his pecs, I had no intention of moving. But once my brain stopped being clouded by phero-mones, I realized that the order had been for the dog, not me. With much reluctance, I peeled myself from him and looked at my phone screen.

Whatever Curtis had texted me about five times had better be dang important.

Hey short stack—Khalil just sent me these photos.

You might want to call your sister.

Monroe's parties are always wild. No way that's not getting busted.

There were pictures in the last two texts, but from their thumbnails, all I could see was a dark room filled with people. I tapped to zoom in, and there was Rory in full Lydia-esque glory, sitting beside Monroe on the edge of a stage. In the second photo, she was laughing and standing between Styrofoam columns. "I knew she was lying!" I grumbled as I texted back Do you have an address?

"That's the theater. Hero High's theater." I hadn't realized Fielding was so close until I heard his voice over my shoulder, his breath ghosting across my cheek as he studied the photo on my phone. "What's going on?"

"I don't suppose they're supposed to be there?"

"No. The theater should be locked. There wasn't even rehearsal today. Someone stole all the costumes last night, so the director canceled practice. They'd have to have broken in. Who'd be stupid enough to go to a party at the school?"

Curtis's response came then—the answer filling my screen. Here's what Khalil sent:

It was a screenshot of text followed by five pictures. The two with my sister, then one of the stage with Monroe front and center, and two group shots of smiling people holding red cups. Above them read: Party of the year is going on now @ Hero High theater. Romeo was a rebel. Are you? #RogueRomeo

"Who's stupid enough? All these people. And my sister apparently. Plus Monroe. Do I have great taste in exes or what?" And, *really*, was it necessary for Rory to go so literal with her Lydia impersonation—running off with Monroe/Wickham and putting herself in a compromising position? I mean, I guess not *compromising* like Lydia's was compromising—it's not like she agreed to elope with a man who had no intention of marrying her—but nothing about this was smart. I'd have accused her of reading the book and doing it on purpose, except Rory never read anything without a grade to her head.

"Let's go," said Fielding. When he pointed to his car, I didn't hesitate to load Gatsby in the backseat and grab shotgun. I knew my parents wouldn't worry. They'd assume Gats and I had run into Toby on our walk.

I thought of my copy of *Pride and Prejudice*, patiently waiting on my pillow. I guess finding out whether or not book-Lydia got rescued would have to wait until we'd saved the real-life one.

35

Sometimes Gatsby got carsick. My pup was like me—he had a delicate stomach. Luckily he seemed content to rest his head on top of Fielding's seat and pant heavily. I was turning around from checking on him when Fielding's phone pinged in the cup holder. I wasn't planning on text-peeping, but once I *did* glance (involuntarily) at the screen and saw that it was a picture of Rory, all bets were off. (Other people's privacy didn't exist when it came to my sisters' well-being.) I grabbed his phone—it was a close-up of Rory, which made me wonder how many people were actually at this party if all the pictures were of my sister. In this one, she was holding a paintbrush. And the black and yellow smudges on her face, arms, and shirt—my shirt!—made it pretty clear that she'd actually been using it.

Vandalism. We've got her. She's totally kicked out. Goodbye interlopers.

It didn't matter who'd sent it—okay, it did. Ava. But it definitely mattered that she was sending this message-photo combo to the headmaster's son. That she assumed there was a "we" between them and they had a common goal of getting my sister—and I'm sure me as well—*out*. It mattered that just three minutes ago I'd thought a different "we" might be possible: me plus Fielding.

I may not have *been* a mistake, but I'd certainly made one.

"Stop the car!" I yelled.

"Merri?"

It was the first time he'd gone nickname on me, and I would've been delighted if ten seconds prior I hadn't decided to hate him again. "Stop the car, I'm getting out."

"But it's closer to the theater if I park by the gym. We're barely even on campus."

"Fine, don't stop, but I'm still getting out." I reached for the handle, and he swore, applying a tyrannosaurus stomp to the brakes. In the backseat, Gatsby yelped as he slid along the seat, claws scrabbling and drool slinging.

I shoved Fielding's phone at his chest, willing myself *not* to feel the sparks when his fingers closed over mine. "Was it all some sort of trick?" I demanded. "Make me fall for you or trust you so that you could get us kicked out?"

I didn't wait for his answer, just yanked my hand from beneath his and then threw the door open and myself out into the night. Gatsby leapt over the console and followed.

"Merrilee! Merri! Wait!"

Nope. No way. I didn't follow orders from backstabbers.

Campus at night was *weird*. The avenue of trees, which looked so dignified in the day, was spooky instead of stately. The branches all felt like they were reaching down to grab at me instead of guiding me down the road to classes. Gatsby barked at every shadow. The sound of it made things skitter away in the dark.

I ran. And while I was grateful to cross-country for new speed and endurance, I was less grateful to past-Merri for thinking it was a smart idea to take Gatsby out in her bathrobe because *It's not like anyone will see me.* And even less grateful for past-Merri tying that bathrobe over a tank top and sleep shorts. Short sleep shorts. And *just* a tank. While I wasn't as curvy as Lilly, it was less than comfortable to be running across campus without a bra.

I was going to kill Rory when I found her. In fact, I had a whole list of people I wanted to kill. It started with Fielding, but Monroe and Rory were on there too. And past-Merri as well, since flip-flops with socks were not comfortable or appropriate footwear for this adventure.

"Merrilee!" Fielding caught up. He reached out like he might grasp my arm, but then pulled back without touching me. "Please stop. You've got it wrong."

"Because I'm too dumb to understand your nefarious plan?" I glanced at his feet. No flip-flop sock-toe wedgies for him. He was wearing sneakers, but not with uniform khakis. With jeans. I hadn't noticed the jeans before. And I refused to notice them now. I definitely didn't want to buy a Ouija board just to call up the spirit of Levi Strauss and thank him for inventing denim. "How long have you been colluding with Ava to get us kicked out?"

"Merri—"

I was whispering. He was not. And while my whispers didn't quite qualify as actual whispers—Toby said my volume only ever turned down to a five—I was still quieter than him.

"Would you mind shutting up and disappearing so I can go find my sister?"

"I'm coming with you."

"No, you're not."

"I am."

"No—" I had a feeling we could stand there all night going back and forth. Voices edging up and toes inching toward each other until we were nose-to-nose and my cells were all crackling with a euphoric warning. I shook my head to clear the image. And turned down the path to the theater. "Fine. Do whatever you want. Just stay out of my way."

I reached for the door to the theater, and that's when I saw it:

Rogue Romeo

The paint on the sign was still wet, but I'd recognize the lettering anywhere. It was the same handwriting that graced the store's windows. Only instead of puppies and pumpkins, this sign had balconies and a curly-haired boy.

The only thing missing was a Juliet.

And I was dang sure not letting my sister be trapped in that character, or Lydia Bennet, or any role but herself.

36

When Toby and I had gone through our movie-making phase in middle school, we'd been obsessed with green-screen technology. We'd film ourselves in superhero costumes, then change the background so we were under the sea, or on the moon, or behind news desks. The scene that greeted me when I opened the doors to Hero High's theater reminded me a lot of that.

It had all the trappings of any teen party from any teen movie: kids with cups and cell phones in laughing clusters. A couple kissing in a corner. A trio tossing a football. An idiot doing a stupid stunt for attention. But it all felt superimposed onto a theater background. The football toss was taking place across aisles. The kissing couple were leaning against the door to the ticket booth. The groups of revelers were standing and sitting around auditorium seats. And the idiot? He was trying to climb the stage curtains.

The major difference, however, was what was taking place onstage. And while most people weren't paying attention, there was a small clump of partygoers who were focused on the drama going down at center stage, where my sister and Monroe stood like gunslingers in a duel. She was armed with a paint cup. He had a bound script, which he was mangling in his clenched fist.

"Fine. We'll skip ahead," he seethed. He wasn't enunciating for an audience, but I'd joined the group around the front row and could hear him fine. "See if you can manage this: Act two! Scene two! Your line is 'Ay me!'" Monroe thrust the script in her direction.

"Get away from me! That's *not* my line," Rory snapped, taking a step backward. "I have no lines. I'm not doing this."

"Yes, you are. Why else do you think I invited you and your freshman friends?" Monroe edged into her space again and shook the script in her face. "Who needs the school play. Or Merri. If I can't have your sister, *you* will be my Juliet."

I winced. That wasn't subtle or kind. No girl wants to hear she's a consolation prize—I doubted even Wickham had told Lydia that she was a substitute Lizzy.

But my kid sister wasn't as flighty as Lydia, wasn't as easily flattered or conned. She was not a girl who'd fall for the empty charm and persuasion of a Wickham. Or succumb to the pressure and insults from the jerk in front of her. And with a surge of pride, I realized she'd *never* be a Juliet either—never tie her identity so tightly with some boy who seemed like her only reason for living. I didn't just have a good role model above me in birth order—my little sister was pretty impressive too.

It occurred to me I should actually tell her as much—after

we'd gotten out of here and I'd given her an epic lecture on being stupid enough to attend this party in the first place.

I watched as she snatched the script from his hand and chucked it offstage. It landed on the floor by the front row— right where Ava was sitting, her eyes glued on my ex. Not that I wasted any time glaring at her or looking around to see if Fielding had spotted her yet. No, my attention was pretty much riveted on the stage, where Rory had followed up her game of script-toss by flinging the contents of her paint cup over the boy invading her personal space.

Rory dropped the empty cup but brandished her brush like a weapon. "I have no interest in being your revenge on my sister or whatever your messed-up plan is. Do not try and touch me again."

Monroe was gaping, spitting out yellow paint that had apparently gotten in his mouth. It spattered onto the red velvet doublet of what could only be the stolen Romeo costume. "I could get any girl—"

"Good," I interjected from my spot on the floor. I tugged on Gatsby, who was in pup heaven with all the new smells and strangers to lick. "Then find one who's actually interested, and leave us alone."

Heads swiveled my way. There was way more interest in the stage than there'd been a few minutes ago. Phones were out and up. I was giving a performance I hadn't auditioned for and didn't want. And as an added bonus, I was doing so while wearing an outfit not fit for public consumption.

"You!" Monroe snarled. "You had your chance. You

weren't invited to my *Rogue Romeo*. You're not fit to play Juliet."

"And I don't want to." Gatsby spied Rory and jumped on the stage. I climbed awkwardly after him, trying to keep my robe closed. While I was careful to avoid the pool of paint at Monroe's feet, Gatsby was decorating the floor with yellow paw prints. "No offense, Monroe"—which was a lie, because I totally meant offense—"but you're not that good an actor. I'm not here for you; I'm here for my sister. And I'm going to walk out of this theater and forget that you even exist; because let's be real, you're not that memorable."

He gave an exaggerated scoff, paired with an exaggerated eye roll, his overacting so egregious that the audience snickered louder than his over-enunciated "You. Wish."

I couldn't believe I'd ever found him attractive. Yes, he had all the right pieces and they fit together nicely, but every part of him felt performative. He was like the lollipop version of grape—artificial and kind of gross. I shook my head. "No, I really, really don't."

The guy who'd been attempting to climb the curtains jumped down and started a slow clap, and a few other people joined in. I might have looked to see who, but I was distracted by Rory's tackle hug. "I'm so glad you're here."

For a second, I thought we were going to have a sister moment, but then she followed up with a panicked scan of the room. "Is Toby? Oh no, did you come with Toby? And what are you wearing? You're so embarrassing."

"Yes, I made Toby do his Tin Man knee-brace walk all

across campus." I ignored her criticism, because really there was no defense for my ugly-robe, braless, socks-with-flip-flops glory. Instead Gatsby and I followed her off the stage. "Are you okay?"

She nodded. "He said it was a 'Rogue Romeo Party.' I thought it might be some sort of avant-garde performance. He said he wanted my help with signs and sets—" Her voice cracked. "But Monroe only invited me to get back at you."

I was half tempted to climb back on that stage and slap his stupid, painted face. I might've if Gatsby hadn't chosen that moment to spot Fielding down the aisle and lunge for him like a long-lost friend.

"Heel," I hissed, and, "Rory, grab your stuff before this gets busted." I noticed the other students were doing the same. Apparently my and Monroe's showdown was the big finale, though he was still on the stage.

"Don't leave," he shouted. Though I was absolutely certain he was addressing the group of six chugging the contents of their cups as they headed for the back door. Not me. "I'm just about to get started. Sit down. I don't need anyone else. I'll do the whole show myself. Sit. Down!" He stomped from one side of the stage to the other. "Huck, get your butt in a chair. Mariah, I see you leaving. Get back in here. *'Two households, both alike'* . . ."

"And that is our cue to go," I told Rory.

"I'll drive you."

Gah. Fielding was like a mosquito that wouldn't stop buzzing around. If mosquitoes could look breathtaking while they betrayed you. Where was his coconspirator? I didn't see Ava anywhere, but she could've left in the first exodus.

I wanted to say no. Or say nothing at all. Or swat at him like he really was an insect. But a guy called out, "Security's coming!" and really, what choice did we have?

I grabbed Rory's arm and turned to Fielding. "Fine. But you're not doing *me* a favor. You're doing *her* one. Let's go. Go. Go. Go."

I took a step toward the entrance I'd used to barge into the theater—the heavy double doors at the top—but Fielding said, "No, this way."

And clasped my hand in his.

Clasped my hand in his.

My hand. His.

If lightning and carbonation had a baby, that's what it felt like when our skin met. His fingers folded over the back of my hand and mine did the same. My lungs stopped working, and so did my feet. Gatsby bumped into the backs of my legs and gave my bare knee a lick. I ignored him. I wanted to ignore *everything* but fingers and those sensations. To hold my breath and examine why there were fireworks detonated by his touch—why it had short circuited my brain, so that I was still saying, "Go, go, go," while I wasn't actually moving.

His thumb stroked the back of mine, and I wanted to purr. But instead I leaned into the tug he was giving me—and blinked back into the moment. Right. Party. Sister.

Security. And I still didn't know what role—if any—Fielding had played in all this.

He led us up onto the stage, around the paint puddle, and between several sets of curtains, each of which presented such a personal threat to Gatsby that he had to be cajoled to go through them. Then out a door I never would've found, which dumped us onto a dark path.

"Merri," he whispered as the door shut behind us. "I need you to know that I didn't—I wouldn't—I had nothing to do with Ava's text. Whatever her motives were—they weren't mine."

I wanted to believe him. To cling to his words like I was to his fingers. To bring his explanations into the light and examine them all. But first we needed to get through these dark woods. "We'll talk about it later," I said. "Now go."

In front of me, Fielding led us off the sidewalk and through the woods. Beside me, Gatsby was snuffling and whining to explore. Behind me, Rory was complaining. Above me, trees menaced with grabby skeletal branches. Beneath me, roots vied to be the ones to trip us. Around us, the air had chilled, and all the animal sounds I loved during cross-country had disappeared, wrapping us in silence—except for the fact that I hadn't stopped whispering "Go, go, go" under my breath as I clung to his hand and the leash and glanced back every couple of feet to make sure Rory was following.

When we stepped out of the woods and onto the main avenue, I exhaled. I could see Fielding's car. Which meant we were almost free. I turned around one last time, one last trio of "gos" on my lips—and crashed into his back.

"Stop," whispered Rory in a sigh of defeat as she bumped into me, jarring my hand from Fielding's. Gatsby gave a weak woof of protest.

I pushed Rory off me so I could push off Fielding. Undoing our train-wreck collision and blowing a strand of hair out of my face, I looked up, and immediately wished I hadn't. Wished hiding my face on Fielding's back was an option.

"Misses Campbell, Fielding, I am so disappointed to see you here."

The headmaster was backlit. The streetlamp pooled on his shoulders and bald head, but his eyes and mouth were obscured. Not that I needed to see his expression to know his disapproval; it dripped from his voice like mud and stung where it landed.

"Father, I can explain."

"You told me you were at Tobias May's house—not breaking and entering."

"We weren't," I said. And if he thought my "we" applied to Rory . . . well, so much the better.

"Are you trying to convince me there's not a party? Because I'm not an idiot, Miss Campbell. Campus security is breaking it up right now."

"Oh, there was a party all right," said Rory. "Monroe's *Rogue Romeo* thing—but it was stupid, and she wasn't even invited."

Rory *really* needed to get a handle on times when sibling rivalry was and wasn't appropriate, but at least for once, she might be helping, not hurting? Go, Lydia-instincts, go.

"If Monroe Stratford was throwing a party, you really want me to believe that you weren't invited?" He pointed a long finger at me. "It's a shame you didn't heed those warnings about your behavior, Merrilee; this school had so much it could've offered you."

My breath whistled out at his use of the past tense, and Gatsby's leash slipped from my hand.

"She wasn't," insisted Fielding, snatching it up and tugging my dog to his side. "I was. Ava invited me."

"Ava? As in daughter of the head of the school board?" His father's voice went up in surprise. And I winced, remembering just how that invitation had been framed.

"Yes. Merri was walking her dog when I got Ava's text. I dragged her along to pick up her sister. I mean, *look* at her—does she look like she's dressed for public?" I grasped the collar of my bathrobe and pulled it a little tighter. I knew I was a tie-dyed fashion nightmare, but had he really had to use *that* much disdain in his voice? While everyone scrutinized me and I wanted to die a chenille-covered death, Fielding added, "Her socks don't even match."

I whirled at him, hands on my hips. "What is it with you and my socks?"

It wouldn't have surprised me if Headmaster Williams assumed I was the type of person who thought bathrobes were appropriate party wear. From the way he looked at me, it wouldn't have surprised me if he thought I was the type of person who ate hair from shower drains.

But my parents could vouch that I'd been home all night, which they did after they got over the shock of their doorbell ringing at midnight and finding both their daughters on the wrong side of it, along with the headmaster *and* his son.

I snuck glances at Fielding throughout the interrogation. He was sitting on the opposite side of our dining room table—as far from me as he could get. And he didn't look back once. Not even when I was explaining how I ran into him on our street or ran *from* him at the school.

Whatever I'd thought I'd imagined between us must've been a jolt of adrenaline. Because all that was left now was the dull ache of those memories. I rubbed my hands together and waited while the adults sorted out our punishment.

"I have to ask, Headmaster Williams, is every student at the party going to merit a middle-of-the-night visit from you? Or have you singled out my daughters for any particular reason? Because while I appreciate you bringing them home, perhaps it's best to delay talk of punishment till the morning or Monday, when cooler heads prevail."

Headmaster Williams turned the color of Mom's tablecloth—red. "The handbook is very clear on matters like this."

That danged handbook . . . I wanted to gather up every copy and create a big bonfire. But I bet even if I did—even if I deleted every backed-up copy off every network—it'd still come back and haunt me like Sleeping Beauty's spindle.

He paused, and I felt like it was supposed to be for

dramatic effect, but really it just made me want to "accidentally" knock his cup of tea into his lap. "Expulsion. Underage drinking is an automatic expulsion."

"I see," said Mom, but she sounded way too calm. And while she wasn't a lawyer, she was Lilly's law school inspiration. This calm meant, *get out a fork and put on a bib, because you're about to eat your own words.* "Rory, were you drinking?"

"Only water," Rory answered. When Headmaster Williams blew out a breath, she continued. "Breathalyze me if you don't believe me. Was anyone else drinking? I don't know. I wasn't exactly conducting a poll. I spent most of the party painting."

"That's another thing," the headmaster argued. "Rory admitted to vandalizing school property by destroying the theater department's sets for the fall play."

"Destroying?" I snorted. "Oh, please. If Rory painted on them, then they're a thousand times better than they were before."

"Merri," Dad said. "Not helpful." But Rory looked over and mouthed "thanks," so I was still calling it a win.

"They were still trespassing," the headmaster insisted.

"They were," Mom agreed. "But if you set a precedent for expulsion for anyone who attended that party—even as briefly as Merri—then you'll also have to include your own son. And apparently the head of the school board's daughter. Who knows how many other students were apprehended by the campus security, but judging from what I've seen in the photos Merri was texted, it looks like dozens. Can you afford to lose dozens of students, Headmaster Williams?"

He gritted his jaw with a stubbornness I'd recognized in his son, but when I looked at Fielding, he was all raised eyebrows and deep exhales. He put a hand on his father's arm. "Dad."

Headmaster Williams shook him off. "Fielding, stay out of this."

"I *can't* stay out of this. It involved me too. Whatever punishment you give Merri, I'll need the same one, if not worse, since I'm the one who drove there." Even when saying my name and defending me, he wouldn't look my way. I wasn't sure what that meant, but it couldn't be good. "Maybe Mrs. Campbell is right—this is a decision better left for when you've had time to talk to the discipline board."

"Fine," Headmaster Williams said, rising to his feet. "I'll let you all get to bed. Enjoy your weekend. I'll see you girls Monday morning in my office."

37

f they gave awards for the longest, stressiest weekend, that one would have won gold, silver, and bronze. I was too anxious to sleep, to eat without gagging. Too stressed to *read*. I was a zombie at the store. I barely managed a "that's great" for Christina and an ear scratch for Marcie when the Makrises stopped by for a Howl-ween costume and so Christina could tell me about her soccer tournament.

I'd never been so relieved for a Monday morning, because there was no punishment worse than suspense.

It was somber on campus, and very little was happening by way of instruction. How could it, since every few minutes students were being fetched from or returned to class? Some came back weeping. Others silent and serious. Some had clearly imagined worse and were floppy with relief.

I would've loved to have known what Fielding thought—what *his* weekend had been like. I'd checked my phone and email obsessively, waiting for his full explanation of Ava's text. It hadn't come. And he was avoiding me. No, maybe "shunning" me was a better word? Because we'd passed each other on campus three times, but he hadn't looked my way or spoken to me once.

Maybe he blamed me for us getting caught. Maybe he remembered that he'd hated me and decided first impressions were the truest. Maybe my luckiest socks—purple with gummy bears, red with dragons—offended his sensibilities to such a degree that he couldn't stand to look at me.

Maybe he hadn't been innocent. Maybe he and Ava *had* had a nefarious plot to get rid of Rory and me. Maybe he was pissed it hadn't worked.

Gah, I hoped not. But I didn't know what else to believe.

The other person I didn't see was Monroe. But Hannah had an answer for that: he'd been expelled. His locker was already cleaned out. Hannah had a surprising amount of knowledge for someone who hadn't been at the party. So did Curtis. Lance looked bummed that he'd slept through the whole thing. Sera just looked embarrassed. Each time someone came back to class, she ducked in her seat—like she was afraid they'd blame her for her father's lectures and punishments.

As for Eliza—she was predictably annoyed that I'd gotten myself involved. "Is there a reason you didn't just *call* her? It's not like you actually *prevented* Rory from being punished, so what good came from you trespassing too?"

"I did. She didn't answer. And thank you for the pep talk." I turned around at our bio lab bench to face Toby. "Your turn. Feeling lecture-y? Because I definitely haven't had enough of those in the past forty-eight hours. Feel free to warm me up before I go for my sentencing with Headmaster Williams. I swear he's saving me for last on purpose."

Toby shook his head. "Stupid knee. I wish I could've

come with you." I laughed, because that was Toby to a T. He'd never cared about the punishment as long as he got to join me for the adventure. "I still can't believe Fielding went. I don't think he's ever gotten in trouble. Not even for, like, talking in class or forgetting homework."

"Great, and now he probably blames me for the big black mark on his record." Though I refused to care if he did or didn't. Not until I had answers.

"You didn't force him." Eliza shrugged, clearly considering the matter closed.

I hadn't forced him, that was true. I also hadn't listened when he wanted to tell me his *why*.

"My only regret is that Monroe got expelled before I could tell him off," added Eliza.

"Oh, no worries there. Rory and I both took care of that. You would've been impressed." But before I could elaborate or stage a reenactment, another office aide walked into the classroom. And this time, the name that was called out was mine.

I'm not sure why Headmaster Williams called for me when he clearly wasn't ready. There were two people sitting in chairs outside his office when I arrived, one wild-eyed and the other thumping her head against the molding. A third stood near them, red-eyed and makeup smeared. The plus side of this backlog of people was the gossip. Everyone knew his punishment before he went in. The downside was that we still *had* to go in.

The partygoers got two weeks of Saturday detentions. While this wasn't exactly what I'd call "fun," at least they were together. At least they weren't suspended or worse.

News of Monroe's expulsion was a perspective check that made *any* other punishment seem lenient. Word of his sentence spread through the campus like a chattering rush of floodwater. It curled around our ankles in whispers and messenger bubbles. People splashed in the news—titillated, shocked, scandalized, outraged, smug. It made my stomach turn.

As I waited in a chair outside Headmaster Williams's office, there was a small guilty part of me that exhaled with relief. I wouldn't have to run into Monroe on campus anymore. Wherever he ended up next, I hoped he was happier. And I hoped his parents finally started paying him attention or got him some help.

"Come in, Miss Campbell. Take a seat." After thirty minutes of being parked in the world's worst waiting room—without anything to read but the Reginald R. Hero High handbook—it was my turn to sit opposite Headmaster Williams's desk. I was fully prepared for my sentence. Sure, it might be tough for my parents to be without Rory or me in the store for the next two Saturdays, but as long as Lilly was available, they could make it work.

"Merrilee, as you and my son kept emphasizing, Friday night, you weren't attending the party."

I wasn't sure what sort of response this statement

required, so I just shifted in the giant chair. There'd been no offerings of beverages today, and there was no veneer of politeness to cloak his condescension.

"Ergo, it doesn't make sense for me to hand down the same punishment as the students who participated."

Wait, that wasn't how this was supposed to work. Spoilers, not surprises. Knowing what to expect had been the only thing keeping me vomit-free. My stomach somersaulted and I burped into my hand. "Excuse me."

Headmaster Williams curled his lips in disgust. "One week of after-school detention. During which time you are suspended from all sports practices."

Again, I wasn't sure if a response was required. If it were my parents, I'd have tried to bargain—but Headmaster Williams didn't look open to negotiation. I doubted he wanted my "That sounds fair" either. In fact, I was pretty sure my opinion was irrelevant, so I settled on an unsatisfying "Thank you, Headmaster."

Apparently they were the right words, because he nodded. "I do hope that now that Mr. Stratford is no longer a Hero High student, we'll see improvements in your behavior. If so, I'll be willing to forget all your indiscretions and attribute them to youthful ignorance." He paused again, but there was no way I was saying thank you for his insults. "But if your behavior continues to impact others, then you'll soon be joining Mr. Stratford on the path out of Hero High. Understood?"

Finally! A question! A clear indication of the type of

response he was looking for. I was so busy celebrating this fact that I almost forgot to answer. "Oh. Yes, sir. I understand."

He gestured for me to stand. And while I hadn't swallowed an etiquette book like his son, I was pretty sure politeness dictated that Headmaster Williams stand also. He didn't. Instead he said, "Please send in the next student on your way out."

I quashed my urge to bob a curtsy in his direction and instead gave a stiff nod before marching my gummy bear and dragon socks across the floor and out of his room. "You're up," I told the boy with messy hair sitting with his head bowed in the chair beside the door, "Don't worry, it's—"

But when the guy raised his head, I shut up and started worrying. Because Fielding looked wretched. Besides the uncharacteristically chaotic hair, he had under-eye circles that rivaled my own. And above them his eyes searched my face like a treasure map. He opened his mouth twice before asking, "Are you okay?"

There was so much to say, but no time. I looked at the closed door. Making the headmaster wait wouldn't count as being a good influence. "I'm fine. But you should go talk to your dad."

He stood, his body taut and tense as an unread book—and just as tempting. But he was a book I'd had to return to the library unread. I'd missed my chance.

"Merri, you have to hear me," he begged. "I didn't ask Ava for that text. She and I talked—way back over the summer—about how you and Rory shouldn't have been admitted. Not since I got to know you. I swear. Believe me."

"I do," I answered, but his father's warning about being a bad influence and Toby's comments about Fielding never having been in trouble before echoed as loud as my relief. "I'm glad. But go see your dad."

"Merri . . ." he said, raking a hand through his hair.

I shook my head. "Don't make him wait. I'll talk to you later."

38

B y "later" I had meant a general "time other than now."
But I should have assumed that if *I* received detentions for my role on Friday night, then Fielding would
receive identical detentions for his identical role.

I hadn't. And since I hadn't, I did a double take when
I walked in the small room off the library and found him
already sitting at one of the two rows of tables. We both offered
stiff waves and stiffer expressions as I took a seat at the table
in front of his. The proctor—the only other person in this den
of awkwardness—explained the rules: we could do homework,
or read, or nap. No talking. No phones.

I didn't know what Fielding was doing behind my back,
but my shoulder blades were creeping in and up, as though I
could form my own sort of turtle shell to hide inside.

The proctor, who I believe was also a math teacher, looked
back and forth between us. "Well, I'm not going to have a
problem with you two socializing, am I?"

"No, sir," Fielding said instantly. I shook my head.

"Good, then I'm going to get coffee."

Which made everything worse. Because now there was
no excuse for not talking, and there was so much to say—so

much potential—that I didn't want to say anything at all. I'd rather live in this state of anticipation and hope—make it my permanent mailing address—than open my mouth and risk everything falling to pieces if we said the wrong words. Because he and I were so good at saying the wrong words to each other. But either Fielding was functioning on a whole different wavelength or he'd swallowed a porcupine, because he cleared his throat four times. And I could feel his gaze on my neck like a laser beam. I tried to ignore it, truly I did. I got out my math book, my notebook, flipped to the right page, and even copied out the first problem.

He.

Cleared.

His.

Throat.

Again.

"Do you need a cough drop?" I asked without turning around. "I don't have one, but I bet you could go to the nurse."

"No." He sounded sheepish. "Merrilee . . ."

I turned halfway and met his gaze. And maybe he was just practicing my name, because he didn't follow up with anything else *or* look away. I couldn't either. But had I missed the part where I signed up for a high-intensity staring contest? One with no prize except stomach knots and sweaty palms?

I blinked. Then turned before I could get ensnared in that eye trap again. "Do you think you could turn down the volume on your glower? I'm trying to do math, and it's my hardest class."

"Oh. Right. Sorry." He tapped his hands a few times on the

edge of his table—the first time I'd ever seen him fidget. "Well, I'll just be back here."

If I could have any superpower it would be perfect comebacks. Well, speed-reading, then comebacks. Since my brain was ignoring all my demands that it *Be clever and quippy! Do it NOW!* I didn't say anything. Just did my best imitation of ignoring him while getting cozy with precalc.

I knew he was hunched forward on his table—could feel him so close behind me—but I wasn't sure why since I was absolutely, *absolutely* not turning around to look. But after the detention proctor popped in and looked us over and offered a thumbs-up before popping back out, Fielding climbed over the table to the seat beside mine. He tapped a pencil on my math notebook. "Those are actually—they're all correct."

I snatched the notebook away and then smoothed out the wrinkle that the snatching had created. "I said it was my 'hardest class,' not that I'm bad at it."

"You are very clearly *not* bad at it."

The surprise in his voice felt like a cheese grater on my confidence. He looked again at the paper in my hand and shook his head. Like, if he hadn't witnessed the miracle of me writing down numbers, he wouldn't have believed it could've occurred. Clearly he didn't even *need* to use words to insult. I'd thought we were past this.

I ground my teeth and slapped my notebook down on the tabletop. "I can't believe I'm going to pull this card, but—do you know what I scored on my entrance exam? I mean, you seem to know everything else about me, so did you look in my file? Do you know my IQ? Because the evaluator told me that it was 'so high that it would make all the so-called genius-dot-com code junkies cry into their matcha lattes.'"

His mouth twitched. "I'm pretty sure those weren't his exact words. But please do use that quote on your college apps or future business cards."

I glared at him.

He . . . smiled. Which was my own form of kryptonite. It froze me in place, and all I wanted to do was memorize that expression and live in the glowing feeling it created in my chest. "Merri, I didn't mean it as an insult, I promise. I was impressed. I barely managed a B in that class—by the skin of my teeth and with a few begged-for retests. It's not just *your* hardest class; it's the hardest class on campus."

"Oh." I offered him a tentative smile of my own and shifted my chair to the side so I could face him.

"I know you're smart, Merrilee. You can lump me in with the dot-com code junkies—because clearly you blow me away too."

"I didn't mean—I mean, I don't care about IQs and stuff like that. At all. I shouldn't have—"

"Do you believe me about Ava?" Fielding in interrupting mode was both startling and intense. I felt my eyes widen at the solemnity in his. "I swear the only conversation we had about you and Rory was back before the school year started. And we were *wrong*. I shouldn't have ever implied that you weren't intelligent enough to come here. I don't even know what a matcha latte is."

"Well, maybe after—" But my invitation was interrupted by the door opening. By the proctor blustering in with all the indignation in the world on his face and a boatload of spittle on his *"Shhhhhush."*

I needed a distraction, something that could actually pry my attention off the boy beside me and his sunshine smile. There was only one thing in my bag that could provide that, and it had about thirty unread pages. I pulled out *Pride and Prejudice* and settled in, tucking my feet up on the chair as I sank into the story—the vile Lady Catherine had just showed up uninvited at Lizzy's house, demanding that Lizzy assure her that she and Darcy weren't an item. Lizzy refused—out of stubbornness and dislike for his aunt, sadly not because she and Darcy had anything going on. But Lizzy's refusal set off a chain reaction—Lady Catherine then turned to Darcy to refute the news. And Darcy? He clung to this opening and went to see Lizzy—demanding to hear if her feelings had changed. Could she, would she return his love?

It's possible I sighed and swooned aloud as I reveled in pages where Lizzy and Darcy surrendered their prejudice and their respective pride, realized how false their first impressions were, and finally got together. In the movie in my mind, Lizzy wore the face I saw in the mirror every morning. And Darcy—he smiled like the guy beside me when Lizzy promised to be his.

They didn't even kiss. There was nothing actually steamy in their nineteenth-century courtship. Except there was. This was way more romantic, way more goose bumps and tingles and swoony than anything Blake and co. had ever done. Romeo didn't even belong in the same library as Darcy. But Fielding did.

Fielding deserved his own shelf or card catalog, because he was *like* Darcy, like I was *like* Lizzy—except, *more*.

Better. Truer. Realer.

And by the time our hour had run out, so had my confidence. My hands were sweaty. My throat was parched. My cheeks were sunburn red and eye contact with Fielding was out of the question, because what if he could guess what I'd just been imagining—about *him*? Instead of asking him to come try matcha with me, I ducked my head and wiggled a couple of weak fingers in his direction, squeaked out a "bye," and fled.

39

t was Lilly and Trent who picked me up. He told me about his own first detention—for speaking exclusively in pig latin for a whole day on a dare. A surprising, un-Trent-ish story, which made Lilly giggle. It made me like him more, especially when she said, "Say something in it," and he touched her face and responded, "Ouyay areyay ymay orldway."

And while he wasn't standing on benches in Convocation or sneaking into her bedroom to commit decorative-candle arson—he *was* romantic. Way more romantic, because his gesture was for Lilly, not for show.

This story might make its way into my MoH toast. But his detention story had reminded me of the Rhodes's connections with the school. I leaned forward from the backseat, interrupting the lingering red-light swoony-glance thing they had going on. "Change of plans. I need to stop at your mom's office."

"My mom?" asked Trent. "Do you mean *your* mom? The store?"

"Nope. Your mom. I need to talk to her."

"But—"

Lilly interrupted him with a hand on his arm. "She's got her stubborn face on; you might as well give in."

He did. And Lilly went on a coffee run while Trent sweet-talked his mom's assistant into squeezing me into her double-booked schedule. He turned around and smiled. "You're in."

I gave him an impulsive hug. "Trent, you are such a Bingley!"

He coughed and patted my back awkwardly. "I'm—I'm not sure if that's a compliment."

I pulled back and almost upended a table full of campaign buttons. "Oh, it is. I mean, maybe you're a Darcy to Lilly, but in my story, you're a Bingley, and he's a really good guy—just like you."

Trent beamed, and for the first time, I noticed it wasn't quite a plastic Ken doll grin. When he smiled big—smiled genuinely—it was a little crooked. I liked him better for it.

A freckled woman in a dark suit stepped around the corner. "The senator's ready for you now."

I took a deep breath and stood up, knitting my fingers together to keep from fidgeting or knocking anything else over.

"Wait," Trent said, and I paused, expecting something cheesy or sentimental. Instead he tipped his head. "You said—'in your story.' You've got Ms. Gregoire this year, don't you?"

I nodded.

He grinned again and gave a small nod of comprehension. "She's the best—we'll have to share *stories* sometime. I never would've met your sister if it weren't for her."

"But . . ." He and Lilly hadn't met in high school. Had they? And his emphasis on "stories"—did he mean that like I thought?

The assistant cleared her throat and tapped her watch. It might not have been subtle, but it was effective. I shot down the hallway after her.

Senator Rhodes was on the phone when I walked in. She nodded in acknowledgment and held up a finger for "one minute." I studied the walls while she finished her call. They were covered in photos and awards from local businesses, schools, scout troops, and politicians. Lots of people sure did like her, Fielding included. Had I ever even given her a chance?

"Merri. Hello. What can I do for you?" I wondered if she expected everyone who walked through her door to make a demand. How awful. Though I guess I was just as bad if it was a demand for info. She was looking at me with eyes that practically had the second hand ticking. Time was money or votes or something. And I didn't have the first or the eligibility for the second.

"Hi. I wanted to ask you something."

She spread her hands in a "go ahead" gesture.

"Could I have gotten into Hero High without you?"

I appreciated that she didn't answer right away. She took her time weighing the question—like it was as important to her as it was to me. Finally she rested her hands on her desk and met my eyes. "No."

I deflated a little. I'd assumed as much, but I hadn't truly wanted to hear it.

"Your scores, your entrance interview, all of your

paperwork was outstanding. Those alone should have granted you entry, and in a fair world they would've. But no, if I hadn't interceded, you and Rory would not have been admitted."

"Both of us?" Rory was a ridiculously gifted artist. There weren't many fourteen-year-olds who'd won art awards and had their work shown in fancy places I would be able to name if I was a better sister.

"The financials didn't work. When I went to the finance commitee and said that they would find the money—I had meant that I would endow you myself. They didn't take it that way, and they scraped together their aid packages, but I'm sure that's caused some resentment. Especially since you're girls."

There were so many things I needed to question, but that last one seemed oddest of all. "Because we're girls?"

"Financial aid is disproportionately awarded to males. When I saw they were actually going to support the entry of two wonderful young women without my intercession, I let it stand. But I'm sorry if that's been a problem."

"Why would you have paid for us?" This was perhaps most baffling of all. She hadn't even wanted me to be maid of honor, but she wanted to fund my tuition?

"You remind me of me."

I might have recoiled, but she just laughed. "Not in personality; I was never as much fun as you. But because I see in you something I saw in myself. You're special, Merrilee. Girls like you are going to change the world someday."

"*I'm* not going to be a politician." At least I didn't plan on it, but since I didn't have a plan for something I *would* do, maybe I shouldn't rule any option out. "And how can you sit there and act like you support me—you told me I wasn't even fit to be maid of honor and meddled in my love life."

"You may not believe this, but I'm sorry to hear you had a breakup."

"You're right," I said coolly. "I don't believe it."

She looked stricken. "My objection to your relationship with Monroe was purely apolitical. I've encountered the younger Mr. Stratford at a few events . . . and, well, he seemed rather like an apple off his father's tree. You deserve better than him, Merrilee."

"I don't mean to be rude," I said—but maybe I did mean to, because my voice was tight and my teeth were grinding. "But why do you even care?"

"Why—I like you. I love Lillian, but I really care for you and Aurora too."

I raised an eyebrow. Fine, both eyebrows. Curse Eliza and her magical one-eyebrow dexterity.

"I know I come across as cool. I know my reputation is that of an ice queen."

If my eyebrows kept climbing at their current rate, they'd be off my forehead before she ran out of startling revelations.

She sighed and studied her nails. They were shaped and filed, painted a half shade darker than nude, but something about their perfection made her frown. "Do you know that I've seen Senator Deacon cry five times? And Mike and Tom, and all the other representatives—I've seen them drunk, or weepy, or pissed-off, red-faced, cursing. But you don't hear about any of this—or if you do, it's spun in a way that's positive. They're

364 | TIFFANY SCHMIDT

'passionate' or 'fired up.' I get bad press for frowning. In fact I get *more* lines in the papers for what I'm wearing, if I gain or lose five pounds, if I wait a week too long before getting my roots touched up, or if I run to the grocery store with minimal makeup than I ever do for the bills I sponsor or any of my political stances. Trent's wedding seems to be far more interesting to my constituents than my platform."

Well, of course it was—who *wouldn't* pick vows over votes? Not that I told her this, because clearly this was only inter-mission in my lecture.

"Which is why I didn't want you to be the maid of honor. I didn't want you to have to deal with that sort of public scru-tiny. D.C. is still a boys' club, Merrilee. I'm there to do a real job, but so often they try and reduce me to a photo caption. The best way to fight that is to ignore it. To keep going. I'm not an unfeeling monster, but . . ."

"You just play one on TV?"

She laughed, and the sound startled me. I was expecting it to be a sharp bark or a high pitched "hee-hee-hee." Instead it was warm and inviting. The kind that made me dissolve into giggles too. She stood and squeezed my arm. "I truly am sorry about your breakup. I hope the next person you date realizes just how lucky he is to have you. The best decision Trent ever made was to fall in love with your sister—though how could he help it? She's extraordinary too."

I wasn't sure if I wanted her to stop—because it was weird to see Senator Rhodes act warm and approachable—or tell me more. Instead I thought of Fielding. He was nothing like Monroe. He was a thousand times better, and if I ever had the chance to prove to him just how stupid and judgmental I'd been when I rejected him, I would. In the meantime, I'd take his advice. "Is there any way I could get involved or help out around here? I don't know much about politics—but if it's okay, I'd like to learn."

Senator Rhodes smiled—it was different from the one in the photos on the wall. This one matched the photos on her desk, the ones where she was surrounded by family members. It was a little crooked, just like Trent's. "I'd love that. Too many people think they're suddenly blessed with political acumen when they blow out eighteen candles. But the best thing someone as intelligent, passionate, and creative as you can do is get informed, get involved. Your future will be shaped by the way your generation chooses to step up or step aside."

It felt like a speech another woman I really admired would have given. "Do you remember Trent's old English teacher Ms. Gregoire?"

She nodded. "Her class was transformative for him. I'm sure he'll be happy to tell you about it, but right now I really have to get on a conference call. Let's talk soon."

"I look forward to it." And shockingly, I did. More shockingly, if I hadn't, I wouldn't have felt pressure to say so—somehow this office, this person I'd also judged so harshly, had become a haven where there was no use for pretend politeness. No use for apologies either—because while I normally would've said "sorry for interrupting," I didn't. I didn't think she'd want me to. Like Eliza—and maybe like me now too—I bet the senator didn't believe in women apologizing for existing. "Thanks for meeting with me."

"Thanks for dropping in. I do hope you'll come back."

"I will. Could I maybe volunteer for your campaign?"

Her eyes widened and softened. She blinked and nodded. "Yes. Yes, I'd like that very much." And for a moment, I thought she might want me to hug her—but I wasn't sure we were there yet. Maybe we'd start at a handshake and work up through fist bump first.

I grinned at her. "I'll have my people call your people."

And in the smile she returned, I caught a hint of the feisty pixie that she used to be. Or maybe still was.

40

How awful is it?" Curtis asked at lunch on Tuesday.

I looked up from my yogurt to find them all staring, so clearly this was aimed at me. "How awful is what?"

"Detention," prompted Hannah.

"I've heard it's just you and Fielding. I still don't get how you ended up in his car Friday night . . ." Curtis paused, but if he was waiting for me to spill, he'd be waiting a long time. "Since you two are like cats and dogs, want me to get detention so I can play referee? I'm good at it."

"Getting detention, or refereeing?" Lance asked.

"Both." Curtis shrugged, and I got angry for a moment, thinking he was picking on Fielding . . . but then I realized he wasn't choosing sides so much as seeking gossip. And he was wrong. We were both dog people, thank you very much.

Eliza rolled her eyes at Curtis, then turned back to me. "You've been strangely quiet about it. Is it terrible?"

Sera looked like she was holding her breath for my answer. I attributed it to the awkwardness of it being *her* "awful" father who'd assigned the punishment and *her* brother whom everyone assumed I'd hate being alone with.

If they only knew.

My cheeks felt hot as I answered. "It's fine. No big deal." It's not like I'd spent half the night watching the *Pride and Prejudice* miniseries and mentally replacing Colin Firth's face with Fielding's. No, nothing like that. I yawned.

It was closer to two-thirds of the night.

I was the first to arrive at detention, which meant I had to do all the high-pressure things, like: pick where to sit and wait for Fielding to arrive. Since I'd finished *Pride and Prejudice* and my last response journal, I didn't even have those to distract me. Or any homework, since I'd done it all during media. But I did have my laptop, and I did have Ms. Gregoire's words in my head, the ones she'd said when I handed in my last journal.

"Keep writing, Merrilee. Just write, whether or not you choose to join the lit magazine. A story, a poem, an essay, a novel. Put your words on paper or a screen—see what you can create. I bet it'll be wonderful."

And I was. I had been writing even before she gave me the pep talk. I'd been up at night and up early in the morning, pressing keys and filling pages. Because I'd found it. My yearning. The thing I wanted to do. The thing that made skipping sleep worthwhile and made me even spacier than usual. I was going to write.

And when another distraction—in the form of a tall, devastatingly beautiful boy—made his way into detention and into the seat beside mine, I smiled my hello, and I got back to work.

Or at least I tried to. I was starting to think that detention was a psychological experiment. Put two people with epic amounts of tension in a room, tell them they can't talk—and leave. Because it was only ten minutes, ten of the longest minutes in the history of minutes, before today's proctor, art teacher Mrs. Mundhenk, stood and exited the room. She didn't even give us a heads up about making a coffee run or whatever, so I had no clue how long until she'd be back.

I looked at Fielding. He was already looking at me. He nudged a scrap of paper across the table. **What are you writing?**

I dug a pen out of my bag and scribbled back: **A story.**

His eyes widened and a hint of a smile flickered on his face—appearing just long enough for me to miss it when it was gone. Just long enough for me to think about what Senator Rhodes had said yesterday, to think about the plot of *Pride and Prejudice*, to think that maybe I didn't need to be Lizzy-like when it came to waiting for her Darcy. That maybe I could be the one to initiate.

While I'd been lost in my head, Fielding had torn another scrap out of his notebook. He slid it down the table. **Can I read it?**

My anxiety made an appearance like a pop-up book. Turn the page, and look! There it was! Only instead of puppy holding a heart or a dump truck, mine was sweaty hands and a dry throat. I took a deep breath and tilted the screen toward him, like a poker player revealing all her cards—which was maybe exactly what I was doing. His slid his chair closer, and closer still.

Oh, I couldn't look. I couldn't watch as he read the feelings and thoughts I'd poured onto that page. I hadn't even read it myself. I hadn't even hit spell check. What would he think of my complete inability to spell the word "appreciate" without trying to stick in an *h*? I probably would've descended into pure panic, the kind that involves lip chewing and rocking and unconscious humming. Oh, wait. I was already lip chewing and humming. Rocking would've been next if his shoulder hadn't grazed mine. I thought it was an accident. The type of accident that made every cell in my shoulder buzz and made every cell in the rest of my body jealous. But it happened again—blazer against blouse—and this time his shoulder stayed against mine as he scrolled down.

He leaned closer, his breath and voice warm in my ear. "This is really quite good." The room had been silent for so long, his whisper felt explosive. It made my heart jump and race.

I turned to reply, but he hadn't moved, so now we were shoulders touching and noses touching, and all the oxygen had disappeared from the atmosphere, because I straight up felt like I was drowning—if drowning was a form of euphoria.

"What is going on in here?"

That wasn't Mrs. Mundhenk, not unless she'd filled her travel mug with something that made her voice drop several octaves. Fielding reacted first, spinning away from me and sliding his chair back. "Dad. What are you doing here?"

"Get your things, Fielding. You can finish this detention

in my office." He turned, and for a moment, I thought I was off the hook. That this humiliation—which, granted, felt like plenty—was going to be all that was served up that day. But after his son had ducked by him through the door, Headmaster Williams turned back to me. "I want you to stop by my office when you finish your detention. We need to talk."

If he'd had a villain's cape, I'm sure he would've flung it dramatically over his shoulder as he swooped out the door. Instead he clicked his heels loudly on the floor as he stormed off.

"What was that about?" asked Mrs. Mundhenk, who'd returned from her wherever break about two minutes too late to be helpful.

I was going to shrug and offer a noncommittal answer, but maybe it was time to stop worrying about polite and start worrying about myself. "He doesn't like me. He resents that Senator Rhodes used her influence to get my sister and me enrolled. Especially since we're here on financial aid."

"Oh. *Oh.*" I could practically see the Rube Goldberg machine going on in her mind as she made these connections. "Well, I hope that's not true."

I deflated like a fluffy dog dunked in water. I'd taken a risk and stood up for myself. And I hadn't been believed.

"But . . ." she continued. "If that's the case, then the very best revenge would be for you and Rory to excel here. You're certainly intelligent and talented enough. I've heard about you from several teachers already. They're impressed."

"Really?"

"Yes, really. And I don't need to tell you how artistically

gifted Rory is. The two of you should thrive here—make Headmaster Williams regret every ounce of grief he directs your way."

"I'll do my best." No pressure there.

"Good. Now run along. And I'll see you around campus."

I ran, literally, because I wanted a pee break before the headmaster's office. That interaction was going to be uncomfortable enough without adding in a full bladder. The bathroom was near Ms. Gregoire's room, and when I exited, her classroom door was open and my little sister was sitting across from her.

I always forgot she was Rory's teacher too. Probably because Rory had done nothing but complain about hating her class, and I just didn't even see how that was possible. But seeing her scrunched in a chair, red-cheeked and miserable as a shaggy Newfoundland on a hundred-degree day made it all pretty clear. And brought to mind the academic warning I'd accidentally kept secret the previous weekend because I'd been too distracted by our potential expulsion.

I paused at the doorway, not sure if I should intrude but also not wanting Rory to show up to the detention hall and think I ditched her. "Excuse me?"

Ms. Gregoire smiled at me. "Well, if it isn't the school's most creative Austen scholar. Before my meeting with your sister, I was just finishing up your last response journal." She squeezed her hands together and pulled them in to her chest. "You have made this story your own in a wonderful way."

Rory slumped down even farther in her chair. The tips of her ears and nose were bright red—the way they got when she

BOOKISH BOYFRIENDS | 373

was trying not to cry. I wanted to ask if she was okay. To push my teacher out the door and close it behind her—trapping Rory in until I got some answers. If she were Eliza, I'd have been able to do the whole BFF ESP thing—but Rory and I had never really been tuned in to the same channel.

Instead I gave her space, turning to Ms. Gregoire and responding to her compliments with a crinkled nose. "I wish. Instead of getting a Darcy, I've got detention and now another meeting with the headmaster." I turned to my sister. "So I'm going to be later than I thought. Sorry."

Rory blinked at me with glassy eyes. "But . . . I'm done now." She jumped out of her seat, knocking a book off the corner of Ms. Gregoire's desk. "You know what, I'll go wait with you by the office."

"Oh, you don't have . . ."

I trailed off, because Rory had bent over to pick up the book, but the second her hand touched the cover, she yelped and dropped it again. She blinked down at it, looked at her hand and the book. She slid her sleeve over her fingers, then picked it up again. Before she could place it back on the desk, Ms. Gregoire intercepted it and flipped it over to reveal the front cover.

"*Little Women*. Hmm . . . interesting."

Rory didn't answer. Her face had gone white, and she was staring, unblinking at the book in our teacher's hand. We all jumped at the knock on the door. I let out a nervous laugh when I saw it was just Toby standing there.

"Hey," he said. "I just finished practice and I'm heading out. I wanted to see if either of my favorite little ladies . . . er, women, right? That's what Eliza's always saying I should call you? I wanted to see if either of you wanted a ride home."

"Me, please." My sister did yoga and meditation, not sports that required speed, but if it had been a race to the other side of the room, she would've won.

"Lose the diminutive and you'd get Eliza's approval," I said. "Women, not *little* women."

Ms. Gregoire hummed to herself and flipped the book over in her hands. She drummed her fingers on the cover. "Interesting. Rory, you should go with Toby." She put that book down and picked up a duplicate of the fuschia-covered novel that had consumed my past two weeks. "And you, my dear, should get to your meeting with the headmaster."

"Oh. Right." I'd managed to forget about that for half a minute, but now anxiety was stomping around in my stomach again. Making me wonder if maybe I shouldn't make another pit stop in the bathroom to vomit before heading into the office of polished furniture, plaques, and pretension. "Time for a showdown." But unlike Lizzy and Lady Catherine de Bourgh, I didn't feel at all confident I'd come out of this triumphant . . . or even tear-free.

"It's not over yet, Merri." Ms. Gregoire curled the book between her fingers and pointed them both at me. "And when you go in there, be assertive, be brave. Be *you*."

41

I wasn't sure if following Ms. Gregoire's advice had been the best decision. If the goal had been to make Headmaster Williams shout and turn clown-nose red, then mission accomplished. The goal certainly couldn't have been to make him like me—but why did I need him to? Why was that my default? It wasn't his role to be my buddy, so why should it be mine to worry about if he thought I was nice or good enough? I hadn't been disrespectful.

But I hadn't capitulated either. When he asked questions, I answered them with honest directness. And when he'd roared and blustered, I'd shrugged.

The only thing I was regretting as I hummed and made my way across campus to where Mom was waiting in the car was that I hadn't finished that moment with Fielding. And because my future detentions were to be solo ones, I wouldn't have that chance.

Since my homework was done, I wasn't quite sure what to do with myself after dinner. I could go bug Toby and see if he wanted to watch a movie. I could write another guest blog post for Hannah, or keep poking at the story I'd started. I could do another pass through the club fair flyer—though with cross-country, my job, lit magazine, volunteering for Senator Rhodes, and homework, I wasn't quite sure what else I could squeeze in. I could read, but none of the other books cramming my shelves felt right.

What I really wanted was a *Pride and Prejudice* sequel. *Humbled and Open-minded*? I wanted to know what happened next. I wanted to know how Lizzy and Darcy lived out their happily ever after. I wanted a road map for my own.

I had just about decided to go be indecisive in Toby's room, when there were footsteps on my balcony and a knock on that door.

"I was just thinking about you," I said as I pulled it open.

"You were?"

Oh, that was not Toby. That was so not Toby.

Fielding looked as jittery as I immediately felt, and the only thing I could think to do was lie. "No. Not at all. I wasn't—" I took a deep breath. "I was. So much."

"I can't believe I'm doing this. I can't believe I'm up here instead of at your door, but . . ."

"But?" I prompted after several epic seconds of silence. "But!"

"But did you tell my father—" He cleared his throat. "Did you tell him that it was none of his business if we dated and that he didn't have the authority to tell you not to date me?"

I nodded. That was a pretty accurate recitation of my words. Because how dare Headmaster Williams use his office or title to intimidate me about my social life? If he'd wanted to yell at me for breaking the rules and talking in detention, sure. But to tell me to stay away from his son, or end things when we hadn't even started? That was out of line, and I wasn't going to be bullied into agreeing. I'd squared my shoulders and met Headmaster Williams's eyes when I said, "Well, you know, sir, I'm pretty obstinate. Some might even call me headstrong. And I'm not interested in your opinion on my love life."

Fielding hesitantly brushed a finger over the back of my hand. The gesture brought me back to this moment with a rush of electricity. "I thought I'd ruined any chance of us ever happening." He took a step closer. "But I couldn't help but think that if there was really no chance you'd ever consider me that way, why wouldn't you have told my father? Why wouldn't you have laughed in his face and said I was the last person on campus you'd ever want to date?"

Wow. Headmaster Williams really was Catherine de Bourgh. This really was my Darcy moment. Every little Lizzy part of me had converged on my heart in one giant squish. But—I could pay attention to the bookish parallels and play that game, *or* I could pay attention to this moment and the handsome boy in front of me with his feelings up for offer. The handsome boy with beseeching eyes who'd asked me a question that I hadn't bothered to answer. I chose *now*. I chose us.

I licked my lips; my tongue was weighted with the implications of what I was about to say. "Because you're not. Not the last. You're the first."

He shut his eyes and inhaled deeply, like it was his first taste of oxygen and it tasted like ice cream. When he opened them, they glowed. He glowed. Brighter than my twinkle lights as he followed me from the balcony into my room. "You really mean that?"

"I do. Have you changed your mind? Are you sure I'm smart and . . ." I searched for the right word, and the closest I could come up with was "Boring? Proper? Enough for you? You're not going to be embarrassed by me? Because this is me—hideous robe. Antics, hijinks. I'm an adventure."

I'd thought I was joking when I started speaking, but all the laughter had evaporated from my voice by the last squeaky word, and I was scrunching my toes against my rag rug, desperate for him to reassure me.

"Merrilee . . ." He sighed and reached out toward me. "May I?"

I wasn't sure what I was giving permission for, but I was all for it. And the fact that he was the type of guy who asked— well, that was how it should be. "Sure."

He slid his fingers through my hair, cupping the back of my head as his thumbs stroked down my cheeks. I shivered—a whole-body shudder that probably proved the point I'd just made: I was highly embarrassing.

"I'm sorry," he said. "I'm sorry I ever said otherwise. I was entirely wrong."

I tipped my face into his hand, luxuriating in his touch. "I have a feeling you don't say that often. Should I have you repeat it so I can record it as your personalized ringtone?"

He smiled. *My* smile. "How about this? I'll take out an ad in the school paper raving about your brain?"

I laughed.

"Or I'll stand on a bench in Convocation and proclaim your superiority."

I wrinkled my nose. "Been there, done that. Bought the T-shirt—threw it in the trash."

"I'll—" He groaned and exhaled slowly, sliding his fingers through my hair and letting them rest by his sides. "I'll wear two different socks, and when people correctly point out that they don't match, I'll tell them my brilliant girlfriend says they're not supposed to."

"That one!" I clapped my hands together and pointed at him. We were so close that the tips of my index fingers brushed against his shirt. "Oh, definitely that one. I pick option C. And I'll pick out your socks too, if you let me."

"Really?" He crinkled his forehead like he was in pain, then laughed. "Oh, fine."

I threw my arms around his shoulders. He stiffened, then relaxed. At least a little bit. I had a feeling that even on my best posture day, I wouldn't match Fielding on his worst. I pressed up on tiptoe so we were nose-to-nose. "Girlfriend, huh? So if I go with you to Fall Ball, am I going to get to see those slick dance moves you told me about?"

He laughed again. "If I say yes, will you?"

I inched closer to him and nodded. "Maybe you should kiss me and make it official."

"You are going to be my favorite adventure," he whispered, bringing his mouth close to mine.

"Shut up and kiss me," I answered.

"Yes, please." Or really, it was more of a "yes, plea"—because that was absolutely the limit of my patience and I trapped the "-se" between our lips. This wasn't a soft first kiss. Not gentle or tentative, slow or gradual. It wasn't stiff or formal, or anything tame.

It was a fierce thing, a wild thing, a please-let-this-be-real and please-don't-change-your-mind melding of mouths, and lips drinking, parting, tongues skating, pulses soaring, hands on faces, and clutching shoulders. Elbows in tight points and bodies so close molecules couldn't fit between us.

We stepped apart and stood there. Chests heaving from breaths skipped and not missed until now. I reached for his hand, tying his fingers in mine. He eased me back against my desk, lifting me to sit on top so our heights were more evenly matched. Like, even in this moment of breathlessness and tingles and anticipation, he still wanted to make sure I didn't end up with a strained neck or cramped calves. How very Fielding. I grabbed his collar, crumpling it horribly, and pulled him back to me.

And then, because Fielding would always, always be Fielding, just like I was always going to be me—he pulled his lips off mine and stepped back. If I was his adventure, he'd be my anchor—um, in the holding-me-steady way, not that he'd be dragging me down.

"What's wrong?" I asked, because I was more than willing to spend all night on my desk or even my tiptoes. Heck, I'd turn ballerina and borrow a pair of Sera's pointe shoes if it meant fusing my mouth with his.

"While I'm very much enjoying *this*"—he paused to give me a thorough demonstration of what *this* was, then broke away again, this time placing a chair between us and gripping on to the back of it with white knuckles—"I refuse to be some creep who's sneaking into your bedroom with your parents down the hall." He let go of the chair, but not to reach for me. Instead he grasped the doorknob that lead back out to the balcony. "Meet me downstairs? I'd like to reintroduce myself to your parents and try and mitigate the damage my father and I did to the name of Williams last time I was here."

I groaned and rolled my eyes—but my toes were curling in giddy little C's. This was the move of someone who wasn't here for just a day. This was the move of someone who recognized how important my parents were to me—and who respected them.

Still . . . "*Yay*, manners and all that, but I don't want to play family meeting or Spanish Inquisition. I want to be alone."

He smiled at me, and concertos could have been written for that smile. Sonnets could have been penned about it. It was possible that global warming could have been solely attributed to the way it lit up the room. "After I meet them, maybe we could take Gatsby for a walk."

And just when I thought he couldn't get any better, he had to go and invoke my favorite four-legged creature. I beamed at him. "You remember his name?"

"Of course I do. You shrieked it when he trussed us up with his leash last week."

"I didn't shriek it." I paused to consider. "Okay, I did."

"Have I mentioned that was my favorite part of the night and I really, really like your dog?"

"Have I mentioned that you're my favorite part of *this* night, and I really, really like you?"

I crooked a finger at him and he groaned. "Play fair, Merrilee. I'm trying to be a good guy here."

"What if we set a timer for five minutes," I suggested. "You can be a good guy—the best guy in the world—once it goes off?"

"Deal." He crossed my room faster than I thought possible, his mouth on my neck in the perfect type of distraction as I fumbled with my phone's timer.

I set it for seven.

42

Much, much later, we said good-bye for the night. But first we sat down for a mug of tea with my parents—okay, mine was cocoa. Then we took Gatsby on a romp through several neighborhoods, with several stops for sidewalk kisses—each interrupted by a wet nose. After saying good-bye, we texted good night. Then I sat at my computer and typed the whole thing up so I wouldn't forget a single swoony moment.

I hit save on the file and ventured downstairs to say sweet dreams to my parents. Back upstairs, Lilly pulled me into her room and confessed, "I totally eavesdropped when he was meeting Mom and Dad. I really like Fielding."

I grinned and hugged her, squealing, "Me too."

"Manicure tomorrow so you can fill me in?" Lilly suggested. "My treat."

I wiggled my chipped nails at her. "Sounds perfect. Good night."

On my way back to my room, I made an impulsive detour and knocked on Rory's door. I expected her to be painting or sketching, but when I opened the door she was glaring at a textbook. "Hey," I said cautiously. "Lilly and I are going for manicures tomorrow—want to come?"

She rubbed her forehead and blinked at me in surprise. "Um, yeah. Sure. If that's okay."

"Yup." I glanced over her shoulder at her notebook and had to fight a wince. There would be *many* redo asterisks if Mom got her hands on that page. "So, um, do you want any help with that?"

I braced myself for her defensive response, but she just sighed and ducked her head. "Yes, please."

I grabbed a pencil and moved a sketchpad so I could sit down next to her. "So you're going to start by changing these to decimals . . ." And, because tonight was made of miracles and magic, we worked through the rest of her problem set without any bickering. Well, barely any.

After all this, I was still too starry-eyed to sleep, so I grabbed the blanket from the foot of my bed and walked out on my balcony. I tossed it up on my roof, monkeyed my way up after it, spread it beneath me, then wrapped the extra around me, burrito style. I pulled my phone out of my pocket, but before I dialed, I glanced at the dark bedroom of the boy next door. I'd have to tell him soon. Fielding had already mentioned it on our walk—only he seemed to think Toby would feel some sort of matchmaker pride. Um, notsomuch. But I'd let him sleep tonight. Maybe tomorrow we'd have that conversation. Maybe while sitting right here. Maybe it'd even go well.

But right now I had a different person to tell. I pressed send.

"Merrilee? Is this an emergency?" I pictured her jack-in-the-boxing up in bed, hair askew, cheeks drowsy red. "Merri? What's going on? Spit it out."

"Fielding kissed me."

"What? *What*?" Funny how I'd wanted those exact words as a reaction, but I'd wanted her to dip them in confetti; I wanted a parade, a skywriter. Instead she was giving me anger and disgust. "Have you called the headmaster and reported it? Or if you don't feel comfortable talking to him about his son's egregious behavior, we can call the school board or talk to a teacher. Are you okay?"

"No, no. No!"

"Right. Of course you're not okay. Do you need me to come over? I—"

"No, I mean I'm not not-okay. Er, I *am* okay. I'm not reporting it. I *participated* in it. Encouraged it. I might have even instigated it."

"Merrilee, it's one a.m. My pulse is racing and I'm fairly sure it's currently pumping excessive adrenaline and cortisol through my bloodstream, which is making it hard to concentrate or sit still. Could you please explain what's going on in a manner that makes sense to people other than you?"

"I really, truly am okay. This is *good* news." I could hear her exhaling against the phone as she calmed down. "Remember how I said boys are better in books?"

"Yes. '*So much* better,'" she quoted dutifully.

I took a deep breath and prepared to share my secrets with her and the stars. To thank the universe for all the dots that had connected to get me where I was right now—cozy and warm beneath the constellations, with a fiercely loyal best friend sacrificing sleep and paperwork to hear this story, and a boyfriend across town who was probably dozing with perfect posture in starched pajamas. The thought made me giggle.

"Eliza, I was wrong. . . . While I'm definitely a Darcy fangirl—Team Fitzzy, *Lizzwilliam?* forever—boys are much, much better in real life."

ACKNOWLEDGMENTS

It is a truth universally acknowledged that no writer creates in a vacuum. Or . . . at least this writer doesn't. I hope you've no objection to hearing my loud shouts of gratitude, because I want to tell you.

Let's get the biggies out of the way first: Thank you, William Shakespeare and Jane Austen. Not only would *Bookish Boyfriends* not exist without you, but my world has been made so much brighter by your characters and stories. You will forever own places on my bookshelves and in my imagination.

Thank you to my parents, who let me have free run of the town library (shout out to Stevens Memorial Library!), helped haul home stacks of books (then hunt them down when I misplaced them), and didn't blink when I switched back and forth between the Baby-Sitters Club and the Brontës.

To my teachers—many of whose names appear within this book—you have inspired and encouraged me more than you know. The same appreciation goes to all the librarians who steered me toward the classics and taught me the power of interlibrary loans and old-book smells. To my real Mrs. Gregoire, your class was a game changer in my life. I suspect many students feel the same way. Thank you.

And to my dearest Anne Heltzel, an editor by any other name wouldn't have been as perfect for this book! Thank you for championing it for so long. To Andrew Smith, Susan Van Metre, Masha Gunic, Alyssa Nassner, Samantha Hoback, and everyone at Abrams! I'm so lucky to have you behind *Bookish Boyfriends*. Thank you for everything you do!

Barry, you have been beyond heroic when it came to this

book. If I could spell out THANK YOU with cookies on your stairs every morning, I would. I'd bake a second mammoth batch for everyone in the Goldblatt agency community because you all are my favorite corner of this industry.

To Courtney Summers, Emily Hainsworth, Annie Gaughen, Patricia Riley, Tricia Ready, K. M. Walton, Elisa Ludwig, Kelly Jensen, Nancy Keim Comley, Jen Zelesko, Stacey Yiengst, Claire Legrand, Heather Hebert, Jenn Stuhltrager, Kristin Wilson, Jessica Spotswood, Lauren Spieller, and Bess Cozby—you are the reason I understand the power of strong female friendships. Seriously, if I could create my own Bennet sisters girl gang, you would all be in it.

St. Matt, you are Darcy, Gilbert, Knightley, Laurie, and Tilney rolled up in one handsome package. But the swooniest thing about you is how much you believe in me. I love you.

To the twins—thank you for tolerating hours of *Romeo and Juliet* and *Pride and Prejudice* on audiobook. Thank you more for making me laugh with your interpretations of Shakespearian and Austen quotes. "Sad hours feel long" will always be better than "Are we there yet?"

To my very Bookish Baby, who was born on Shakespeare's birthday and snuggled in my arms for most of this book's last draft, I love you, Rascal. Please learn to sleep soon.

Thank you to every reader, blogger, teacher, librarian, and bookseller who has cracked this cover or passed this story along to a friend. You are the reason I get to continue in my dream job. You must allow me to tell you how ardently I appreciate you!

And finally, thank you, Leonardo DiCaprio, for peering broodily through a fish tank, and Colin Firth, for diving in that lake.

TIFFANY SCHMIDT

Tiffany Schmidt grew up in Massachusetts, where she split her childhood between the library and the time-out chair. She is the author of several popular young adult novels, including *Send Me a Sign*, *Bright Before Sunrise*, and the Once Upon a Crime Family series. A former sixth-grade teacher, she lives in Pennsylvania with her impish twin sons, their rascally baby brother, a pair of spoiled puggles, and her very saintly husband.